The Kiss That Heals

"God, you're beautiful," he said hoarsely, even before he knew the words were out of his mouth. He grasped her hand in his own, pulling her closer to him, inhaling her fragrance. Desire returned, hot and fast, pushing away the pain to the far corners of his body.

"Why are you being nice to me? . . . Why are you like this? I don't understand." Her voice quavered slightly.

"I don't, either," he said, feeling reason escape him. "I don't understand it at all. But tell me you feel it, too." A strong gust of wind buffeted the house as he brought her hand to his chest and placed it softly over his thudding heart. "Feel this, feel what you do to me."

"Mr. Grant, I—"

"Evan. Call me Evan."

"Evan, I—"

He pulled steadily on her arm, until her face was near his own. "Madeline."

Their eyes locked. Supper and injuries were forgotten. Their breaths mingled as, slowly, inevitably, their lips met.

DIAMOND WILDFLOWER ROMANCE

A breathtaking line of searing romance novels . . . where destiny meets desire in the untamed fury of the American West.

WILD WINDS

PEGGY STOKS

DIAMOND BOOKS, NEW YORK

This book is a Diamond original edition,
and has never been previously published.

WILD WINDS

A Diamond Book / published by arrangement with
the author

PRINTING HISTORY
Diamond edition / December 1993

ISBN: 1-55773-965-X

Diamond Books are published by The Berkley Publishing Group,
200 Madison Avenue, New York, NY 10016.
DIAMOND and the "D" design
are trademarks belonging to Charter Communications, Inc.

PRINTED IN THE UNITED STATES OF AMERICA

10 9 8 7 6 5 4 3 2 1

For Grandma H.
and
Grandma T.
I miss you both.

ACKNOWLEDGMENTS

I am greatly indebted to John and Susan Gross and to all the other folks at the Gross-Wilkinson ranch who helped so much in the creation of this book. If you need any help branding again next year, let me know.

Ann Nelson from the Wyoming State Museum deserves a big thank-you for so promptly answering each of my requests for information. While I must admit to taking liberties with such things as the weather and moon tides in the writing of *Wild Winds*, I did otherwise strive to be as historically accurate as possible.

There are several other important people whom I wish to credit for their assistance. First and foremost I would like to thank Jeff, Jenna, and Allison Stoks for enduring several months of instant food, country music, and living with a terribly preoccupied wife and mother.

Hey, guys, are you ready to do it again?

To my critique group—Kathy, Carol, and Paula: If not for your unique strengths, insights, and talents, I could not have grown as a writer. Thank you.

I would also like to acknowledge all my faithful friends who hung in there with me, as well as the gang on 65, the Man with the north woods cabin, and my faithful proofreaders Jackie and Sunday.

Finally I wish to thank my editor, Judith Stern, and my agent, Meredith Bernstein, for taking a chance on me. Your kindness and encouragement throughout this project will always be remembered.

WILD WINDS

one

"I HAVE A GRANDFATHER LIVING IN SAN Francisco," Madeline Spencer explained to the laboring cow before her, shaking her head with disbelief. "Emmett Brinkman. I never knew about him, but now he writes and says he wants to become acquainted with me. And my brother isn't really my brother. He's my father."

The cow turned her great brown head at the sound of Madeline's voice and lowed commiseratively.

"Oh, what do you know about it?" Madeline retorted, though her voice was heavy with sadness. "At least you knew who your mother was. The person I thought was my mother is my grandmother!"

A brisk breeze whipped through the fat-budded branches of the small stand of willows. Faint green color already tinged the winter-brown grassland, a testimony to the recent spell of mild weather. She shifted on the saddle, closing her eyes and turning her face to accept the sun's warm radiance.

But even the bright spring sunshine and equally bright
sounds of the first returning songbirds on the morning air
could not dispel the pensiveness that gripped her. With the
arrival of the letter from San Francisco a few weeks before,
hand-delivered directly to the ranch by paid messenger,
all the absolutes governing her life had been shockingly
rearranged. Her parents weren't her parents; they were her
grandparents. Her brother wasn't her brother; he was her
father. And her mother—her real mother—was a young
woman from San Francisco who had died after giving birth
to her.

It was all so unreal, so hard to believe. She was no
longer the daughter of Albert and Elsie Spencer; she was
the daughter of Nathaniel Spencer and some woman named
Sara Brinkman. . . .

"Hey, Miss Maddie, whatcha doin' sitting there all by
yerself?" shouted ranch foreman Willis Reed, approaching
her on horseback. "First it looks like yer talkin' to a cow,
and now it appears yer tryin' to catch forty winks sittin'
upright. You got the makin's of a fine rancher, all right."

She managed a small smile and shrugged her shoulders.

"Oh, honey, you know I'm just kiddin' with ya," he said
gruffly, stopping his horse beside hers. He fiddled with his
reins. "You doin' okay? You don't have to be out here today,
ya know. Not too much goin' on right now." He made a face.
"How 'bout you go on back to the house and put up your
feet an' sew on one of them frilly little samplers?"

Despite her heavy spirits, she smiled at the burly foreman's rare show of solicitousness. "Thanks, but I'd rather
be out here talking with the cows than making a pincushion
of my finger." Her expression grew serious again. "Besides,
with Nate gone, I know you can use my help."

He lifted his hat and scratched his graying head. "Yeah,
you're right." The reins once more became a source of
interest to him. "I know you're hurtin' bad now. Got the
rug pulled right out from under your feet when that damned
letter came. But for what it's worth, Maddie, I've known the
truth about you for prit-near ten years now, and I know your
pa loves you somethin' fierce. Don't think he don't. He just
didn't think he could do right by you." He cleared his throat.

"Well, I said my piece and now I'll shut my yap." He pointed to the gravid longhorn, abruptly changing the subject. "Are ya thinkin' she'll calve soon?"

"I don't think so," she replied uncertainly. "She's just standing here." Not that she knew two hoots about calving. Since her arrival at her brother's—correction, make that *father's*—ranch last summer she had acquired a wealth of information about cattle ranching. But her knowledge of calving was still extremely limited.

"Her water ain't broke, is it?" Reed stroked his stubbly chin thoughtfully at the negative shake of her head. "Prob'ly got a while, then. I noticed several more in the herd gettin' springy, too. We got another mess of calvin' coming up here. We're gonna be damned busy." He winked. "I hope yer not too fond of sleep."

"Sleep? What's that?" she joked sadly. "I haven't found too much of it lately."

"Aw, Maddie. Things'll work out just fine, you'll see. Your pa's gonna take care of things out in San Francisco."

Take care of things? She'd never seen Nate in such a rage as when she'd shown him the letter she'd received from Emmett Brinkman. After the eruption, the story had come from his lips, sentence by strained sentence.

"I'm your father, Madeline," he'd begun bluntly.

He'd told her how he led a wagon train westward in the early fifties, just after the gold rush. "The Brinkmans were part of the train," he'd explained, "and from the first moment Emmett Brinkman laid eyes on me, he decided he hated me. To make a long story short, I . . . " He'd stopped then and rubbed his hands over his face before finishing his sentence. "I fell in love with his daughter."

Despite her shock, Madeline had listened intently to Nate's words, watching the emotion on his handsome, lined face.

"Brinkman didn't think a hired man was good enough for his daughter," Nate said bitterly. "Sara—your mother—loved me, though," he went on, his voice softening, "and once we got to San Francisco she promised she'd wait for me to come back for her. I had to go back east. . . ."

He sighed then, a deep, empty sound. "I came back, all right, just like I promised. In the spring. The old man all but threw me off his property, screaming at me that Sara was dead. Dead of the fever. He didn't even tell me about you. She must have given birth to you and died afterward. And then the—" He broke off, his voice thickening.

He was quiet a long moment. "And then," he started again, "Brinkman packed you off to Independence to be raised by my folks. I don't know what perverse pleasure it gave him to do that, to send me away without telling me about you, but he did." His face had darkened then, and he'd sworn foully. . . .

"Oh, Maddie?" Will intruded on her thoughts. "Almost forgot! We got some fellow comin' out later on this afternoon wantin' to talk about a beef contract. Figured as long as Spencer's away, me and you's in charge here. Whaddaya say, you wanna meet him with me? If you're serious about learnin' the business and all . . . "

A beef contract. Normally she'd have jumped at the chance to be included in the business dealings of the ranch. She'd written long letters to her grandmother—not her mother—about life on a cattle ranch in the wilds of the Wyoming Territory. Everything had been fresh and exciting, a series of adventures to be soaked up and savored . . . until the letter from Emmett Brinkman had come.

Now she had another letter to write to Elsie, a very difficult letter. Or should she? Elsie's health had become somewhat delicate in the past months. The loss of her husband last summer had been devastating; and almost immediately after that she'd undertaken the exhausting responsibility of nursing her dying sister in Philadelphia. . . .

"Maddie?"

The wind teased several errant strands of golden blond hair that had escaped from the heavy braid, whipping them across her wind-pinkened cheeks. Exasperated, she lifted her hat and tucked the hair securely beneath it. "Sorry, Will. I seem to be doing quite a lot of woolgathering lately." She sighed and forced her lips into a pleasant smile. "I'll be happy to meet the gentleman with you. What time?"

" 'Bout three. Up at the house."

"I'll be there. And, Will?" she added, her smile no longer forced, but sweet and tentative. "Thank you for trying to make me feel better."

"Aw, wasn't nothin'. Cain't stand to see a pretty little gal with a long face." Abruptly he turned his tall sorrel gelding and kicked it into an easy lope.

The longhorn calved without incident two hours after the sun climbed to its highest position in the sky. Madeline was fascinated with, rather than repulsed by, the birth process and with the enchanting, wobbly-legged calf.

It was a miracle, an absolute miracle, she thought, giggling as the calf struggled to its feet for the umpteenth time, only to be knocked back to the ground by his mother's rough, cleansing tongue. She realized that her spirits had lifted considerably in the past few hours.

Robbie Ashler waved from astride his shaggy brown-and-white mount and rode across the couple hundred yards that separated the cow from the herd. A broad smile creased his young, angular face.

"Hullo, Miss Madeline. Gettin' warm, huh? I was wonderin' if winter was ever gonna end. I just got done up at the barn, you know." He barely paused for another breath, pointing at the new calf. "We got another new one, huh? Reed says we got a heap more that're gonna come soon. Busy time o' year. Too bad Nate had to leave. . . . Jeez, would you look at the tongue bath that poor little fella's gettin'! His ma's learnin' his taste and smell, you know," he added importantly. "She'll know him anywhere now." He lifted his hat and brushed back a long hank of dark blond hair.

She fondly regarded the tall, gangling adolescent. His mouth rarely stopped moving as he switched from subject to subject with the speed of rifle fire, but he'd patiently taught her much of the ranching knowledge she now possessed.

He worked six days a week at the ranch, returning home every evening in time to help his widowed mother with evening chores at their small farm, three-quarters of an hour's ride north. A hardworking and honest young man, his manner was openly friendly. Though his incessant chatter was sometimes irritating, like the buzzing of a pesky mosquito, it was impossible not to like him.

"Do they all calve this easily?" Madeline asked, eager to learn more about the fascinating process she had just witnessed.

"Naw, not all. Ain't exactly a subject for women, but I reckon you're gonna pry it out of me."

A silvery giggle slipped from her throat, floating between them on the fresh spring wind. "*Pry* it out of you? You're always just a-dying to let the cat out of the bag."

"Oh, yeah, and speaking of cats," he said, jumping to another subject and screwing up his face in distaste, "I gotta warn you about that blasted cat of yours. He's gettin' into mischief in the barn again. Tore open another sack of oats. I never heard of no cat that eats oats."

"He likes snap beans, too," Madeline interjected, suppressing a smile, knowing his level of tolerance for her pet was low.

"Beans and oats," he snorted. "Ain't normal. I'll warn you, though, if Reed finds out he's tearing open feed sacks, he's gonna make a potful of cat stew so fast you'll see stars. Don't worry this time. I fixed things up so's Reed won't know." He looked at her pointedly. "Again."

"Thank you, Robbie." She smiled entreatingly. "You do have to admit that Sugar's a good little mouser."

"*Little* mouser? That fat cat weighs fifteen pounds if he weighs an ounce. Prob'ly eatin' sugar, too, when he ain't eatin' oats."

"He's half bobcat," Madeline countered importantly, raising her eyebrows, once more starting up the endless go-around between them. "My"—the correct word came with only a slight hesitation now—"grandfather told me so. That's why he's so big and has that short tail."

"Bobcats can't breed with house cats!"

"How do you know? Maybe they can," she responded waggishly, not truly knowing for certain if the two types of cats could or could not interbreed. Being right didn't matter to her at all in this friendly argument; she simply loved to tease Robbie. It was a pleasure to watch the ever-moving jaw work soundlessly, to see the garrulous youth at a loss for words.

The boy's brows knit together. "Bobcats can't breed on little cats. I know they can't. It just don't work that way, Madeline. You don't see horses and cows breedin' together, do you? Crows and sparrows? Cats and dogs?"

"Well, cats and bobcats are both cats, aren't they?" she shot back, daring him to refute her logic. "And suppose you tell me about how mules can be made, then."

"Well . . . well . . . I . . ." He shook his head, causing the hank of hair to fall into his eyes again. He swiped it away with a snap of his hand. His lower jaw worked noiselessly, finally meeting the objective she had set for it.

Inwardly she smiled.

"Madeline, mules is just a whole different ball of string," he answered after a long silence, frustration evident in his voice. "Your granddad was pullin' your leg about that bobcat business. More'n likely your little lump of Sugar didn't make it out of the barn door fast enough and got his tail slammed off. Or maybe he got too close to the stock and got it stepped on." He stopped and grinned wickedly. "Or maybe a naughty little boy took a knife and—"

"Robbie!" she squealed, a quick wave of horror running through her. "Stop it! I won't listen to any more!"

He chuckled, appearing to be quite pleased at finally finding an effective way to put an end to the disagreement. "Oh, all right. Reason I came out here was 'cause Reed wanted me to remind you about that fellow comin' out about the beef contract. It's headin' on toward three o'clock."

"It is?" Surprised that so much time had slipped away, she glanced at the position of the sun for confirmation. "My gosh, it is." Holding out her arms with an impish grin, she shrugged. "What do you think this fancy man's going to think of my attire? I reckon there's no time to change."

"Well," he replied cautiously, "you ain't dressed like no woman I ever saw, in them baggy pants and chaps and that oversized coat. Except Ma, maybe. Sometimes she wears Pa's old coveralls to do chores when it's cold and windy out," he confided. "But don't tell her I told you so."

Madeline was more than amused by the thought of Robbie's stout mother wearing coveralls. On the one day a week when Mary Ashler came to the Spencer ranch to help with cleaning and baking, it was regular practice for the loquacious but goodhearted woman to drop several broad hints to Madeline about the impropriety of her dress.

"Maybe this fellow won't even notice you're a woman," Robbie offered helpfully. "More'n likely," he continued with barely a breath, "he just wants a chance to meet with Nate and shake his hand, just like every other big-eyed stranger who finds out Nathaniel Spencer's settled in these parts."

"Say," he added, shyly lowering his head, "I didn't say nothin' before because . . . well, because. But I heard—couldn't help it, you know—that Spencer's your pa and all, and, well, I just want you to know that it don't make no difference to me—or to none of the other hands, neither—if you're his sister or his daughter or his great-aunt. We all like you just fine no matter who you are." His cheeks had flushed to a dull red by the time he finished his sentence.

"Thank you, Robbie," she answered quietly, deeply touched by the boy's sentiments. Her grandmother had expressed much uneasiness about Madeline going to live on Nate's ranch and being in the unrelieved company of men. And, as Elsie had told her, most of the ranch workers *were* coarse and poorly educated.

But coarse and poorly educated didn't necessarily mean anything but just that, Madeline had quickly discovered. Most of the men here might not know how to read or write, but they knew everything there was to know about cattle and how to work a cattle ranch, doing their jobs with tireless, good-natured efficiency.

And so what if their grammar wasn't perfect, or if they had a fondness for certain . . . indelicate words and phrases, which they attempted to modify with only fair success in her presence, or if they were incurable braggarts?

These men had helped her, little by little, recover her zest for living after the loss of the only father she had ever known. Over Nate's initial halfhearted protests of impropriety, they had been delighted to teach her all they could about cattle ranching, stumbling over each other to demonstrate such things as roping, and cutting—or separating—certain cows and calves from the large herd with their intelligent horses, working their catch-ropes with fluid accuracy.

They were nothing but kind and respectful and exuberantly encouraging—not to mention amused, she feared—at her clumsy but steadily improving attempts to assist on the range.

They had become a family of sorts to her, these rough-hewn men.

Robbie's words reinforced in her a warm feeling of acceptance. His speech, awkward but obviously heartfelt, meant a great deal to her. He and the other ranch hands liked her just fine no matter who she was, and that was high praise indeed.

The deep sadness she'd been carrying for the past days suddenly lifted, her normally optimistic nature rushing to take its place.

She felt like herself again.

Though there was still much unfinished business as well as a new strain between her and Nate, she at least knew some of the reasons now for the deep restlessness she'd always sensed in him. She suspected, too, that he had undertaken those dangerous exploring expeditions in his younger days for the same reasons.

She had adored and worshiped him as a much older, not to mention famous, brother, enormously enjoying each of his infrequent visits while she grew up. Who knew what he'd be like as a father? Perhaps she should view this long-buried secret as a gift. Though God had taken one father from her, maybe He sought to ease her pain by giving her another.

She offered Robbie a wide smile, unaware of the dazzling beauty of her face beneath the brim of her low-crowned plainsman, or of the fact that he and every other cowboy practically floated on air after one of those smiles.

Seeking to relieve his embarrassment, she admonished him with mock severity. "Don't you think I'm just a little young to be someone's great-aunt?"

His eyes met hers shyly, appreciatively. "Yeah, guess so. Well, gotta go now. Good luck with this beef fella." He kicked his horse into a gallop, his skinny frame sitting tall in the saddle. Smiling after him, she shook her reins and turned her horse toward the house.

Evan Grant checked his direction against the sun's tilt. The Spencer place shouldn't be much farther, he thought, according to the directions he'd received in Laramie City. There were fewer cattlemen in the Laramie City vicinity than around Cheyenne, but Spencer's growing ranch was reported to have over fifteen hundred head of longhorn and longhorn cross after more than two years of operation.

It was usual practice for him and his brother Ben to learn as much as possible about a ranch and the rancher who owned it before a face-to-face meeting ever occurred. Knowing about Nathaniel Spencer wasn't difficult; Evan had no doubt that the man's exploits as a guide and explorer of the West would someday be legend.

He'd been surprised, though, to learn that Spencer had settled into cattle ranching. The frontiersman had just dropped out of sight, disappearing from the public eye, a few years back.

Nonetheless, Evan looked forward to meeting the man. He wondered how Ben had fared today at the Dunlay and Fletcher ranches. His brother hadn't been at all pleased when he had insisted upon splitting up, as usual, and visiting the ranches separately, for Ben had wanted the opportunity to meet Spencer as well.

Evan had had to remind him that time was of the essence, that they were simply able to cover more ground by themselves than together. Normally good-natured, Ben had thrown his fork into the last bits of his eggs at breakfast and stalked from the hotel dining room in a huff, grumbling about bossy, overbearing older brothers.

Recalling his brother's fit of pique, Evan chuckled, knowing that at the hotel this evening Ben would be hanging on his every word about the meeting with Spencer.

Being older did have its advantages.

Bright sunshine from the endless blue sky beat warmly on the side of his face, making him aware of his weariness. He urged his horse on over the surprisingly rock-stubbled ground. Guiding the roan gelding around a deep chuckhole, he hoped a cup of strong coffee would be waiting for him at his destination.

He also hoped that his ride out to the Spencer ranch wasn't in vain.

As representatives of Grant Meats, he and Ben were in charge of securing beef contracts for their family's newest meat-packing plant, currently under construction in San Francisco. Though most cattle headed for slaughter were shipped from west to east, patriarch Hiram Grant was somewhat of a maverick regarding business techniques. He saw great potential on the West Coast and had expanded his Chicago operations accordingly, putting Evan and Ben in charge of the new plant.

Bored with life in Chicago, Evan didn't have to think long on whether or not to accept the opportunity. Also, Hiram Grant, aware of his son's ennui, had gone below the belt in securing a commitment from him, reminding Evan that he had no wife or young family to keep him in Chicago.

Though subtle, Evan knew the message behind his father's words had been sharp. Would the man never be done with his disappointment over his broken engagement, he wondered? More than four years had passed since Evan had severed his relationship with Melissa Morris. . . .

A house and outbuildings appeared in the distance. Putting the unpleasant thoughts of the past from his head, he smiled absently at the thought of meeting his boyhood hero. It would be good to meet Spencer, to be sure, but it was also going to be damned nice to get back to the hotel, have a bit of supper, and crawl into bed.

The horse crossed the distance at a smooth pace. Evan slowed the gelding near the house, lifting his hat and smoothing his dark, wavy hair. The two-story clapboard structure looked empty.

He noticed a tall sorrel hitched to the railing outside the barn and turned his horse in that direction. As he paused a few yards from the open barn door, the sound of hoofbeats carried to his ears. He looked up to see the figure of a boy riding toward him from the great expanse of gently rolling hills on the east side of the cluster of buildings. The boy lifted his arm and waved.

Evan returned the gesture, hoping the boy wasn't coming to make Spencer's excuses. Missing the opportunity to meet the man would be a disappointment, but it would be an even greater disappointment, in his opinion, to miss the opportunity of doing business with the owner of a cattle operation this size. He willed Spencer to be the rider of the sorrel hitched before him.

"Hello!" the boy shouted.

Evan took a sharper look at the boy.

He shook his head slightly, not believing his ears. The youth possessed a very feminine voice, and as the rider came closer, Evan saw that he had indeed heard correctly.

Approaching him on horseback was a lovely young woman fully dressed for work on the range. He hadn't heard that Spencer was married, or had any other arrangements, and he was fairly certain that ranchers in these parts hadn't taken to hiring female cowhands.

He was intrigued.

"Hello, again," the young woman said as she entered the yard, smiling cautiously. She was slightly out of breath, her cheeks pink from the wind and her ride. "Are you the gentleman to see us about the beef contract?"

He knew he was staring, but he couldn't help it.

Lord, she was beautiful. Her face was classically oval, her skin clear and healthy. He studied her features almost hungrily, trying to recall how many months it had been since he'd seen such a vision. Because of the shadow of her hat brim, he couldn't quite decide what color her eyes were, but her lips were pink, so full and pink, framing straight white teeth. He couldn't believe his eyes. Such a woman in the West was scarcer than a pig with wings.

Had she said "to see *us*"?

Evan's brain exploded with questions. Who was she? His eyes didn't leave her for a second as she turned her head quickly toward the barn and yelled, "Will?" A long, dark golden braid swung over her shoulder with the movement.

Her profile was every bit as exquisite as the front view of her face, Evan discovered. Pert little nose; firm, graceful jaw; delicate cheekbones . . .

She looked back at him, catching him at his ill-mannered staring. Her smile faded.

He hastened to reassure her. "Ma'am," he said, politely tipping his hat and flashing her what he hoped was his most charming smile. "My name is Evan—"

"Maddie! You out there?" The deep, booming voice came from the gloom within the barn, interrupting Evan. "That fella here yet?"

"He's here," she shouted back, looking at Evan warily.

Evan was about to ask the young woman how she happened to be on the Spencer ranch when a loud clatter arose from inside the barn. The deep voice bellowed in anger, and another, louder crash sounded.

"Goddamn!" the voice swore thunderously. "I don't believe my friggin' eyes! You worthless, stealin', sumbitchin'—" Another crash. "You're dead! I'm gonna hunt you down and kill you deader than dead!"

The young woman looked with alarm at the barn. "Oh, no," she cried, hastening to dismount. "Sugar! Oh, dear!"

Sugar? Spencer kept sugar in his barn? Had women tend to his cattle? What the hell kind of a ranch was this, anyway?

A loud thump ricocheted from within the barn into the bright afternoon air, accompanied by an eerie, yowling screech. The muscles of Evan's horse rippled nervously beneath him.

Evan tensed and drew his gun.

The voice bellowed again, this time incredulously. "Goddamn cat! Tearing open my feed sacks and eating *oats*!"

An enormous gray cat streaked out of the barn just a moment before a big, extremely angry-looking man appeared, pistol drawn.

"No, Will," the woman begged, hurrying to step in the path of the enraged man.

"Out of my way, Madeline Spencer!" he yelled. "This time he's done for!"

Madeline Spencer? Spencer was married to this beauty, then?

Evan watched in disbelief as the oversized feline lost his balance in the loose, wet dirt, sliding for a moment on his side, claws scrabbling for purchase. His mistress nearly reached him, but the angry man gained on the cat, bellowing the whole while, causing the cat to redouble his efforts to escape.

With a loud screech and a quick glance over his shoulder, the cat regained sure footing and dashed directly toward Evan's horse. The last he saw of the furry, wild-eyed creature was a fleeting glimpse of his bobbed tail as he disappeared between the front legs of the horse.

The roan spooked and jumped sideways. He landed perilously close to the fence, stiffly planting his forelegs on the ground and snapping his head downward, at the same time arching his back powerfully and kicking his rear legs high into the air. The wild movements caught Evan off guard and off balance, throwing him from the saddle and pitching him violently toward the fence.

The two riderless horses also panicked, neighing wildly, turning the yard in front of the barn into a dangerous confusion of screaming, agitated horseflesh and flying hooves.

Goddamn, I've been unseated.

The mortifying thought raced through Evan's mind as he was catapulted through the air. It happened so quickly, yet it seemed to happen so slowly. In the space of a heartbeat, his temple struck the fence rail with a dense crunch just before the ground rushed up to meet him, slamming mercilessly into his left shoulder.

With the danger of being trampled foremost in his mind, Evan scrambled to his feet and began to run, the searing pain in his head and shoulder not yet fully registering in his mind. He was aware of the surprisingly agile movements of the big man, of his daring to come between the fence and the bucking horse, of the big arm reaching for him.

Then his awareness seemed to fold in on itself, the bright afternoon fading to the ebony of a moonless night. A loud buzzing filled his ears, replacing the shrill neighing of the horses, and he stumbled, his legs no longer obeying the messages his brain sent.

He fell into blackness.

two

GREEN. HER EYES WERE BRIGHT, BRILLIANT green.

The thought skittered across Evan's mind as his eyes fluttered open, doubly rewarding him with the dizzying split-second image of a woman's concerned face close to his own and with a burst of pain through the right side of his head. Hot pain gripped his left shoulder, too, radiating down the entire arm.

Warm, feather-light strokes across his eyelids easily convinced him that he would be much better off keeping his eyes closed. "What happened?" he spoke, his words thick, barely understandable.

"Shh . . . Don't try to talk," urged a tear-choked feminine voice. "You had an accident."

He was aware of something pressing against his temple, pressing excruciatingly against the hurt. He tried to lift his head, but the simple task was unachievable. Rivers of pain flowed from indefinite areas of his body, converging into turbulent vortices of agony in his head and left shoulder. His mind was thick, and he felt disoriented; clear thought was utterly impossible through the haze of pain.

Though the sun shone down warmly on him, he became aware, too, in slow degrees, of the chilling cold seeping up from beneath him, leaching the heat from his body. Curiously, though, the back of his head felt warm. Cushioned, almost. A wave of nausea ran through him, bubbling sickly in the base of his stomach.

He heard himself groan.

A warm hand, blessedly warm, moved against the unhurt side of his face, stroking gently. "I'm so sorry," the young woman whispered. "Oh, mister, I am so very sorry. Can you ever for . . . forgive—" Her voice broke. He heard, and felt, a single sob run through her.

His head was in her lap, then?

The sun painted the insides of his eyelids a bright orangey red while the odor of manure and dirt and leather invaded his nostrils. A warm, sweet floral fragrance, too, rode in on the stink. Or did it? He shivered. Pain pounded in heavy waves over him, pain such as he had never known, flowing and receding, making it impossible for him to keep a string of thoughts tied together.

It was quiet now—he seemed to remember the shrill screaming of horses—with only the sound of the wind and the distant bawling of cattle in his ears. Gentle fingers continued to caress the side of his face. The nausea abated slightly, and he realized he could feel the delicate movements of the woman's respirations against him.

He awakened—had he dozed?—to the sound of approaching hoofbeats. Squinting, he opened his eyes a crack to see the young woman's golden head still bent slightly over his own. She was so close that he could feel the soft fanning of her breath against his cheeks. One of her hands rested lightly on his chest; the other continued to apply pressure to his temple. Though tearstains marred her cheeks, she was so very lovely, possessing the caring, exquisite face of an angel. Her eyes, he noticed again, were an absolutely arresting shade of green, bordered by damp, dark-spiked lashes.

The hoofbeats—it sounded like two horses—were louder, nearer.

"Hello," his sad angel said, mustering a small smile, her voice cracking. "You blacked out again. Don't worry, though. Will's coming. He went to get some help to move you."

He nodded his head slightly, indicating his understanding, causing fresh pain to spike through his temple. Closing his eyes, he took a deep breath, pounding in another spike of pain, this time, through his shoulder.

"Move . . . your hand," he managed to say. "My . . . head."

The verdant gaze slid from his eyes to the side of his head. "It was bleeding before, but I think I can let up on it a little now." He felt the pressure gradually melt away and was dismayed to discover that it didn't make his head feel any better at all.

"There," she said with satisfaction. "The bleeding's stopped. Does that help?"

"Not . . . much," he answered tightly, closing his eyes once more. The horses stopped somewhere close to them; he heard the creaking-leather sounds of dismounting.

Madeline.

The woman's name suddenly popped into his head. The memory flashed, too, of a huge gray cat, of being thrown from his horse.

"Miss Madeline!" An excited adolescent voice confirmed the woman's name. "Is he breathin'? Lordy, he's a big feller. Gonna be heavy. He ain't dead, is he? Aw, don't tell me he's gone over the range. Reed, the frost is out of the ground, ain't it?"

"He's breathing," Madeline stated, "but he's slipping in and out of consciousness. I think he's in a lot of pain."

"Oh, good," the young voice said with obvious relief. "You know who'd have been doin' the diggin', don't you?"

Two sets of booted feet approached. Evan opened bleary eyes and recognized the big man from the barn. With him stood a lanky youth—the owner of the flapping lips, he supposed. Dead! It would take more than being tossed off a horse to kill him.

"Grant?" The older man knelt next to him. "Name's Reed. I'm the right-hand man here. Can you understand what I'm saying'?" At his slight nod the man continued. "Good. Your livery horse turned into a high roller when that sonofabitchin' cat ran under it. You got bucked off. Hit the fence. Remember?"

He managed another nod.

"You're bunged up pretty good. Cracked your head wide open on the side there, but it looks like Miss Madeline got it to stop bleedin'." Reed's huge hands were surprisingly gentle as they ran over him. "You hurtin' anywhere else?"

"Shoulder," he answered, his voice pitifully weak. "Can't move my arm."

"I was afraid of that," Reed said, sighing and shaking his head. "You hit the ground dead-on with that shoulder. Prob'ly popped it out of joint."

"Will you have to—"

"Yup," Reed answered the woman before she had finished her question. "And the sooner the better." He barked at the youth to fetch whiskey.

Whiskey. Oh, God, that meant more pain. Evan felt a prickle of dread start in his gut. As if sensing his anxiety, Madeline gently stroked his forehead. "It'll help," she whispered reassuringly. The look in her eyes, though, told him that she didn't believe her own words.

When the footsteps had receded, the ranch foreman addressed Madeline, this time in a low voice. "I'd have preferred to have McCaleb help with this, but I ran into Robbie not too far out. Guess he'll have to do. I warned that boy to keep a hold on his lip, else I'll take a running iron to his hide."

"He'll do fine," she answered loyally.

"Grant?" Reed said, stooping over, his voice painfully in Evan's head.

For God's sake, Evan thought, nearly jumping out of his skin. He was injured, not deaf.

"We're gonna go ahead and sit you up here now, me and Maddie. Whiskey's comin'. We gotta put yer shoulder back into place." Sympathy was evident in the older man's face. "I won't blow no sunshine up your ass: it's gonna hurt like the devil."

Though the pair was as gentle as possible, he nearly passed out when they sat him up. Pain slashed all through him, and the scenery swung wildly in front of his eyes for a long moment before settling back into place. Planting his right arm on the ground for support, he leaned heavily upon it while his left arm hung useless at his side.

At Reed's suggestion, Madeline knelt behind Evan, providing support for him should he lose his balance. A moment later she wedged her knees tightly against his buttocks, whispering, "Go ahead and lean on me." Gratefully, he allowed himself to sink back against her, giving her lithe form a great deal more of his weight than he intended.

Robbie returned with a nearly full bottle of clear yellow-brown liquid and held it to Evan's lips. He took three long pulls of what the boy referred to as coffin varnish, grimacing at the taste. The liquor burned a trail to his stomach, nearly causing the organ to empty itself on the dirt before him.

"Gonna keep it down?" Reed asked.

"Yeah," he croaked, a shiver running through him.

"While we're waitin' for it to work, we gotta get your coat and shirt off. Give me a hand here, Ashler."

Evan closed his eyes, feeling the whiskey and the warm, intimate contact of the woman begin to relax him. The pleasant glow was rudely interrupted by the efforts of the two men to remove his coat, however. Jolting agony caused him to gasp and cry out. In his distress he was aware of Madeline's hand slipping down over his unhurt shoulder to his upper arm, giving it a compassionate squeeze.

"Got your coat," Reed announced.

"Yeah, but what about his shirt?" Robbie asked. "He about went out on us with the coat."

With supreme effort, Evan managed to say, "I . . . don't care. Just . . . cut . . . it."

"He says to just cut it, Reed. I guess we should just cut it offa him. Ain't got no scissors, though, so what are we—"

"Shut up, boy, and give me your knife," Reed interrupted.

A moment later the cold, smooth hardness of a blade slid inside his sleeve. The man's rough sawing motions sent waves of pain through Evan's shoulder.

"Jesus, Ashler!" the foreman swore, "is this all the better you take care of your knife? It's about as sharp as my dick." He threw the knife down in disgust and gave the fabric a great rending tear with his big hands. "There."

"You shouldn't take the Lord's name in vain in front of a lady, Reed, you know," the youth admonished. "Didja forget Miss Madeline was right here? You're lucky my ma didn't hear you. She'd be takin' you to task right now. Shouldn't be talkin' about no dicks, neither. Beg pardon, Maddie," he added apologetically.

Evan saw the irritation flare in Reed's eyes, but the man only threw a quick displeased look in the adolescent's direction, as if to say, "I'll deal with you later." Callused hands ran expertly over his shoulder, feeling, testing.

"Robbie, help Madeline support his body," the burly man ordered. "No, the body, not the arm. There." He paused, looking directly into Evan's eyes. "You ready?"

Madeline watched as Will Reed silently manipulated the useless arm and shoulder. The injured man's shirt, ripped from cuff to neck, hung crooked, baring an expanse of lean, smooth skin. She noticed that the muscles of his chest were spectacularly defined, but his shoulder . . . Oh, dear Lord! Instead of being centered, it leaned grotesquely toward his back. A tremor of horror ran through her. Robbie, too, looked as if he might be ill.

With a grunt from Reed and a scream from Evan, the top of his arm found its socket and snapped into place. The man's weight slumped hard against Maddie, nearly knocking her over. His head lolled back, resting heavily against her chest. Was he breathing? Her own breathing stopped until she noticed, with great relief, that he was.

"It's done," Reed said unnecessarily. "Now we gotta bind his arm down and get him in the house."

It was just as disturbing to look upon Mr. Grant as he lay in her father's bed as it had been out in the yard, Madeline thought. Though he was still unconscious and presently beyond pain, she wanted to weep at his suffering.

The room was in twilight. The man's handsome profile was outlined sharply by the fading light from the window. A length of linen had been tied about his shoulder and torso, firmly securing his arm to his abdomen, his elbow bent at a right angle, in the proper position for healing.

Unease filled her at the prospect of caring for the man by herself. His life had been literally in her hands since Will had gotten an urgent summons to assist with a cow struggling to give birth to a breech. He was thankful he and Robbie had gotten the injured man inside the house and into bed before one of the hands had ridden in from the range, calling for him.

"Give him a little whiskey if he comes to," Will had said to her, grabbing his hat. "This calving's gonna wear me into an early grave. Damned heifers . . . It'll probably be a hard pull," he had grumbled, striding out of the ranch house with long steps.

Robbie, too, had since gone home.

The man stirred slightly, exhaling deeply. A grimace flitted across his features and was gone. She studied his face for the hundredth time, thinking that she had never seen such a man. He was more than handsome; he had presence. Even severely wounded and unconscious, there was something compelling about him, something that drew her attention and utterly possessed it.

Not able to help herself, she reached out and put her hand first on his chest, feeling the rise and fall of his respirations, then gently touched the lock of dark hair that had fallen on his forehead, marveling at its softness between her fingers. Dark flecks of dried blood were visible on the side of his forehead, reminding her of the ghastly wound just under his hairline. The wound *she* was responsible for.

Wretchedness swept through her. All of this had happened because of her pet . . .

Pulling back her hand but still feeling the sensation of his silky hair on her fingers, she vowed to take good care of this magnificent man, even if it killed her. Looking around her father's room, she wondered what Nate was doing at this moment. She realized she hadn't thought of him—or her other troubles—since setting eyes on Evan Grant. With a last long glance at the man, she sighed and left the bedroom to put on a pot of coffee.

This promised to be a long night.

three

 IN THE SPACIOUS AND RICHLY APPOINTED MONT-
gomery street offices of Merritt, Walters, and
Stewart, Basil Merritt removed his spectacles and
massaged his temples, surreptitiously releasing
a nearly silent but vexed sigh.

The tall, distinguished-looking visitor sitting across from
him positively exuded hostility. Dressed in wrinkled travel
clothing, the solid, powerful man, about forty years of age,
Merritt guessed, glowered at him, his large form seeming
to fill the room. A fine porcelain cup of fragrant tea sat
unsipped on the desk in front of the angry man.

"Spencer, we've been over and over this," Merritt tried
again, his patience wafer-thin. "Emmett Brinkman's will
cannot be executed unless all three beneficiaries are present.
Madeline will have to come here to San Francisco."

"She will not."

The equally spaced, carefully enunciated words hung
between them.

"Dammit, Spencer," Merritt swore, uncharacteristically
heedless of decorum. "I'm having the devil's own time

with the third beneficiary the way it is. You do realize that if I cannot bring the three parties together I cannot execute the will in accordance with the wishes of the late Mr. Brinkman."

"Piss on Brinkman's grave," the big man ground out, a muscle jumping in his jaw. "I refuse to let Madeline accept one cent of his money."

Merritt's deep baritone rose as he spoke, and he felt an unbecoming flush break out on his neck. "The will cannot be executed if I can not—" he paused, then all but shouted, "bring the three women together." He swung his short portly form away from the desk and threw out an ace. "The Miss Brinkman here in San Francisco has been apprised of, ah, all the facts and is most eager to meet your daughter."

Merritt wasn't fully prepared for the crackling intensity of the man's deep green gaze upon him. Never in all his years in the courts had he felt so much like a bug on a pin as he did at this moment. Tension invisibly churned on the late afternoon air between him and the big man, and he felt a churning begin in his stomach as well. He began pacing behind the polished mahogany desk.

"What exactly do you mean by 'the Miss Brinkman here in San Fransisco'?" Spencer asked, his soft words carrying all the menace of a growling, crouched panther. His eyes had narrowed, giving him even more of the look of that dangerous predatory beast. "Brinkman had only one other daughter—Caroline—and I saw her not more than an hour ago."

"I shouldn't be discussing this with you," Merritt said with calculation, precisely choosing each word, "but simply put, the *other* Miss Brinkman—the one in France—is rejecting her inheritance in a most unmistakable fashion."

Having played his trump card, the attorney stopped pacing and reached for his glasses. It had to be done, he told himself, as he watched the color drain all at once from Spencer's face. Though Merritt had regained the upper hand, he felt no satisfaction, only a grim determination to see the thing through to the finish. He took a sip from his own teacup, hoping to settle his stomach, and waited.

His words had the same effect on Spencer as a blow to a vital organ.

"Oh, my God," the frontiersman whispered, closing his eyes, his forehead creasing into furrows of pain. "Tell me," he said weakly after a long moment, swallowing with great difficulty, "the given name of the Miss Brinkman in France."

"I think you know."

Spencer crumpled before him. A giant fist struck the desk fiercely, causing papers to spill from neatly stacked piles and tea to splash from both cups. "Nooo! Oh, God, no!" he cried in a raw voice, sounding wounded. "Sara's *alive*? She's been in France all these years?"

"I had no idea, either," Merritt hastened to say, "until Brinkman came to me to revise his will. He apparently had a turn of conscience in his final months and revealed to me that his story of Sara's death was a deception." He paused and readjusted his glasses, which were again pinching his temples unmercifully. "He confessed that he had disowned her after the baby was born and had sent her to a convent in France."

"Oh, Sara. Oh, sweet Jesus. I didn't know . . . I thought she was dead."

"You couldn't have known." Merritt felt obligated to offer what little support he could. Brinkman covered his tracks well. No one except his wife knew of this. "It's likely what drove her to an early grave." He added the last sentence under his breath, appalled by his old friend's lies.

"Brinkman knew he was dying. He tried to reunite his family while he still lived, but his time ran out," he went on to explain. "In the event he failed to do this, it was his most fervent wish that his family could be united through his death. He also hoped to atone for his many mistakes by dividing his estate equally among his descendants."

"You mean the fucker tried to buy his way into heaven," Spencer snarled roughly, the color rapidly returning to his face.

Merritt shrugged noncommittally, inwardly satisfied at the younger man's recovery from the cruel shock he had dealt him. But how best to proceed? He needed all three women in San Francisco.

"What was Sara's response to all of this?" Spencer asked, the green gaze again fixed intently on the older man.

"Brinkman wrote her, wired her. She never responded. I wired her, too, of course, after her father's death," Merritt said. "Handy business, being able to wire across to the Continent."

"And?"

"I informed her of her father's passing, as well as of her being named as a beneficiary. I instructed her, too, to return to San Francisco with all haste so the will could be executed."

"And?"

"And I received a reply. Perhaps you would like to read it?" Merritt reached into the top desk drawer and removed a sheet of paper, handing it across the desk to the large outstretched hand.

Nate Spencer took less than a second to scan the sheet of paper before throwing it down. Landing in the spilled tea, the one-word message—"*Never*"—spread and became blurry. He rose from his chair in an angry, fluid movement.

"Now, Mr. Spencer—" Merritt began.

"No, you listen to me, Mr. Lawyer." The hostility was back, emanating in waves from the imposing, broad-shouldered form. "Pardon me if I don't share your exalted view of Emmett Brinkman. Twenty years ago the old man told me Sara was dead and all but threw me off his property. He didn't even tell me I had a daughter! *Do you understand?* I didn't find out about my daughter until the next time I visited my parents, and there she was, already toddling around."

"I know that," Merritt affirmed quietly. "Emmett confessed to me, I believe, the whole of his deeds."

Spencer grabbed his head between his hands with such force that his knuckles stood out in bloodless relief. He turned sharply, presenting his back to the attorney. "And what kind of woman is Sara?" he very nearly roared. "In twenty years she never once tried to contact me. Oh, God, forget about me! What kind of woman could turn her back on her baby? Her own flesh and blood?"

Ah, the heart of the matter. So there was still a spark there. Merritt calmly folded his hands in front of his own rounded belly. "She didn't know about the baby. Still doesn't."

"Doesn't know she had a baby? How could a woman give birth and not know she had a baby?" The pictures on the walls rattled from the volume of Spencer's voice.

"Another deception," he replied, shaking his head, certain that this sin would weigh heavy on his friend's soul for all time. "The perfidy of Emmett Brinkman extended beyond telling you Sara was dead. He made certain, too, that Sara was told her baby had died at birth. It's a miracle, I suppose, that he just didn't do away with the child. Instead he hired a wet nurse and sent the child to your parents in Missouri."

Spencer had turned slowly back around at his words. Merritt knew he had his full attention. "To Brinkman, Sara *was* dead. He disowned her and put her aboard a ship to France before she was even well enough to travel. Installed her in a nunnery."

"And she just accepted it?" The words were bitter, cynical.

"She had to!" Merritt's voice boomed back. "She was warned, under the pain of *your death*, never to try to contact you or return to her home country."

A faint gleam of hope dawned in the proud green eyes before Spencer looked away.

"You'll be wanting the details of exactly where in France you may find your Miss Brinkman, I imagine," Merritt stated quietly, reaching into his desk. "Let me get them for you."

four

MADELINE AWOKE WITH A START, THE TASTE of old coffee clinging foully to the inside of her mouth. She hadn't meant to sleep! The high-backed wooden chair tipped precariously with her sudden movement, nearly depositing her on the floor before she caught her balance and planted the legs of the chair down firmly. Her pounding heartbeat slowed when she saw that the dark-haired man slumbered peacefully in the center of the bed.

Finally.

The dingy light of a gray morning washed the bedroom in drab tones. She stood, rubbing her kinked, aching lower back, recalling the worry and anxiety she'd experienced during the seemingly endless night. Her eyes felt gritty from lack of sleep, and a dull throbbing in her temples promised to grow into a skull-splitting headache.

From just after sundown until somewhere in the wee hours Evan Grant had muttered and moaned and thrashed about, never fully waking, initially causing her near-panicked distress. Will had returned around midnight and had managed

to get a little whiskey, mixed with several drops of laudanum, down the semiconscious man's throat. Bone-tired
and voicing his opinion that the injured man would be "just
fine once the snake juice hit him," the ranch foreman had
retired to the sitting room floor with his bedroll and then
had punctuated the night with loud bursts of snoring. Rising
shortly after four o'clock, he had been satisfied to see that
Evan was resting more calmly. He'd dosed him with another
shot of laudanum-laced whiskey before heading out the door,
admonishing her to get some sleep herself.

But she had found it impossible to leave Evan's side.
Every movement, every sound had filled her with worry, stretching her nerves to their limits. What if his head
wound should open up and begin bleeding again? What
if he thrashed about so much that he fell out of bed and
further damaged his shoulder?

What if he should *die*?

She was pulled from her thoughts by the sound of loud
male voices outside the house. Will's shouting was instantly
identifiable, but the other man's voice was one she had
never before heard. Evan stirred slightly and mumbled as
she stepped quickly to one of the windows and peeked
outside.

At the same time, she heard the kitchen door open and the
owners of the angry voices enter. Was Will in some kind of
trouble? Had something happened to Nate? Licking her dry
lips, she ran an ineffective hand over her baggy, wrinkled
garments before attempting in vain to smooth out the waves
of messy, tangled hair spilling over her shoulders.

"Where is he?" the unfamiliar voice demanded. "Dammit,
I'll have the law out here—"

"I told you, you impatient whelp, that he's laying flat
on his back in Spencer's bed and he'll be just fine after
his shoulder sets back together."

Evan Grant stirred and groggily opened his eyes at the
sounds.

Walking swiftly to the bedroom door, Madeline was
nearly knocked aside by a tall, dark-haired man bearing
a strong resemblance to the supine man in her father's
bed. Flashing blue eyes first searched the appearance of

the injured man, then swung piercingly to her.

"Who the hell are *you*? What the hell did you do to my brother?" There was a frantic note in his shouted demands. He looked from her to Will, who now stood behind him in the doorway, then turned his attention again to the man on the bed. "Oh, God, Ev, what did they do to you? Can you talk? Can you sit up? Don't worry, I'll get you out of here. . . . Hey, there's dried blood on his head—" He broke off and stared accusingly at Will. "You never told me anything about his *head*! What did you do, bushwhack him?"

"Now hold on for just one minute, you wet-behind-the-ears little scrapper," Will angrily interjected, making the wounded man, who was having difficulty keeping his eyes open, wince at the eruption. "For chrissake, Grant, I told you your brother came out here yesterday and got tossed off his horse. Listen to me: your ever-lovin' brother bit the dust. His head's cracked open because it hit the fence afore he hit the ground." He shook his head and pushed his way past the young man. Irately gesturing toward the bed with a plate-sized hand, he continued his harangue. "If we was gonna do him in—an' why the hell would we wanna do that?—do you think he'd be layin' here in the middle of Nate Spencer's bed like the goddamn queen of England?"

"So . . . loud."

All three heads swung in Evan's direction. Beneath the tangle of dark hair, pain shone on the man's features as he attempted, in slow movements, to inch himself higher in the bed. His eyes had again closed, and his face had blanched from his efforts. He sank back against the pillows. "Can't hardly move. . . . Can't stay . . . awake," he said weakly.

Watching the man who yesterday afternoon had sat tall and commanding in his saddle, Madeline felt her heart contract painfully. She remembered how he had looked at her when she had first ridden up. She remembered the dazzling smile he had flashed her, remembered the fluttery feeling that had started in her breast. He was so handsome that she'd felt, when she first saw him up close, as if she had fallen from the stars and landed flat on her back; the sight of him had sucked the very air from her lungs. And then Sugar had—

"Maddie, are you listenin'?" Will questioned. "I asked you if he's had any more of the potion I fixed up."

"What kind of potion?" the younger Grant demanded. "So help me, you'd better know what you're doing."

Will sighed. "Just whiskey with a little laudanum mixed in. Nothin' else, so don't get your drawers all bunched up."

"He hasn't had anything since you dosed him at four o'clock," Madeline wearily answered Will's question, "and he's been resting fairly comfortably since then." Extending her hand and a wan smile to the angry, distressed young man standing near the bed, she said simply, "I'm Madeline Spencer, Mr. Grant. We're very sorry for what happened to your brother, but we're doing our best to take care of him."

For a second it looked as if he might ignore her gesture, but he slowly reached out and met her hand with his, the fire rapidly fading from his blue eyes. "Ben. Ben Grant." Studying her, he removed his hand and held it against his chest. "You stayed up the whole night with him, didn't you?" he asked in a subdued voice.

"Well, I—"

"You did, didn't you? You look as though you haven't slept in a week—pardon me for saying so, ma'am. Aw, I can be such an idiot sometimes. Can you forgive me—both of you—for barging in here like I did? It's just that I was so worried about Evan not coming back last night . . ."

"It's all right," she said, feeling a small portion of her tension drain away. "You must have been worried sick about him."

"We'd have got word to you, except we didn't know there was two of you," Will gruffly explained. "Your brother's been pretty much out of it since the thing happened."

As if on cue, Evan snored softly.

"Can I make you some coffee, Mr. Grant?" Madeline asked, remembering her manners. "Have you had breakfast yet?"

"Well, no," he hesitated.

"Reckon I could eat a little more at that," Will interjected. "Let's get on outta here and let your brother do the sleepin' for all of us. Miss Maddie is a fairly decent cook, Grant," he added, deadpan, "when she don't get a notion to petrify the egg yolks."

The meal she and Will shared with Ben Grant had been quite pleasant, Madeline reflected, washing quickly at the pine dry sink in her upstairs bedroom. Over strong freshly brewed coffee, crunchy bacon, and fried eggs, the tired but relieved young man had been a charming, lively conversationalist, causing even Will to break into guffaws a time or two at his entertaining anecdotes. He told them a great deal about the expansion of Grant Meats and the plans for Evan and him to head up the San Francisco operation.

"Mrs. Spencer," he'd called her once, wrongly assuming she was Nate's wife. Will had raised his eyebrows slightly but had said nothing, continuing to chew thoughtfully on his bacon, allowing her to correct the man or let him believe what he would.

She had taken a sip of coffee and a deep breath before correcting him. "It's *Miss* Spencer. I'm Nate's daughter," she'd said, looking directly into the merry blue eyes.

"I didn't know he had . . . Oh, never mind." A slight flush had risen on his lean, handsome face before he recovered his wits. "Miss Spencer, it is," he'd said gallantly, briefly nodding his head. "I'm pleased to know you."

"I'm pleased to know you, too, Mr. Grant," she'd replied, feeling great relief at his polite if slightly awkward response. She'd smiled wryly, adding, "Although I fear your brother may not be pleased to know any of us after what happened to him yesterday."

Ben had winced at her comment. "Ah, yeah. Evan will most definitely not be pleased when he comes around. He can be a mite . . . er, grouchy when things don't go the way he wants." He'd grinned and leaned toward her. " 'Overbearing' describes him nicely," he had whispered conspiratorially, "but he's also bossy, arrogant, domineering . . . Oh, and I can't forget that he's always right, too." He'd rolled his eyes. "I wonder if everyone's older brother is the same way?"

Madeline smiled, patting her shoulders and torso dry with the towel, shivering in the chilly air, remembering her answering grin and the saucy words that had tumbled from her lips. "Well, might makes right around these parts, and I'd say that in your brother's condition, he doesn't presently have much might at his disposal. Just think about it. He'll have to do whatever we tell him to." She'd raised her eyebrows impudently, cocking her head to one side.

"Lord above!" Ben had exclaimed, laughing. "I hope you never meet up with our little sister Annalisa. The pair of you would turn the country on its ear! You out in the middle of nowhere wearing trousers and probably punching cows, and her, if she had her way, on the next train to San Francisco and up to her elbows in the new business."

"For your information, Grant, Miss Madeline ain't a bad cowpunch," Will had asserted, finishing his coffee in a large gulp, "and her ropin's comin' along nicely." He'd pushed his chair away from the table and stood. "Well, I gotta get back out there. I set Robbie to doin' a bunch of chores up around the barn, so holler at him if you need anything. Thanks for breakfast, Maddie. Nice to meet you, Grant. Spencer's away, but you're welcome to stay as long as you like. I'd say your brother's gonna be here a good coupla weeks."

A couple weeks with Evan Grant in the house. The man was barely conscious and as weak as a babe, but the thought of him living under her roof for the next two weeks gave Madeline an odd giddy feeling in the pit of her stomach. Just as curiously, though Ben Grant was nearly every bit as handsome as his brother, his winsome manner and appealing smile had no more effect on her senses than did the innocent and endearing Robbie Ashler.

She finished patting herself dry and donned a clean chemise, the sweet fragrance of the French-milled, floral-scented soap clinging softly to her freshly scrubbed skin. After slipping into a sensible green-on-green calico print dress, she briefly studied her appearance in the mirror and frowned. Her eyes were tired-looking, complete with dark circles beneath them, while her hair sprouted untidily in all directions about the high, delicate bones of her oval face and spilled messily over her shoulders. Heavens! And she'd sat through breakfast looking like that! She picked up her brush and attacked the unruly locks with strong merciless strokes until they gleamed like polished gold. Anxious to get back downstairs and check on Evan, she quickly plaited the thick silky strands and wrapped the fat braid into a neat chignon at the nape of her neck.

Evan had been sleeping peacefully when the others had finished breakfast, so Ben had decided to return to Laramie City to wire his parents and possibly keep one of his appointments at an area ranch. He planned on returning to the Spencer ranch at the end of the day.

"I won't tell you to take good care of Evan because I can see you're already doing that," he'd said before he left. "But if he comes to, don't mind his bark. As the saying goes, it's much worse than his bite. Ever since . . . well, let's just say he's not as lighthearted as he used to be." He was quiet for a moment; then his seriousness had lifted and he'd laughed, raising his eyebrows. "If he tries to bite you, Miss Spencer, just bite him back. Or better yet, slip him another dose or two of that concoction to keep him docile."

Descending the stairs, she pondered Ben's words. What had he meant by Evan not being as lighthearted as he used to be? Ever since what? Had something terrible happened to him? An old injury that wasn't readily apparent? He'd certainly looked healthy enough yesterday afternoon. *Too* healthy, in fact, she concluded, remembering the intensity of his eyes upon her. But perhaps there was a tragedy in his background. Countless thousands of persons and families had been touched by the terrible War between the States. She made a mental note to discreetly bring up the subject to Ben this evening when he returned.

Walking to the doorway of Nate's bedroom, she saw that Evan still slumbered restfully. What to do next? The dishes? She could heat extra water, too, and sponge away the crusty, dried blood from the area around his head wound. She told herself it would do Ben's heart good to see his brother looking more presentable, but she knew her peace of mind would greatly benefit as well.

A half-hour later the dishes were done, and she stood in the bedroom. Setting down the pail of warm water, she walked to the bed and gently shook the man's good shoulder. "Mr. Grant?" His skin was warm and slightly damp. He sighed deeply but made no other sound or movement in response to her presence.

"Mr. Grant?" she repeated.

Still no response.

Her eyes searched his face. In repose, even with black-stubbled cheeks, he looked relaxed, friendly, and devastatingly handsome. Her gaze drifted downward, watching the gentle rise and fall of his bound chest. A pulse beat strongly in his neck, reminding her of his strength and vitality.

Her own pulse quickened in response. The memory of the intimate contact she'd had with him, of wedging her body tightly against his before Will had set his shoulder, leapt into her mind. Through two sets of clothing and two leather coats, her thighs and belly and breasts had ached at the weight of his muscular body leaning against hers. She remembered the clean smell of his glossy hair. . . .

A queer feeling twisted inside her chest and shot down through the center of her, making her knees weak with some undefinable emotion. She stared at his face again, memorizing each feature, until she resolutely tore her gaze away and busied herself with pouring water into the basin and soaping a washcloth.

Her hands trembled.

What on earth was the matter with her? Her feelings and emotions were running amok, rushing about in frenzied violence inside her. Maybe she was coming down with something. That was it, she told herself, she must be coming down with something. A spring cold, perhaps. Because it was craziness, sheer craziness, to think that a man she didn't even know could cause such turbulence within her.

Evan swam up through thick layers of sleep, gradually becoming more alert, sense by sense. Each breath he drew caused his shoulder to move slightly, sending regular surges of white fire burning through the injured joint. In addition to the pain in his shoulder and the generalized stiffness and soreness of his body, his head ached terribly.

With great difficulty, he opened his eyes and struggled to focus on his surroundings. Gray daylight entered through two curtained windows, causing him to blink several times. Although befuddled with pain and somnolence, he realized he was alone and that this room was one he had never been in before. His right hand gingerly explored the wounded shoulder and the snug wrappings encasing his chest and arm before ascending to touch the throbbing area on the side of his head, while his unusually laggardly mind tried to piece things together.

In addition to the obvious fact that he was lying in someone's bed, where was he?

It wasn't until he rested his arm on the bed again that he realized his face was clean-shaven. Who had done that? Footsteps of worry scurried through him at the realization he'd been out so cold that he had been unaware of having his wounds tended and of being moved and shaved . . . and bathed?

He raised his right arm again and cautiously sniffed it. The scent of soap on his skin was unmistakable.

A slight squeak at the door drew his attention. Large pieces of the puzzle fell into place when he saw the delicate feminine face peering at him with great concern. Spencer's woman. The Spencer ranch. The beef contract.

He remembered being thrown from his horse, remembered the burly foreman reaching for him, then later setting his shoulder while the young woman had all but held him up. He searched the hazy corners and recesses of his mind, but found he remembered nothing from that point on.

Standing in the doorway, the woman who had before been dressed like a man now wore a simple work dress. Though plain and unadorned, the bodice fit neatly over square, proud shoulders and a full bosom. She was remarkably tall for a woman, he noticed, but proportioned perfectly. Spencer was one lucky son of a . . .

His eyes grew heavy from the effort of taking in such a magnificent, appealing sight. But at least he had forgotten all about the pain for a moment. He closed his eyes briefly and opened them again. Two Mrs. Spencers stood slightly apart from each other and slowly blended to become one luscious figure.

This time he noticed that fatigue hung heavy on the fresh beauty of her features, staining the area beneath her eyes with dark smudges of color. She looked exhausted.

"Hello," she said, smiling tentatively, running a hand self-consciously over the top of her head. "Are your eyelids going to win the battle this time and stay open?"

"I'm not sure," he replied, disgusted with the infirm sound of his voice. His shoulder pained him terribly. He tried to reposition himself, but a fresh bolt of pain caused him to abandon the effort. Sucking in his breath sharply, he sank back heavily against the pillows. A film of sweat broke out on his forehead, and he closed his eyes once more; the effort of blinking seemed overwhelming at the moment.

"You're in pain!" he heard her exclaim. "Let me get you some laudanum."

"No . . . laudanum. Just get me whiskey."

"I really think—"

"I don't care what you think." The pain rolled and swelled over him. "Just bring me some damned whiskey."

"All right," she answered quickly, placably.

He heard her footsteps move out of the room. In only moments, yet an eternity, she was back. He felt a slight disturbance of air in front of his face as she stepped over to the bed. On it drifted a light, flowery fragrance, personalized with the warm, still-unfamiliar scent of this woman. In spite of his agony, he breathed more deeply, drinking in the wonderful aroma of sweet-smelling femininity. His shoulder throbbed horribly, but he hadn't smelled anything so delicious in . . . how long?

"Here's your whiskey, Mr. Grant," she said, her voice soft and soothing in his ear.

Her tempting perfume and gently spoken words fueled him with enough strength to open his eyes. She stood next to the bed, leaning over him. Her full lower lip was caught between her teeth, while concerned green eyes looked straight into his own. Wispy tendrils of golden hair hung beguilingly about the perfection of her face, bordering it as finely as a gilt frame would a priceless painting. He sensed the lush, ripe curves of her breasts rising and falling with her respirations, felt their heat only a fraction of an inch from his upper arm. In her hand she held a tumbler with two fingers of dark amber liquid.

"H-here's your whiskey," she said, breaking eye contact and looking, instead, at the glass in her hand. "Do you still want it?"

"Yeah." He struggled to lift his head from the pillow but found it impossible. "I don't think I can sit up. . . . You'll have to help me."

He winced when she eased her hand behind his head and helped him raise it. Misjudging the angle, she tipped the tumbler too soon and spilled some of the strong-smelling liquid down his chin and neck. He muttered an obscenity, which brought a flush of color to her pale cheeks.

"I'm sorry," she said miserably. "Here, let's try it again."

A little dribbled from one corner of his mouth, but a healthy swallow of the whiskey wound up where it was intended. "Arghh." He shuddered, gooseflesh rising on his arms. He took another grand gulp, emptying the glass. "Jesus H. Christ," he swore, the raw taste of liquor lending strength to his voice. "What the hell kind of home brew is this?"

She straightened up, her lower lip still caught between her teeth. "I'm sorry," she said.

"Sorry? Sorry for what?"

"Sorry for . . . everything, Mr. Grant."

"Well, if you're so sorry, why don't you go get me some decent whiskey?" He hadn't meant to sound quite so surly, but he felt frustrated and powerless lying here helpless, at the mercy of a mere slip of a woman.

She stiffened when his words struck; green sparks jumped in her eyes. "Certainly," she replied. Turning on her heel, she walked from the room without another word, her backside swaying bewitchingly beneath her skirt.

He waited expectantly for her to return, intending to apologize for his rough words. Waves of drowsiness washed over him while he waited, each swell sending the pain a little farther away. In fact, he almost seemed to be floating. God, that repulsive home brew had quite a kick to it.

It also seemed as though she was taking an infernally long time to get the good whiskey.

Ah, so that was her game, he realized foggily, grudgingly admiring her strategy. Thought she was clever by not coming back, did she? Well, he could outwait her, he thought, valiantly holding his eyes open for three more seconds before slumber claimed him.

five

Holding the knob for support, Madeline leaned heavily against the door of her father's bedroom. Mr. Grant was finally asleep again; the laudanum in the whiskey had done the trick.

Ben hadn't been kidding when he said his brother had a bark. She had a very good idea, too, that Evan's bark would turn into a lion's roar if he knew he'd received a generous dose of laudanum mixed in with the whiskey. Home brew, indeed! According to Nate, the liquor she'd served Evan Grant was a very fine scotch.

Had Mr. Grant suspected? she wondered uneasily. The tincture of opium was extremely bitter. . . .

No, she decided, he hadn't suspected. He just thought the whiskey was terrible. She might even be able to get another dose or two into him before he figured it out. Honestly, the way he'd barked orders at her! She let out her breath with a short, exasperated sound. It served him right to be deceived.

Her satisfaction at outwitting the cross, foul-tempered man crumbled when she recalled the incredible pain in the depths of his blue eyes. And such eyes the man had been blessed with! Light sky-blue irises spread mesmerically, with variegation, into deep azure outer rings. They were, without question, eyes to become totally and completely lost in. Framed by a generous fringe of dark lashes and elegant brows, they were enough to arrest the heartbeat of any warm-blooded female hapless enough to look into them.

And many souls had doubtless succumbed, she told herself severely. A man who looked like Evan Grant probably didn't have a moment's trouble finding female companionship.

In fact, a man like Evan Grant probably had women lining up down the street, painted and powdered, tittering and teasing, all flounces and flirtation. . . . Oh, why did that idea produce such a miserable, sick feeling inside her? Was it because a man like Evan Grant would be so, so . . . so what?

She sighed. It was fortunate, indeed, that his seductive blue eyes had been closed while she sponged his face. There was no telling what effect they might have had upon her. Effect. Affect. Why did this man affect her so? She didn't know, either, why or where she'd gotten the courage—or was it presumptuousness?—to shave his face and wash his upper torso. It was most imprudent, really, but she had wanted to tenderly minister to his needs, to care for him, to make whole the magnificent man she'd had such a great part in disjointing.

She shook her head. Her foolish thoughts even punned themselves.

Ben would return to the ranch house at the end of the afternoon, as would Will, she was certain. What was she to do in the long hours until then? She was unused to being indoors and remaining idle for a whole day. She walked through the large, attractively furnished sitting room and looked out the window. Though the day was gray, a dose of the outdoors might clear her head.

But she dared not leave the man unattended. What if he should cry out? What if he should need something? She sighed and let the curtain fall back into place.

Will would take his evening meal at the mess hall with the other hands; no doubt he'd invite Ben Grant to partake of Old Roger's delicious cooking as well. Then Robbie would run a plate of the cook's savory supper up to her. . . .

The morning meal had been so pleasant and companionable with the three of them around the rectangular pine table in the kitchen, sharing food and laughter and conversation. It had been that way back home in Independence before her . . . grandfather died. Since she'd arrived at the ranch she hadn't exactly been starved for mealtime companionship, but Nate had often eaten his meals out at the cookshack. She ate there from time to time, too, but sensed it was awkward for the men to have a woman at their table. Conversations became stilted or broke off entirely when the men realized they had headed into improper territory. Despite their valiant efforts to keep their language decent, her vocabulary had increased greatly, as had her stock of colorful and unrepeatable sayings.

Walking to the bedroom door, she peeked inside. Good. He was still sleeping. She watched the easy rise and fall of his chest for a long minute, noticing that the lines of pain had been erased from his face. Tiredness washed over her. Loneliness, too, ached within her breast.

She missed Elsie, missed Albert, missed Nate.

Elsie's raisin squares came to mind, a symbol of the older woman's love and comfort. As she remembered the taste of the rich, delicious pastry, her mouth nearly watered. She often craved sweet foods around the time of her monthly, but her woman's flow had ended a few days before.

Why, then, did her mind continue to conjure up thoughts of plump, juicy raisins, or of rich cream flowing over a delicately browned crust?

Comfort, she answered herself, *that's what you crave.* And if today wasn't a day for self-indulgence, she didn't know of a better occasion.

Stepping briskly into the kitchen, she pulled down a baking pan and a large mixing bowl from the shelf. Busying herself with gathering flour and sugar and salt and lard and the other ingredients she needed, she settled on the idea of having Robbie fetch down a nice cut of meat to roast from the covered carcass on the meat pole. Roast, browned potatoes and carrots, hot buttermilk biscuits, raisin squares—it would be a meal to rival Old Roger's best.

Ben and Will would share the evening meal with her, she decided. She wanted—no, *needed*—the company, needed to find out more about the compelling man lying in her father's bed. And who better than the man's brother would be able to tell her what she wanted to know?

And just what *did* she want to know?

Only everything.

She wanted to know what he'd been like as a child, if he'd had any pets, what subjects he'd studied, if he'd pulled any little girls' pigtails . . . or if he'd pulled any big girls' pigtails.

She swallowed hard. Maybe she didn't want to know everything. Maybe the thing Ben had alluded to this morning had involved a woman. "Ever since," he'd said before he stopped himself.

Ever since what?

Her mind—and heart—ached from the leapfrog route her thoughts had taken. The dull throbbing in her temples that had been present the whole day long erupted into full pain, causing her to set the grater and container of curled cinnamon bark down hard on the table. Sliding into a chair, she bent her head forward, resting her elbows on the table and her head in her hands, and massaged her temples in slow, therapeutic circles.

Touch. That was another thing she sorely missed. Elsie had often stroked her head, brushed her hair, massaged her shoulders, her neck. Albert had also been generous with his affection, frequently pulling her into a great bear hug or chucking her gently under the chin or planting a loud kiss on her cheek when he walked by her.

She had felt so loved, so cherished, by the grandparents who had raised her as their own. As her older brother, Nate, too, had been free with his demonstrations of love.

All that had changed with the arrival of the letter. Before Nate left for San Francisco he'd been nothing but stiff, automatic, distracted, and very, very grim. Her thoughts leapt again, this time toward the shocking revelations her father had made.

What kind of woman had Sara Brinkman been? she wondered. Tall? Short? Plump? Willowy? Talkative? Reticent? Nate had said she was beautiful, but that didn't answer the questions Madeline had. Gooseflesh prickled on her arms when she realized—really, truly, deeply realized—that Sara had died after giving birth to her. Sara Brinkman, a woman she didn't know but had once been a part of—a part of—had suffered untold agony and had lost her life because of her.

Her eyes filled with moisture at the enormity of her thoughts. Sara must have numbered fewer years than her own twenty when she had borne her. She had been a girl, just a young girl, in a catastrophic situation. She must have been so frightened.

A tear slipped down her cheek. Her whole world had rocked off its axis. Why did everything have to change? She no longer knew what to think, what to feel. She pressed harder on her head with her fingers and wiped her face with the sides of her thumbs. Had she really been so immature, so naive, as to take the good things in life for granted?

Granted.

Grant.

Oh, damn, back to him again.

She stood, wiping her eyes and sniffling one last time, and pulled an apron on over her dress. She set a pan of water on the stove in which to simmer the raisins and measured two heaping cups of flour, a generous pinch of salt, and a chunk of lard the size of a small apple into the bowl, thinking all the while of the flushed, tremulous feelings that seized her each time she looked into the strong, finely sculptured face or upon the great, imposing body of the man filling her father's bed.

Lost in her thoughts, she thrashed the crumbly mixture around in the bowl with a fork, added a little water and thrashed some more, unmindful of every painstaking pastry-handling lesson Elsie had ever given her.

By late afternoon the aroma of roasting meat filled the lower story of the ranch house. Commingled with the mouth-watering fragrance was the spicy, unmistakable smell of cinnamon; its source, a perfectly browned rectangular pastry, rested invitingly on top of a many-times folded towel on the sideboard.

Compared with the oppressive gray skies that hung low over the plains and caused a premature dusk, the homey, comfortable kitchen radiated warmth and cheer. Under the table's neatly laid dishes rested a crisp blue-and-white cloth, while matching napkins sat with uniform precision on three plates. A pan of baking powder biscuits sat near the stove, unbaked and covered with a towel, ready to be set in the oven at a moment's notice.

The yellow glow of the lamp banished to the corners of the room the late afternoon dismalness and also set to gleaming the coiled mass of tawny golden hair belonging to the sleeping woman who leaned forward in her chair, resting her head in her arms on the end of the charmingly set table.

It was this scene that Ben walked in on, opening the door and stomping his feet, calling loudly, "Hello, the house." A fine sheen of moisture glistened on his hat and coat, and he set down the bags he carried, rubbing his hands together briskly. "It smells like heaven in here! Good to get indoors. It's getting darned cold out there. Misting, too. A cup of hot coffee would sure—" His voice broke off when he noticed the relaxed figure at the end of the table. "Oh, jeez, I'm sorry, ma'am, I didn't know you were sleeping."

Madeline raised her head, looking with unfocused eyes at the red-cheeked young man. A draft of chilly air hit her, chasing away a good deal of her dopiness, and she shivered, mortified that she had fallen asleep at the table. To add to her embarrassment she became aware of a runner of drool dribbling from the corner of her mouth. Hastily she wiped it away with the back of her hand.

"Ma'am, if you need some more sleep, I can see to my own supper," Ben said earnestly. "I'm really sorry I came in here jawing at the top of my lungs. Anna and Ma used to give me heck for that all the time." He walked to the oven and peeked inside. "Looks like everything's about ready to go." He lifted the towel from the baking pan. "Biscuits, too!

Lordy, you surely know the way to a man's heart." He let go of the towel and splayed his hand across his chest. "Good looks, and she can cook, too."

He bounded over to where she sat, theatrically dropping to one knee. "Will you marry me, Miss Spencer? Please, won't you marry me and cook for me every night? We could be so happy together. You cookin' and me eatin'. I can see it now." He made a face. "Evan can't cook at all."

She giggled at his foolishness, while at the same time feeling her cheeks pinken under his regard. "No, I won't marry you, Mr. Grant, but I will make us some coffee." She pushed her chair back from the table.

"Aw, darn," he said, returning to his feet. "I'm always having to settle for second best." His gaze remained on her. "Pardon me for commenting on this, ma'am, but you have the cutest dimple in your cheek when you smile. And you're wearing a dress like a woman!"

Her eyebrows rose in mock outrage. "Well, what did you think I was?"

"Well, um, you were wearing those denims this morning, and your hair was all messed up, and I thought . . . Well, shoot . . . you're a woman, all right." He cleared his throat uncomfortably. "How's Evan doing?" He walked over and pinched off a corner of the pastry between his thumb and forefinger. Popping it into his mouth, he rolled his eyes. "Mmm, raisins." Licking the fruit and rich filling from his finger, he added, "I would have asked about him sooner, but I smelled the food and then I saw you . . . and I got sidetracked." He shrugged helplessly, looking as pitiful as a lost puppy. "It's always happening to me." He raised his eyebrows, tilting his head to one side. A wide, appealing white smile appeared. "My mother never knew what to do with me."

"I can see why!" she answered, realizing she was smiling back. Busying herself with filling the coffee pot, she began relating the details of Evan's condition to him. "Your brother's been sleeping most of the day, but when he wakes up he asks for whiskey. Both times I offered him laudanum instead, and he about bit my head off. You weren't kidding about him having a bark. Is he always like that?"

If she thought Evan was cross the first time he awoke, he had been nearly ferocious the second time he came around, in the middle of the afternoon. Really, it was a most unpleasant situation, and she had been hard pressed to hold a civil tongue in her head.

"Did you give him the whiskey?"

"Of course." She paused for effect. "With a good healthy dose of laudanum mixed in."

Ben chuckled. "Well, that was probably for the best, but he's going to be hopping mad when he finds out. I'm surprised he didn't taste it."

Her smile increased, causing the dimple to appear again on her cheek. "He just thinks we have rotten whiskey. Home brew, he called it."

"Probably for the best he goes on believing that. Think I'll go check on him till supper's ready. Is that okay with you? I take it Reed'll be joining us, unless your pa is expected back." His eyes were hopeful. "Is the third place set for your pa? It would really be something to meet Nate Spencer."

"My father's gone to San Francisco on . . . on business." A pensive feeling rose in her chest. "We don't really know quite when to expect him back, but it won't be in the next few days."

"Son of a gun! San Francisco! That's where our new plant's going to be. Does he have business out there often?"

"No." She shook her head. No, she thought to herself, her father didn't have business in San Francisco often.

Only once every twenty years.

"Evan! Hey, Ev! Are you in there somewhere? You're looking a little better than the last time I saw you. Got a shave, anyway. Come on, Evan, open up those baby blues. All right, so you're not going to wake up. I think I'll sing your favorite song. Remember your favorite song? Evan, Evan, drew a seven—"

"Shut up, Ben." Evan stretched his legs in the bed, remembering just in time not to move his upper torso. A terrible taste coated his tongue and the inside of his parched mouth. He felt stiff and sore all over, as if he'd been dragged over miles of rough ground. His shoulder hurt a great deal, and the confining wrapping that held his arm in place against his chest was most irritating. A heavy sleepiness lingered in his head, trapping and encasing the wicked pain in his right temple. He willed himself to open his eyes, but they felt so heavy.

"Oh, so you *are* awake. Nice voice you have there." Ben imitated Evan's croaking, scratchy command. "Shoot, brother, I think you sounded better when you were thirteen." Evan felt Ben's touch on his good wrist. "Come on, you lazy sack of bones, open up your eyes."

"Then I'd have to look at you." Evan eased his eyes open in the fading daylight. For all of his brother's smart-alecky words, the young man stared at him with great concern, lines of worry furrowing his forehead. Evan was surprised, too, at the relief he experienced at seeing the familiar face.

The blue gaze that nearly matched his own anxiously roamed over his face. "How are you feeling?"

"Like shit," he said flatly.

"That good, huh?"

"Ben," he said wearily, "as soon as I get out of this bed . . ."

A dark eyebrow rose rakishly. "Yeah? Problem is, you won't be getting out of bed for a while." He grinned. "Think I'll have a little fun with you while I can."

"Well, have yourself some fun and find me something to whiz in." The pounding of his full bladder was nearly unbearable. "Unless you'd like me to humiliate myself by wetting the bed."

"No, I'd say you humiliated yourself enough by getting thrown off your horse." The tall young man walked to the dresser, chuckling, quite pleased with himself, Evan knew.

Ben fingered several items on the dark walnut dresser, keeping his back to Evan. "Now, what could we use here for the poor, broken-down old man to whiz into? *Whiz?* Really, Ev." He picked up and immediately set back down a comb and brush set. "Those won't do at all, will they? No, you can't *whiz* into them. Hmmm, it *was* you who told me a man should always have complete control of his mount, wasn't it? Yes, I do think I recall you saying that a time or two—"

"Now isn't the time, Ben," Evan warned with a surge of annoyance, his urgency increasing with every second. "Get me something and get it fast."

Quickly looking around the room, Ben shrugged and grabbed a large crystal vase from atop the dresser. Wrinkling his nose with distaste, he helped position the vessel beneath the covers, grumbling, "I think this goes just a little beyond the call of brotherly duty, don't you? There. All set. Guess it'll do the job." He stepped back from the bed and whispered loudly. "I won't tell Miss Spencer if you won't."

"Won't tell me what?"

At the same time Madeline appeared in the doorway of the bedroom, a door banged farther off in the house. Will's booming voice was unmistakable, calling, "Anybody home?"

"We're back here in the bedroom," Madeline called. "Come on back. He's awake again. Ben's in here with him, too."

"Me, too, Miss Maddie?" a young voice asked. "I been kinda worried about the feller since he fainted yesterday. I been real glad, though, that he din't die."

"Sure, come on in, Robbie, you can come pay your respects," she called over her shoulder. Two sets of footsteps clomped toward the bedroom. Extending a steaming mug to Ben, Madeline said, "Here's that hot coffee you asked for." Her eyes regarded Evan for a long moment before returning to Ben's face. "How's he doing? He looks a little better. Now what were you saying? What didn't you want to tell me?"

She talked over him as if he weren't there! And if that wasn't bad enough, she'd just invited two more people into the room to stare at him. The ice-cold vase lay heavily between his legs, shriveling his testicles. Oh, God, the pressure in his pelvis was unbearable. He couldn't ever remember a time in his life when he'd had to urinate so badly.

Ben shot him a helpless look. "Uh, Miss Spencer," he said, turning to the quizzical blond woman, carefully balancing his coffee in one hand and taking her arm with the other, guiding her out of the room. "Do you think you could wait out here for, um, just a few moments?"

"Why?" she asked.

Evan saw her staring at him around her brother's tall frame before Ben released her arm and thoughtfully pulled the door closed. He heard her voice, Ben's voice, Will's voice, the boy's voice. They were all standing just outside the door. Inconsiderate bunch of . . .

Relax, Evan, relax.

After what seemed like an eternity, he was able to relieve himself despite the noisy conversation taking place just outside the room. And such sweet, blessed relief it was. Though he still felt the pain of a thousand hammers banging busily away inside his body, he found he felt better and could think more clearly now that this most elemental need had been met. "Ben?" he called.

His succorer returned. Ben opened the door a little way and clumsily edged around it, telling the assembled group, "It'll be just a moment." He shut the door in the faces of the three individuals who stood just on the other side, each straining for a glimpse of Evan.

After opening a window and emptying the contents of the vase on the ground outside, Ben thrust the ornamental receptacle under the bed and awkwardly straightened the covers. "They all want to come in now, Ev."

"No kidding. I'm surprised you didn't let them stay and charge them all admission."

"Aw, come on, Ev, don't be such a bear. They're all concerned about you." He lowered his voice. "Miss Spencer, especially, has about knocked herself out taking care of you."

Evan wondered at the soft look on Ben's face when he spoke of the young woman. "Mrs. Spencer, you mean?" He snorted. "I've had commanding officers who didn't give orders like that woman." Fragmented recollections of her tender ministrations . . . and stern, unyielding words drifted into his mind. If he hadn't been so sick, so weak, so utterly helpless this afternoon, he could have given a good deal more appreciation to the sight of the finely made woman, arms akimbo, green eyes flashing, breasts rising and falling tantalizingly against the bodice of her dress, first reasoning with him, then lecturing him uncompromisingly. But that line of thinking was wrong. She was a married woman. He erased the figure of the beautiful woman his mind had drawn and announced, "Poor Spencer's got his hands full with her."

Ben shook his head, a smile playing about his lips. "You gave her a bit of trouble, eh? I warned her that you could be a real . . . oh, and by the way, it's not *Mrs.* Spencer, it's *Miss* Spencer. She's Spencer's daughter, not his wife." He waggled his eyebrows, then an earnest look appeared on his young face. "I think she's the most magnificent thing I've ever seen. Out in the middle of nowhere! Can you believe it? She's tall, but did you notice that neat little figure she's got on her? I think I died and went to heaven when I came in the door today. And such a great set of . . . Well, she really fills out her dress. And you know what else, Ev? She can cook! Take a whiff of that dinner she's got going out there!"

Surprise ricocheted through him at Ben's disclosure. Spencer's daughter? He wasn't aware that the man had ever been married or had children.

Still wondering at that news, he became aware of a pleasant mixture of cooking aromas on the air. And he had done more than Ben by noticing Madeline's luscious breasts; his head had rested against them when she helped hold him up before his shoulder was set. He'd had crazy dreams throughout the day, imagining the weight of them filling his hands and the smooth feel of their silky softness. He'd wondered, too, if their centers were rosy pink or rich brown, and if the areolae were pert little berries or wide and generous . . .

She wasn't married! That threw a whole new light on things.

But he didn't like the light he saw in his brother's eyes, even though the young pup was always imagining himself in love with one woman or another. Because Ben wore his heart on his sleeve, it had gotten to be a game among the Grants to make bets and predictions about which woman Ben would be in love with during any given week. And that was about the duration of his infatuations, a week, before his head was turned by another pretty face.

For some reason, though, the thought of his brother looking on Miss Madeline Spencer with a healthy male interest disturbed him.

The voices outside the door broke off. "Hey, Grant?" Reed's voice came clearly through the door. "You gonna let us in one of these days?"

Ben looked at his brother questioningly, and Evan nodded. He owed a lot to the big man who had risked his life for him and tended to his wounds. The chatterbox boy? Well, his heart was in the right place, he supposed, though Evan wondered how much of the young man's relief was due to not having to dig a grave rather than to any real concern for him.

Out of nowhere, a surge of anticipation ran through him as he thought of Madeline and spending the next several days recuperating at the Spencer ranch. He resolutely squelched the pleasant thought, wondering if his brains had been softened by the blow to his head.

His mind should be on getting on his feet as soon as possible and going back to work. Time was tight; the San Francisco plant was opening, and they needed beef contracts. Ben would be working doubly hard.

The door opened. Quiet now, Reed and Robbie solemnly filed in. He couldn't stop his gaze from flicking past them, searching.

She came in last, her eyes meeting his shyly. Even in the dim light, her beauty struck him with a potent force. With his head clearer than it had been in who-knew-how-many hours, he sharply studied the flawless lines of her face, felt his heart pound more quickly, against his will, as her pink tongue moved quickly to moisten full, shapely lips.

Reed began to speak, and Evan unwillingly dragged his eyes away from the innocent yet stirring sight to look instead at the lined, experienced face of the ranch foreman. While answering Reed's queries about his shoulder, he noticed out of the corner of his eye as Madeline slipped from the room.

Why did she leave?

Why did it matter to him why she left or, for that matter, what she did? he asked himself angrily. *Get on your feet, Grant, and get away from here. There are plenty of women in San Francisco who don't have fathers known for their strength and daring.*

six

 RIVULETS OF COLD WATER MET IN THE VALLEY of the roof above the kitchen and ran to the ground in a steady, diagonal stream in front of the four-paned window. It had rained all through the past night and straight through the entire day as well.

A blast of wind shifted the torrent of water wildly away from the house. Madeline stared out at the storm, ineffectually swiping at a single frustrated tear making its way down her cheek, thinking that if her mood was as gray as the weather, then Evan Grant's was as black as the middle of the moonless night was sure to be.

She shivered and hugged herself. Tears! Once yesterday and twice today. She wasn't easily given to weeping; it simply wasn't her way to whine or fret or carry on. She sniffed, searching her pockets in vain for a handkerchief. Why was it so difficult to keep track of a little square of fabric?

Sighing and stepping back from the window, she lit the lamp on the table, wearily giving thought to what she might prepare for the evening meal. Something warm would probably be best for the injured man, but if it had been up to her she wouldn't have bothered. She had no appetite at all.

And no wonder, with the tension in the house.

Poor Ben. After the roast beef supper last evening, he'd unwittingly mentioned the "special" whiskey within earshot of his brother. Evan's wits were sufficiently clear for him to deduce that his excessive sleepiness was due to more than the aftereffects of the injuries he'd sustained.

To say he'd been furious was a gross understatement.

Will had spoken up and told Evan he was the first to doctor the whiskey and that he wasn't sorry, not one little bit. He'd done it, he explained, because Evan's injured body had *needed* the pain-relieving and relaxative properties of the laudanum—no ifs, and no buts about it. He'd added that he'd instructed Madeline to administer the potion at intervals throughout the day yesterday as well.

Ben, realizing he had made a dreadful mistake in joking about the narcotic-enhanced whiskey, hurried to the defense of both Madeline and Will, telling his brother he knew of the opium tincture and had approved of its use. Evan had demanded to know how Ben could know such a thing, which led Ben to explain about being at the ranch earlier in the day—and Evan to be further upset by not having any recollection of Ben's first visit.

From then on, an unpleasant tension had existed in the comfortable ranch house. It was even worse now that Ben was gone, for his lighthearted, comical manner, though somewhat forced last evening, had served to chase away the worst of the gloom.

Staring at the frying pan that seemed to have materialized in her hand, Madeline shook her head and set it on the stove. Evan Grant. His name lingered on her tongue, his face in her mind. Why?

How he must hate her for the accident that had caused his injuries. It was also evident to her that he hated not having control of any situation, hated having to ask for things, hated depending on others. She knew he was in great pain, knew his sleep was restless and fitful. She knew he also worried about the new plant in San Francisco not opening on schedule; she had overheard part of his conversation with Ben last evening. How could she ever begin to make amends to the man for inflicting on him a set of circumstances of this magnitude?

Ever since last night his magnificent blue eyes, filled with anger and pain and silent frustration had bored holes through her each time she was in his presence. His only words were spoken in short, clipped sentences. What a metamorphosis he'd undergone since his arrival two afternoons before, since that warm afternoon filled with bright sunshine when he'd ridden up to the ranch and flashed that cocky, self-assured smile at her.

Lord, how that smile had affected her.

Paying only slight attention to the potato she was slicing, she let the paring knife skid sideways from the top of the slippery vegetable and felt it cut deep into the side of her thumb. With a strangled cry of pain and surprise, followed by a particularly foul—and most inadvertent—combination of words, she threw down the knife and wrapped her bleeding hand in a towel, applying firm pressure to the injury.

From nowhere, a sob rose in her chest. The cut was not the cause, however. Tears pooled in her eyes and ran warmly down her cheeks while desolation and hopelessness swelled within her. Too many problems had come together from too many different directions and now weighed heavily upon her.

One thing was certain, though: she wasn't going to give Evan Grant the satisfaction of knowing she was about to indulge in an overwhelming and disgustingly female bout of tears. Favoring her injured hand, she threw her coat loosely over her head and stepped outdoors into the rain.

What had she said? Evan blinked in surprise, a grin pulling up the corners of his mouth despite his surly mood. Furthermore, why had she said it? Had Miss Madeline Spencer gathered her courage and decided to tell him what she truly thought of him—from a distant room? He heard a clatter and the sound of the outside door closing, none too gently at that.

Now what? Had she left him to his own devices?

After the way he'd treated her since yesterday he probably deserved worse. But dammit, it was such an unnerving, appalling, *helpless* feeling to know he'd been drugged for the better part of a day.

A sudden brutally sharp pain in his shoulder made him wonder if he might have dismissed the merits of the medication too hastily. Gritting his teeth, he awkwardly readjusted the pillow beneath his neck, attempting to stuff a little of its plumpness beneath his upper arm. The entire right side of his head ached atrociously, causing dizziness to wash over him with the minor exertion. How many more days would it take to heal the harm that was done in the space of a few seconds?

No, there would be no more head-muddling laudanum and no more whiskey. They did nothing but weaken a man. And he admitted to himself that he was indeed pitifully weak. He couldn't even sit at the edge of the bed without assistance. Once last evening and once this morning, each time with Ben's help, he'd tried the simple feat. Both times he'd had to admit defeat before attaining a fully upright position, his body sweating and trembling. The pain was just too overwhelming.

A blast of wind drove needles of rain into the window, making him think of his younger brother. What miserable weather for him to be out in. Regretting the harsh words he'd spoken to him, he hoped Ben would understand that he just wasn't himself right now, that pain and frustration were doing a lot of the talking for him. He also hoped that no trouble would befall the young man while he was out on his own. If anything happened to his brother he'd never . . .

The door opened and closed again. Madeline? He heard what he thought were the sounds of her booted feet, the noises of a heavy coat being removed and shaken. She and Ben seemed to have hit it off very well in a short period of time, he thought with annoyance. To listen to Ben talk, a person would think the sun rose and set in Madeline Spencer. Just wait until the impetuous, impressionable young scamp learned that his paragon could curse as efficiently as any of her daddy's ranch hands.

He heard her movements farther off in the house and wondered what she was doing. Drugging some food for him, perhaps. Though he was fairly certain she had operated with what she thought were his best interests in mind, he was still outraged that she had been a party to doping him. Ben, too.

Why did he give so much thought to Madeline Spencer? In a week or two he'd be gone, never to set eyes on the woman again. She could swear to her heart's content and rope cattle and drug any damn fool she wanted to—she and that blasted fat cat of hers.

He exhaled sharply, looking around the unpretentious yet tastefully furnished bedchamber for the ten-thousandth time, knowing deep down that Nathaniel Spencer's daughter was about as hard-bitten and calculating as a fluffy little kitten. There was simply something about her, despite a few unladylike attributes, something in her eyes, her manner, that made him sense—no, made him *know*—deep down, that she was pure of spirit, unspoiled, untainted.

Madeline Spencer was innocence and spunk rolled up into a most inviting, enticing package.

His mind pictured her perfect beauty, her delicate movements. Why couldn't he have had a horsey-faced caretaker or, if not downright ugly, at least someone plain and efficient? Or why not a sturdy, no-nonsense matron measuring a few ax handles across the rear end?

Someone who didn't make him think of unintelligent pursuits.

Why did he have to be in the care of a woman who smelled like a tempting garden of summer flowers, a woman whose voice was soothing and melodious while at the same time slightly husky and unintentionally provocative?

What had he done to be punished in this way?

Why did Madeline Spencer have to have stunning green eyes that made him think of verdant banks along a softly babbling brook? Silky golden hair that his fingers itched to touch? Why did she have to possess the face and form of a goddess?

He uttered an ugly oath to himself. Hadn't he learned anything?

Four years ago he had learned that packages didn't necessarily contain what the pretty ribbons and eye-pleasing
outer wrappings promised. He'd learned about illusions,
about beauty and true character, and that beneath impeccable breeding and good bones resided all things rotten
and spoiled. He had learned that love between a man and
a woman was only a word, a concept, and more than likely
a fallacy.

He'd also learned that the woman who had agreed to
become his wife, the woman he'd once fancied himself in
love with, the beautiful, sophisticated, raven-haired Chicago
socialite from the right side of town and the right family,
had played him false.

During a midsummer's party at the home of an acquaint-
ance, in a private moonlit garden, he'd discovered his fiancée
on her hands and knees, her skirts tossed high over her back,
being serviced by their host, Charlton Stimson. He'd come
upon them quite by accident while seeking a quiet moment
of contemplation away from the noise and crowd.

Every illusion he'd had of love, of loyalty, had shattered
as he watched the frenzied, copulating pair. Sickened, yet
unable to tear himself away from the sight, his heart first
rent, then hardened as he waited for the pair to finish before
announcing his presence—and the end of his engagement.

Love. He knew all about it.

"Mr. Grant?" Madeline stood in the doorway of the room.

For her height she looked so small, so vulnerable and sad,
as if invisible lead weights were fastened to her shoulders
and arms. Had his churlish treatment of her wrought such
heavy heartedness within her? She was just a young girl,
really, probably no older than Annalisa. Feelings of self-
condemnation, mingled with an odd protective tenderness,
came unbidden to him.

She stepped hesitantly inside the bedchamber and walked
to the bed, keeping her eyes on the covered plate she
held in her towel-wrapped hand. Hot food. Despite his
frequent bouts of nausea, his mouth actually watered at
the smell of—

"It's stew," she said, confirming what he'd already
guessed. "Old Roger down at the cookshack made up a

plate for you. I hope it didn't cool off too much." She removed the lid from the deep plate and looked at him. "Do you think you'll be able to sit up a little?"

"I don't know," he answered truthfully. "You'll probably have to help me."

Her eyes appeared dark and luminous in the shadowed room. They widened in surprise at his civilly spoken words, though she didn't immediately answer. Instead she nodded and looked away, setting the plate down on the bedside table. He noticed that dampness clung to her hair and eyelashes and the sleeves of her simple blue dress. Her face was flushed from the cold, and he had a crazy urge to reach out with his good hand and warm the end of her pert nose.

He also noticed that the wet kitchen towel was still wrapped around her hand. She grimaced slightly as she toyed with the edge of the cloth. "How do you want me to help you?" she asked, standing uncertainly before him.

He thought a moment before replying. "If you could help me sit up some, and stack a few pillows at the head of the bed, maybe I could scoot myself backward." It was going to hurt like hell no matter what they did, he knew, but this seemed like the best way to get him upright, or at least partially upright. "Stay here on my good side," he instructed when she started to move around to the other side of the bed. "Give me your hand."

She hesitated. "It's cold," she said apologetically, shyly extending her hand. "Sorry."

Her hand *was* cold, as frigid as an ice block. It must be freezing outdoors. The uncharacteristic tenderness that had begun within him when she appeared at the bedroom door thumped at his heart once more. "Give me your other hand, too," he ordered, "and I'll warm them up for you." It was the least he could do after she'd braved the elements to get him a meal.

She looked uncomfortable, as if she might bolt. "No, really, Mr. Grant, I don't think—"

"Well, I'm not good for much else, lying here under a pile of quilts," he said more severely than he'd intended. "You're damp, too. You're going to catch cold if you don't get out of those wet clothes." He dropped her chilled right hand and reached for her left. "Why are you keeping hold of this wet towel? It's soaking the bottom edge of your sleeve."

She made a small cry when his hand closed around the towel. Holding both arms against her chest, she took a step backward. "I have a slight injury that needs attention, Mr. Grant," she said tartly. "It's good of you to be concerned about me, but your needs come first. Now, let's get you situated in bed before your food gets stone cold." She moved toward him again, determination written on the tired but still lovely lines of her face.

Something suddenly made sense. "Just hold your horses. You didn't by chance injure yourself in the kitchen a short time ago, did you?" he asked, raising one eyebrow, now knowing the reason for the string of curse words he'd heard.

"Oh, dear." She refused to meet his eyes, and the flush on her cheeks became even darker. Flustered, she thrust her hands behind her back. "You didn't . . . I, ah—"

"You what?" he interrupted sternly. "Where did you learn to talk like that? Do you know what those words mean?"

She peeked at him from beneath her thick lashes. "Well, sort of," she answered, catching her lower lip between her teeth.

"Sort of!" He snorted, his perturbation fading as he tried to hold back a smile. Was she totally unaware of what a charming picture she presented? It was impossible to further chasten her. Besides, that was a duty best left to her father.

He looked at the dark spot of wetness the towel had left on her bosom. He couldn't tell for sure in the dim light, but her nipples appeared to be erect beneath the fabric of her bodice. Given his present condition he would have thought it impossible, but he felt a most unfatherly surge of desire streak through him, accompanied by a tightening in his groin.

Was she as affected by him as he was by her?

The rain beat steadily on the house while the moment stretched out between them. Slowly she released her bottom lip from between her teeth and brought her hands up across her chest. Wetness gleamed on her full lower lip. He longed to first run his thumb across it, then to capture it with his own mouth. He pictured her lips yielding to his, her pink tongue parrying with his own. A vivid picture of green eyes, heavy-lidded with passion, flashed in his mind.

His gaze dropped to her chest once more, and his imaginings stopped abruptly. Despite the room's dimness, a dark red stain was plain to see on the towel wrapped around her hand.

"My God," he swore, "your hand is bleeding. What the hell did you do to it?"

She turned her hand over and looked without expression at the red splotch on the towel. "I cut it," she said, covering the bloody area with her other hand. "It's nothing, really."

Concern for her sharpened his voice. "That's *not* nothing. Unwrap your hand and let me see. What did you cut it on? Did you wash it?"

"I said it was nothing," she snapped, her eyebrows drawing together. "Why do you care, anyway? You've done nothing but snarl at me and tell me what to do since you came around yesterday, and I'm sick and tired of it. You were just awful to your brother, too, and to Will. Not one of us has done anything to you except try to help you, you know!" She shook her head angrily, dark green fire glimmering in her eyes. "I'm sorry you got hurt, Mr. Grant, but nothing can be done to change that now. The accident was my fault—I'll take the blame for it—but that doesn't give you call to mistreat people."

The kitten had claws.

"You're right, it doesn't," he said softly, feeling more than a little ashamed of his boorish behavior. She'd undoubtedly been through hell herself in the past few days. Too, it seemed she'd wrongly assumed the blame for his accident.

That unfamiliar tenderness tugged once more at his heart-strings and made him wish he could take back all the harsh words he'd spoken. "I owe you an apology, Miss Spencer," he said sincerely. "Now will you *please* let me see your hand?"

"No . . . I . . . It's too dark to see anything."

He heard the vexation—and puzzlement—in her voice. Christ, he didn't understand himself or his changing moods, either. His eyes followed her movements as she turned and efficiently lit the lamp on the dresser. The mellow glow of the flame accentuated her exquisite face and turned her hair to molten gold. "There," she said, walking back to the bedside. Her tone was crisp, her jaw set determinedly. "Now let's get you up a little higher in bed."

"God, you're beautiful," he said hoarsely, even before he knew the words were out of his mouth. He grasped her good hand in his own, pulling her closer to him, inhaling her fragrance. Desire returned, hot and fast, pushing away the pain to the far corners of his body.

"Why are you being nice to me? . . . What are you doing? I don't understand." Her voice quavered slightly.

"I don't, either," he said, feeling reason escape him. "I don't understand it at all."

Their eyes locked. Supper and injuries were forgotten. Their breath mingled as, slowly, inevitably, their lips met.

seven

 THE KISS, SWEET AND GENTLE, SEEMED TO GO on for an eternity. Surprise and confusion and disbelief mingled with pleasure and other new, unknown, unnamed emotions within Madeline's breast. Her legs grew weak. *My God*, she thought with shock, *I'm kissing a man.*

Suddenly out of breath, she pulled back. This was madness, sheer lunacy. Her voice shook. "Mr. Grant . . . we shouldn't be doing this. . . . Your injuries—"

"To hell with my injuries."

"But this is wrong!" she whispered, her body refusing to obey her mind's sensible command to retreat, to run.

"Kiss me again, Maddie," he commanded roughly, his breathing sounding ragged.

Powerless to do anything else, she again lowered her head to his. Her uncomfortable, chilled dampness was forgotten, as was the stinging cut on her hand when his mouth opened beneath hers, his tongue coming up to trace a tingling line between her lips. A streak of heat ran through her body at the intimate contact, and she parted her lips slightly.

"Ah, Madeline," he groaned softly, "that's it, open your mouth for me."

His tongue swept into her mouth, engaging her own, causing the heat within her to build and the area between her legs to throb strangely.

"Oh, God, you're sweet," he muttered against her mouth, "so sweet. Have you ever been kissed before?"

"Not . . . like . . . this . . ."

She was breathless, practically mindless.

"How about like this?" he growled, capturing her mouth hotly, savagely. At some point his hand released hers and moved to cup the back of her head, guiding the kiss, teasing her, teaching her, torturing her.

The sound of rain and kissing and harsh breathing filled her ears, her senses. She moved closer to him and of its own accord her right knee came up and slid onto the bed. Half bent over but ignoring the strain in her lower back, she gripped the edge of the mattress for support as best she could with her towel-wrapped hand. One of her breasts brushed against his arm, and she realized her nipples were as hard as the buttons down the front of her dress.

Evan's hand released her head and moved to trace sensuous circles on her face and neck. Her skin tingled—no, positively *burned*—at the contact. She closed her eyes and absorbed each new sensation—the pressure of his mouth, his tongue, his hand—all the while feeling her heart pound crazily. His searing hand dipped lower and lower, finally coming to rest on the upper swell of her breasts. Her nipples thrust outward even farther, it seemed, against the damp fabric of her bodice. She knew she should stop him, knew that his touch was much too familiar, but she couldn't. The ache within her intensified, and a small sound escaped from her throat.

He ended the kiss. Sighing deeply, he whispered her name as if he were in pain. Her eyes snapped open, searching his face. "Am I hurting you?" she asked, belatedly mindful of his injuries.

"No," he lied.

Pain was written on his features. She rose slightly, but his hand snaked down her arm, his fingers brushing full against one aroused breast, and caught her wrist.

"Don't move."

"But I'm hurting you!"

His fingers laced tightly with her own. "You make me forget my pain," he said gruffly, his incredible blue eyes looking deep into hers, his forehead furrowed with an intense emotion.

She gathered the courage to touch his handsome face, thinking of the sunny, windy afternoon two days before when she'd cradled his head in her lap and done the same.

His eyes closed at the gentle contact. "Madeline Spencer," he said, the lines in his forehead deepening instead of fading away, "do you have any idea how lovely you are? Your face. Your hair. Your voice." He sighed. "Your *smell*. Do you know that I wait like an eager schoolboy for you to walk into the room just so I can smell the air that drifts in around you?"

"You do?" She was surprised and flattered at his disclosure, but she remembered breathing in his hair's clean fragrance before his shoulder was set—and how it had made her feel. It was ridiculous, really. How could the sight or smell or even the thought of someone produce such nerve-jangling effects? What was happening to her? Her body was consumed by a strange fever, a restless yearning for . . . for something she didn't understand.

"What *is* happening?" she whispered, more to herself than to him.

Blue eyes searched her face. "Something that shouldn't be, sweetheart."

The sound of a door opening and closing had the same effect as a bucketful of creek water being poured over her head. She gasped and jumped backward.

"Miss Madeline?" came Will's deep voice. "You back there with Grant?"

"Yes," she answered, knowing her voice sounded unnatural. Panic made her legs feel boneless, but somehow they carried her away from the bed and over to the doorway. Will's deep, distinctive cough rang out, followed by the loud trumpeting sounds of the older man blowing his nose. She trembled. What if he suspected what had been going on in the bedroom? Did she look as if she had been kissed? What if he had seen something?

Her mind refused to contemplate that last horrible possibility. All she knew was that she had to think, had to collect herself, had to get out of the bedroom and away from Evan Grant as quickly as possible.

"Madeline." His voice was barely audible over a strong blast of wind that shook the house, but she heard him as clearly as if he'd spoken into her ear. The sound of her name on his tongue was compelling. Irresistible. Gooseflesh rose on her arms.

Keep going, her sensible self shouted. *Don't turn around! Don't look at him! Get away from him!*

Her feet stopped moving.

Slowly she turned and drew her shaking, uninjured hand across her face. The wind gusted again, harder, and the flame in the lantern on the dresser flickered, patterning the ceiling and walls with weird shadows.

"Madeline, look at me." Evan's voice was low, commanding, not at all the voice of an invalid.

"I can't," she answered helplessly, near tears. How could she ever look him in the eye again after the shameless way she'd acted? Kissing him. Being kissed by him. Touching him. Being touched by him. And, truth be told, not wanting any of it to stop.

Worst of all was the fact that he was a seriously injured man. She had a responsibility to care for him, to heal his wounds. She could have caused him further damage—she'd nearly crawled into *bed* with the man! What had she been thinking of? He'd had a severe blow to the head; perhaps his brain had been bruised, and he could no longer control his impulses. She'd heard of things like that happening. And from what she understood of men, given the large number of sporting establishments in Laramie City and Cheyenne, lust was a simmering, below the surface, but nonetheless prevailing appetite.

Lust. Was that what she'd had a taste of today? Was that what had caused her blatantly shameless behavior? Thoughts spun and collided in her head. Only a few minutes before, she had blocked out everything except the feeling of his lips on hers. All she wanted to do was get closer. Feel more.

At this moment she wanted to fall through the floor. He must think she was the lowest sort of woman . . . completely amoral.

Will honked again in the kitchen. Wind and rain continued to strike the house with violence as night fell across the mountains and grasslands. The nearly cold plate of stew sat on the bedside table, uncovered and untasted, giving off a zesty fragrance.

"Madeline . . . Maddie?" He was persistent. "We need to talk—"

"How's Grant doin' tonight, Maddie?" Will asked, approaching the bedroom with booted steps. "I hear Roger sent him up a plate. You manage to get a little food poked into him?"

With relief she turned and greeted Nate's best friend with the details of Evan's condition. She was too animated, she knew, but she could feel the intensity of Evan's stare on her back; it irritated her senses and caused the nape of her neck to prickle unnervingly.

She could barely concentrate.

Will stepped into the room. "Well, son, now you're lookin' only a quarter dead instead of half dead. Miss Spencer must be doin' a fair job of tendin' to you. Say, what's that there?" He pointed to the area of the bed where Madeline had gripped the edge of the mattress with her wounded hand. "Your head break open and start to bleed again?"

Madeline looked down in horror at her left hand. More blood had soaked through the towel—and must have smeared on the sheet when she'd been in Evan's embrace. Her eyes took in the red-daubed mess next to Evan's shoulder and head, and despite herself, she glanced at his face. His dark blue gaze hit her with the intensity of twin bullets, making her stomach pick itself up and flip fully over. Did he raise his eyebrows slightly? His face was unreadable, yet so *knowing*.

She looked back down at her hand. How Will had failed to notice the red-stained towel when he came into the room she'd never know. It seemed nothing escaped his shrewd eyes. Only by the grace of God this had.

She had to leave. Immediately.

She didn't wait to hear Evan's response. She couldn't watch those full, sensuous lips part or listen to that smooth, deep voice that altered her senses—and every last bit of her common sense.

eight

THE STORM HOWLED AND MOANED THROUGH-out most of the night, finally tapering off to a light drizzle by early morning. Madeline didn't easily find sleep, and the few hours she did slumber were fitful and plagued by vivid dreams.

"Didja survive the storm, Miss Madeline?" Robbie asked from the doorway, holding a cloth-covered bundle. "We was out there all night! Them dumb cows just keep on calvin' and calvin'—they ain't got no good sense. I hope my ma ain't worried about me. I'm gonna try to be home a little early for supper tonight. And can you believe this crazy weather? Now since lunchtime the sun's out and it's gettin' nice again. Still wet, though. How's Mr. Grant doin'?"

"Fine," Madeline said, answering his last question distractedly, unable to keep up with the speed of Robbie's mouth. She sat at the kitchen table with a long-neglected pile of mending in front of her. Anything to keep her occupied. Anything to keep her away from the man in the bedroom and her mind off what had happened in that room last night. . . .

Robbie's voice broke into her thoughts. "Boy, did Roger have a spread and a half set out for us this mornin'. Almost made last night worth it." He yawned and extended the bundle to her. "Here. He sent you some ham an' fried potatoes an' half an apple cake. Said it's time to start puttin' some meat on Mr. Grant's bones. Okay if I take my coat off an' come in for a while? I could take Mr. Grant a plate an' help him with it." He looked at her hopefully.

"Mr. Grant is not entirely helpless, Robbie," she said more sharply than she'd intended, unable to stop a rush of explicit memories. She rose and took the bundle from him, setting it down with a bang on the table next to the pile of clothes. Tempting smells rose from the parcel, but her stomach was much too unsettled to think of eating anything. Returning to her chair, she sat down heavily. After a nearly sleepless night, her disposition was quite sour.

"Well, I wasn't thinkin' I had to spoon-feed him or nothin'," he answered, his eyes widening. "I just meant if he needs help sittin' up or anything, I could help him."

She heard the hurt in his voice and was immediately contrite. She sighed and snipped off a thread with her embroidery scissors. "Oh, Robbie, I'm sorry. I don't mean to be cross with you. I didn't sleep very well with the storm last night . . . and I'm a little out of sorts."

A *little* out of sorts? That was almost laughable. Her emotions were as snarled as the ball of threads in the bottom of her sewing basket. She'd spent a good deal of time in her bed last night, every nerve in her body still tingling, pondering the mysteries of human mating and analyzing what had occurred in the bedroom below.

Truth be told, she'd always had an improper curiosity about these matters and about the physical differences between men and women. Elsie had told her only that what went on in the marriage bed was a special and wonderful thing, but that if a man ever tried to "take liberties" outside of marriage, she should scream bloody murder.

She had a feeling that what had gone on last night qualified as liberties.

And, damn her soul, she hadn't screamed. She'd been too busy assuaging her curiosity, too busy soaking up every feeling, every sensation.

She'd wondered, too, if this same wonderful thing had happened to Sara Brinkman. Though it was impossible to think of Nate doing the same things to her mother that Mr. Grant had done to her last night, she wondered if Sara had caught the same fever of the flesh with which she was now afflicted. Had Sara's every waking and dreaming moment been occupied with thoughts of Nate?

Nate had said they were in love.

Well, *she* definitely wasn't in love. She didn't even really like Evan Grant, though a part of her sensed that he would be a much different man, given a different set of circumstances. What was it that shadowed his past? she wondered. What had changed him? She'd never had the opportunity to ask Ben.

Serving Mr. Grant breakfast this morning and facing him in the daylight had been the sorest trial of her life. It was plain to see he was feeling much better; he had eased himself to a sitting position in the bed without any assistance whatsoever. His eyes had nearly crackled with life and vitality. His mien had been cool and remote, however, his manners impeccable, and somehow that made her feel worse than if he'd tried to continue with what he'd started last night.

She had appeared cool and remote herself until his movements in the bed had moved the quilt aside—and exposed the brown bloodstains on the sheet. In an instant she'd grown flustered and self-conscious. It had been humiliating.

A quick grin lit Robbie's tired young face. "Shoot, Maddie, it's nothin'. Lotsa people get owlish when they don't get their sleep." He removed his coat and hat and hung them on the long row of pegs near the door, then walked over to the table and studied her face. "Ya know, you are lookin' kinda peaked today. Your eyes are all puffy, and they got them bluish-purple bags underneath—"

"I'm sure Mr. Grant would be very happy to see you, Robbie," she interrupted. "Why don't you go on back and talk with him for a while?"

"Hey, Madeline, you been cooped up in here for what, three, four days now? That ain't like you at all. You're just not one to stay indoors. And didn't you say you hated to sew? Like my ma says—"

"Robbie!"

"Well, never mind what she says. Guess I'll go on back and see what I can do, huh?" He picked up the package of food and bounded off to the first-floor bedroom.

The pile of mending grew steadily smaller over the next hour. Madeline's eyes burned, and the muscles between her shoulder blades ached, but at least the cut on the side of her thumb hadn't broken open at all today. The small bandage she'd applied to the wound last night was still dry and intact. Threading the needle for what she hoped would be the last time, she frowned at the sound of male laughter coming from the back bedroom.

Just what on earth was so funny?

And why was Robbie still back there? Since he'd gone back to visit Evan he'd made several trips out to the kitchen. First he'd needed a plate and some utensils. Then he'd wanted some pepper. Next had been a cup of coffee. He'd put some water on the stove when he got the coffee, too, telling her to continue with her stitching and not to bother getting up, that he'd take care of things. Then he'd gone back to the bedroom and come out to the kitchen again with his hands full of dirty dishes.

She knew it had been too much to expect that he'd roll up his sleeves and use the warm water for washing the dishes. Instead she'd watched the long-legged youth carefully carry the large kettle off toward the bedroom and had heard the door close.

Each time Robbie had appeared in the kitchen and puttered about, her patience wore a little thinner. Each time she heard Evan Grant's deep voice, her hand shook, and her needle missed its mark. Her composure was slipping away as quickly as corn went through a goose.

Needle in, needle out, pull the thread tight. *Concentrate, Maddie*. An unwanted thrill ran through her as her mind again settled on the events of last evening. Merciful heavens, how many more days was the man going to be here? She didn't think she could retain her sanity for even the remainder of this one.

"Hey, Miss Madeline! Come here! I got a surprise for ya!" Robbie called out.

She heard the low murmur of Evan's voice but couldn't make out his words.

"Oh, come on, Mr. Grant, she'll be proud of us," Robbie replied to the man in a slightly lower voice. "Don't you go gettin' all grumpy on me now, too. This'll probably get her back in a decent mood. Madeline don't get bearlike too often, but when she does . . ."

Bearlike? That was it! Annoyance flooded through her. Robbie had gone too far in discussing her temperament with Evan Grant as if it were the weather. The last thing she wanted was to be within fifteen feet of the man in the bed—nay, even fifteen miles was too close—but Robbie had simply crossed the line.

"Maddie? Come on—"

"I'm coming!" She flung down the shirt she'd been repairing and stamped across the kitchen and sitting room. *Bearlike*. She'd show them what "bearlike" meant.

She was brought up short by the sight of Robbie's grinning face in the doorway of the bedroom and by the sight of Evan's clean-shaven face farther behind him. "Oh" was the only sound that escaped her mouth as she took in the straight, clean lines of Evan Grant's upright body. He sat in a chair next to the window, the planes and angles of his face highlighted by curtain-muted sunlight. Her breath caught in her throat, her heart seemed to stop beating, and she forgot entirely what she'd been so angry about.

He was dressed in brown woolen pants and a well-worn collarless blue cotton shirt. The shirt was unbuttoned and hung open, exposing his linen-wrapped torso and a strip of flat, muscular belly below it. A thick line of dark hair ran vertically between the horizontal boundaries of his waistband and the sheeting that supported his arm.

She swallowed hard and raised her eyes, only to meet Evan's stare. His eyebrows rose slightly—this time she was certain!—but again his expression otherwise remained the same.

Oh, dear Lord, he thinks I was staring at his private parts.

Well, weren't you? her inner voice questioned.

"Whaddaya think, Maddie? Look at the bed! I changed the sheets all by myself." The pride and excitement in the young man's voice were unmistakable, and she gratefully focused on his bright face. He grabbed a breath and gestured to the pile of wrinkled sheets on the floor. "Ma always says to soak bloodstains in cold water. Throwin' in a little salt can't hurt, either, but you prob'ly already knew that, huh? Guess I got no call to be tellin' you how to do the wash."

"Robbie." Evan's deep voice rolled around the bedroom, his tone sounding remarkably patient after nearly an hour in the company of the loquacious boy.

Madeline covertly watched his full pink lips move as he spoke to Robbie, thanking him for his help and asking him to pick up the sheets and clothing that lay strewn about on the floor and, if he didn't mind, fetching him another cup of coffee. She'd thought Evan looked dangerously handsome this morning with his face covered by black stubbly whiskers, but she had been dead wrong.

He looked much more dangerous—no, he looked devastating—with his lean face free of the dark bristles. The urge to flee came over her again. So did the conflicting urge to press her lips, once again, against his.

Clumsily she stepped aside as Robbie came through the door with his arms full of wadded-up clothes and bedding. "You want this out with the other wash?" he asked, waiting to see her affirmative nod.

Evan noticed Madeline's tentative steps backward. Though he had become quite fatigued by the exertion of washing, shaving, and being out of bed for the first time in days, it was time to confront the skittish Miss Spencer with what had happened last evening and reassure her that nothing of the sort would happen again.

Because it wouldn't.

He'd lain awake well into the night, damning himself for a fool. What *had* happened last night? He still didn't understand it himself. Hell, he didn't understand himself right now. Trifling with young girls wasn't his way.

His only defense was that there was something irresistible about the fresh-faced and very beautiful young woman who tended to him. For all her swaggering about in range dress and possessing the ability to cuss quite competently, he sensed not only a vulnerability beneath her surface but also an uncertainty.

Was that innocence?

Innocence? In his experience womankind and innocence mixed like oil and water.

Whatever it was, though, it—and she—touched something deep inside him. After last night, at least he was certain of her sexual innocence. Her lips had been unskilled and unknowing—and somehow very, very exciting. He remembered with satisfaction how quickly the passion had risen in her smoldering green eyes, how quickly she'd learned to kiss him back.

"Wait, Madeline—Miss Spencer," he said, not allowing his train of thought to continue. "We need to talk."

Her deep green eyes widened. She cast a nervous glance over her shoulder, causing her braid to swing and several unruly wisps of shining blond hair to flutter with her movement.

His eyes were drawn to the loose tendrils around her face, tendrils that he knew would be as soft beneath his fingertips as spun silk. "Don't worry," he reassured her. "The boy will be occupied for a while. I want to—"

She didn't let him continue. Her head snapped around, anger flashed in her eyes, and she marched determinedly over to him. Her whisper was outraged. "You want to *what*? In broad daylight? With a young boy in the house? What kind of miscreant are you?" She folded her arms across her chest. "There is nothing I could ever possibly want to discuss with you, Mr. Grant, and it is certain that nothing akin to what happened last night will ever happen again." Her hands moved momentarily from her breast to push back the wisps of hair that had fallen onto her forehead. "I'll not have you thinking I'm some little soiled dove you can amuse yourself with while you heal. Do you understand?" Pink patches had risen in her smooth cheeks by the time she finished her speech, but she met his eyes squarely.

So she took him for a mindless lecher, did she? A matching irritation rose in him. His wounds pained him greatly, and it was getting harder and harder to remain upright, but dammit, all he had wanted to do was apologize for his actions and ask her forgiveness for his lapse in judgment.

She turned on her heel before him.

"Hold up right there, Miss Spencer."

She looked over her shoulder at him, her pert nose in the air, and took a step toward the door.

If she thought she could get in the last word *and* defy him in the space of a few short seconds, she was sorely mistaken. His anger burned hotter. "I said stop!"

"You can't make me." She positively *sashayed* one, two, three more steps forward.

"Don't be so sure." Vexation propelled him to his feet, causing the chair to scrape the floor noisily as he rose.

He heard her intake of air, saw her turn. A wave of dizziness assaulted him, but Madeline Spencer's scorn and her flagrant dismissal of him were too much to let pass. He took two steps forward. Oh, God, he was so dizzy. He leaned heavily with his left arm on the dresser, unable to walk any farther. Despite his anger, his legs felt as feeble as those of an octogenarian, and he was certain his face was a resplendent shade of green.

He was wrong about the color.

"Oh, my goodness, you're so white!" Concern replaced the alarm that had crossed her face. Even if he fainted dead away, Evan felt that his effort would have been worthwhile. At least he'd had the satisfaction of seeing that righteous look wiped from her face when she spun around and saw him standing on his own two feet.

"Whatcha hollerin' about, Maddie?" Robbie called, his footsteps carrying him rapidly toward the bedroom. "Ouch! Blasted hot coffee!"

"Hurry, Robbie! I think he's about to collapse."

Evan didn't lose consciousness, but he came within a hairbreadth of it. To his frustration, the two of them had to assist him back to bed, where he spent the next several minutes taking deep, slow breaths in an attempt to regain his equilibrium.

Oh, he'd shown her all right. Now she thought of him not only as a horny wretch who couldn't sit a horse but as a weak-tit horny wretch who couldn't sit a horse or even stand on his own two feet. And he hadn't even gotten a chance to tell her he wasn't remotely interested in her.

That's because you're interested in her.

No. Not true. He wasn't interested. What had happened between them had merely been a mistake, an aberration due to his head wound, months of sexual deprivation, and an enforced recovery in the company of a good-looking woman.

She's a damn sight better than good-looking.

He closed his eyes and willed his body to heal.

Images of Madeline's face hovered in his mind's eye. He remembered the feel of her breast against his hand, the sight of her nipples standing out against her bodice. Against his will, his thoughts slid toward undressing that perfect body and taking those nipples in his mouth . . . running his hands over every square inch of sweet-smelling skin . . . burying himself deep inside her. He imagined her eyes, half closed and drugged with passion; her voice, urging him on, whispering his name.

But all he had was one good hand and a tendency to black out. Given the opportunity to experience his fantasies—which she had made abundantly clear he *wouldn't*— he would no doubt find a way to embarrass himself at that, too.

The waxing moon rose clear and bright in the cloudless night sky. Madeline lay awake in her bed, listening to the night sounds. Her mind and body ached with tiredness, but sleep once again eluded her. *Just lie here quietly and rest.* Sooner or later, she told herself, a body just had to succumb to exhaustion.

Now that Evan was getting better, she was going to take Robbie's advice and get out of the house tomorrow. Maybe she'd hunt for Sugar, the traitorous little troublemaker, just to make sure Will hadn't carried through on his threats to kill her cat. She hadn't seen her pet since the accident. It wasn't like Sugar not to come around to the house in so many days, but maybe he had enough sense to lie low for a while.

Mr. Grant, if he didn't try to stand or walk, would be fine by himself for a couple hours. His color had still been poor at suppertime, and he hadn't eaten much.

He was back to glaring at her again. He didn't speak to her, either, which was fine with her. She remembered the fury that had risen in her when he'd told her to come to him, that he wanted to—

Wanted to what?

The strange, unfamiliar stirrings deep within her body that had plagued her of late leapt to life once again. Her thoughts turned toward last night's incident, and the stirrings intensified into a restless wanting. She had to face the fact that she was terribly curious about the goings-on between men and women.

After a fashion, she fell into a fragile, troubled sleep. Waking suddenly, she felt every bit as fidgety and jumpy as she had before. Her heartbeat pounded in her chest. Had a noise of some sort awakened her?

A loud thud below made her jump. What on earth? Had Evan tried to get out of bed? She jumped to her feet and ran to the stairs. He'd probably fainted dead away. What if he'd broken his head wound open again? How on earth was she going to pick him up and get him back into bed? She'd have to go to the bunkhouse for help; she didn't have the strength to lift the man by herself.

The smooth wooden planks of the stairs were cold on her bare feet. Her flannel nightgown swirled around her ankles and threatened to trip her; she swept up an armful of fabric and hurried down the rest of the stairs, unimpeded.

Moonlight streamed in through the sitting room windows, illuminating her path to the partially open bedroom door. She heard a deep sigh and a muffled curse come from beyond the door. At least he wasn't out cold, she thought with relief.

Moonlight bathed the bedroom as well. Pushing open the door, she was brought up short by the sight of Evan sitting straight up in bed, his head turned toward her. It wasn't light enough to clearly make out his features, but judging from the word he'd uttered, she was sure his mood wasn't congenial.

Suddenly she regretted her impetuosity in rushing downstairs. Now that she knew he wasn't lying on the floor in a heap, she felt self-conscious and rather stupid. Besides that, her feet and lower legs were ice cold. She dropped the hem of her nightdress.

He still hadn't spoken.

She cleared her throat. "I, ah, came to see if you were all right." Did she smell liquor?

"Oh, I've never been better, Miss Spencer."

Her eyes narrowed. The man knew just what to say to provoke her. Before he'd come to the Spencer ranch, she never would have described herself as bad-tempered. Taking a deep breath, she quelled the urge to fire back an equally sarcastic rejoinder.

"Well, if there's nothing you need, I'm going back to bed," she said evenly, keeping a tight rein on her temper. She *did* smell liquor, she was sure of it. Damn him, anyway. The way she felt inside, like a coiled spring, there was no way she'd find sleep again anytime soon.

"As long as you're here, I guess you could pick up the bottle." His tone was only slightly less rude.

The reins slipped. "That's what that noise was? You're lying in bed and *drinking* in the middle of the night?" She sniffed loudly. "It smells like a still in here. What did you do, spill the whole bottle? Don't you know that's got to be mopped up right away? It'll ruin the wood!" She strode angrily to the dresser, opened a drawer, and pulled out a towel. She knew she was being terribly peevish, but she couldn't help it. Slamming the drawer closed, she stalked back across the room. "Where is it? I suppose you weren't even going to tell me—Oh, dammit, it's right here."

She gasped when his fingers closed tightly around the tender area just above her elbow.

"Someone needs to teach you and your foul little mouth a lesson."

"Let go of my arm!" Her heart seemed to rise in the back of her throat. Was he drunk? What was he going to do? "I said to let go," she repeated. Her voice didn't sound at all firm anymore, but weak and breathless.

He pulled hard on her arm, causing her to stumble and land on her bottom on the mattress next to him. "Does your daddy know you talk like that?"

"What my father knows or doesn't know is no concern of yours." She felt the heat of his body through her nightdress. Every nerve in her body tingled. "Now will you please let me go so I can wipe up your mess?"

His tightly worded exclamation was much more profane than any of the language she'd used in his presence. His grip tightened, making her cry out. "So help me, woman, but you have a way of getting under my skin."

"Me!" It seemed he was confused as to who got under whose skin.

Something in the night air changed.

His grip loosened, turning instead into a soft caress.

"Yes, you."

Though his grasp was now loose enough from which to free her arm, she didn't move. She couldn't. His stroking fingers sent hot shivers up and down her limbs, and she sighed, a deep, ragged sound. "You're going to take liberties again, aren't you?" she helplessly asked.

His hand stopped, and he made a noise that sounded suspiciously like a snort. "Liberties?"

"Elsie always said that if a man tried to take liberties, I should scream."

His fingers resumed their motions, sliding up over her shoulder and neck to linger at her jaw. "Who's Elsie . . . and why aren't you screaming?" His voice was as seductive as his fingers, his whiskey-scented breath warm in her face.

"Elsie's my . . . grandmother," she replied, "and . . . I . . . don't know."

The silence of the night hung between them, broken only by two sets of uneven respirations.

His hand slipped around to the back of her neck and pulled her head to his. Their lips fused in a soul-stirring kiss that seemed to disable a large portion of her mental capacity. What was she doing? It was as if someone else had stolen into her body.

The bold stranger within her met Evan's mouth and tongue with willingness, even eagerness, tasting the bite of the whiskey. Though she knew what was happening was terribly wrong, there was just something so right about it.

Her hands came up, needing to be occupied, and settled gently around his neck. Hot winds of desire blew tempestuously through her, causing reason and all caution to be whisked away.

He broke the kiss. "Maddie—"

She reconnected her lips to his and teased his mouth open. He made a noise deep in his throat and took control of the kiss. His thumb explored the side of her breast, sending explosions of feelings in all directions. He loosed her mouth and spoke against the side of her face, pressing kisses on her cheek, her jaw. "You're more than under my skin, Madeline. You're like a bad fever I can't shake. I was going to tell you this afternoon that what happened last night was a mistake . . . that I wasn't interested in you." His hand moved to fully cup her breast. "And you know what? That's a damn lie. So if you know what's good for you, sweetheart, you'll find me another bottle of whiskey and run back up to your safe little bed."

"Could you just kiss me one more time?" Had she said it aloud?

She must have. His mouth came to meet hers. Shock and pleasure mixed when he lifted her breast and lowered his head to nuzzle its peak. Lord, he sucked at her nipple right through her nightdress! Her breathing came in short gasps, and she couldn't help her exclamation. "Oh, God, do the other one. Please!"

"Am I making you hot, little one?"

"You're making me . . . something. I feel so . . . so . . . yes, 'hot' *is* a good word."

"It is," he agreed, and devoured the hard crest of her other breast.

"Ahh, Evan," she whispered, "that feels so good."

He lifted his head from her breasts. His eyes were dark, shadowed, beneath the dark slashes of his brows. The wet fabric over her nipples grew cold almost immediately, feeling uncomfortable and stimulating at the same time.

His hand cupped her chin. "I want to see you, Madeline. I want to touch your bare skin. I've been lying in this bed all the damn day and night thinking about . . ." His voice dropped to a low whisper. "Open your nightdress for me."

Of their own accord, her shaking fingers began working down the row of buttons. She hesitated when she reached the level of her breasts.

His index finger traced a heated line down her breastbone. "More."

Finally she reached the last button at her waist. The feel of his hand on her bare flesh was heavenly. He stroked and caressed her breasts and belly, murmuring about how flawless she was. Flawless, her? She'd never thought of herself as more than fair.

Somehow her arms were out of her sleeves, and the nightdress was at her waist, leaving her entire torso bare. The chill air struck her skin, but it felt bracing, invigorating. She was emboldened.

"Get on your knees." The covers rustled as Evan drew up his legs and pushed himself to the head of the bed. He sat, legs splayed wide apart, with his back against the headboard. "Crawl over my leg and get on your knees in front of me, sweetheart."

The nightdress around her waist hampered her movements and was caught underneath her as she moved. The garment slipped down low over her hips, exposing nearly her entire body to his view. "Oh, Lord!" she exclaimed, attempting to tug her gown back into place.

"Nothing underneath." His voice was tight, and his hand stilled the movements of hers. "Leave it down. . . . Oh, God, you're beautiful." Almost sorrowfully, he muttered, "One hand. All this, and I've only got one hand."

He might be temporarily one-handed, but his one hand had spread a powerful fire within her. Would two hands create twice the pleasure? She didn't think a person could withstand a double measure of what she was feeling right now. Her private parts felt inflamed and slick. Throbbing, actually. Aching. Needing.

Did his feel the same?

His hand eased over her flank and hip, steadily moving the fabric down to her knees. "There, that's *much* better." He stroked her abdomen, making wide circles between her hipbones, then smaller circles as his hand strayed into the soft hairs at the base of her belly. "I can see you in the moonlight, Madeline. Your body is exquisite. So perfect, so feminine."

It was supremely difficult to think. Was he going to touch her . . . there? What he was doing had to be leap years ahead of liberties. By fractions of inches, his fingers moved lower. Oh, yes, she wanted him to touch her there, wanted him to stroke that aching area between her womanly lips. She whispered his name, whispered encouragement.

His hand hesitated. Did it tremble?

He took a deep breath. "Madeline, I'm not made of iron. I'm only a man, and sometimes not a very strong one. Do you know what's going to happen if you don't bundle yourself back to bed?"

His hand *did* tremble. It lent her bravery . . . or was it recklessness? She settled her hand on a hard-muscled, long underwear–clad thigh. "Sort of."

"Oh, God, not that 'sort of' again." His hand held its position, moving neither up nor down. "If you stay here, we're going to make love. Do you know what *that* means?"

Tentatively her fingers explored the hardness of his thigh. "Sort of . . ."

"That's it." His hand moved boldly over her mons, sending pleasure skittering through her limbs. "You've been warned. Now you're going to be—" His words broke off as he separated her folds and stroked the soft, damp flesh within.

"I'm . . . going to be . . . what?" Feelings she had never known existed grew and intensified. Was his finger moving *inside* her? It was! She spread her knees farther apart, allowing him greater access. Her breath caught . . . She couldn't breathe. Nothing had ever felt so good.

Evan's breathing was rough. "You're going to be . . . Oh, hell, you're going to be made love to."

"How . . . do we do this?" She had a feeling he'd been about to say something different. Involuntarily her pelvis rocked in a tight circle, sending a wave of pleasure through her as the heel of his hand rubbed deliciously against the sensitive nub of flesh between her folds. "Ohhh," she half-whispered, half-moaned, "don't stop."

His swallow was audible. "How do we do this?" he dryly repeated her question. "I'd say we're off to a good start."

"No . . . I mean . . ." Another of his fingers gently sought her opening and eased into her. "Oh, Evan," she implored, shuddering at the incredible fullness, not knowing what it was that she asked. Clumsily, with one hand, she freed her lower legs of the tangled nightdress and tossed the garment aside.

Evan's mouth sucked first at one taut nipple, then the other, causing the fire and the wanting within her belly to rage. Everything, absolutely everything, revolved around the central point of his fingers and hand. The hot, tight, ticklish, tortured, yet delicious feeling in her privates grew as her hips continued to make circular motions around his adroit hand. A small cry escaped from her throat.

"I'm only going to ask you one more time, Madeline. Are you absolutely certain—"

"Yes!" she cried impatiently. "Please . . ." Something was close, just out of reach. She was panting, her breath coming in short, hard gasps. "Please!"

His hand slowed its motions.

"Please, pretty please . . . Evan . . . you have to."

A hard yet tender smile touched his lips. "Such a demanding miss. I'll do my best to accommodate you." He withdrew his fingers slowly, leaving her aching with emptiness, and fumbled near his waist. "If you're in a hurry, sweetheart, you may have to help me."

"I'll help you," she whispered with frustration, brushing his hand away and assisting him in removing his long underwear. The crisp hair on his legs was foreign to her fingertips, and she tentatively touched a bare thigh once he was divested of the garment.

"Touch me here," he said, taking one of her hands in his and moving it to his hardness. "Touch me as I touched you."

With his hand over hers, she explored his male contours. "It's so hard," she exclaimed, "and so . . . big. Kind of like a bull's before . . . you know."

"Why, thank you," he replied with what she was beginning to learn was his typical brand of dry humor. His hand slipped away as hers grew bolder. "Ah, Maddie, that's it. . . . Why were you watching the bulls?"

"Just curious."

The sound of his breathing changed. "I like curiosity."

"Evan?" The more she touched him, the more the appetite inside her grew. Instinctively she knew where his maleness would go . . . but how to go about it?

"Yes?"

"How are we going to . . . ah . . . accomplish this?"

"Straddle me, sweet, and I'll show you."

He guided her above him, at the same time moving himself into a recumbent position, his hand gliding teasingly over her buttocks and into the crevice between her thighs.

"Evan?" she asked, his touch inflaming her. "Is it a sin to want something this much?"

"Probably," he replied, "but it's a sin that'll take us to heaven long before it takes us to hell." His hand moved to squeeze the side of her thigh. "I want to tell you . . . Damn, I want you in the worst way, Madeline, but I have to tell you . . ." He breathed deeply through his nose. "I have to tell you that the first time will probably hurt you."

She didn't care. Her emptiness needed to be filled. "Just put it where it's supposed to go," she whispered.

He rubbed the smooth tip of himself back and forth across her sensitive swelling before sliding into her virginal entrance.

Pleasure and pain mixed. "It's so tight."

"I know."

"It's not going to fit."

"I believe . . . it will.

It did.

Evan remained still, not moving a muscle, while she allowed herself to sink slowly down his shaft. Something inside her gave way, tore, but she resolutely kept going until his flesh was joined fully with hers. At last she was full, gloriously full.

"Am I hurting you?" he asked, his voice strained.

"Sort of."

"Hell, Madeline, you're nearly killing me. Is that a yes or a no?"

She moved, discovering the friction, the pleasure. "Ohh . . . I think it's . . . ahh . . . no."

Her thighs, accustomed to the rigor of riding astride, quickly adapted to this new type of riding. And in the moonlit chamber she finally discovered what awaited her at the end of her sensual journey.

Instead of being relaxed, Evan's senses were on edge. Madeline Spencer lay with her backside snugged up tight to his body like a tired, worn-out little kitten. Her gentle breathing told him that she had found sleep.

What a stick of dynamite she'd been.

His heart twisted in that uncomfortable way again. Guilt? She'd been a virgin. Though he knew it was wrong, pride and gladness mingled in his chest. After the garden incident with Melissa, he was sure he'd never been where no man had gone before him. Not that Lissa had been his only lover; there had been others before and after her. Discreet, practiced others. But Melissa was the only one who had dared to pretend she was untried. The calculating bitch. A scowl twisted his face. No doubt she'd bedded half of Chicago by now. How she'd deceived him, set her hook into him, and nearly reeled him into matrimony like a stupid, pop-eyed fish.

He sighed, staring at the ceiling, Madeline's sweet scent filling his nostrils. She stirred slightly and snuggled more tightly against him. Madeline. Sweet. Pure. So hot. What she lacked in experience she made up for in eagerness to learn. She'd excited him and satisfied him in a way no woman ever had.

And he'd pleasured her in return. His virgin lover.

He found himself wanting to possess her, wanting to know everything about her.

Wanting her again.

He slid his right leg over hers.

Nate Spencer will kill you if he ever finds out.

It didn't help. The thought of an enraged father stalking and charging him had absolutely no effect on his erect organ, nor did he have the willpower to continue to fight his need for the woman next to him. His mind, instead, chose to think of Madeline sitting astride him, to remember her tight spasms and inarticulate cries as she reached her peak.

Though she lay in the crook of his arm, his hand was free, and it began exploring the texture of a plump, rounded breast. The nipple tightened immediately. God, how this woman excited him. Briefly, with a flash of uneasiness, he wondered in what net he was now ensnared.

That was his last questioning thought before the simple act of feeling overrode all else.

nine

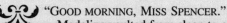 "GOOD MORNING, MISS SPENCER."

Madeline vaulted from sleep to consciousness, her heart pounding, as Evan lifted her arm and pressed a series of hot, wet kisses against her palm and wrist. The room was still dark, with only a hint of predawn light.

Evan's words were gentle, regretful. "Much as I'd like you to stay, sweetheart, we can't take the chance of Reed walking in."

"Oh, my God!" she cried, remembering exactly where she was. She snatched her hand away and sat upright, the realization of what she'd done sending a lightning bolt of shock through her middle. It was so unreal, so unbelievable.

You've made love to a man!

The hair-roughened leg of the man next to her wasn't unreal, though. It felt very real. She became aware of the cold air striking her bare torso, and she belatedly remembered she had not a stitch of clothing on. Where had her nightdress gone? Oh, Lord, where had her modesty gone?

The same place your virtue's gone.

"I didn't mean you had to run out of here right this second." Evan's voice was still kind, but it contained a trace of amusement, much to her horror. Was he laughing at her?

"I-I've got to go," she said dumbly, scooting out from beneath the covers in a hasty motion. Spotting the light-colored nightdress on the floor, she wailed when she picked it up, the slight smell of whiskey on the early morning air turning bitingly strong. "Oh, no!" she cried, gingerly holding the sodden, reeking garment. The motion caused the bottle beneath the nightdress to scuttle noisily across the wooden floor. Hot tears came to her eyes and spilled down her cheeks.

"Just slow down, Madeline." Coming across the shadowy bedchamber, Evan's voice was as gentle and deep and smooth as velvet. "Reed's not here right now. Everything's fine."

"Fine?" The word, mixed with a sob, came out as a choking sound. "I don't think so," she added in a whisper. The magnitude of what she'd done with Evan Grant seemed overwhelming. Twice last night their bodies had been joined as one, and after the first time her virginity was a thing of the past. What had she done? What could she have been thinking? The area between her thighs felt sticky and swollen and slightly aching, testimony to her innocence lost.

"Aw, hell, Madeline, you're not crying, are you? Don't cry." The covers rustled as he struggled to sit up. "Please don't cry. Oh, damn it all anyway, did I say the wrong thing? I only meant to tell you that what happened between us was . . . very good." His voice deepened, and she saw the dark shadow of his arm being extended toward her. "Please don't have any regrets, Maddie. Such a thing between a man and a woman is natural and should cause you no shame."

"Maybe not for a man," she managed to say through her tears, hugging the spirit-soaked nightdress to her torso. "Oh, why did you have to drink yourself silly in the middle of the n-night?" she asked miserably, painfully conscious of her nudity. "And why d-did I have to come down here?"

The chilly air and the cold floor beneath her feet couldn't be ignored any longer, either; it was difficult to keep her teeth from chattering. She knew she should leave right this second, but for some curious reason, perhaps due to shock, her legs wouldn't move.

"I wasn't drinking myself—" His voice broke off. "You're shivering, Madeline. You're going to catch your death. Here, take this," he said, pulling the top quilt from the bed and extending it toward her. "We can talk about this later," he added gently.

She accepted the proffered covering and wrapped it around her shoulders, her legs suddenly regaining their ability to move. Exiting the room in a quilt-wrapped flurry, she felt as if she could run a hundred miles without stopping. *You can run, but you can never escape what you've done*, came the righteous, reproachful voice within her as she mounted the stairs two at a time, to the silent upper story of the house.

Reed didn't stop by the ranch house until after ten o'clock. Instead of coming in and visiting, though, the busy foreman only poked his head into the kitchen door and asked what kind of night "that Chicago feller" had had.

A night you'd hang him for, Madeline thought while attempting to answer him in a normal tone of voice. He was satisfied to learn that the injured man had rested well and breakfasted heartily on eggs and griddle cakes. After she added that Evan was dozing again, Reed nodded and said he had to go to the Matthews ranch to help with a stuck calf. With a brisk good-bye, he immediately left.

You've made love to a man.

All morning long, the thought echoed again and again through her brain, causing her to stop whatever she was doing and stare blankly. Thinking, analyzing, trying to tell herself it really hadn't happened, Madeline continued to wash and dry the breakfast dishes in fits and starts, though it was nearly noon. Her tears were gone for now, but the terrible confusion inside her was not.

What had she done? Why had she done it? She dried another spoon and realized she had no answers for herself.

She'd certainly satisfied her curiosity about what went on between women and men. Lord, she'd never imagined such a glorious thing could exist between a woman and a man, not to mention such all-consuming physical pleasure.

A different man, given a different set of circumstances.

The words jumped into her head. She remembered thinking them while she was mending yesterday, while trying not to think of Evan—but while thinking of Evan. She remembered, too, his concern and consideration of her both times they'd made love. The tender Evan Grant who had single-mindedly pleasured her last night was an entirely different man from the Evan Grant who had lain in the bed and scowled at everyone and everything.

Different circumstances, different man.

Her heart flip-flopped in her chest, and, setting down the spoon she had forgotten was in her hand, she took a deep breath. Though Evan Grant was the handsomest, most compelling man she had ever seen and though what they shared last night had been the most earth-shattering experience of her life, she had made a terrible mistake. One that she wouldn't repeat.

Removing her apron and pacing back and forth through the kitchen and sitting room, she realized she was full of nervous boredom. The dishes were finally done, the bedroom floor had been scrubbed of the strong-smelling spirits, the pungent nightdress had been rinsed and was soaking in the washtub along with several other garments, and nothing was out of place in the ranch house. Mrs. Ashler would have an easy time of it tomorrow, she thought, glad she'd been able to lighten the older woman's work load.

Walking quietly to the door of the first floor bedroom, she saw that Evan still slept, his chest rising and falling gently. An unwanted thrill passed through her as she gazed upon his handsome features and tousled dark hair. She had dreaded facing him again earlier this morning, but there had been no choice. He'd needed food, and the floor needed to be scrubbed.

She had fully expected his mood to be black once again, but he had further rattled her with his gentle words and continuing tenderness. She'd discouraged his attempts to draw her out, and somehow she'd managed to serve him his breakfast and wash the floor without acting like a senseless ninny, leaving the room quickly when she was finished.

How much longer was he going to be here? she wondered. How soon would he be strong enough to move on? Guiltily, she realized she had barely given Nate two thoughts since Evan had come to the ranch. At first her worry for the injured stranger had pushed thoughts of her father and Sara Brinkman from her mind; now it was these new, discomposed feelings she had for the tall, handsome man in her father's bed.

What *were* these new feelings?

How she wished for a best friend, an older and wiser confidante to whom she could confess the strange feelings and flutters and stirrings within her, one who could sensibly explain this whole business to her. Her odd habit of talking to the cows when she was by herself sometimes helped her to sort things out, but she knew she was beyond the benefit of bovine bolstering in this situation.

Leaving the doorway, she walked back to the kitchen and looked around.

Nothing to do.

Her eyes were drawn to the sky beyond the window, a bright robin's-egg blue dotted with only a few puffy clouds. It was a beckoning sky, if she'd ever seen one. Pulling up on the window sash, she was delighted to feel a fresh breeze blow into the room. The cool weather of the past few days had evidently departed, and spring had returned. The pure, clear music of robins and meadowlarks drifted in on the warm, temperate wind that promised a beautiful afternoon.

Madeline felt as if she *had* to get outdoors, had to get away. Slicing several pieces of bread from a loaf, she hurriedly arranged them on a plate and filled a little pot with raspberry jam, thinking with relief how glad she was that Pete Matthews hadn't come to the house this morning. She didn't think she could have faced him after what had happened last night.

The small-time neighboring rancher had been sweet on her since the instant she had arrived in Wyoming Territory and been introduced to him. A loud show-off, he was ever trying to sidle up to her and capture her attention. He wasn't so bad-looking, she supposed, with his straight yellow hair and strong features, but his personality was nothing but overpowering and offensive. On the other hand, his younger brother Jack was as polite and well-mannered as they came. Men. They certainly came in all types and sorts.

A quarter of an hour later she had changed from her dress into comfortable denims and a loose blouse. Before slipping on her work boots, she tiptoed into the first floor bedroom and set the plate of bread and jam, a large glass of water, and a note on the bedside table. Evan still slept soundly; the cadence of his breathing didn't change at all while she was in the room or while her eyes studied his face.

Just an hour, she told herself, quietly backing out of the room, torn between craving the heat of the warm sunshine and remembering the heat of eyes bluer than the sky.

Moist, smacking, chewing sounds rudely penetrated Evan's indecently immoral and immensely pleasant dream. Aroused and nude, Madeline was poised above him, her blond hair spilling about her soft shoulders and full, forward-thrusting breasts. *Hold on just one minute*, he told himself. She wasn't *eating* anything, was she? There was nothing in his dream for her to eat—except him.

The smacking continued.

No, he firmly told his subconscious. She wasn't supposed to be eating anything, she was only supposed to be moaning his name in heated abandon.

The noises stopped.

Impatiently, without opening his eyes, he swiped at an itch on his nose and tried to immerse himself in the dream once more.

Slurp, slurp, slurp-slurp-slurp.

"What the hell?" he said sleepily, causing the slurping sounds to cease and the delightful dream to be lost. He sensed—no, he *knew*—someone was in the room with him. Opening his eyes, he saw only an empty room.

"What the hell?" he repeated, feeling overly heated and confused and irritable. "Madeline?"

No answer. Where was she? What was going on?

A thin, uncomfortable layer of perspiration coated his body, and he kicked the covers down to the foot of the bed. Eyeing the window opposite the head of the bed, he wondered if he had the endurance to make it there, lift the window, and stumble back to bed without collapsing in a feeble heap.

Well, damm it, he was sure as hell going to try. After a night like last night, a full breakfast, and a morning-long nap, he should be ready to tackle the world.

A tiny sound drew his attention as he prepared to hoist himself to a sitting position, a delicate noise that almost sounded like someone licking his or her lips. He turned his head and jumped when his eyes met the wide, unblinking gaze of the enormous gray cat that sat on the bedside table, a gaze in which he could see twin images of his face reflected.

"What the hell?" Evan said for the third time, amazed at the feline's intrepid stare.

Unconcerned with the affronted man before him, the great cat slowly blinked his green eyes and swirled his tongue again around his long white whiskers and gray-furred chops. Lazily, but without breaking eye contact with the man, the beast bent his front legs and settled into a comfortable position next to the plate and glass on the little table.

Evan opened his mouth, but speech eluded him. This . . . this—he couldn't think of an adjective vile enough—*cat* was the reason for his dislocated shoulder and his head wound, the sole reason he was laid up in the middle of Wyoming Territory.

He sat up in the bed, rubbing his eyes with his good hand. Another jolt of awareness hit him, increasing his indignation tenfold. The corpulent gray cat had evidently eaten a snack Madeline had set out for him.

"Get out of here!" he snarled, lunging toward the bed-side table.

With the clatter of plate against glass, the cat bounded down from his perch, lit upon the floor, and sprang up onto the dresser in a series of graceful movements. Regally setting his haunches down on the wood surface, the feline fixed him with an arrogant stare and began washing one of his front paws.

"How the hell did you get in here anyway, cat?" Evan's tight, angry voice increased in volume. His feet found the floor, but he dared not rise; his head was filled with that damnable dizziness again. "So help me, you fat, furry son of a bitch," he continued hotly, "if I ever get my hands on you or your ugly stub of a tail, you're done for. Do you know what you did to me? Do you even care? Do you just know, too, that I can't get up and chase you out of here, you little—"

He broke off, realizing he was bellowing at a cat. Not that it mattered; the gray ears hadn't so much as flickered. He thanked God that no one—Madeline, in particular—was here to witness him making such a fool of himself. For pity's sake, he was sweating and panting for breath.

Gradually the dizziness passed, but the anger still burned in him as he watched the cat continue to groom his paws sedately. He decided to try another tack.

"Here, kitty," he crooned with false sweetness. "Here, Sugar. That's your name, isn't it, you fat ugly fur-face pus-gut kitty?" At that, the cat's ears twitched, and his tongue paused a moment in mid-lick before continuing.

"Aha!" Evan said with dangerous, syrupy satisfaction. "Sugar *is* your name. Much as I like your mistress, what a *stupid* name she gave you." A bead of sweat rolled from his temple down the side of his face, and he forced himself to smile. "Why don't you come over here, Sugar, and let Uncle Evan pet you?"

He couldn't believe his eyes when the monstrous tom slowly raised himself to a standing position. Did the senseless tabby have sugar for brains as well as for his name? This was going to be as easy as taking candy from a baby.

"That's it, nice kitty," he said, holding his breath and patting the bed. "Jump right over here next to me so I can send you into next week." Drat, this was almost too easy. A pang of disappointment whiffled through him at the lack of challenge. But then, how much challenge could an obese, bobtailed house cat with the name of Sugar present to a man?

Sugar took a step toward him and stopped, arching his back and yawning.

"What? Am I boring you? Don't stop now, pussycat. Come over here." Impatience crept into his voice. "Come here, Sugarbutt." He slid a portion of his weight onto his feet, testing his legs and his equilibrium. So far, so good. His lips curved into an evil grin. "Would you like me to come to you, Your Royal Highness? That can be arranged." He estimated Sugar had about three seconds to say his kitty prayers before he reached the dresser.

Evan stood up. Sugar finished his yawn and looked down his nose at him, lifted his short tail, and made a most indelicate sound. In a great leap, the cat jumped from the dresser to the doorway and was gone.

Fury washed over him. How long had it been since he had felt such impotent rage? Since Lissa? He took four staggering, rubber-legged steps to the doorway. "Sugar! Come back here, you little pecker! Don't you *dare* do that and run off! God *damn* it, you miserable wretch. I'm going to find you, if it's the last thing I ever do!" Grabbing hold of the doorknob for support, he leaned against it, gasping for breath.

"Evan?" Madeline's voice was far off. He heard booted, hurrying steps on what he assumed was the porch. "Evan? Are you all right?" He heard a door open, and a moment later she was standing before him, looking alarmed. "Evan! My goodness! What are you doing out of bed? What was all that shouting?"

She was a vision to behold. She wore a man's clothing once again, but her garb did nothing to detract from her beauty. Her face was clear and fresh, and her cheeks bloomed with color. Wisps of golden hair had again worked themselves loose from her long, thick braid and conspired with her shining face to present a totally radiant picture.

"Evan?" she asked, breathing hard, bringing her hand up to rest over her heart. "What's the matter? Are you in pain? Can I help you?"

He felt a good deal of his anger melt away at her obvious concern for him, but he couldn't stop the slightly accusing "Where were you?" that tumbled from his lips.

"Outside." Her gaze dropped to the floor. "Didn't you see the note I left you?"

"What note?"

"The note I left you on the nightstand, right next to the plate."

He turned his head and noticed a piece of paper, inscribed with neat handwriting, lying on the floor next to the wooden stand. "Oh."

"I just needed to get a little fresh air," she explained, backing away from him. "I wasn't even gone an hour. Did you need something while I was out?"

He shook his head.

Glancing at him briefly before turning her attention back to the floor and taking another small step backward, she asked, "Are you unwell? You're acting most peculiar."

"I'm fine," he answered shortly, leaning heavily on the knob. The little energy he had was fast fading, and he felt a sweat break out on his face. Closing his eyes for a moment, he struggled to summon his strength.

"Oh, dear, your color is terrible again." He heard the anxiety in her voice, heard unwilling feet step forward. "Let me help you back to bed."

Her arm slipped hesitantly around his waist, and he put his good arm about her shoulders, pulling her closer to him than was perhaps necessary, but, damn, she felt so good. Her nearness and clean outdoorsy fragrance, as well as her surprisingly strong arms, lent him the strength he needed to make it back to the bed. Inhaling deeply of her scent as he lay down on his side, he felt a contentment steal over him, a sort of peace that smoothed all the spiny edges of his nettled disposition.

"Thank you," he whispered, lost in the depths of the concerned green eyes that looked down at him. What the hell was the matter with him, anyway? Had he gone soft in the head? He didn't need complications like this. He'd already damned himself a thousand times for what had happened last night.

"You shouldn't be up by yourself, Evan," she chided in a businesslike way, extricating herself from his grasp and stepping backward. "Remember what happened yesterday? You almost fainted."

"Men don't faint," he said with mild outrage, easing himself onto his back. His shoulder ached like hell, and he tried to shift his arm beneath the binding.

"They don't?" The impertinent Madeline briefly returned. "What is it they do, then, when their faces turn white and their eyes roll up into their heads and their legs buckle and they fall down?"

"Men don't *faint*," he repeated distinctly, countering the amusement he heard in her voice. "Occasionally one of us might *pass out*, but we most definitely do not faint. And for your information," he added, "my eyes did not roll up into my head, yesterday, nor did I fall down."

"Mm-hmm," she responded, folding her arms across her chest. "Whatever you say."

His gaze traveled down her form, and he totally forgot what he had been about to say. The impish grin and beguiling dimples that had momentarily appeared on her face just as quickly fled, replaced by the uneasy, remorseful look she'd worn this morning.

"Well, if there's nothing else you need . . ." She let her voice trail off, then clasped her hands before her and looked again at her boots.

"Madeline—" he started to say, wanting to put her at ease. Damn, he wanted to make things right with her, but he knew he probably never could.

"I need to go," she said abruptly. "Let me know when you want your supper."

She was gone then, leaving him alone with the weightiness of his thoughts.

ten

"I WANT A BIG CHICKEN, ROBERT JAMES, AND a decent-sized basket of eggs—at least a dozen and a half. Don't you be skimping on me or go favoring that short little runt cook of the Spencers. And don't you be telling me, not even one more time, about Roger Reilly's pickled peaches or corn bread dressing or gingerbread or apple pie—"

"It was apple cake, Ma, not apple pie, and Old Roger said he'd write down the receipt for you. I'm sorry you're mad, Ma," Robbie Ashler said earnestly, "but that was about the tastiest cake I ever did have." He reached down and furiously scratched at an itch on the back of his knee while keeping his eyes fixed on his mother. "You know you're the best cook there ever was. Everyone says so. Even Reed was sayin' the other day that he could hardly wait until the Fourth o' July picnic so's he could get his jaws into one of your pies. I believe he mentioned your pork and beans in the same conversation, too, ma'am. You remember that, don't you, Miss Madeline?"

Madeline answered the pleading, help-me-out look in

Robbie's eyes. "I most certainly do," she said to the older woman. "Will talks about your cooking frequently, Mrs. Ashler."

"He does, does he?" Mary Ashler said as if she didn't believe it. "Hmmph. The July picnic's a long ways off. Ain't even May yet—"

"If you'll excuse me, Ma and Miss Madeline," Robbie interrupted his mother, "I gotta get goin' so's Reed don't have my hide. Sun's already been up a good hour. You wouldn't want him to have my hide, now wouldja, Ma?" He grinned. "It's the only hide I got." Pausing in the doorway, his wiry form exuding restless adolescent energy, he rapidly shifted his weight back and forth from one foot to the other. "Do I gotta pluck the bird, too? You ain't gonna make me do that, are ya? You know how I hate doin' that."

"I'll pluck it, Robbie," Madeline volunteered. "You just bring it up here."

"Thanks, Miss Maddie," he answered quickly, and was gone.

Mary Ashler placed her hands on her stout hips and shook her head. "You're too soft on that boy, Madeline Claire." As she patted her neatly coiled graying hair, her stern look gave way to a soft smile. "But I'm glad he's got good work with you good people. Both Nate and Will have taken extra pains with him since he's been workin' here. It's a shame my Henry passed on afore seein' the boy to adulthood, but what's a body got to say about that? The Heavenly Father's got his own plan for things." Abruptly she changed the subject. "You heard anything out of your pa yet?"

Madeline shrugged and shook her head. "Nothing yet."

"Nothin'? Well, it ain't been a month yet, has it?" Kind blue eyes studied her face. "What are you thinkin' about this whole business, dear? You ain't said much about Nathaniel Spencer goin' from bein' your brother to your father in one fell swoop."

"I don't know what to think, ma'am," she answered honestly.

"Mm-hmm," Mrs. Ashler said thoughtfully. "And what's this business Robbie's been tellin' me about some Chicago man layin' smack-dab in the middle of Mr. Spencer's bed

with a busted-up shoulder?" the older woman asked, bustling past Madeline toward the oven. "Gotta get the old girl
fired up good and hot, here. Yeah, I heard he's mendin'
nicely. Anything special you want me to make today?"
Without giving Madeline a chance to answer either question, she stood up and sniffed. "That man ought to be out
in the bunkhouse. I don't know what that big ox Will Reed
was thinkin' by puttin' him up in the house. It ain't proper.
Especially with that man bein' one of them big-city gents.
I know their type . . . and you here all by yourself."

Crickets of nervousness jumped in Madeline's chest. Like
Will, Mary Ashler had been born with the gift of uncanny
perception. Could the woman look into her eyes and know
how forcefully her pulse thrummed from just the mention of
the man? Could she tell what had happened in that bedroom
just two nights past?

"Dear?" Mrs. Ashler asked. "I asked if you wanted me
to make some of them sticky buns you like so much. Long
as I'm makin' bread, it'd be simple enough to do. Your
cheekbones are standin' out, child. Have you been eatin'
properly? No, don't answer that. You haven't, have you?
You're a tall one, but I always said you could stand to put
a little meat on your bones." She patted her hips. "Padding,
I call it. Wards off ailments, yes, indeed, and keeps a body
warm in the winter. I just bet you were cold all winter.
Uh-huh, you were, weren't you? Don't even try to tell me
you weren't. You gotta eat more, girl. Plump yourself up a
little."

Terribly self-conscious under the older woman's obser-
vant gaze, Madeline smoothed her hands over her own hips.
"You don't need to fret about me, Mrs. Ashler, I've got
a little padding. I-I just haven't been too hungry lately,"
she answered. Suddenly the air in the kitchen felt stifling.
"Well, I think I'll go on out and see to that chicken so
Robbie can get to work," she said, clasping her hands
in front of her nervously. Her palms were moist, sliding
against one another uncomfortably. Heading toward the
door, she added politely as an afterthought, "Some sticky
buns would be nice, though—with raisins."

"Hold your horses a minute, young lady. You plannin'

on hangin' around the house much today, or you gonna be
out punchin' cows or whatever it is you go out and do in
them god-awful britches?"

Out of nowhere, Madeline remembered what Robbie had
told her about his mother wearing coveralls in the winter-
time. The comical mental picture did nothing to disperse her
near-panicked anxiety, however. She didn't think she could
stay in the house even one more minute.

"We've been real busy with calving, Will tells me," she
said, inching ever closer to the door. "I'll go out and see
if he needs any help. I know he went over and gave the
Matthews brothers a hand with a hard pull yesterday." She
stopped moving, feeling a sweat break out on her back.
"That is, of course, ma'am, if you don't mind taking Mr.
Grant his meals."

Sighing, the older woman shook her head. "Run along,
dear. Robbie tells me you been cooped up here for quite
a few days now. He's been talking about that hurt fellow
quite a lot, too." She walked to the pantry, her words harder
to hear as she bent over and pulled bread tins from a drawer.
"I know all about tendin' to the sick, that's for sure, and
how it tires a body. I nursed my Henry for the better part
of a year, God rest his soul." She stood and turned, her
round cheeks flushed pink from her movements. "You just
run along, now. I expect I can feed the man."

Them big-city gents. I know their type.

The words set Evan's teeth on edge. What was that supposed to mean? And now Madeline was arranging for his
meals to be brought in my Mrs. Ashton . . . Ashwood . . .
or whatever her name was. The lovely blonde was certainly
doing a fine job of avoiding him. Now she was leaving for
the day without so much as a how-do-you-do. Where was
she going?

Why do you care, Grant?

He stretched, his movements choppy and frustrated. A
biting ache burned deep in his shoulder socket, and his
stomach growled emptily. Perturbed, he realized he had
always been the one to set the boundaries of a relationship. When, where, how, and how long had always been

his decision. Now here he was, nearly as dependent as a babe, having been loved and left by a slip of a girl who apparently had chosen the companionship of chickens and cows and horses this morning over being in the same house with him.

Woman, his mind protested. *She's not a girl; she's a woman.*

Girl, woman, combination of the two—whatever she was, Madeline Spencer did and said what she pleased. Rankled, he mentally ticked off her faults. She swore, she was opinionated, she wore a man's clothes, she rode astride . . . She rode astride. The events of two nights past played in his mind, and his list immediately vanished. He swore softly. How sweetly the woman rode astride.

How sweet she was, period. Sweet, gentle, soft, winsome . . .

Hell and damnation, he realized he wouldn't have her any other way. *Have* her? She wasn't his to have. With consternation, he realized that the idea of *having* her sounded uncomfortably possessive.

Studying the pattern of the dim, curtained light on the ceiling, he decided he'd had enough of lying in bed like an invalid, doing nothing but sleeping, eating, and staring at the four walls. He had important business to attend to, a new plant to open. He was going to get up out of bed and out-of-doors today if it killed him. Too many days had already been wasted . . .

"If you keep scowlin' like that, your face just might freeze in that position." A short plump woman in a nononsense black dress filled the doorway. "What in the name of David are you making such a sour puss about, young man? You been layin' back here suckin' on lemons or somethin'?" Bustling into the room without giving him a chance to answer, she continued, "Since there ain't no other big dark-haired men layin' around here, I take it you must be Mr. Chicago." She nodded. "I'm Mary Ashler. Live over in the next valley. You met my boy Robbie already. He's been tellin' me all about you."

One of the sashes of her apron appeared at her side briefly as she reached up to open the curtains, then disappeared back into the generous rolls at her waist as her arm came back down.

Evan winced at the bright light that entered the room.

"Yeah, I heard all about you gettin' up and tryin' to take a turn around the room by yourself the other day. Stubborn, eh? Durned near fainted, too, the way I heard it." She shook her head. "That's just what you need is to pop that shoulder out again. You know, mister, that shoulder could be a problem for the rest of your days. Once they pop outta joint like that they rather have a tendency to keep doin' it at inconvenient times."

She changed subjects without so much as a pause. "It was like a tomb in here." She pulled the window up, allowing a current of cool air to enter the room. Sniffing loudly and planting her hands on her sturdy hips, she turned back to face him. "It don't smell none too fresh in here, neither."

"Nice to meet you, too," he said shortly, watching her through slitted eyes.

The blue eyes crinkled at the corners. "Oh, we got us a touchy one here." A broad, amused smile followed. "Well, don't you worry none, boy, it's washday. We'll have you scrubbed up and fresh as a daisy in no time."

Like hell. There was no way this woman was coming near him with a washcloth. "With all due respect, ma'am, I can do for myself." To his embarrassment, his stomach chose that moment to growl loudly.

"Well, now. I suppose you'll just be jumpin' outta bed and makin' your own breakfast, then. And while you're at it, I need some water hauled and some wood brought in." Her smile became one of patience. "Don't be silly. You *can't* do for yourself right now. You know, young man, askin' for help don't mean you're weak or incompetent. It just usually indicates you got more smarts than the next person. Now, I'll ask you again: what'll you have for your breakfast, Mr. Chicago?"

"My name is Grant," he said tightly. His stomach growled again. "And I'll eat whatever you're making."

"My, don't you sound excited to eat Mary Ashler's cooking. . . . Honey, didn't your mama ever tell you that you could catch more flies with honey than with vinegar?

Lord, but you're a sour one. Is your arm painin' you this mornin'?" Concern and determination were written on her round features. "You know, you're going to feel about twelve times better once we get some breakfast into you and get that smelly old wrap off you."

"Reed said it wasn't supposed to come off for at least a month."

"Ain't no one who could stand to be around you in a month," she said matter-of-factly. "It's comin' off today, and you're gettin' a new one, so don't even try to argue with me. Now, that Will Reed, he knows plenty about his cows, and he fancies he knows quite a lot about doctorin' on people, too, but he ain't Wyoming Territory's leadin' authority on everything."

The patient, comfortable smile remained on her lips. "Don't you worry, Mr. Chicago, this won't hurt the healin' process none. I didn't raise nine young'uns without tendin' to my share of scrapes and sickness and broken bones. You just let me take care of you today and you'll be fine. How's a pile of griddle cakes sound? There ain't none better around these parts; you can ask anyone. Light as clouds, they are, and I can have them for you in no time. Then we can get on to the business of cleanin' you up for the day."

Evan opened his mouth to argue that he didn't need her to fuss over him, but realized that trying to tell this woman anything would be as futile as trying to empty Lake Michigan with a teaspoon. Mrs. Ashler was obviously in her element and loving every minute of it. He suspected that if he opposed her, she would just talk and talk until he eventually agreed, out of aural exhaustion, to whatever she was determined to accomplish. His head, which hadn't yet pained him this morning, began to throb dully.

Mrs. Ashler continued to look at him expectantly, miraculously silent for the present time. Her plump, benevolent face seemed to be the type, he noticed unwillingly, that smiled often, judging from the wrinkles that fanned out from the corners of her eyes.

He closed his eyes briefly. The day was young, and Madeline continued to shun him; now this woman had

managed to make him feel as if he was all of eight years old.
If he got any softer, he might as well tuck his man-parts up
between his legs and put on one of the dresses that Madeline
damn near never wore.

It was just too much to take.

Nodding, he opened his eyes and found himself saying
that, yes, griddle cakes would be fine.

Two hours later Evan had been washed, rinsed, shaved,
and fluffed into weariness. He sat in the padded armchair
Mrs. Ashler had dragged into the room, feeling a little
buzz-headed and very much like a small boy, wondering
at the strength in the older woman's stout form.

Breakfast had been delicious. Mary Ashler's flapjacks
were every bit as tender and light as she'd promised, and
he'd eaten two large stacks of the cakes smothered in
butter and maple syrup. She'd made all kinds of approving
comments while he ate, nodding in satisfaction as her fare
disappeared.

After giving him some time to digest the food, she'd
hauled him out of bed and begun her work on him. First
she'd efficiently shaved his face. Then she had removed the
offensive linen wrap from around his torso, and he'd been
helpless to do anything but hold his injured arm in place
while she attacked him with soap and a washcloth, hum-
ming the whole while. She had even insisted upon washing
his hair after she'd dried him off and replaced the binding
around his torso, positioning him with his head bent forward
over the basin, exclaiming at the healing wound behind his
hairline while she gently soaped and rinsed his scalp.

Though he'd just been treated like an invalid, it still felt
mighty good to be clean, he thought, closing his eyes and
inhaling the mouth-watering aroma of what he guessed was
an apple pie.

"I plumb tuckered you out, didn't I?"

"No, ma'am," he answered dryly, "I'm just checking to
see if you left any soap on the insides of my eyelids."

She laughed, a rolling, rich sound that washed over him
pleasantly. "Impertinent youngster. You'd best mind your
manners or I'll feed you a bowl of oatmeal for dinner."

"Ma'am, if your flapjacks are an accurate measure of your cooking ability, I think you'll find I can exhibit the finest manners known."

"Silver-tongued devil," she said, smiling as she walked past him and tossed the used sheets through the doorway. "Just keep up the sweet talk and see where it gets you." She turned and faced him with suddenly serious eyes. "You know, with those black stubs scraped off your face you're rather a handsome rascal, Mr. Grant." Walking back to the bed, she snapped a clean sheet across the mattress. "No, sir, your cracked-open head and crippled arm don't count much with me. It's not at all seemly for you and Madeline to be alone together in this house. She's an innocent, while you, young man, most undoubtedly are not."

He coughed to cover his sudden discomfort. "With all due respect, ma'am, look at me. Do I look capable of ravishing a young woman?"

Shrewd eyes studied him a long moment. "Maybe, maybe not. I don't know. I ain't so old, though, that I forgot about how it can be between a man and a woman. Nope," she said, shaking her head, "I ain't forgot a'tall. It just ain't right for the two of you to be alone. I'd stay on here myself," she added, smoothing a wrinkle from the fresh bottom sheet, "excepting I have my own place to tend."

A cloud passed in front of the sun, momentarily dimming the room's brightness. "There's no need for that, ma'am. Miss Spencer is taking very good care of me."

"I didn't say I was worried about Madeline not properly takin' care of you, young man, and I'm pretty sure you know what I was aimin' at," she said crisply. Patting her neat braids, she warned, "I may be short as a stump and gettin' on in years, but so help me, if I find out that you've made so much as one improper advance toward the girl, I'll track you down and make you more than sorry. Madeline's a good, decent girl. The poor lamb's been dealt more than her share of troubles of late, and I'll not see her harmed." She concluded with a tender note in her voice, "She's become quite dear to me."

"Mrs. Ashler—" he began.

She cleared her throat, effectively cutting him off. "Oh,

Lord! I got to get back to the kitchen. Got a pie in the oven, and the bread's probably ready to be punched down." She bustled out of the room, her black skirt swishing about her feet.

Evan felt as if he'd been standing in front of a cyclone that had blown off to the south suddenly at the last minute. He expelled his breath, feeling totally worn out, and willed his body to hurry and heal itself. He needed to put a couple hundred miles' distance between himself and the Spencer ranch, the sooner the better.

Her place. That's how Madeline had come to think of the grassy, sloping bank at this certain bend in the creek. She'd discovered the spot one day last summer while exploring Nate's land on horseback. That particular afternoon had been hot and windy, and both she and her horse had grown thirsty, so she'd headed for a stand of willows in the distance and come across the meandering creek. It was an area she had headed back to time and time again for its peace and simple beauty.

After dismounting, she walked down the bank, her thoughts as turbulent as the spring-swollen waters of the creek. The toes of her boots quickly turned dark with moisture as she moved over the damp ground. Though the morning was sunny and warm, she could both smell and feel the coldness of the water as she approached the mountain-fed stream.

She picked up a stick and tossed it into the water. It was carried away in an instant by the swirling, surging flow. *Just as you were carried away the instant you saw Evan Grant.* She sucked in her breath. It was true. From the first glimpse she'd had of him, she'd been gone. Lost. Out of control. Swept away.

As much as she tried to tell herself that it wasn't possible, that it couldn't be possible, she wondered if she had fallen in love with him. She blew out the breath she'd been holding. *Love?* Could it happen so quickly? She'd thought of a variety of reasons over the past days to explain away the flutters and tingles and palpitations she'd been experiencing since the man had arrived, but none had rung true. It was even harder to rationalize the seeming preoccupation she had with him. He was ever on her mind, invading her thoughts, invading her dreams.

And for God's sake, how could she ever explain away or justify what she'd done with him in her father's bedroom? *Love*?

The feelings she had for Evan were like nothing she'd ever known before—and they scared her to death. She had never suspected, never imagined a person could experience such intense feelings for another, feelings that made a body so excited and breathless and quivery inside.

Nor had she suspected the magic that two bodies, together, could make.

A large branch turned up and over in the seething flow before her, negotiated the curve, then quickly shot by. Following its progress with her eyes until it was out of sight, she realized that the tranquillity she had expected to find here at her private place would not be found.

It was up to her to find her own tranquillity.

And where would it be found? Where *could* it be found? With Evan Grant? Did he feel any of the same things she did?

No, her mind insisted. *He'll stay here until he's well enough to leave. And leave he will, make no mistake about it*. Anguish filled her at the thought. Why did it have to be this way? Had her innocence of the love between a man and a woman led her to believe that what they had shared was a special thing? Or in her naïveté did she not see their love-making for what it truly was—an ordinary slaking of lust?

She needed to stay away from Evan Grant. Being around him only served to muddle her mental faculties. First of all, though, she needed to make it perfectly clear to him that nothing of the sort was ever going to happen again. Then she needed to keep herself as far away from him as possible.

Having made a decision of sorts, she felt hunger gnawing at her belly. She thought longingly of Mrs. Ashler's sticky buns and realized she hadn't eaten any breakfast. Glancing at the sun, she saw that it would be close to noon by the time she returned to the ranch.

The thought of a chicken dinner with all the fixings tempted her sorely . . . or was it the excitement of being near Evan? She resolutely pushed that possibility away. She would take her midday meal in the cookshack, away from the befuddling nearness of Evan Grant and the sharp eyes of Mary Ashler. Then she'd throw herself into whatever work Will assigned her for the afternoon.

Briefly she wondered what kind of day he and Mrs. Ashler were having.

Why do you care?

She told herself she didn't care, not one little bit, about what kind of day Evan was having. As she walked back up the creek bank, the wind caught her full in the face and threatened to tear off her hat. Bordered by the purple-gray mountains that rose in the near distance, the ocean of rolling grassland before her also rippled with the wind's force.

Again she thought of Evan and wished he could be here with her to share the beauty of this rugged land. She imagined him standing beside her, strong and proud, with his arm around her shoulders, taking in this magnificent scenery.

Stop it, Madeline. Breaking away from her reverie, she mounted her horse, the sound of creaking leather being whisked away by the stiff breeze. She was in trouble— more trouble than she had ever been in in her whole life. She could no more stop thinking about Evan Grant than she could fly to the moon.

With a last look at the lovely spot at the creek, she headed back toward the ranch feeling very unsure of herself, very small, and very alone.

Mrs. Ashler. Her husband had no doubt gone to his final repose just to give his ears a rest. A crooked smile touched Evan's lips. After cooking and baking her heart out and giving the ranch house—and him—a thorough scrubbing, she'd gone home. Robbie had hitched up their wagon and come for her an hour or so earlier.

Sitting at the kitchen table nursing a cup of coffee, Evan supposed the day hadn't been a total waste. He'd made a lot of progress physically, and that had to count for something.

Though the dizziness was still frequently with him, the spells didn't strike with the same viciousness or intensity as they had during the past few days. He could now walk from the bedroom to the kitchen without assistance, and he had even taken a few turns outdoors with the sturdy support of Mrs. Ashler.

What he'd done mostly, though, was think of Madeline and wonder what she was doing, what she was thinking. She hadn't come home to check on him even once during the day. Taking a sip of his coffee, he thought maybe it was for the best for the two of them to stay apart. Things were just a little too hot between them.

Setting the mug down, he brought his hand up to his forehead and raked his fingers through his hair. A *little* hot? Things had been blistering hot between them. He'd never known a woman like her before in his whole life. Beautiful, fun, full of surprises, innocent, a wildcat in bed— she was the kind of woman a man could think about settling down with.

A feeling ran through him at that idea, a feeling as disquieting as the sound of a fingernail skidding across a slate. Settling down? What kind of nonsense was that? Damn, but Madeline Spencer was the kind of woman who sent a man's mind revolving in all sorts of uncomfortable directions.

The day's light was just beginning to fade. He looked around the comfortable kitchen, wondering about the owner of the house. Nate Spencer. What manner of man was he? Evan had heard plenty about him, but he suspected that a good deal less than half of it was true.

He was curious as to why Spencer had settled into something as mundane as cattle ranching after the kind of life he'd led. And what was he doing in San Francisco right now? Though Mrs. Ashler had mentioned that he was out there on business, she had remained silent on the subject after that. What kind of business would Spencer have in San Francisco?

Evan suddenly remembered Mrs. Ashler mentioning that Madeline had had more than her share of troubles lately, too.

What kind of troubles? Was there trouble between father
and daughter? And where—who?—was Madeline's mother? She'd mentioned her father and her grandmother, but
never once had she mentioned her mother. This house and
its outbuildings weren't more than a couple of years old.
Where had she grown up? With whom had she grown up?

He didn't like not knowing things.

Sighing, he told himself that he shouldn't care. At this
rate, in another week or so he would be well enough to
leave. He'd briefly considered going back to Chicago to
recover, but had decided against it, thinking of the time
that would be wasted in travel when he was up to returning
to the West.

Or was he reluctant to leave because a certain blond
caretaker would no longer be at his beck and call?

The sound of a horse in the yard interrupted his musings.
Against his will, a surge of anticipation ran through him at
the simple thought of seeing her again. His emotions warred
with his common sense as he tossed down the remainder of
the coffee and waited for her to enter the house. *Calm down,
Grant*, he told himself. *She's just a woman; she could be
any woman.*

"Hello, Madeline," he said softly, struck anew by her
fresh appeal as he watched her enter and hang up her hat.
You damn well know she's not just any woman.

"Hello," she said just as softly, walking toward him.
Determination set the angle of her jaw. "We need to talk."

"I agree."

"We . . . ah, the other night . . ." She stopped just out of
arm's reach and folded her arms across her chest. Taking
a deep breath, she looked up at the ceiling and tried again.
"I mean . . . when we—"

"When we made love?" he gently supplied, wanting to
spare her the painful feelings she was obviously having.

She nodded vigorously.

"I wanted you, Maddie," he said simply, "and you wanted
me. I'm not very proud of myself for allowing things to go
so far, but it's that way sometimes between men and wom-
en." Sighing, he added, "A better man probably wouldn't
have . . . Oh, hell, I can't say I wouldn't do it all over again,

given the same set of circumstances."

Her eyes shone big and luminous. "Why did you want me . . . in that way?" Her voice caught on the last word, and her strong jaw quivered.

Tenderness surged up inside him, pushing aside the sexual desire that had flared to life at the sight of her. He stood, leaning against the table with the side of his thigh. Madeline's delicate face was sunburned and streaked with dirt, but he'd never seen anything more beautiful in his life. He longed to cup her trembling jaw with his hand and kiss away every last bit but of her sadness and regret.

Now close enough to touch her, he reached out and gently stroked her cheek with his index finger. "I don't know why I wanted you," he replied honestly. "I just did."

She took a deep breath and spoke, her voice shaky. "I told myself today that I wasn't going to . . ."

Edging his body closer to hers, he let his fingers glide from her cheek to her shoulder. "I know," he said. He was close enough to catch the faint, familiar floral scent, mixed with the smell of salt and leather and the outdoors. Something strange was happening inside his chest. "I told myself the same thing."

"What's going to become of this, Evan?" she murmured. "I feel as if you've turned me absolutely inside out."

He knew the feeling as her dark green eyes met his. Questioning eyes. His thigh brushed hers, and his hand closed over a small, cold fist. "Let me hold you, Madeline," he said with a deep sigh, confused at the depth of his feelings. "I don't know that we can sort anything out, but you have my word that I won't force you to do anything against your will."

Stiffly at first, she yielded to his one-armed embrace. "We can't . . . do that . . . ever again, Evan."

"I know, Maddie," he whispered, stroking her hair. "I know." Allowing himself the small pleasure of resting his cheek against the silky golden mass, he closed his eyes and inhaled deeply of her unique fragrance, while around them the dimness deepened to dusk.

eleven

OVER THE NEXT DAYS EVAN'S HEALTH CONtinued to improve. He still suffered from random dizzy spells and headaches, though Madeline knew he tried to disguise them from her. She was thankful that his shoulder seemed to be healing properly—neither the sensation nor the blood flow to his hand was impaired—and Will Reed predicted a full recovery.

True spring had come to Wyoming Territory, efflorescing under the pure blue skies and bringing the land alive with green newness. Since that night in the kitchen, Madeline felt as if she had bloomed as well. The shame and shyness she'd felt around him had gradually melted away, and a fragile, tacit understanding now existed between them, for he continued to make good his word that nothing improper would happen between them.

He was a perfect gentleman as well as a surprisingly entertaining companion. When she was about the house or grounds, he would turn up at her side at odd moments to regale her with a story or a silly joke, and it became apparent to her that he had more of Ben's lighthearted nature than she ever would have guessed.

She knew great pleasure whenever she was around him, but it was mixed with great pain. He would be leaving soon, she knew, and she couldn't bear to think of how empty her life would be without him in it. Each wire he received from Ben carried the realization to her that he would soon be gone. And after he left the ranch and moved on to San Francisco, would he ever think of her again?

"Why are you frowning, Maddie?" Evan sat cross-legged on the ground at the edge of the vegetable garden she was planting. The collar of his brown cambric shirt was open, exposing his neck and the top edge of the wrap around his torso. The left sleeve flapped emptily in the breeze.

Looking up at him, she felt her heart turn over. The warm wind ruffled his dark hair, and she noticed that his handsome face had bronzed considerably in the past days. He looked so boyish, so carefree. As she stared at the strong column of his neck, another surge of bittersweet pain rolled through her.

Glancing skyward, she swallowed hard and tried to speak in a normal tone of voice, but it was difficult to get the words past the lump in her throat. "Was I frowning?" she asked lightly, forcing her lips to curve into a pleasant smile. "I just remembered that Will is going to turn Robbie loose at noon so he can help me put in the garden. It's got to be almost twelve now." She rose and dusted herself off. "We can take our noon meal at the cookshack today."

"You mean you're not going to cook?" he asked, raising an eyebrow and gesturing with his arm toward her dirty hands. "There's nothing like a little grit—"

He broke off at the distant sound of several sets of hooves. For a man prone to dizzy spells and lacking the use of one arm, he rose quickly. "Who's that?" he asked, squinting toward the northwest.

Lifting up the brim of her hat, she studied the riders moving toward them. "It looks like the Matthews brothers and their foreman. They're coming from the right direction. I don't recall Will mentioning a visit, though. I wonder if there's trouble."

"You know these men?"

"Yes. Pete and Jack Matthews have a small spread north and west of here. Jack's the younger of the two brothers, and he's very pleasant. I don't know too much about their foreman except that his name's Rendner and he's supposedly from Texas." The riders were nearer now, close enough for Madeline to positively identify them. "Yes, it's them." She waved in greeting.

"What about the other brother? You didn't mention him."

"Pete?" She tried to keep the distaste from showing on her face when she spoke his name. The man clung to her side like a burr whenever he happened to catch sight of her. She remembered, too, the long, loud, self-important discourses he was wont to launch into. "He's . . . he's probably quite decent." She watched Evan's brows rise questioningly at her lame remark. Pausing, she searched for something kind to say about Nate's neighbor. "One might find his personality . . . a little strong."

The galloping horses came to a stop in the yard. "Howdy, Miss Madeline, I was hoping you'd be about." A medium-sized man all but leapt from his horse and doffed his hat, exposing a longish thatch of straight yellow hair. A bright red-and-blue-plaid shirt competed strongly with his brown-and-green-plaid trousers. Tucking his hands in his pockets while swaggering forward, he paid her a loud compliment. "Don't you just look about as lovely as one of those there flowers you're planting." A sickly sweet fragrance wafted from him on the warm breeze, making the inside of Madeline's nose itch unpleasantly.

She forced a smile. "Good day, Mr. Matthews." Pointedly she added, "We're planting vegetables today."

"Oh. Well, you're certainly prettier than a turnip." He slapped his knee and shifted a wad of tobacco from one side of his mouth to the other, laughing loudly at his own joke.

"Good day, Miss Spencer," Jack Matthews said, politely removing his hat and giving his brother an exasperated look. He dismounted in a fluid motion, his long form lean and graceful. "Good day to you as well, mister," he added to Evan, who had been standing silently beside Madeline, his face impassive. "I'm Jack Matthews, and this is my brother,

Pete. Over there's our foreman, Aaron Rendner."

Unsmiling, Rendner remained seated on his horse. He touched the brim of his hat. "Miss Spencer. Mister." Though he was a solid beefy man with dark hair and dark eyes, his voice was curiously thin. During the few times she'd seen him, Madeline didn't think she had ever seen a smile cross his face.

"We heard about your misfortune," Jack continued addressing Evan, sympathy evident on his pleasant features. Short sandy hair crowned his golden-tanned face. He smiled kindly, exposing straight, even teeth. "It looks like you're coming along pretty well, though."

"Not too bad," Evan said, extending his hand to the young man. Though he didn't quite smile, the tight look on his face eased. "Name's Evan Grant."

Madeline watched the older Matthews take in every detail of Evan's appearance, his expression growing more and more sour as Evan and Jack made small talk. Unexpectedly, his eyes flicked to her and caught her staring. The sour look was immediately replaced by an expression she couldn't interpret.

"Are you enjoying the springlike weather, Miss Madeline?" Pete asked loudly, interrupting the men's conversation. He jammed his hands into his pockets and rocked back and forth, from heel to toe. "I'd sure like to come around some evening and take you for a turn in the fresh air."

Madeline heard Evan's voice break off in mid-sentence as he turned his attention from the younger Matthews brother to the older. He regarded the shorter man with blue eyes as frigid as an outcropping of granite in January.

"My place ain't as grand as Nate's, but it looks real pretty in the moonlight," Pete continued, still wearing the half-earnest, half-smirking expression. "You remember that moonlight ride home we had last fall from the social at St. Matthew's, Miss Madeline? Remember how you thought it was kind of funny that me and the Episcopal church shared the same name?"

Madeline wondered what Pete's game was. She had never thought of him as particularly clever or cunning, but now she wasn't sure. Did he suspect some sort of relationship between her and Evan?

As if sensing the tension, Jack cleared his throat. "The cattle, Peter," he reminded his brother.

"Oh, yeah. We're here to see Reed," Pete announced importantly, pulling his hands from his pockets. "Unless Spencer's come back." At the negative shake of her head, he continued, "We figured Reed mighta come in to have a bite of lunch. We got us a little trouble we need to talk to him about."

"What kind of trouble?" she asked, concerned. Rendner continued to sit on his horse, looking sullen and impatient. Jack opened his mouth, but Pete's loud voice trounced over his brother's.

"It's nothing you need to fret your pretty head about, little gal." He laughed patronizingly. "Why, it's hardly important at all."

Jack spoke up, looking at Pete with annoyance. "I think cattle rustling *is* rather important, brother. We've had a fair number of losses. I also think Miss Spencer has a right to know what's going on in the valley." Turning to her, he asked, "I know you haven't been out on the range much of late, Miss Madeline, but has Reed mentioned anything to you on the subject?"

"No, not at all," she answered, shocked and dismayed that the despised thieves were in their area. "In fact, whenever Will's talked about rustling in the past, he's always remarked on how fortunate we've been around here *not* to have had trouble with it."

"Well, not no more," Pete said with disgust.

"How many have you lost?" Evan asked.

Pete spat a wad of brown juice on the ground. "Butt out, Grant. It ain't your business."

Jack clamped a hand on his brother's arm, but Pete jerked away. "It ain't his business, Jack. We don't need no outsider knowing our affairs. Especially some outsider who thinks our beef ain't good enough for his highfalutin slaughterhouse in San Francisco. San Francisco? Whoever heard of shipping cattle west? And why didn't he have one of his little appointments with us, huh, brother? Do you s'pose our cattle ain't good enough for him?"

"Exactly what the hell is your problem, Matthews?" Evan asked in a low and angry voice.

"Now, Pete," Jack began, "we're just a small operation—"

Madeline clamped a restraining hand of her own across Evan's good arm. The muscles of his forearm worked tensely beneath her fingers. "I believe I need to get out of this hot sun, Mr. Grant. I'm suddenly quite fatigued," she managed to say with honeyed breathlessness, though all she wanted to do was give troublemaking Pete Matthews a good swift kick in the shins. "Perhaps you'll find Will down at the cookshack," she said to Jack, not trusting herself to even look at Pete.

Over the simultaneous, concerned offers of assistance from both brothers, Madeline shook her head and said, "No, no, you gentlemen go on. Mr. Grant can assist me to the house. You have urgent business with Will. . . ." She let her voice trail off as she dug her fingernails into Evan's uninjured forearm as hard as she dared. "Please, Mr. Grant, I really must get indoors."

He resisted just long enough to let her know of his displeasure at being manipulated, but allowed himself to be led away toward the house.

"So long, Miss Spencer. Hope you're feeling better soon," Jack called. She heard him say, "Come on, Pete. Grant can walk her to the house. She'll be fine once she gets out of the sun." She couldn't make out Pete's grumbled reply, but she heard the two of them remount their horses and ride in the direction of the cookshack. Turning her head slightly, she was able to watch the three riders from the corner of her eye until they were well beyond the corral. Pete turned his head once and looked in their direction, but he was too far away for her to see his expression.

What made Pete Matthews so disagreeable? Will classified him as all gurgle and no guts, and furthermore pronounced that the man had a case of calf-eyes over her. She uncomfortably realized that Will was probably right about the infatuation, especially after Pete's display in front of Evan. She hoped he and Evan wouldn't cross paths again.

Silent the whole way to the house, Evan turned on her when they got to the porch steps, shaking her arm from his. "Fatigued, my ass. There's nothing the matter with you. Don't ever do that to me again, Madeline," he said in the same tight voice he'd used to speak to Pete Matthews. "I don't take kindly to a woman interfering like you just did back there. I kept my mouth shut because I don't know anything about your relationship with your neighbors, but I'm warning you, if that man gets within a mile of me during the rest of his natural life, he'll be damned sorry. You might think I'm only half a man right now, but I don't need to hide behind a woman's skirts." He stabbed a finger at her trouser-clad lower body and sarcastically added, "Figuratively speaking, of course."

Anger rose hot and fast inside Madeline's breast, and the words were out of her mouth before she could stop them. Stepping backward onto the first step, she faced him, her chest heaving, her eyes nearly level with his. "Are you looking to get yourself laid up again? You know, we've put a hell of a lot into getting you put back together, Mr. Grant, and now you want to get yourself into a fight? Isn't that just dandy? Reed says your arm isn't going to be fully healed for a long time . . . Oh, never mind." Breaking off, she let out her breath in a huff. "Isn't it just like a man?" she added sarcastically, turning on her heel. "A half a man, a whole man, whatever you are—"

A sweat-dampened hand grasped her arm with the strength of steel, pulling her close. "I'm *all* man, Madeline, and don't you ever forget it."

As if I ever could. His warm male scent invaded her nostrils, mixing with her anger and doing crazy things to her insides. The width of his shoulders was imposing at this close distance, making her very aware of the differences between them. She wasn't sure how much of his anger was directed at her, but she sensed that Pete's braying about wanting to take her for a moonlight ride had raised his dander as much as Matthews's other inflammatory words had.

Releasing her wrist, he reached up and removed her hat. The air was charged between them as they stared into each other's eyes. Madeline's breath caught in her throat as she heard the change in his breathing, saw the ice in his eyes soften, then run liquid blue. Hot stirrings of desire ran through her, making her legs feel weak, and she let out her breath in a long sigh.

"Would you care?" His voice was a caress. Tilting slightly, his head moved toward hers.

"Would I care . . . what?" She swallowed hard, shifting her weight, causing the porch step to creak.

"If I was laid up again . . . Oh, hell." Abruptly he pushed her hat toward her hands and stepped backward, the softness in his voice disappearing. "Hell, Madeline," he repeated, breaking the spell between them and running his hand roughly through his hair. His gaze left her and settled on the barn. "I'm going for a ride," he announced curtly.

Watching him stalk off toward the barn, Madeline quelled the urge to ask him how he thought he was going to saddle a horse. A dangerous shiver scooted down her spine as she considered what had just happened—and what might have happened after that.

Evan had been about to kiss her, she knew. Her heart still pounded wildly from the potency of his nearness. Feeling shaky and strangely disappointed, she walked up the porch steps and pushed open the kitchen door.

Why had he asked if she would care if he was hurt again? Was it because he cared about her? she wondered. Was it too much to hope that he might have feelings for her? Maybe the hot sun *had* touched her, she thought wryly, shaking her head and hanging her slightly rumpled hat on its peg.

Another wire from Ben arrived for Evan that afternoon. Along with it was a second envelope, the outside bearing Madeline's name. Generously tipping the towheaded lad who had delivered the telegrams, Evan took the envelopes indoors and set the one belonging to Madeline on the kitchen table, wondering if it was from Nathaniel Spencer.

Madeline had been gone when he returned from his ride. Robbie labored away in the garden, announcing that Maddie had ridden out to find Reed and learn what she could about the reports of rustling in the area. It was probably just as well she was gone, he told himself.

Though restlessness scratched at him, he sat down on one of the kitchen chairs and read through his brother's brief message. Ben proposed meeting him in Reno and wanted a return wire from Evan setting a date for the meeting. Rereading the words in front of him, he worked the fingers of his injured arm with frustration, closing his hand into a fist several times.

It was time to leave, he knew. He had already spent too much time here, too much time with Madeline Spencer— playing with fire, he amended—but these few weeks of stolen pleasure had been the happiest he could ever recall.

Don't leave, then.

The thought crept sneakily through his mind, providing a childish solution to a complex problem. He pondered the idea for a moment. He knew virtually nothing of ranching. What would he do if he stayed here? Learn to punch cows?

Why not?

To tell the truth, he'd fallen in love with the wild, rugged beauty of the mountains and the wide open spaces of the West since he and Ben had embarked on their journey. There was room here, room for a man to breathe and stretch his elbows. He had made several wise investments in the past and had more than a tidy sum in the bank. Why not start up a place of his own? From all appearances, Spencer had made a go of his ranch in only a few years.

Glumly he realized that trading life in Chicago for life in San Francisco was, in essence, an even swap. Both cities were busy, populous, smelly places. Now more than ever before, he knew that living the next several years of his life in San Francisco wasn't really what he wanted to do. But did it matter? For so many years life had held only responsibility and purpose for him. Maybe a man simply wasn't entitled to a small measure of joy in his life.

Sighing, he read through Ben's message once again. His damned sense of responsibility reared its head and snorted, blowing away the mists of his daydreams. He couldn't leave everything on the shoulders of his little brother. Poor Ben.

He must have been going through hell out on his own while Evan had been here with a full belly and a roof over his head.

Reno. Set a date.

He had to leave; he simply had to get back to business. Though the intervals of weakness still plagued him, he was well enough to travel. Actually he was learning to conquer the dizzy spells quite neatly; he hadn't had one that had taken his feet out from under him out for at least a couple of days now. And the headaches . . . well, he supposed a man had never died of a headache or, for that matter, a little pain in his shoulder.

What about your responsibility toward Madeline? a disturbing voice inside him asked as he rose to prepare his message to Ben. *She deserves better than what you did to her.*

Pausing, he mentally justified his priorities. Family and business. They had to come first. Surely she would understand that, just as she understood that he couldn't stay at the Spencer ranch forever. Looking out the window at the flawless spring day, he suddenly felt as joyless and grim as he could ever remember feeling. Could he live without the pleasure of being warmed by Madeline's sweet smile ever again, or the quiet thrill of losing himself in her brilliant green eyes? Or smelling her warm, unique floral fragrance or touching her . . .

Stop, he sharply told himself. He could live without those things; he'd lived without them his whole life. And she could live without him, as well. Her fate was to marry some local rancher—*like Pete Matthews?*—and have a brood of little ones. He couldn't change that.

Ignoring the peculiar pain in the vicinity of his heart, he scribbled a message to his brother. He'd leave in the morning. Robbie could take the message to town and find out what time the westbound train departed.

Forgetting all about the telegram for Madeline and his curiosity regarding its sender, he walked out the door and down the porch steps. A picture of Madeline's alluring face appeared in his mind when the bottom porch step creaked. Funny, he'd never noticed the creak before today.

Heading toward the garden with large, determined steps, he gruffly called out, "Hey, Ashler. How'd you like to get out of doing that woman's work for a while? I'll make it worth your while."

Robbie's face popped up, bright and shining as a new penny. "Sure, Mr. Grant. What can I do for ya? You know I'm always happy to help you out if I can. And you know what else, Mr. Grant?" he continued, looking at him eagerly, taking a deep breath.

Evan watched the tall, skinny boy brush the dirt from his hands and fill his lungs with enough air to sustain him through what would likely be several rapid-fire sentences. His young body was so full of exuberance, so full of expression, so full of life.

Christ, he wasn't going to miss *him*, too, was he?

More than half a continent away, Nate Spencer stood amid the bustle and clamor of New York Harbor, estimating that his sparsely worded message would be in his daughter's hands by this time.

Remembering the shock on her lovely face when she'd learned of his long-kept secrets, he vowed to make things right with her just as soon as he got back from France. And with Reed, too. He'd deserted the ranch at one of the busiest times of year.

He should have contacted Madeline long before this, he reflected guiltily. She must be out of her head wondering what was going on. Heaven knew he was out of his head *knowing* what was going on. His only excuse was that the events of the past weeks had seized him like a sharp-taloned hawk, and carried him helplessly away.

Dear God, Sara was alive.

A salty, fishy breeze blew unpleasantly in his face, making him long for the familiar smell of dust and cattle. The enormity of what he was doing had eaten at him during every minute of the nine exhausting days he had spent traversing the continent by train, but he was determined to see this thing through to the end.

He was going to France to find Sara.

What would she look like after all this time? he wondered. More than twenty years had passed since he'd last seen her. Would she still have feelings for him? Would he for her?

Would she even agree to see him?

Spying his ship, he squared his shoulders and melted into the crowd, hoping to hell he was doing the right thing.

twelve

"WE'RE LOSING CATTLE, TOO." MADELINE strode into the kitchen well past suppertime and threw her hat onto the table, ruffling several papers haphazardly spread out in front of Evan. "Will didn't tell me because he didn't want me to worry about it." Dusty, disheveled, and disheartened, she began to pace about the kitchen, perilously close to losing control of her emotions.

"How many have you lost?" Evan looked up at her, concern written on his tanned face.

She threw up her arms and turned on her heel to walk the length of the room again, remembering the grim look on Will's face. "I don't know exactly, but enough to be noticed."

"What's Reed doing about it?"

"He's put more men on the watches, but so far . . ." Her voice cracked, and burning tears stung the corners of her eyes. She stopped in front of the window and stared outdoors, fighting for control. After a long moment she was able to continue. "But so far, nothing. I can't believe he didn't tell me. He just told me not to worry about it."

"I wouldn't worry about it either," Evan said soothingly, corking the ink bottle and setting down his pen. "Knowing Reed, I'm sure he'll—"

She spun to face him. "Evan, how can a person *not* worry about something like this? Especially now, while Nate's away."

"Hold on, Madeline, something came for you this afternoon." Evan dug among the papers on the table and extracted an envelope. He held it toward her with a fleeting smile, eyebrows raised. "Maybe it's word from your father."

A surge of optimistic anticipation squelched her beaten and forlorn feelings, bursting from her lips in an excited exclamation as she all but snatched the envelope from his fingers. She felt his eyes upon her as she opened the message and eagerly devoured the words with her eyes. Disbelief was her first reaction; then came a deep, cutting hurt.

"Maddie . . . is something wrong? What does it say?" Evan was out of his chair and at her side. She felt his arm around her and numbly leaned against his hard form.

Nate doesn't want you. Her inner voice was quick to have its say. *He never did and he never will. He'll just keep running and leaving you his whole life.*

" 'Brinkman is dead,' " Evan read aloud over her shoulder. " 'Have gone to France to attend to business. More later. Tell Reed.' " He took the paper from her hands and threw it on the table with disgust. "What the hell kind of message is that?" he asked, guiding Madeline to a chair. "Who's Brinkman? What kind of business does Spencer have in France?"

"I don't know why he's in France," she answered flatly, still standing.

Awkwardly he patted her shoulder. "Well, try not to worry about it—"

Pulling away from his one-armed embrace, she exploded with anger. "Try not to worry? *Try not to worry?*" Her voice grew in volume. "What else am I not supposed to worry about? My father—pardon me, I mean my grandfather— dies, and I come to my brother's ranch only to have my whole past yanked out from under me. Then my new father disappears to San Francisco, for all I know to kill my other grandfather. We hear nothing from him—nothing!— for weeks while cattle rustlers are taking their pick of his herds, and now he wires us that he's gone to France, of all places. You don't think I should be at all concerned about that?" She couldn't hold back the tears any longer. Hot and fast, they blurred her vision and coursed down her cheeks. She was able to get out one last, choked sentence before she buried her face in her hands. "You'll have to forgive me if I worry just a little, Mr. Grant."

She felt his warm hand rest hesitantly on her shoulder before he pulled her close. He felt so good, so comforting. "Madeline," he said with the same degree of concern, but also with a generous amount of caution, "I don't know if this is a good time to tell you this, but you're not making any sense."

Sobs racked her chest, making her breastbone hurt. Or was it her heart? Barely hearing Evan's words, she realized her anger was already gone. Instead her head whirled with the implications of Nate's message. "If he went to France," she reasoned tearfully, her lips resting against his chest, "he had to pass right through Laramie City on his way east. Why couldn't he have at least stopped? He must have gone right on by. Why would he do that? I . . . I . . . just don't understand."

Feeling her dissolve against him in a fresh bout of tears, Evan understood the agitated feelings inside him about as well as he understood what was going on. Though he'd spent much of the afternoon trying to figure out the best way to tell Madeline he was leaving, seeing her hurt like this made him want to stay at her side. Why, he wondered, did seeing her in such pain make an answering hurt echo deep inside him? He only knew he wanted to make her feel better; no, he wanted to beat the hell out of whoever was responsible for making her cry like this.

Who was this brother she referred to? How many children did Nate Spencer have? Was it the brother who had caused her this grief? She'd never mentioned a brother to him, but she hadn't talked about her family much at all. And what

was the business with the fathers and grandfathers and new
fathers? Those questions and tens more crowded his brain,
each demanding an answer. Something was going on here,
something he didn't understand, and he was determined to
get to the bottom of it.

No one was going to get away with riding roughshod
over Madeline's feelings, not if he could help it.

Stroking her tousled, silky hair beneath his fingers, he felt
an arrow of some sharp emotion land in his heart and stick
fast. A sheen of perspiration broke out on his forehead, and
with no small amount of panic he considered whether or not
he'd been struck by a dart from a certain cherub's quiver.

Love? Was what he was feeling for Madeline Spencer
love?

No! his mind protested. *Love between a woman and a
man exists only in fairy tales. Remember Melissa? You
thought you loved her.*

The middle of his back grew sweaty.

Madeline isn't Melissa.

He let his breath out, unaware he'd been holding it. His
thoughts sped and collided crazily in his head, making the
well-healed wound on his temple throb. He couldn't argue
that he *liked* Madeline one whole hell of a lot; she wasn't
anything like Melissa Morris at all. No, Madeline was good
and sweet and pure.

His quick-thinking mind turned down an avenue of escape.
Maybe he was confusing pity with love. *That's it.* He con-
gratulated himself for seeing the answer so swiftly. He felt
about as sorry for Maddie right now as one human could feel
for another, but that didn't necessarily mean he loved her.

His next thought chilled him, bringing a shiver to his
damp skin.

*What's it going to do to her when you tell her you're
leaving?*

His eyes traveled around the comfortable kitchen, a
room that bespoke Madeline's gentle touch. Her fragrance—a delicious, distinctive essence he'd know anywhere—filled his nostrils and senses as completely as
she filled his embrace. She felt so natural and right in
his arms.

Could he really tip his hat and walk away from her without so much as a backward glance?

Family first, Grant. Family and business. Think of Ben.

Her weeping quieted, and she slipped from his embrace to sink into the chair in which he'd been sitting. Staring straight ahead, she didn't speak. Strangely unwilling to break physical contact with her, he slid his hand beneath her heavy braid and soothingly massaged the tight cords in the back of her neck. She sighed and leaned forward, resting her face on her hands, allowing him greater access. A snuffling hiccup caused her back and shoulders to jerk, but her taut muscles soon became pliant under his kneading fingers.

Do you love her?

"I didn't know you had a brother, Madeline," he said slowly, banishing the disturbing introspection from his mind by forcing himself to sort through her confusing words. His hand stole farther inside her collar to rub her shoulders and upper back while he shifted his left arm impatiently beneath its binding, wishing it were free to join its mate. The day's light had begun to wane, saturating the room with faint blue-violet shadows, and the thought crossed his mind that the color of her hair had never looked so beautiful as it did at this moment.

"A brother?" she asked in a peculiar voice, pausing a long moment before she answered herself. "I don't have one anymore."

"He died, then?" It struck him as soon as the words were out of his mouth. Now he understood. Oh, God, Brinkman was her brother—Brinkman Spencer. She'd just gotten word of her brother's death. Sympathy surged through him, and he wished he had the power to shield her from the misery she must be feeling. "Oh, Maddie, I'm sorry. I didn't know. Hell, I didn't know Spencer had one child, let alone two. Were you close to your brother?" He bent and kissed her temple, tasting the salt of her tears and perspiration. "Oh, honey, I'm so sorry," he whispered against her hair, "so very sorry."

The tenderness and compassion might have been her undoing, or perhaps it was his delicate kiss—she wasn't certain, and furthermore she didn't care. Though it was too new, too fast, Madeline was past doubt. She loved this man. While the other, formerly solid areas of her life crumbled one by one and blew away like so much dust in the wind, Evan was her strength, her support. With him, she could bear all else.

A serenity settled over her, soothing the distress in her soul. She felt safe with this man, cherished. His familiar scent wrapped itself around her like a well-worn blanket, giving her comfort and warmth. Instinctively she knew he would never hurt her.

"Evan," she began, intending only to correct his misassumption. Under the soothing rhythm of his hand, however, his quiet acceptance, his murmured encouragements, she said a good deal more than she had intended to say. She told him everything. The entire story of the circumstances of her birth somehow came tumbling from her lips, and with it her shock, her pain, her uncertainty. After a few perceptive questions from Evan, the reasons she knew for Nate leaving as he had, pitiful few that they were, followed.

Anger gripped Evan while he listened, a slow and seething anger. While in San Francisco last summer, he'd heard of Emmett Brinkman. He'd heard, as well, of the man's reported wealth—and of his harsh and unscrupulous business tactics. Learning that Brinkman dealt with flesh-and-blood concerns the same way he handled business matters made Evan's stomach turn. As for the letter Brinkman had sent to Madeline, he believed the old man could have changed coats as well as a horse could change colors.

Poor Madeline—he knew the only purpose she'd served, as far as Brinkman was concerned, was that of a living pawn to hurt Nate Spencer. That she was unwanted and rejected by her mother's family was something she should never have had to learn.

Now she felt unwanted and rejected by her father, too.

Breaking contact with her for a moment, he pulled another chair alongside Madeline's and took her hand in his. His mind searched for comforting words to speak while he wondered, putting himself in Nate Spencer's boots, what he would have done given the same set of circumstances.

"Though I don't necessarily agree with some of the other choices your father made in his life, sweet," he began, "I think I can understand his reason for going to San Francisco the way he did. If you were my daughter, I probably would have done the same thing." *No, I would have gone to California and killed the bastard years ago*, he added to himself.

Her luminous eyes studied his face, their color appearing as deep green as moss that grew in the shaded depths of the forest. "Nate's done nothing but leave me my whole life. If that letter hadn't come, do you think he ever would have owned up to the fact that he's my father?" Her last words were so soft he had to strain to hear them. "And now that I know, why did he have to go and leave me again?"

"I don't know," he answered truthfully, feeling distressed at the naked hurt he saw on her face. "Because he's a fool, maybe. Or maybe because it hurts him too much to face you."

"Maybe so," she said in the same quiet voice. "There is so much that is unspoken between us." The hurt on her features faded to a tender, tentative look that made him feel distinctly uneasy. Clear green eyes fixed on him. "There is much unspoken between us as well, Evan."

Unable to say anything, he nodded. He felt as though he were swimming in a river, a lazy but dangerous river in which his legs had just felt the first tug of the undertow. He watched her take a deep, steadying breath, feeling as though he needed more air himself.

"When you came here," she began, "it seemed like everything was too much to take, especially after you were injured." Tears shone again in her eyes. "I know it sounds ridiculous, especially since I didn't know you, but during those first few days I was so afraid you were going to die."

He squeezed her hand reassuringly, feeling the forceful undercurrent yank at his body again. "I'm still here in one piece," he attempted lightly, hoping to steer her away from where he feared she was headed.

A small smile touched her lips. "For that I thank God." She took another deep breath, releasing the air delicately through her nostrils. "I blamed myself at first for your accident. In fact, I still can't shake the guilt I feel for ruining all your business plans and forcing your brother to do the work of two. But you know what else?"

"Madeline, it wasn't your fau—"

"No, I know it wasn't my fault. This is going to sound horrid, but I'm glad you ended up here. Then we . . . well—"

Anxiety grew to apprehension, and fresh prickles of sweat broke out between his shoulder blades. "Madeline—"

"I think I've fallen in love with you, Evan."

Apprehension burst into alarm. His fingers ceased their motions—freezing, actually—and his hand fell away from hers. Green eyes locked with his, searching, beseeching. A long moment passed, during which his jaw latched tight, and he found himself unable to speak.

Now what, Grant? She thinks she loves you.

He tried to swallow but failed at that, too. There was nothing to swallow. Her declaration had acted not only as a paralytic but also as a desiccant.

Say something, you idiot.

His mind raced, but he still couldn't seem to find his tongue. The silence stretched out between them while the radiantly hopeful look on her lovely face was rapidly transformed into one of despair.

She turned her head to the side and picked up one of the papers on the table with deceptive idleness. Her voice was small and shaky. "You don't have to say anything."

"Maddie—" he started hoarsely.

"What's this?" she asked, looking more closely at the paper she was holding. "A map?" She shuffled through the other papers on the table before slowly and deliberately setting them in a neat stack before her. "Maps," she said in the same small voice, shaking her head. "How could I have been such a fool? You're leaving now, aren't you?"

She turned back toward him, straightening her shoulders and meeting his gaze squarely. Her face looked swollen and puffy. Anguished. Terrible. "When?"

Never had he felt as low as he did at this moment. "Maddie . . . let me explain. . . . I got a wire from Ben this afternoon . . ." He faltered under her gaze.

"I don't think there's anything to explain," she said, rising stiffly. "Are you going tonight?" she asked, as though she were asking if he'd like another cup of tea.

"In the morning," he mumbled, thinking that weeping and hysterics would be less difficult to deal with than the quiet control she held over her emotions.

You're a coward, Grant, his inner voice berated him, *a low son of a bitch. Just say it. Tell her you have feelings for her, too.*

"We can write to each other, Maddie," he offered as a concession, realizing how asinine the remark sounded the instant it left his lips.

"Write? You'd like to write?" Her eyes pierced him for a second, then dismissed him. In a graceful, proud movement she turned her back on him and reached for her hat.

"I think not," she said, and then she was gone.

The light cast by the moon and stars was faint. Thank goodness the buckskin she'd hurriedly saddled at sunset seemed to know his way back to the ranch. Madeline knew she would have had trouble finding her way in the dark.

Don't go back. Just bed down somewhere and stay away until he's gone.

She'd gone to her sanctuary by the creek and sat until well after sunset, cursing herself for being a thousand times a fool. The things she'd done with Evan . . . the intimacies they'd shared . . . and now he was picking up and leaving as if none of that had happened.

She'd further humiliated herself by telling him she loved him. What had she expected? That the man would fall to his knees, propose marriage, and offer to take her to San Francisco with him? Or that he would give up his interest in Grant Meats to be a cattle rancher?

Or that maybe he'd say he loved her, too?

How could she have been so terribly, incredibly stupid? One of Elsie's sayings came to mind, increasing, if possible, her sense of shame: "Why buy the cow when the milk's free?"

The air had cooled, and she felt nearly frozen. She had no coat; in her haste to get away from the house, she had not thought to grab one. Her hands were numb on the reins, and her lips and face felt brittle enough to crack.

But if her face did crack, it would only follow the lead her heart had already set. The damaged vital organ lay heavily in the center of her chest, broken into two jagged, bleeding pieces. The memory of her declaration of love, and the stricken look on Evan's face afterward, loomed before her mind's eye while her inner voice continued to castigate her.

He doesn't love you. You were just a pleasant diversion while he recuperated. Nothing more, Madeline, nothing more.

The night air, damp and scented with new-growing things, rushed past her face. As she noted the position of the Big Dipper in relation to the North Star, she judged the time at well past midnight. How was she going to get through the hours until he left? And past that, how was she going to get through the next days—and the rest of her life?

Heartsick. Heartrending. Heartbroken. Words she'd used in the past now held entirely new meanings. Oh, God, she hurt inside. She felt cast off, discarded, first by Nate and now by Evan. She wished she could cry, but she had no more tears left.

Would anyone ever want her? Where was her place in this life? What was her purpose?

The buckskin picked up his pace, and she hoped the animal wouldn't step into a chuckhole in his haste to get back to the barn. Straining her eyes, she could make out the dark shapes of the house and outbuildings. No welcoming light shone from the house. In her heart she hadn't expected that Evan would wait up for her . . . but she had hoped.

Accept it. He's out of your life.

"Who goes?" a harsh male voice suddenly demanded to know.

"It's Madeline," she said wearily, pulling on her reins, too numb to even be startled.

"Miss Madeline! What are you doin' out this time o' night?" The odor of tobacco smoke drifted to her at the same time as, off to her left; a red eye winked in the night. "It's me, Wilkes, ma'am," the man said. Spurs jingled and leather creaked as his horse moved toward hers. "Glad I din't shoot first an' ask questions later," the older cowboy said. "What're ya doin' out, miss? I don't recall as you pulled a watch tonight, did you? In fact, since that eastern feller got hurt, we ain't seen much of you a'tall."

"I . . . couldn't sleep. I just needed a ride tonight, I guess," she responded dully.

"It ain't safe around here to do that no more, Miss Madeline, not that I'm sayin' it's ever wise to go out for a nighttime ride by yourself." He took another drag of his cigarette, his weathered face faintly illuminated by the glow of the burning tip. "We ain't had any Injun trouble 'round here, but we got us some cattle rustlers now, and I'm tellin' you them brand artists can be right nasty fellers when crossed. They're mean and desperate . . . and," he added grimly, "they're still out there somewhere. We ain't caught 'em yet."

"How late is your watch?" she asked, trying to turn the conversation.

"Till two," he answered, "same as usual. Say, are you all right, Miss Madeline? You sound kinda funny, you know?"

"I'm fine," she lied, trying to keep her teeth from chattering.

"You better get in an' get some shut-eye," he said kindly. "Mornin' comes quick, especially this time o' year."

"It does, doesn't it?" she commented distractedly, thinking that the next morning couldn't come quickly enough for her. " 'Night, Wilkes," she added before letting the impatient buckskin have his head.

The house had been dead silent when she entered. Evan could already have departed for all she knew, but she'd bet all she owned that he was still here. Her nerves felt his presence just the same as they reported any other sensory signal to her. He was here in the room below her.

Still wearing her dirty clothes beneath a thick blanket, she sat in a chair next to her window. The first ridges of dawn's light appeared in the eastern sky, and she thought of the first night Evan had been here, the night she'd stayed up watching over him. Was it during that night she'd fallen under his spell?

She heard movements from below. Rustling. Scraping. Drawers opening and closing.

Would he come upstairs?

What for? her mind asked, adding bitterly, *One last good-bye tumble?*

She had her answer when, a half-hour later, he hadn't come. Pink streaks crisscrossed the sky above the mountains to the east, and she heard a cock crow. She'd thought herself incapable of ever producing another tear, but hot wetness stung her eyes when she heard the kitchen door open and heard his boots cross the porch and go down the steps.

This is it. He's going.

Desolation swept through her. He came into view a second later, his long legs carrying him swiftly across the yard toward the barn. Even from her perspective, his tall, broad-shouldered form looked impressive. No, she corrected herself. His form was perfect.

A hot tear overran its dam and trickled down the side of her nose. She noticed that he carried his bag slung over his right shoulder; his other arm swung at his side. It took her a long moment to comprehend that his *left* arm swung at his side.

He must have taken his binding off, the fool. His shoulder couldn't have completely healed yet. According to Reed, it needed to be kept immobilized for another week or two. She nearly opened the window to shout to him, but stopped herself.

He doesn't need you to worry about him, she told herself harshly. *He sure as hell isn't worrying about you.*

He walked inside the barn and reappeared a short time later, leading the livery horse by its reins. His left arm still worked, she noticed; he apparently hadn't done the shoulder any damage by saddling the tall roan. He secured his bag and, for the first time this morning, looked up at the house.

It was impossible to make out his expression, but his glance was brief. He mounted the roan, and with a sharp "g'yup," which she heard clearly through the closed window, he was off.

Gone, gone, gone. Her mind repeated the word over and over. *He's gone, just like that, without so much as a good-bye. You really meant a lot to him, Maddie.*

thirteen

FOR MADELINE, THE FOLLOWING DAYS WERE filled with numb suffering. Difficult as the days were, however, the nights were worse. Darkness and loneliness consorted cruelly with countless bittersweet memories and taunting, elusive dreams, hour after endless hour, until she had to throw the covers aside and rise for another day.

The trick was to involve herself in strenuous ranch chores, she quickly learned. Physical exhaustion went a long way toward deadening the senses and blunting the sharp edge of the terrible hurt within her. Though she was sure the ranch hands sensed she wasn't herself, not one man commented to that effect. They welcomed her back into their midst as if she had not spent any time away from them at all.

But through her despair she detected a level of tension among the men that had not been there before. They were tired, too, and their rough-and-tumble joviality was strained. Calving was in full swing, and the continuing cattle thefts by the still-uncaptured rustlers despite the increased patrols greatly troubled and frustrated them.

Will Reed, by far, was the most affected. To Madeline he appeared to be a man with the weight of the world on his shoulders. Was it her imagination, she wondered, or did he have more gray hair than he'd had a mere two weeks ago? Nate's friend looked older every time she saw him, and so very weary. To his credit, he spoke not one word of complaint about Nate's absence. "The man must have his reasons" was all he'd say about the matter, effectively closing off any further discussion.

Two days after Evan left, a long, chatty letter came from Elsie in which the older woman gently hinted that the gap between letters had been much longer than usual. Was everything all right? Elsie wondered. Madeline wasn't ill, was she? Was it just that the springtime was so busy and Nate was keeping her occupied? Judging from the light tone of the letter, Madeline realized Elsie apparently knew nothing of Emmett Brinkman contacting her, or of Madeline knowing the truth of her parentage. It was also obvious she assumed Nate was still at work on his ranch.

So he hadn't told his mother anything, either.

Her respect for Nate dwindled while a thick callus developed over her feelings for him. *Run, Nate, run and hide*, she thought bitterly. *How long before you come back this time?*

Long before you'll see Evan Grant's face around these parts, her mind promptly hissed, sending a fresh shaft of pain through her at the realization that while Nate would have to come back sometime, she'd probably never see Evan again.

Not ever.

The door to Nate's bedroom had remained closed since the day Evan had departed. More than once she'd been tempted to open it and step inside, but she'd never gotten any farther than putting her hand on the knob. Half of her wanted to throw herself onto the bed and wrap herself in his remaining essence, but the other half wisely advised her to give the room a wide berth. Grimly she thought that if two men had conspired to cause a person grief, they couldn't have caused even a tenth of the emotional pain that Nate and Evan had caused her.

Evan. His eyes, his glossy dark hair, his smile, his broad shoulders, his long legs—*Don't*, her aching heart cried. *Stop it! Don't think of him*!

The day was a beauty, full of sunshine and bright blue skies, but Madeline scarcely noticed. Her eyes roved over the hundreds of cattle before her, many of them full-uddered, with yet unbranded calves at their sides, and she wondered how many more of them would fall prey to rustlers before the thieves moved on or were captured. For a few moments she allowed her lower back to rest heavily against the saddle's sloping cantle, yielding to the fatigue within her.

Though the date for spring roundup to begin was still a week away, the Spencer hands were bringing together as many head of cattle as they could in order to make sure the calves, as well as their mothers, would be safe from theft. Keeping watch on a few tight herds would prove much more efficient than patroling miles of open grazing land with cattle scattered here, there, and everywhere. Madeline suspected that roundup would take place early before the week was out; she knew Will had been speaking to the owners of the smaller neighboring ranches and that a meeting between them was set to take place in the morning.

Another meeting had been planned, she knew, for the end of May, to formally organize the Wyoming Stock and Wool Growers Association. A recent article in the *Wyoming Tribune* had mentioned that "the Association will have a general fund to be expended in the detection, arrest, and conviction of stock thieves, and in the purchase of rope with which to hang them."

Will strongly favored organizing with other stockmen. Already they had pooled their manpower and resources with the Matthews brothers, their closest neighbors. She guessed that Aaron Rendner, their foreman, must be every bit as busy as Will, for nearly every day she caught sight of him riding somewhere, talking to someone, or grabbing a quick plate of grub at the chuck wagon.

Though she didn't see Jack often, his brother, Pete, was a frequent visitor to the range, always making a big show of coming to visit with her after he'd bent Will's ear. In fact, Pete Matthews made a show of everything, she decided one afternoon, listening to him bewail his cattle losses and spout off about what he was going to do to the rustlers when he caught them red-handed. An unkind thought sat on her tongue—if he was so worried about his cattle, why wasn't he back home helping his brother tend to them?—but she hadn't said as much. Yet.

He was pursuing her, she knew, showing off and, worse yet, pressing his suit more strongly than ever. Much to her relief, she hadn't seen him since yesterday morning; today she simply didn't have the energy to deflect his much too avid gaze or to discourage his much too possessive attitude toward her. How much longer would it be, she wondered, until he grew bold enough to mention marriage?

Thinking of married life with Pete, she shuddered. Never. Not in a million years would she join with the man. She'd rather spend the rest of her days tending to cows, unmarried and heartbroken. Though she tried not to think of Evan, tried not to compare Pete with him, she couldn't help it. If Evan was the yardstick by which she could measure a man, in her opinion Pete stood well below the first inch mark.

She straightened in the saddle. This afternoon she and Robbie and Joe McCaleb were responsible for keeping order among approximately four hundred head of peacefully grazing cattle. Short, bandy-legged Joe—Joker Joe, as he was commonly known—gave her a tired salute from across the herd. Given the present state of affairs at the ranch, McCaleb's usual outpouring of wisecracks, wry witticisms, and jokes of all kinds had slackened to a slow trickle.

Beyond the herd, the heavy chuck wagon sat at the base of a gentle swell in the terrain. Off the back end of the wagon a tarpaulin had been rigged atop crooked, spindly poles to provide an area of shade for the cook and for those who were eating. She watched Old Roger's white-aproned form move back and forth slowly between the wagon and the fire. It didn't seem to matter where Roger did his cooking; his meals tasted equally delicious whether he prepared them at his stove at the cookshack or in Dutch ovens over an open fire.

But delicious as Old Roger's cooking was, Madeline hadn't had much of an appetite for the past few days. Her baggy trousers had become even baggier, last evening, sliding dangerously low on her hips under her chaps as she'd dismounted her horse. This morning she had taken a hammer and nail and pounded another hole in her belt, as well as another in the belt of her chaps, so she could cinch herself more snugly. Unwittingly exposing her southern half to the view of any cow—or—cowboy—who might happen to be looking was a thought she didn't relish.

The remainder of the afternoon passed uneventfully. Exhausted and seated beneath the tarpaulin, she and Robbie, ate their final meal of the day. Around them were the sounds of quiet conversation, the clinking of utensils against plates, the bawling of cattle. Steam billowed out of a large, brewing pot of coffee, filling the air with a tantalizing odor. The wind had quieted to a gentle occasional breeze.

Mopping up the last of his stew with a half-eaten biscuit, Robbie looked longingly at her plate. "You plannin' on finishin' there, Miss Maddie? I got a little more room if you're filled up already."

"Go ahead." She handed her plate to him. "Roger gave me too much, I think."

"What's the matter? You got a sick stomach or somethin'? You could always eat that much before. Seconds sometimes, too." Concern shone in his friendly hazel eyes. "You know, Maddie, you just ain't been yourself lately. I don't wanna hurt your feelings and tell ya you ain't been no fun, but you really ain't been no fun since that Grant feller was here. You ain't even been teasin' me or nothin'." He shoveled a spoonful of meat and potatoes into his mouth and chewed rapidly. "I told Ma you been quiet and mopeylike, and you know what she said?"

Madeline wanted to hear Mary Ashler's opinion of her present condition about as much as she wanted this unwanted attention from her son. "Robbie, I—"

"She says you been bit by the lovebug," he went on, shyly dropping his gaze for a moment before looking at her with frank curiosity. "Gosh, is it true, Maddie? Didja go and fall for Grant?" Another giant spoonful of stew went into his mouth. "Do you love him?" he managed to ask rather clearly despite having a mouthful of food.

She dropped her own gaze, not knowing what to say.

"Ain't none of your business, boy," Will answered for her, walking up behind them.

"Reed!" Robbie exclaimed, the plate jumping in his hands. "Didn't see you ride up. Anything happen this afternoon?"

"Nope." Dust and grime covered Will's clothes in much the same way that thick gray-black stubble covered his face and neck. He took his hat off and ran his fingers through his hair. "Thought I'd have a plate of chow, then ride you back to the ranch, Miss Madeline. The rest of us'll be beddin' down out here under the stars till this thing is over, but I'm puttin' a man or two on duty back there to keep an eye on the place and tend to the regular chores." He cast a meaningful glance at Robbie. "I was plannin' to rotate that duty, Ashler, same as I been rotatin' roustabout, but—"

"I'm doin' a good job out here, Reed," Robbie said quickly. "You can ask anyone. I'm pullin' my fair share, and I ain't talkin' too much . . ." He looked between Will and Madeline, and his words trailed off. "Oh." He swallowed nervously. "Guess I was outta line there. Aw, jeez, Miss Maddie, I din't mean to pry into your private business. Forget I even said anything. In fact, I don't even remember what we was just talkin' about. Nope, not at all." He shrugged his shoulders with attempted casualness while the brown and gold flecks in his green eyes appealed to her for forgiveness. "Can't even remember the feller's name."

A feeble smile crossed her lips at the young man's earnest attempt to smooth things over. "Apology accepted, Robbie." Looking up at Will, she added, "I think he might have just saved himself a week's worth of wrangling horses and doing Roger's bidding. What do you think?"

A deep "Hmmph" was Reed's only reply as he filled a plate with hot, fragrant stew.

"Long as you're scoopin', you s'pose I could have a little more?" Robbie asked with a relieved grin, scrambling to his feet and extending his plate toward Reed. "You know, some days I just can't get filled up. I figure those are the days I'm growin', but Ma doesn't think so. She says I got a hollow leg."

"Ain't all that's hollow," Madeline heard the foreman say in a low voice, depositing a generous portion of stew on the adolescent's plate with a thunk.

If it was warm in Wyoming Territory, it was just plain hot in Reno. A sheen of perspiration sat uncomfortably between Evan's clothing and his skin as he crossed first the Truckee River bridge, then the threshold of the Lake House. His shoulder ached miserably, and for approximately the five-hundredth time since leaving Laramie City he wondered if he hadn't made a grave mistake in removing the binding.

"Evan! Hey, Evan! Is that you?"

Blinking, trying in vain to make his eyes instantly adjust to the hotel lobby's dimness, he turned his head at the sound of his brother's voice.

Kawump.

His breath left him in a whoosh when, a split-second later, he was crushed in Ben's rough embrace. A jaw-clenching bolt of pain shot through his shoulder, nearly causing him to cry out.

"You made it!" Ben exclaimed, pulling back but keeping hold of both his brother's arms, beaming at him with a smile as big and bright as the sun overhead. "Son of a gun, brother, it's good to see you again! And your arm! Holy smokes!"

Abruptly the younger man let go of Evan's arms, the smile falling away into an expression of concern. "Your arm! Oh, gosh, Ev, I'm sorry. Did I hurt your arm? Hey, how come you don't have it tied down anymore? It hasn't been long enough yet, has it? It can't be—"

"It's fine," Evan said shortly, resisting the urge to hold the all-but-screaming joint with his good hand until the pain subsided.

Ben folded his arms across his chest and snorted. "Yeah, I can see by the look on your face just how fine it is, old man. You're not fooling me. Did I ever tell you what a pig-headed, stubborn—"

"That'll do, unless you care to have this old man kick your hide into next week." His eyes adjusted to the indoor dimness, and he studied his younger brother's face, frankly surprised at how good he looked. Well rested, in fact. The lines of overwork and worry and fatigue he had expected to see simply weren't there.

Suddenly he felt exactly like an old man, old and tired.

"You look like hell, Evan." Ben stared back, a grin playing about his lips. "Maybe you need some more doctoring from a certain blond caretaker to make you feel better. Say," he asked, raising his brows, "did you two ever get along any better? When I left, you were about at each other's throats."

A vivid rush of recall assailed Evan, a memory of Madeline nuzzling at his neck, her soft breasts pressing against his arm and chest. He recalled, too, the silky warmth of her throat, the feel of her pulse beneath his lips, the floral, musky, womanly scent that was hers and hers alone.

Damn. There it was again—just exactly the sort of thing he'd been trying not to think about.

But he couldn't help it.

Ever since he rode away from the Spencer ranch—no, ever since that late afternoon in the kitchen—all he'd done was think of her. Of her beauty, her gentleness, her independence, her feistiness. Of her love . . . and her pain.

Now, every time his mind turned toward her, his chest felt hollow, his spirit empty. The essence of a long-ago learned Democritean maxim leapt to mind: Happiness resides not in possessions and not in gold—and not in the expansion of Grant Meats, he added, seeing a disturbing truth in the next portion of the aphorism—the feeling of happiness dwells in the soul.

For a brief time, with Madeline, he had tasted perfect happiness. What kind of fool had he been to walk away from it?

Another thought roughly shoved its way to the front of his consciousness, a thought that had plagued him over and over since he'd left Wyoming Territory: *What if your seed found purchase?* He had not sired any children in the past, to the best of his knowledge, but what if—

"Evan? Hey, Ev? How come you're not answering me?" Ben looked at him with concern—and something else on his lean, handsome face. "Come on, brother, and I'll buy you a beer. You look like you could use one." He dropped his voice, glancing at the clerk who sat behind the counter with indolent posture but nonetheless very interested eyes. "Besides, we have something more urgent to discuss than business."

"What?" The word came out sounding flat and dull, and Evan closed his eyes, feeling utterly spent. The past days had taken a heavy toll on him, both physically and emotionally, and now his brother was telling him that they had something more urgent to discuss than business. A groan rose in his throat at Ben's next words.

"It seems Annalisa's run away."

An hour, two fat pork chops, and three beers later, Evan had learned of their father's attempt to push Anna into marriage with Milward Thurman. "The man's got to be all of Father's age—or more," he said with disgust, feeling greatly revived by the food and libation. "And I suppose it's purely coincidental that Mil owns Thurman Leatherworks."

"The old man saw a nice little opportunity in that arrangement, all right," Ben agreed. "I don't blame Annalisa for running." Turning his glass this way and that, he watched bubbles rise in the golden brown liquid. "What do you think, Ev? Did he try to marry her off to keep her from going to San Francisco, or did he have this idea in mind all along?"

"With him, it's hard to tell." He took a sip of beer, enjoying the bitter taste on his tongue. With bitterness as well, he thought of Hiram Grant. His father had transformed himself from a penniless man to a very rich one with determination, grit, and nearly uncanny business acumen. He had been a good father in many ways, but his will was inflexible, and his mind, once set, was unchangeable.

"Maybe we should have taken a stronger stand against him," Ben said, sighing. "You remember how much Anna wanted to be a part of the expansion, don't you?"

"Our protests wouldn't have mattered," he commented, feeling both worry and irritation for Anna and her latest and largest escapade. Mixed with that, though, was a grudging respect for his baby sister. This time she'd defied Hiram Grant but good. What he wouldn't give to have been a fly on the wall when their father discovered she'd fled. "Did she know the two of us were meeting in Reno?" he asked.

"I think so" was Ben's response. "I've been in contact with Father frequently since you and I split up."

"Well, then, brother, one of us had best stroll five or six blocks up the street to the depot and give her description. It seems we're going to have a three-way partnership after all."

"Well, I half thought she might . . . Naw, she wouldn't come west all by herself, would she? I bet she went to Aunt Minnie's in New York. Minnie always spoiled her rotten, indulged her, gave her whatever she . . ."

Ben's voice trailed off at Evan's semi-amused stare. "Careful, Ben, your childhood jealousy is showing. Of course Anna is coming west. And if she doesn't turn up here in Reno, she will in San Francisco."

A thousand delicate tones of mauve and violet painted the western sky as Will and Madeline rode back to the ranch. Will was the first to break the companionable silence between them by announcing, "We're gonna start roundup."

She glanced at the big man riding beside her. "That's the talk," she replied, lapsing back into silence. The air had begun to cool, and she retrieved her coat from where she'd tied it behind the saddle.

The horses covered another mile while Madeline recalled the bone-wearying work of the roundup she'd been a part of last autumn. That had been a fun, festive time, though. Her first day out, she'd watched the hands brand strays that had been missed during spring roundup. Before she quite knew what was happening, Joker Joe had put a hot branding iron in her gloved hands and was instructing her on the subtleties of where, how hard, and how long to hold the iron to the cow's side. Then she was branding cattle, first with Joe's help, then by herself.

"You gotta take a little better care of yourself, honey," Will commented, pulling her from her memories, "or you're gonna get yourself sick. You ain't been eatin' enough to stick in a gnat's ear, and your cheeks are about as hollowed out as a creek bed in August."

She raised a hand to her face self-consciously.

"I liked Grant plenty myself," he went on, "and it ain't my business any more than it was Ashler's, but I'd lay even money that the man trounced on your heart but good." Her horse followed suit as he slowed his tall roan to a walk. "Did he hurt you, Maddie?" His dark eyes were penetrating. " 'Cause if he did, I'll fix whatever needs fixin'."

Torn between shame and embarrassment at her case of unrequited love and a need to swallow her pride and confess her misery to someone, she hesitated. Seeing the hard look on Will's face, though, she thought better about admitting her feelings. "I-I think I'm just out of sorts, wondering what Nate could possibly be doing abroad." The half-truth was bitter on her tongue, but she continued. "Part of me wonders, too, if Brinkman was dead when Nate got to San Francisco or whether Nate helped him along. And then there's the rustling . . ."

"You sure that's all?" The dark eyes remained fixed on her, waiting, questioning.

"Isn't that enough?" There. Maybe if she turned the tables on Will, he'd back away from the topic of Evan Grant. "Or does a person need better reasons to suffer a case of melancholy?" she added.

"That's some case of melancholy you got goin' there."

Will paused a long moment, during which Madeline realized she'd broken out in a sweat. He knew she was lying. Wishing she could take off the coat she'd just put on, she tried instead to move some air inside the garment by nervously fanning its bottom edge.

"Aside from the matter of your pa," he said with a sigh, "which is a weighty matter indeed, and the rustlin', which is another weighty matter entirely, I got just one more piece to say." Will dropped his gaze from her and studied the reins wound around his gloved hand. "Over the years I had more'n one gal throw her loop at me, but I was a quick stepper and never got roped. Kinda like Grant, I suspect. I'll tell you right up front I ain't much good in matters of the heart, Maddie, but I'd be a good listener if you ever feel like talkin'." He looked up at her and nodded briefly. "Now, let's get you home,'cause I'm plannin' on workin' you tomorrow like you ain't never been worked in your whole life."

Madeline flashed a small, relieved smile in his direction and kicked her horse, thinking that for all of Nate's faults, he was a mighty good judge of a true friend.

Will left after he'd seen her safely into the house. Dusk was rapidly falling, and she lit the lamp in the kitchen to chase away the dark shadows. Dark or light, though, the same final scene with Evan played over and over in her mind whenever she was in the kitchen. She wanted to fall through the floor when she remembered what a fool she'd been. How could she have been so stupid as to think he might love her?

Lost in her thoughts, she wandered into the sitting room, running her fingers over a small ornamental table as she walked by it. The faint residue of Mrs. Ashler's linseed oil furniture polish made her fingers feel slippery, and absently she rubbed them together as she walked. *Just go to bed*, she told herself. *You're tired.* But somehow she found herself standing once again in front of the closed bedroom door.

Remembering.

After wiping her hands on her pants, she touched the knob. It was stupid, she told herself, to be frightened of opening the door to an empty room. Mrs. Ashler would come to clean in a few days, anyway. And the house wasn't haunted. Gripping the cold knob more tightly, she turned her hand and pushed the door open.

She had been wrong. The room *was* haunted—*she* was haunted—by memories of Evan Grant. Though the light was dim, in her mind's eye she saw him. In the bed. In the chair. Standing in the doorway. Her heart contracted painfully in her chest while her fingers continued to cling to the doorknob.

A faint, stale odor of lye soap and . . . whiskey hit her, bringing back in a vivid rush of recall the night she'd lost her virginity. Looking around the room, she saw he'd left it immaculate. Not one thing was out of place. The edges of the quilt hung parallel to the floor, and . . . wait. She paused in her visual examination. There was something on the bed.

A piece of paper?

A note.

Walking over to the bed, she snatched up the paper and read the neat black letters silently, her eyes straining in the twilight gloom. "Dear Madeline," it began. "I'm sorry, possibly sorrier than I've ever been in my life. You deserve better. Evan."

Her hands and knees trembled, so she sat heavily in the chair near the window. He was sorry? Her mind whirled with questions. Sorry for what? Sorry for taking advantage of her? Sorry for hurting her? Sorry he'd ever met her?

The sound of a team and wagon interrupted her disturbing thoughts, and she pulled the curtain aside, wondering who would be calling at the ranch at this hour. It was too dark to make out any details of the two figures on the buckboard, other than that one was a man and one was a woman; she could tell by their hats. Curiosity overcame caution, and she set the note on the chair as she hurried from the room.

Entering the kitchen and blinking at the lantern's bright glow, she paused a moment to run a smoothing hand over her messy hair and dirty garments. Well, there was no help for it now, she decided hopelessly as delicate footfalls ascended the porch steps.

The footsteps stopped, and an equally delicate knock sounded at the door. Sliding the bolt aside, she opened the door to a tall, rumpled-looking but well-dressed young woman who appeared to be on the verge of tears. Even in her wearied, untidy state, the woman's uncommon beauty was plain to see.

As was the resemblance.

"Good evening," the woman said in a clear but unsteady voice, extending her hand toward Madeline. "My name is Annalisa—"

"Grant," Madeline interrupted, staring at the woman and feeling as stunned as if she'd fallen into a deep gorge. "You're Evan's sister, aren't you?"

fourteen

THE DARK-HAIRED WOMAN NODDED. "EVAN'S long gone, isn't he?" she asked, her voice cracking.

Madeline felt a surge of sympathy for the young woman who appeared to be holding on to her emotions by a single frayed strand of rope. The light from the kitchen lantern cast a gentle glow on Annalisa's features, and for a long moment Madeline simply stared at her, the shock she felt upon opening the door and seeing a feminine version of Evan standing before her fading in the face of the woman's obvious distress. "Yes, he's gone," she answered gently.

To her surprise the young woman didn't burst into tears. Instead Miss Annalisa Grant, presumably of Chicago, Illinois, smacked a fisted hand in the center of her forehead and let loose with a deep sigh, followed by a blunt curse that would have done any cowboy proud.

Before Madeline could respond, a deep male voice she recognized as Tom Lang's called from outdoors, "Who goes there? State your business." She remembered that Will had mentioned that Lang was taking duty at the ranch tonight.

"Glidden here, from town," the livery driver answered quickly. "Brought a lady out visiting. She's on the steps trying to make up her mind if she's staying or not. Maybe she'll manage to make it up sometime in the next decade," he added sarcastically, further making his impatience known by clearing his throat. "Then I'll be on my way."

Annalisa paused while untying her bonnet strings and turned her head. "Well, pardon me for wasting *your* time, Mr. Doughhead," she shot back, "but which one of us didn't think to mention the fact that he 'maybe remembered' my brother leaving your godforsaken little town until we were nearly all the way here?" Her fingers worked once more at the strings, and she slipped the bonnet from her head, exposing a pinned-up mass of glossy dark hair.

"Lady, if you—" the driver started, but Lang interrupted, walking from the yard to the foot of the steps.

"Save it, Glidden. You expectin' company, Miss Madeline? You know this woman?"

Annalisa turned back to face Madeline. Despite the young woman's bold words, Madeline saw in her eyes the deep shadows of fatigue as well as a flicker of fear and uncertainty. She stuck by her initial impression that Evan's sister was perilously close to exhaustion.

"It's all right, Tom." Madeline couldn't clearly make out Lang's features, but she looked past Annalisa and smiled in his direction, trying for an easy, reassuring tone of voice. "I know her, and she's most welcome. Would you give Mr. Glidden a hand with her bags?" Under her breath, she asked, "You do have bags, don't you?"

"Only two—and thank you so very much," Annalisa whispered to her with obvious relief, the stiff set of her shoulders relaxing as Madeline ushered her into the house.

After the bags had been deposited just inside the kitchen door, with a good deal of grousing and complaining from the sour driver, who insisted he didn't need any help from Lang, the two women were finally alone. Simultaneously they released long sighs, their eyes tentatively meeting in the lamplit room.

"Thank you for taking me in." Annalisa was the first to speak. She twisted her bonnet nervously in her hands. "I don't know what I would have done if I'd had to ride back to town with that awful man."

"You're quite welcome to stay here," Madeline responded politely, tamping down the urge to ask a rush of questions.

"I-I suppose you're wondering why I traveled all this way alone," Annalisa began as if she'd read Madeline's mind.

"Well, the thought had . . . Heavens! Where are my manners? You must be exhausted after the day you've had. Please sit down." Madeline pulled out a chair, her own tiredness forgotten. "Please sit down. Are you thirsty? Hungry? What can I get you?"

"A drink of water would be nice," Annalisa said with a grateful smile, settling herself into the chair, "and you're being extremely gracious to a body who just showed up on your doorstep unannounced. If our positions were reversed, I would have asked a score of questions of you by now." Her smile was both sweet and friendly. "May I ask just one? So we can become properly acquainted? I know this is the ranch of Nathaniel Spencer . . ."

Madeline found herself returning the smile, struck by how much she had missed having female companionship. "It is, and I'm his daughter, Madeline." While getting a glass of water for Annalisa she couldn't contain her curiosity any longer. "Evan didn't mention that you were coming for a visit."

Annalisa smiled humorlessly, then dropped her gaze to study the bonnet in her hands. "Ah, well, he . . . ah . . . didn't exactly know I was coming."

"Oh."

"It's worse than that." The words burst from her lips in a torrent as she raised her head. "Oh, dear, I can't believe Evan is gone already. Now what am I going to do? I did . . . something, and I need his help. I'm afraid I've really made a wretched mess of things this time."

"Surely it's not as bad as all that," Madeline offered, feeling great sympathy for the young woman's misery and something near a physical pain deep in her chest as she looked into a pair of blue eyes nearly identical to Evan's.

"It's bad," Annalisa assured her, shaking her head. "You don't happen to know where Evan went, do you?"

Silently Madeline shook her head, memories of that last awful afternoon flooding back.

"Well." Annalisa took a sip of water and a deep breath. "Perhaps I will just have to travel on to San Francisco and meet up with him out there. Why not?" She gave a hopeless shrug. "I'm in the mud up to my armpits already—pardon my indelicate language."

"Why don't you stay here for a few days to rest and think things over?" Madeline offered, thinking of all the dangers that could befall a woman traveling alone. "If you've run away, which I suspect you have," she said, knowing from Annalisa's shamefaced cast that her assumption was correct, "the damage is already done. Besides, things never seem quite as bad when you're well rested." *Most* things, anyway, she added to herself.

"I couldn't impose—"

"I insist. Roundup is starting tomorrow, so you'll have the house to yourself."

"You're going to a cattle roundup?"

Madeline grinned at Annalisa's wide-eyed expression. "I'm doing more than going to a cattle roundup, I'm going to be part of it." She gestured to her clothing. "Just as I was today."

"Really! I didn't want to say anything about your . . . attire, but you're the first woman I've ever seen in trousers."

"Oh. Well," Madeline began, unsure of what to say, then settled for the truth. "It's much more practical."

"Is it conventional for women in the West to wear such apparel?"

"I don't think so," she said, thinking of Mrs. Ashler's comments, adding with a sigh, "nor do I suppose I am a conventional sort of woman."

"Well, I admire you for it." Annalisa's white, even smile was genuine. "I should think it would be an . . . an adventure to live out here as you do."

Madeline's next words were out of her mouth before she thought about them. It had been too long since she'd enjoyed the company of a young woman her own age. "Why don't you come along with me tomorrow?" she said. "As long as you're already in it up to your armpits, as you say, why not? It'll be a long day in the saddle, but—"

"I'd love to," Annalisa said without hesitation. "This may be the only adventure of my entire life." Her expression was wistful.

Madeline felt a rush of comradeship with Evan's younger sister. In the West, where decent females were just about as scarce as upper teeth in a cow, it was a natural thing for women of all types and sorts, by mere virtue of their sex, to bond quickly. But had she found something more than a woman with whom to pass a pleasant time? she wondered. A kindred spirit who felt as constrained by convention as she? A new friend who was as equally frustrated by the endless rules and regulations and dictates of civilized society? A flutter of optimism stirred within her breast.

Maybe the next days wouldn't be as hard to get through as she had thought.

It was a short night. Morning dawned cool and clear while the two women rode to the roundup camp. A heavy dew sat on the ground, and the cheerful sound of birdsong filled the air.

Despite the small amount of sleep she'd—they'd—gotten, Annalisa's good nature was infectious. She had been delighted to don a pair of denims, hurriedly stuffing her finely made pantalets into the legs of the garment so she could fasten the buttons and admire her appearance in the mirror in Nate's bedroom.

"If I'm going to have an adventure in the West with my new friend," she'd said cheerily, as if she didn't have a care in the world, "I must wear trousers to make it complete."

Holding the lamp aloft, Madeline had laughed out loud while Annalisa giggled at her reflection in the mirror, turning this way and that. She'd forgotten all about the note from Evan, not even thinking of it when she'd tiredly shown Annalisa the room last night. When her eyes rested on the piece of paper still lying on the chair, she had felt a moment of panic. Had Annalisa read it? And if she'd read it, what conclusions had she drawn from her brother's words?

She'd had a moment of indecision while she considered her options. In the end she'd decided the wisest course was simply to leave the note where it was and hope Annalisa had not seen it. Calling attention to the note, and to herself, by retrieving it in front of her new friend would be worse than inconspicuously slipping the paper from the room later on while Annalisa was otherwise occupied.

The pair of horses traveled swiftly across the rock-studded grassland. Annalisa spoke, pulling Madeline from her thoughts. "I've never seen mountains like this before," she exclaimed, looking about, "or so much wide open space. I can see why you live out here and do this, Madeline. It's positively exhilarating. Much more fun than being married to some old man and having a pack of children hanging on your skirts, which would have been my . . . Oh, never mind."

After a long moment, she grinned. "This is really rather fun. I haven't ridden astride in years—and I've never worn chaps. Mother would fall over in a dead swoon if she could see me now. Father, too. When we were growing up, the boys taught me how to ride like this. You should have heard our parents when they discovered that Evan and Ben were teaching me all sorts of unladylike pursuits." Her dark hair swung in a long braid down her back, in the same style as Madeline's, while an amused, remembering smile lingered on her lips.

Studying her new friend's appearance, Madeline was pleased. She'd raided the empty bunkhouse for the hat and chaps her new friend wore, adding those articles to the others she'd loaned her. Because Annalisa's feet were a size larger than hers, she'd had to make do with a pair of sensible shoes she'd brought with her. It was the only small flaw in the otherwise complete outfit of a cowpuncher.

"What will we be doing today?" Annalisa asked, glancing over at her.

"Oh, probably shagging cattle out of the brush," Madeline replied reassuringly, "which isn't too difficult if you have a good horse."

"Do I have a good horse?"

"You do." She smiled at Annalisa's look of uncertainty. "Don't worry, you're just along for the ride today. Your only job is to stay on your horse—and I can already see that you're a good rider."

"Don't worry, I'll stay on," she replied bravely.

"Of course you will. Now, the first part of your adventure is about to begin." She pointed ahead. "Just over that rise is the valley—and breakfast. Have you ever eaten grub from the back end of a chuck wagon?"

"A chuck wagon?" Annalisa flashed Madeline a skeptical but game grin. "No, I can't say as I have."

"This is absolutely delicious," Annalisa commented, popping the last bit of a honey-smeared baking powder biscuit into her mouth. "I don't think I've ever eaten a better breakfast." The two women sat on the ground, plates in their laps, feasting on Old Roger's plentiful fare while cowboys hovered about them like flies. The lovely brunette's presence had made quite a stir among them; several faces had been freshly washed in her honor, and a single comb had made the rounds, neatening the hair of just as many heads.

"Would you like some more coffee, Miss Annalisa? Or another biscuit? I'd be happy to—"

"How 'bout some more eggs?" Wayne Johnson interrupted Jim Culvert. "They'll stick to your ribs better'n—"

"Look, Miss Annalisa," Artie Hamilton exclaimed, elbowing his way in front of the men and kneeling before them. "The bacon's gone, but I saved my last piece for you." He set it on her plate reverently, as though it were a rare and priceless gift.

"Why, thank you." Annalisa's smile was dazzling as she looked up from beneath the brim of her hat at Artie, then at the other men assembled before her. "Thank you all. I believe I have only enough room left for this one piece of bacon, but perhaps if it isn't too much of an imposition, you other gentlemen could fix my plate at the next meal."

She fluttered her lashes prettily, and Madeline smothered a smile at the deft manner in which her new friend managed to make each man feel as important as the next.

"Time to get going, men," Will's voice boomed out loudly. "By noon or so we're gonna be officially starting the roundup we already unofficially started." The men quickly dispersed, depositing their cups and dishes in a tub near the chuck wagon. Madeline and Annalisa rose as well.

"I understand you two wanted to cover some countryside today, so why don't you follow the crick three, four miles up and see what you can find?" He gestured to the northwest. Repositioning his hat, he scratched a bushy eyebrow as he took in Annalisa's appearance. His voice was stern. "You sure you're up to this, young lady? You can ride, can't you?"

"Yes to both, sir," she answered with an engaging grin, not appearing at all intimidated by the burly foreman. She tipped her hat jauntily and twiddled the fringes on either side of her chaps. "I'm all set."

"We'll be fine, Will," Madeline reassured him. "She rides well."

"Hmmph," came the muttered exhalation. "I'm not quite exactly sure what she's doin' here, nor do I think her brothers would be too happy to know what she was up to." He cleared his throat. "An' I got me a real sneakin' suspicion her brothers *don't* know what she's up to."

"Mr. Reed, I—" Annalisa began earnestly.

He shook his head and momentarily covered his large ears with even larger hands, knocking his hat askew. "Nope. I don't wanna hear it 'cause I don't want to know about it. I got enough on my old mind the way it is. The two of you are a fine pair, all right, a sight that'd knot up the fine white drawers of every proper old biddy in town."

Madeline felt her heart sink under his disapproving words until he went on.

"But you know what? I ain't seen a genuine smile on your face, Maddie—like the one you been wearin' this mornin'—in more days'n I care to count. So, you two, have at it. Go beat the brush and see what you can find. I'll catch up with you later on to see how you're doin'." Abruptly he turned, spurs jingling, and walked toward his horse.

"Thanks, Will," Madeline called after him, smiling at the don't-mention-it gesture he made with one of his big hands without turning around or even breaking stride.

The morning was a productive one, both in terms of cattle found and in terms of the two women getting acquainted. Madeline found Annalisa's company absolutely delightful, though she was disturbed to learn of the circumstances under which she had left home and set out to find her brother.

Anna, as she invited Madeline to call her, was quite a talker, her personality reminding Madeline a good deal of Ben's. Throughout the course of the morning, Madeline heard several amusing stories of the Grant children's escapades as they grew up, as well as one that had occurred more recently—the details of the marriage Hiram Grant had attempted to arrange for his daughter.

As the two rode along a grassy ridge looking for wayward cattle, Anna confided to her, "I've wanted to be a part of the San Francisco plant ever since Father started talking about it, but he wouldn't hear of it. Even with Ben and Evan trying to talk him into letting me go, he was adamant. After my brothers left, I suppose Father figured the best way to deal with me was to marry me off." Her eyes flashed blue fire. "He figured wrong, though. There's no way in hell I'm going to be married into some business arrangement of his. That's why I set out to find Evan," she explained, her beautiful features softening. "After what happened to him, I knew he'd never allow Father to railroad me into a marriage I wanted no part of."

There it was again. *What had happened to Evan?*

"You have the most exciting life, Madeline," Annalisa said wistfully, "and the most exciting papa that anyone could have. I wish I could live out here like this."

Madeline strove for an offhand tone of voice. "Things aren't always what they seem to be, Anna. The land is rough, and the work is hard . . . and as for my papa . . . well . . ."

Annalisa looked expectantly at her.

"Speaking of papas," Madeline said, changing the direction of the conversation, "I'll bet yours is worried sick about you. The rest of your family, too. You took a big chance by coming here all alone, Anna—any kind of harm could have befallen you. Besides, running away doesn't solve any problems; it just makes more." Her fingers shook on the reins, but she couldn't stop. "It's a terrible thing, too, for a family to wonder where one of its members is, to wonder what's become of him—" To her horror, her voice broke. "Or her," she managed to finish.

"Your papa ran away?" Annalisa cut perceptively to the point, pulling on her reins to stop her horse. Madeline's horse stopped as well.

"Nate Spencer ran away?" Annalisa repeated in an incredulous tone of voice.

Madeline first shook her head, then nodded.

"Oh, dear. And what of your mother?"

"Sh-he's dead." Tears stung her eyes.

"Oh, dear. Oh, dear." Answering tears shone in Annalisa's eyes, and she reached out to clasp Madeline's hand. "You're all alone out here? You poor, poor thing. That means you must have had to tend to Evan without any assistance. You're so brave, Madeline," she said sincerely. "And I admire you all the more for being strong enough to shoulder these heavy burdens. Someday—only if you like, of course—you shall have to tell me all about them. 'Tis much better to share your troubles with a friend than to let them fester inside you."

If you only knew the whole of it, Madeline thought, squeezing the warm hand that held hers tightly, thinking that Anna's unconditional caring and freely offered friendship were enough to calm anyone's spirit, festering or not.

The emotional storm inside Madeline passed without fully erupting, and a long moment later she looked up at Annalisa. "You are truly a friend, Anna—oh, no!" she exclaimed, seeing another of her burdens approaching on horseback.

"What?" Annalisa turned in the direction Madeline was looking. "Is something the matter? Who are those men?"

"The Matthews brothers," she said in a grim voice, rubbing a suddenly throbbing area in the center of her forehead with the pads of her fingers.

"Oh, dear, is that bad? Are they dangerous?"

"Only half of them. Dammit, they've already spotted us. Pete's waving." Madeline lifted her hand and returned the wave, muttering, "Why don't you just eat a huge cow pie, Pete Matthews?"

"*Mad*eline! For shame!" Annalisa squealed in delight, her grin stretching as wide as Madeline had ever seen it.

"Shame, shmame," she said, feeling more like her usual self. "You'll be wishing your horse'd drop a fresh one for him within five minutes of meeting the man."

And she did, just as Madeline had predicted, well before the five minutes were up. After introductions were made all around, Anna was repulsed at what a horrid, overbearing, patronizing, simply *rude* man Pete Matthews was.

"Oh, you're that Grant fellow's sister, huh?" he said. "Yeah, I guess I can see the resemblance. Glad he's gone. Can't say as I liked the booger much."

That and the possessive, high-handed way he treated Madeline made Annalisa want to kick him in the teeth. Poor Madeline, she had to deal with him in addition to everything else?

The other brother, though—Jack, the utterly handsome blond man who hung back a ways from obnoxious Pete and cast her a shy grin that nearly made her heart flip over in her chest—now, he was different.

Good different.

Lowering her head, she shyly smiled back, covertly studying from beneath her lashes the lazy yet masterful way he sat his horse. The overall effect was devastating to her senses, making her forget everything else. She didn't think she'd ever seen a man put together the way he was. Lean, hard belly, broad shoulders, thick-muscled arms . . .

"Oh!" The cry came from her lips as a strong gust of wind tugged her hat off and sent it sailing.

In a graceful motion Jack wheeled his horse and, leaning over so far that Anna's breath caught in her throat, retrieved the errant headpiece. He straightened in the saddle and

dusted off the hat, extending it to her as he guided his
horse next to hers.

"Here you are, Miss Grant," he said politely, bestowing
upon her another shy, disarming smile. His teeth were
straight beneath his neatly trimmed blond mustache.

"Th-thank you," she stammered, knowing she was lost
when she looked directly into a pair of melting brown
eyes.

His voice, soft and deep at the same time, caressed her
ears. "Don't mention it, Miss—"

"Didja hear me, Jack?" the horrible man in the clashing
plaid shirt and pants shouted, interrupting his brother. "I
said it's about lunchtime. Let's accompany Miss Madeline
and her brown-haired twin sister here back to camp and
have us a bite to eat."

Annalisa's head snapped around at Pete's unmannerly
comment. He sat on his horse with a broad grin on his
strong-featured, rather homely face. Next to him, Madeline
wore a pained, see-didn't-I-tell-you-so expression. "We
really don't need an escort," Madeline said stiffly.
"Annalisa and I—"

"No, no, no," Pete dictated. "I insist. Right, Jack?" He
went on without waiting for a response from his brother.
"What's the world coming to, anyway, when that fool
Reed's wastin' two perfectly good women to do his cow
huntin' for him? Doesn't he know there's a shortage in the
county of marriageable—"

"That's enough, Pete." Jack's voice was stern. "I'm sure
Reed is grateful to have himself a couple extra far-swinging
riders." He turned to Annalisa, an apologetic expression on
his handsome face. "We're headed to camp, anyway, and
as my brother so delicately put it, we'd be honored to
accompany you."

Annalisa glanced at Madeline, who shrugged. "I suppose," she said with barely disguised annoyance.

The ride back to camp was, in Madeline's opinion, thoroughly miserable.

Coming over the last rise, she was surprised to see what
a busy place the valley had turned into throughout the

morning—a little town, almost, of cows and horses and men beneath the bright blue sky. Two more chuck wagons had been set up, and even from this distance the smells from the cookfires drifted to them on the breeze. Remudas of horses stood in tight bunches, contained by makeshift corrals fashioned from single ropes stretched tight on poles, and the number of cattle peacefully grazing had increased by half, she estimated.

She was thankful when Pete spotted Rendner. "Gotta go, girls," he brayed.

Jack accompanied them to the Spencer chuck wagon, quickly dismounted, and helped Annalisa from the saddle. In what appeared to be an afterthought, he turned to Madeline, but she had already dismounted on her own.

Almost at once, Wayne Johnson and Jim Culvert descended upon them. "Miss Annalisa! Miss Annalisa! We got a nice place all fixed up for ya to eat. Oh, and you, too, Miss Madeline. Come on with us. So, how'd you do this morning, Miss Annalisa?" The two men effectively nudged Jack out of the way as they crowded the dark-haired woman, firing eager questions at her. "What do you think of ranchin', Miss Annalisa? Did you work up a good appetite this mornin', ma'am? What do ya think of signin' on with us and stayin' awhile?"

Madeline smiled at Jack's crestfallen expression. "Come on, Jack," she said. "Us second and third fiddles can keep each other company."

Lunch was a festive affair. Joker Joe wandered over with his plate while they were eating, commenting that the chaps and hat that Annalisa wore looked awful familiar.

At the young woman's surprised, uncomfortable look, as well as the long stares directed at him by the other men gathered around, he scratched his brown beard and went on, "But I'm proud—no, miss, I mean *honored*— that you're makin' fine use of 'em," he said awkwardly, now embarrassed as well as unsure of how to conduct himself with an unfamiliar woman at mess. "Use 'em for as long as you like, ma'am, with my blessing," he added.

"Thank you, Mister . . . I don't believe I know your name, sir," Annalisa said prettily.

"It's Joseph McCaleb, ma'am," he said, doffing his hat, blushing bright red. "But most folks call me Joker Joe."

"Ask him why," someone hooted.

"Yeah, Joe, give us a joke," another voice said. "You been about as dry as a tobacco box lately. Let's hear a good one."

"You tell jokes?" Annalisa asked, breaking into a wide smile. "Please, do tell us one. I love jokes. My brother Ben was forever telling them."

"Yeah, Joe, come on," several voices said at once.

"Well, I gotta think if there's one I can tell in mixed company," Joe said, quickly recovering his composure. "Miss Madeline, now, she's almost like one of us," he said, pulling on his beard, "but I don't wanna go offendin' your fine eastern sensibilities, Miss Annalisa."

Nevertheless, within a few minutes Joe was back in fine form, much to everyone's delight. Midway through the meal, after Annalisa had been completely taken in by a sincere-sounding story with a punch line, Madeline watched her new friend exact her revenge amid the dying guffaws of laughter that came from all around.

Delicately picking at the contents of her plate, Annalisa looked at Joe and asked, "Wherever does your cook get seafood all the way out here, Mr. McCaleb? I should think it would be impossible to have fresh seafood in Wyoming Territory."

Joe looked puzzled. "Seafood? What the hell—oops, pardon me, ma'am. I mean, there ain't no seafood on your plate, Miss Grant. We eat beef an' we eat pork an' we eat antelope, an' every once in a while someone catches us a mess of mountain trout, but you definitely got something on your plate that once lived on four legs."

"I beg to disagree with you, Mr. McCaleb." Taking another spoonful of what was clearly ham and beans, she chewed and nodded. "This is, most assuredly, sea-food," she said after she'd swallowed. "I do know my seafood, you know," she added, looking at Joe with raised eyebrows.

By now they had the attention of nearly the entire camp. Murmurings of "Ain't no seafood . . . what's she talkin' about?" could be heard from several lips. Madeline knew Annalisa was up to something, but she wasn't sure what it was.

Joe squinted at her, his puzzled expression even more pronounced. Taking a bite of his own ham and beans and chewing vigorously, he pronounced, "This *ain't* no seafood, ma'am."

"Is, too," came Annalisa's immediate response. She took another bite and chewed. "And it's absolutely delectable."

Joe threw down his plate and jumped to his feet. "I don't know what the hell you people eat back east, but that's *ham* and *beans* on your plate, as sure as I'm standin' here." His face had grown flushed, and he paced back and forth on bandy legs. "Ham and beans! Not seafood!"

Annalisa shook her head and stood, still holding her plate. "Oh, dear. You're looking rather purple, Mr. McCaleb, but I must insist. It's seafood. If you think this is ham and beans, you must come and take a closer look." She scooped up a spoonful of the dish in question and held it in the air.

Everyone was quiet now, watching. Even white-aproned Old Roger had wandered over from his chuck wagon to see what was going on. He stood silently, head cocked to one side, arms folded across his chest, with a vinegary expression on his wrinkled face. Jack watched Annalisa intently.

Madeline disguised a smile as Joe stomped over to stand practically toe to toe with Annalisa. Her friend held the spoon in front of Joe's face, turning it this way and that. "Seafood," she said in a determined tone of voice.

"Ham and beans."

"Seafood."

"Ham . . . and . . . beans." Joe's hands were on his hips now, his voice taut with frustration.

Hushed expectancy hung in the air of the camp.

"Mr. McCaleb, this is seafood," Annalisa asserted again in all apparent seriousness, her voice sweet and clear. "Watch." Depositing the spoonful of ham and beans in her mouth, she chewed the mixture a few times, then opened her mouth wide, pointing to the partially masticated contents.

Joe stared at the woman—the woman with a wide open mouth full of half-chewed food standing before him—with an utterly blank look upon his face.

"Oh!" A male voice shouted. "I get it! See-food. *See-food.* Hot damn, she got you good, McCaleb!"

The word echoed around the camp as the first hoots of laughter began, then swelled into waves of loud guffaws, cackles, and hee-haws. Joe put his hands over his face, mock-staggered, and fell over backward, feigning death. Madeline laughed until she thought her sides would split, wondering where on earth Annalisa had learned such a gag, but at the same time delighted that her new friend had bested Joker Joe. Glancing at Jack, she saw he laughed every bit as hard as she did, gazing at Annalisa with obvious adoration.

Annalisa set down her plate and walked over to the still form of Joe, kneeling beside him, having swallowed her ham and beans. The laughter quieted as she said, "Truce?" extending her hand.

Joe pulled his hands away from his face and raised his head. "Truce," he agreed grudgingly, meeting her hand and shaking it once, hard. "Where'd a pretty thing like you learn a prank like that?" he asked, then added with loud dismay, "And how come I never heard that one before?"

"I think you met your match, McCaleb," someone shouted.

"Yeah, Joe, she's gonna keep you on your toes."

The remainder of the midday meal continued on in a merry fashion until Aaron Rendner called. "Time to break it up! Goldie, Payson, Miller, I want you over at the branding fire." While the assembled men dispersed, Madeline watched Jack say his farewells to Annalisa and was again struck by the heat that seemed to radiate from the two.

She was dead-on, she discovered after she and Annalisa had ridden about a mile. "What do you know about Jack Matthews?" Evan's sister eagerly asked. "Don't you think he's just about the most handsome man you've ever seen?"

No, your brother is the most handsome man I've ever seen, Madeline thought miserably, the warm glow she'd felt during the meal turning into cold ashes in her stomach. "Yes, Jack is certainly nice-looking," she answered, forcing a pleasant tone.

"Do you think so? Do you really think so?" Anna asked, looking about as happy as a blind cat in a creamery, to borrow an expression of Will's. "There's just something about his eyes . . . no, his smile . . . no, maybe it's his shoulders . . . Oh, I don't know. I've never felt quite this way before. All flutterylike inside, I guess. Ben is forever falling in love with one woman or another—" She broke off and smiled at Madeline. "Did you know that Ben wrote home about *you*, too?"

"Me?"

"He didn't mention you by name, but he wrote that Evan was 'laid up with a real looker' and said he wished he had been the one to get hurt instead of Evan." She shook her head. "I can only imagine what Evan must have been like while he was here. He can be perfectly awful at times, especially when he's hurting."

A deluge of memories flooded back through Madeline's heart while Annalisa paused, thinking.

"Madeline?" she asked, tilting her head to the side. "Do you believe in love at first sight?"

"I . . . ah . . . I suppose," she answered, taken off guard, wondering what Anna's reaction would be if she knew.

"You know," Anna said musingly, "it's funny. Ben falls in love at the drop of a hat—or should I say handkerchief— and here I am, as crazy as it sounds, wondering if I'm falling in love for the first time—with a cattle rancher in Wyoming Territory, of all things." She shook her head. "And then there's Evan. Except for that dreadful Melissa Morris, poor Evan never seems to fall in love at all. What do you make of that?" Changing the subject once, then again, she went on. "Gosh, it's hot out here this afternoon. Do you suppose we'll find some cows down in that gully over there?" she asked, pointing. "Or better yet, do you suppose we'll see Jack again this afternoon?"

Melissa Morris. The name rang over and over in Madeline's head. Was that why Evan couldn't love her? Had he already given his heart to another?

fifteen

SUNLIGHT SPARKLED THROUGH THE BANK OF west-facing shadows as Evan walked across the room that would be, in a few weeks' time, his office. "It doesn't appear Anna's shown up here either, brother," he stated grimly. His footsteps were loud, echoing along with his voice in the unfinished room. "Damm it, where is she? I checked every hotel I could think of . . ." His voice trailed off as he stared at, without truly seeing, the wind-ruffled waters of the San Francisco Bay.

"It's Sunday, Evan," Ben replied reasonably. "We'll have a better chance of finding her tomorrow." He stooped to pick up a nail from the floor. "You know what I think? I think she's holed up somewhere because she's afraid we'll send her right back to Chicago."

"Maybe," came Evan's slow response. "But I've got to tell you, Ben, I'm worried. I thought for sure she was going to turn up in Reno." He turned his back on the windows. The empty, destitute feeling he'd been carrying in his chest since—*you know exactly when it started*, his inner voice

caviled—grew with each day that passed, making his whole
body feel hollow. "If something's happened to Anna . . ."
he said, unwilling to let himself think of Madeline's soft
kisses, of her gentle touch . . . or of the agony he had caused
her—and himself.

"Nothing's happened to Anna," Ben replied firmly,
standing and stretching his long legs. "We know she
didn't turn up at Aunt Minnie's. We waited a whole
week for her to show up in Reno, so that only leaves San
Francisco. She's got to be out here somewhere. Come on,
Ev, you know how stubborn she is . . . kind of like you, in
that respect. Granted, this is her biggest stunt yet, but I think
she's set on showing Father, in the most painful way possible, what she thinks of his high-handed ways—and she's
just making the rest of us sweat a little in the process."

Evan listened to his younger brother's words, hearing the
reason in them. Not for the first time since they'd met up
in Reno, he was impressed with a side of Ben he hadn't
seen before. It wasn't just the new take-charge attitude,
nor was it solely the knowledge of the enormous success
he'd learned Ben had had while on his own. With pride, he
realized his brother had matured fully into manhood in the
time they'd been apart.

"Anna's fine, Evan," Ben reiterated, tossing the nail into
a corner. "Knowing her, she's planning one of her dramatic
entrances for us once the plant's open, figuring there'll be
so much work to do that we'll fall to our knees and beg her
to stay."

"That would be like her," Evan agreed, feeling a little of
his worry dissipate. "But the girl deserves a sound thrashing
for putting us through this. Poor Mother is nearly insensible
with grief."

"And Father's apoplectic with rage." Ben grinned. "I
always knew she had it in her." He was silent a moment,
his grin fading. "You know, women have a tough lot in
life, don't they? They can't do this, they're not supposed
to do that . . . but, you know, I think they *want* to and *could*
do anything, probably as well as any man. You and I both
know Anna's every bit as capable and intelligent as we are.
And take Nate Spencer's daughter—now, there's one hell

of a woman. I understand she works the ranch about as well as any of the cowhands." The familiar gleam appeared in his eye. "I don't mind telling you, either, that I've spent more than one uncomfortable night thinking of her. You don't suppose Levi's will catch on as a women's fashion, do you? Madeline Spencer looked damn fine in them." Ben made an appreciative sound deep in his throat. "Think of it, Ev, never having to wonder what kind of legs a woman has . . . or, for that matter, what kind of—"

"That's enough, Ben," he said sharply as an image of Madeline's sweetly swaying hips appeared in his mind. Until he met the long-legged, denim-clad beauty, he never would have imagined he'd spend so much time studying the way the human leg joined the rump, but he'd been absolutely fascinated with watching Madeline walk. And stand. And bend over. God, he'd memorized each tiny detail of the way the fabric had creased and tightened and folded under . . . and disappeared into the mysterious cleft between her legs.

"You're hot for her, aren't you?" Ben looked and sounded incredulous. "Holy cow, Ev, you should see the look on your face." His brother clutched his chest and mock-staggered. "Evan, old man, can it finally be? Has your head finally been turned by a member of the fairer sex? I was beginning to think that Morris bitch had gelded you for good." He bounded toward the windows, splaying his arms wide. "Attention, world," he shouted with playful good humor, looking for all the world like a puppyish youngster once again, "my brother has a rock-hard, cock-hard, bona fide boner for a woman for the first time in years!" He threw back his head, laughing loudly. "And it's about damned time," he added, turning to face Evan with a mischievous leer.

Maturity? He'd been greatly mistaken to think Ben had grown up. Anger rose within him, hot and fast. "If you'd like to find your way back downstairs via the window, just keep it up," he snarled. His body tensed, and his hands curled into fists.

"Okay, okay," Ben said appealingly, walking over to him. "Sorry, old man. Just having a little fun at your expense." His serious expression lasted only seconds before the infuriating smirk appeared on his face once again. "But come on, you *have* to tell me what happened back there! My God! You two were all alone . . . and I don't recall that anything was broken below your waist."

"Nothing happened," Evan lied with a tight voice. Abruptly turning his back on his brother, he walked toward the door, Ben's snickering laughter ringing in his ears.

A week passed, then another, without word from Annalisa. Evan didn't know which was worse: the dread for his sister's fate he carried knotted in his gut or his chaotic feelings for Madeline Spencer, which continued to tear up his heart without any sign of easing.

Summer bloomed around them as, slowly but surely, Grant Meats readied itself for opening. No longer confident that Anna would turn up at the plant, a subdued Ben threw himself into the final business preparations. As Ben had things well in hand at Grant Meats, Evan spent large portions of his days combing the city for his sister and, although he didn't admit it to himself, keeping his ears open for any information about Emmett Brinkman.

He knew he'd been surly, uncommunicative, and edgy— or as Ben put it, "mean to the bone"—so it was no surprise to him that his brother didn't waste a proper greeting on him when he walked into his office this afternoon. In fact, Ben didn't even look up from the large ledger he was busily writing in.

"Nothing again," Evan said shortly, announcing another day's failure. "No doubt Father's hired Pinkerton's by now."

The pen's scratching movements slowed, then stopped. "No doubt," Ben agreed, running a hand through his hair before he looked up at him. Gone was his boyish sparkle; somberness sat on the younger Grant's features. "Say, Evan, you got a letter today," he added quietly.

"From who?"

"From Miss Madeline Spencer of Wyoming Territory. It's right here." Not so much as one teasing twinkle could be seen in the depths of Ben's tired blue eyes as he held the envelope toward Evan.

Evan's fingers closed around the mailer, and suddenly he felt as if he couldn't breathe. Why would Madeline be writing to him? Was she coming to San Francisco? A fierce joy rose in him. That must be it. She was coming to San Francisco and she wanted to see him again. By God, he would have another chance with her . . . Hold on! His mind snapped out the order. *You don't know anything of the sort. Maybe she just wants to tell you to go to hell.*

"Are you going to stare at it all day or are you going to open it?" Ben extended a shiny letter opener toward him, a flicker of interest lighting his weary features.

After wordlessly opening the envelope, Evan unfolded the paper and read Madeline's neat hand. Disbelief rose in him first, then white-hot fury. "God *damn* it!" he swore viciously. "I don't believe this! I'm going to wring her worthless little neck!"

"What?" Ben had risen from his chair, concern and confusion etching his lean, handsome face. "Why are you going to wring Madeline's neck?"

"I'm not going to wring Madeline's neck; I'm going to wring *your sister's* neck!" Crumpling the paper in a savage motion, Evan hurled it to the floor. His blood pounded through his body at a furious rate. "Not only has she been at the Spencer ranch since she left Chicago—no doubt having the time of her life—she's apparently taken up with Jack Matthews!"

Relief shone on Ben's face. "Whoa, Evan, settle down. Anna's unharmed. That's the main thing. And why is she always *my* sister when you're angry with her?"

"She'll be unharmed until I get there," Evan threatened, "but after that, she may not be able to sit down for the rest of her life."

Ben grinned widely. "So you're going back to Wyoming Territory, eh? It's about time, old man. Though you're too pigheaded to admit it, it's about as plain to see as the nose on your face that you're in love with Madeline Spencer." He chuckled. "Why don't you just marry her and put yourself— and the rest of us—out of your misery?"

"And why don't you just go to hell?"

As plain to see as the nose on his face? Bullshit! And damn all women for the trouble they caused a man. His first priority was to send Annalisa back to Chicago.

Then, and only then, would he see to any unfinished business between himself and Madeline Spencer.

"You did *what?*" Annalisa wailed loudly into the warm morning air.

Madeline felt her cheeks flame at her friend's accusing question, but she firmly repeated what she'd said: "I wrote to Evan in San Francisco. Someone had to let your family know where you were." Her voice dropped, and she added, "Anna, it's been weeks now. They must be frantic for thinking the worst."

"Oh, Madeline," Anna said miserably, plopping onto her bottom in the garden's soft dirt. She tossed down the handful of weeds and took off her work gloves. "I know I kept telling you I'd contact my family, but I did such an awful thing . . . and it's just that it went so far . . . and they're going to be *so* angry with me." She shook her head, digging her bare fingers into the warm earth. Her voice quavered. "I've been having such a good time here . . . and I guess I just kept trying not to think about them."

"But that was wrong, Anna," Madeline persisted gently.

"I know." She was silent a long moment while her fingers made five-furrowed tracks on either side of her. "Evan will be coming for me, you know," she stated with a shaky sigh. "He'll be coming to get me—and I don't want to leave."

Would he really come? Nervous fear surged through Madeline at the thought of Evan returning to the ranch. *But then again,* her subconscious whispered, *isn't that just what you hoped he'd do?*

"I don't want you to leave either, Anna." She spoke quickly, trying to banish the nagging voice from her head. "And I meant what I said: you're welcome to stay here for as long as you like." Filled with trepidation at the thought of another ugly encounter with Evan and uneasily wondering just what her true motives were in contacting him, she pushed herself rapidly to her feet, brushing off her knees as she stood. A black buzzing filled her head from the rapid movement, and prickles of sweat broke out under her arms.

Her friend's voice continued on, filled with sadness and uncertainty. "And what about Jack? I think I love him—*Maddie!*" she interrupted herself sharply. A second later Madeline was aware of Anna's arm about her shoulders. "What is it, Madeline? Are you ill? I swear, there's not a drop of color in your face. Oh, dear! And you scarcely ate your breakfast! Here, now, sit yourself back down."

That was easy; there was no strength in her legs. Or arms. Or any part of her, for that matter. Her buttocks hit the ground heavily, and she felt the pressure of Anna's hands pushing her head gently forward toward her knees. Her heartbeat boomed loudly in her ears, filling her head with the noise, and what little breakfast she'd eaten threatened to come up.

She moaned.

The control in her friend's voice fled her, her words coming fast and staccatolike. "Oh, dear . . . oh, dear! *Oh, dear!* Honey, I'm going to run and get Will. Can you just sit there for a minute? I'll be right back, I promise! I think he's still up at the . . ."

It seemed as if she was gone and back almost before her words had been carried away on the wind. Madeline heard two sets of pounding footsteps, then Anna's desperate voice, interspersed with rapid, panting gasps, explaining to Will that they'd been weeding the garden, and Madeline had been just fine, except that she hadn't eaten much for breakfast, and then she'd stood up and nearly swooned.

The black whirring in Madeline's head eased slightly, as did the nausea, and she lifted her head to stare blearily at the pair. Will crouched before her, looking at her intently, while Annalisa stood nervously just behind him, biting on the knuckle of her index finger.

"She needs food and drink," Will stated decisively. "Water. Plain bread."

"I'll be right back," Anna promised, taking off at a dead run.

Will continued to look at her strangely, in a way that made her uncomfortable, and Madeline dropped her head back to her knees. Physically she already felt better. The spell she had experienced seemed to be quickly fading.

"Damn your father for putting me in this spot!"

Will's voice was explosive, and Madeline's head snapped up. Sudden fear sent her heartbeat to racing once again. She stared at Will with wide eyes, seeing the expression on his face for what it was.

Anger.

Opening her mouth, she wet her lips. In a sudden motion, Will's big, powerful body shot from a crouch to its full height. He planted his hands hard on his hips and stared down at her. "I got a few questions for you, missy, and you better answer 'em, and answer 'em quick."

Swallowing hard, Madeline nodded. She'd never seen Will this angry, and what was more, his rage seemed to be directed at her. His voice was like the blast from a shotgun. "Have you had your woman's time since that Grant fellow was here?"

"My—my woman's time?" Fear and confusion made her stutter.

"You know, your bleedin' time!"

Madeline was shocked to the core. "You know about that?" she whispered.

"Of course I know about that!" Will's neckerchief had worked itself loose, and Madeline could see the distended veins below his jaw. He threw his arms out to the sides, his booming voice reaching all the way to Cheyenne, she was sure. "Just how the hell do you think a man could run a ranch without knowin' about female cycles? A woman ain't no different than a cow, cyclin' every month . . ." As if he realized he was shouting, he cut himself off. Visibly fighting for control, he continued a moment later in a tight, though much softer voice. "Unless she's breedin'."

"Breeding . . ." She mouthed the word. Sudden understanding poured through her, and she gasped aloud. *Breeding!*

He squatted before her, his sides heaving. For an endless moment their eyes locked, and she knew he saw into her heart . . . accurately reading the truths held there. She saw, too, the effort it cost him to speak quietly. "You ain't bled, have you?"

Madeline closed her eyes, feeling her world threaten to fade to black again. *Breeding.* Thinking back, she realized her monthly flow had not come since well before Evan had arrived at the ranch. With all that had been going on, she hadn't missed it; she hadn't even given it a thought. And now Evan Grant's child grew within her belly? It was simply too much to comprehend. Tears pooled behind her eyelids and ran down her face. She gave her head a quick negative shake.

His curse word was immediate and blunt. "Well, ain't this just a dandy state of affairs?" he went on. "Aw, honey," he said with gruff tenderness as a sob escaped her throat, "don't do that cryin' business. You know I can't stand that . . . an' I ain't mad at *you*, not exactly, an' besides, we already got a little irrigation crick here to take care of the plants," he finished awkwardly. "Here, wipe your face off." She felt him press a wadded-up handkerchief into her hands.

Drying her tears, she opened her eyes.

Will stared back at her with a mixture of compassion and frustration. "Oh, Madeline Spencer, why didn't I listen to myself?" he asked, shaking his head. Knees cracking, he pushed himself upright. His voice increased to its former volume with each successive word. "Why the hell didn't I listen to myself? That man shoulda been out in the bunkhouse. Damn, I seen the sparks between you two, but I just didn't listen to myself." Pacing, he trampled several small lacy-green carrot plants.

"And you an innocent, to boot!" He went on, his voice gaining roughness. "Damn Evan Grant's balls to hell! I oughta take the first train out to San Francisco and geld the sonofabitch with the dullest, rustiest knife I got. I had my suspicions—in fact, I had me a real strong hunch about you two—but I trusted the man. Jesus, Mary, and Joseph, I even *liked* him!"

Now fully wound up, Will continued to rant and pace. "He's gonna do the proper thing, I'll see to that. 'Less I leave him so full of holes he won't float in brine! Who the hell does he think he is? I'll teach him for messin' with young girls . . ."

His voice faded from her ears as she thought of Anna's assertion: "Evan will be coming for me, you know." Would he really come? Anna seemed certain he would. But maybe he wouldn't, Madeline reasoned. Ben could come, or even their father . . .

Will raged on, his large feet smashing a goodly number of new plants back into the earth. She'd never seen her father's best friend in a state such as this. Hearing his infuriated voice without any longer listening to the words, she wondered what would happen if Evan did come . . . What would happen *to* Evan if he came?

A shudder passed through her, having nothing whatsoever to do with her dizzy spell.

sixteen

EVAN *WAS* COMING.

He'd left San Francisco within two hours of receiving Madeline's letter, galvanized into action by the neat handwriting on the page. Feelings of relief and enormous anger roiled inside him at the news Annalisa was safe—and had been fine all along. Whether he was going to give the headstrong little brat the worst thrashing of her life or hug her until she couldn't breathe remained to be seen. Right now, each sounded like an equally fine idea.

But along with those emotions churned something else, something that made him feel electrified and afraid at the same time. Something he'd tried to deny for weeks.

Though you're too pigheaded to admit it, it's about as plain to see as the nose on your face that you're in love with Madeline Spencer. Why don't you just marry her and put yourself and the rest of us out of your misery?

Ben's laughing but incisive comments echoed in his mind. How the hell was it, he wondered with frustration, that his brother had looked at him and simply known what was inside him? Was it really so obvious?

God, he'd acted like a coward when Madeline had told him what was in her heart. *No, you were even lower than a coward*, he told himself harshly. He couldn't blame her if she never wanted to see him again.

Another feeling, much stronger than the simple sense of responsibility, joined the already seething mass of emotions inside him when he realized he very well might have left her in a family way. A picture of her appeared in his mind—teary-eyed and swollen-bellied . . . and all alone.

Oh, dammit, he'd made such a mess of things.

The beauty of the Wyoming Territory landscape was lost on him as the livery horse galloped toward the Spencer ranch. The train trip from San Francisco to Laramie City had been interminable; each of the several stops along the way had caused his vexation to grow enormously. Though he'd been sitting for days, it felt incredibly good to have horseflesh under him, to finally be in control of something.

He desperately needed Madeline in his life. It was as simple as that. Why hadn't he fully realized that before? Hell, he'd even get down on bended knee, and tell her what was in his heart, if that was what it took. Being a bachelor for the rest of his days no longer held any appeal, not since he'd discovered what completeness, what *rightness* a person could feel with another.

Being a part of Grant Meats no longer held any appeal for him, either. Ben was young and eager, and was doing a more than capable job of setting up and running the plant on his own. Evan had seen for himself that his brother didn't need him. Hell, the grinning fool had all but shoved him out the door after he uncrumpled and read Madeline's letter, telling him to go and not worry about coming back.

Maybe he wouldn't go back. The West was full of wide open spaces. . . .

The familiar house and outbuildings appeared. The day was warm and windy, with sunshine spilling from a white-dotted sky. Remembering what had happened the last time he had arrived at the ranch, he made a mental note not to linger on horseback near the barn.

Bringing his horse to a stop in the dirt-packed yard in front of the structure, he dismounted immediately, half expecting his bobtailed enemy to charge him again. Looking around, he saw no sign of the fat gray feline. With any luck, Will had made good on his threats to dispatch Madeline's little Sugarpie.

"Who goes there?" came the big man's voice from inside the barn, pulling him from his thoughts. "That you, McCaleb? Say, where the hell's that bottle of liniment anyway? You know, the new one I had Ashler pick up last time he was to town—"

"Howdy, Reed," Evan interrupted the foreman, an amiable, if not relieved, look crossing his face. He was glad for the chance to talk to the big man alone before seeing Madeline or Annalisa. He'd genuinely liked the gruff, hardworking man and had often wondered in the past weeks whether Reed had succeeded in apprehending the cattle rustlers. "I don't know where your liniment is," he called lightly into the barn's dim interior, "but I understand you know where my sister is."

"*Grant!*" The name burst from inside the gloomy structure like a ball from a cannon, followed by an equally resounding "*You sonofabitch!*"

His immediate thought was that there was no pleasantness in the foreman's voice, a thought that was confirmed a moment later when the burly man appeared from the depths of the shadows, charging him like an angry bull.

Evan was stunned. "What the he—"

His bewildered question ended with a strangled "Oof!" as Willis Reed hit him with a flying tackle, sending them both heavily to the dirt a good distance away from the barn door. Evan's chest constricted when he struck the ground, and his left shoulder felt as though it had been smashed into bits.

He couldn't breathe. He couldn't talk. He couldn't think. With no air in his lungs, pain slashing wildly through his not quite healed joint, and with two hundred plus pounds of beefy man directly on top of him—a man trying like hell to sink a brawny forearm into his throat—he was nearly incapacitated.

His weak, involuntary gasps didn't seem to inflate his lungs whatsoever, and he struggled desperately, trying to rid himself of the weight of the furious man atop him. Though Reed's face was only inches from his own, he wasn't able to comprehend what the man's deafening bellowing was about. A roaring blackness seeped into his head, and he felt his struggles weaken.

Then, mercifully, the weight was gone.

He rolled on his side, gasping in air like a half-drowned man. The blackness in his vision cleared, and he stared dumbly at the burly man who stood before him and brushed the dirt from his unadorned chaps. Fleetingly, he wondered if he was destined to lie in the dirt every time he came to the Spencer ranch.

"I'll let you get your breath back," Reed snarled, sides heaving, " 'cause I won't have it said I don't fight fair." His fingers unknotted the red bandanna at his neck, and he hurled it to the ground. "But you'd best say your prayers while you're tryin' to fill up your lungs, boy," the older man continued, his ham-sized fists opening and closing at his sides, "because if you think I knocked you ass over teakettle just now, you ain't seen nothin' yet." His eyes narrowed. "I guess I should be glad you saved me a trip out to California. Your balls got an appointment with my knife, you worthless—" Instead of finishing his sentence, he jerked his head to the side and spat contemptuously on the ground before continuing. "I'm gonna cut you like a bellerin' calf and stuff your oysters down your throat for what you done to my best friend's little girl."

For what you done to my best friend's little girl?

Oh, God. For what he *did* to Madeline? Evan tried to speak, but his voice sounded like air passing through a broken bellows. Did Reed mean what Evan thought he did? He gasped for breath, finding that the air-starved feeling was slowly abating. Looking up, he met the big man's furious, unflinching gaze. Slowly, laboriously, he propped himself up on his good elbow. Things were finally starting to make sense, but the only possible conclusion he drew caused both a thrill and sheer terror to streak through him.

"Is your thinker workin' yet, boy?" Reed thundered. "By God, you're actin' about as slow as a cow in a boghole. Is any of this sinkin' into your shallow brainpan?"

"I . . . think so, but . . . I don't intend . . . to part with any of my . . . valuables," he wheezed, finally having enough wind to string a few words together.

In a sudden motion, Will grabbed him by the front of his shirt with both hands and roughly hauled him to his feet. "How could you have?" the foreman bellowed at him before swearing foully. "She was just an innocent girl! An' you go payin' back our hospitality by breachin' her! Dammit, it, Grant, I trusted you. I even *liked* you."

A matching anger flared to life inside Evan. Pushing the man's hands away, he stepped back, putting a small distance between them. "Damm it yourself, Reed, I liked you, too! Jesus!" With his good hand he grabbed his screaming shoulder and worked it around in a tight circle, relieved that his left hand clenched into a fist as readily as did his right. "If you're itching for a fight, I'll give you a good one," he shot back, his voice nearly fully restored, "but I've got one question for you before we get down to business, one that you haven't completely answered yet."

Neither of them paid any attention to the two women and two men who approached on horseback from the northwest, or to the women's cries of distress at seeing the two of them thus embroiled. Will Reed lifted a fist and took a threatening step forward.

"Well, Reed," Evan ground out, not moving an inch, "say it. I'm waiting."

The women were nearly upon the yard, having kicked their horses into a full gallop at the sight of Will and Evan facing each other in hostile stances. The two men rode close on the women's heels, ready to spring off their horses and into action.

"So what do you want to know? Ain't I made it simple enough for you?" Reed roared back at Evan, oblivious of the audience of four shocked faces that now looked on from a distance of no more than fifteen feet. "Do you want to know if your seed took? Well, *it did*. Madeline's expectin' your get, if that's what you're askin'."

A shocked female gasp cut the air between them. In unison, Will and Evan turned their heads toward the sound. Madeline's face was bloodless, stricken, and she slowly brought up her hand to cover her mouth. Her eyes locked briefly with Evan's before her gaze slid down to fix upon the reins in her hands. Even from the distance, Evan was lanced by the pain that had been briefly reflected in their shadowed depths.

Quickly his gaze moved to search his sister's appearance. She stared in open shock at Madeline, as did Pete and Jack Matthews. Anna wore pants and sat astride her horse as proud as you please, looking healthy and robust. Amid his inner turmoil and physical pain, he felt a great relief at actually seeing for himself that she was unharmed.

As if Annalisa felt his eyes upon her, she turned her head toward him and shot him a look of pure censure. Except for the distant sounds of the cattle on the wind, a brittle hush settled over the yard. Jack Matthews seemed to have found something interesting to look at in the empty corral, but his brother Pete, like Anna, fixed Evan with a hostile stare.

The sound of Reed's heavy breathing pulled his attention back to the big man. A look of pain crossed Reed's weathered face, and all the fight seemed to go out of him. "Shit in a basket," he muttered in a distressed baritone. "I guess I couldn't have made that none plainer. I was hopin' the two of you could get hitched quietlike."

"What are you saying?" Pete demanded to know, throwing his reins to his brother and dismounting. He swaggered aggressively toward Evan, his chest puffed out like a bantam rooster's. His cotton shirt was an offensive green-and-black plaid, and ill-fitting, brown-striped woolen trousers rode low on his hips. Red splotches stood out unattractively on his ruddy face as he looked rapidly between Evan and Madeline. "What the hell are you saying, Reed?" he repeated, spittle flying from his furiously working mouth. "Are you saying that this . . . this . . . eastern scum here forced himself on Miss Madeline? 'Cause if he did, I—"

"I didn't do anything she didn't want me to do." Evan sounded unashamed and absolutely unapologetic as he cut off Matthews's incensed threat, looking first at Reed, then directly into Pete's eyes.

"Why, you—" Pete Matthews lunged at Evan, but Will Reed caught him, easily restraining the smaller man. Jack was off his horse in an instant, crossing the distance in a few long-legged strides.

"Hold on, boy," Reed commanded Pete. "Dammit, Matthews, will you just stop with your wigglin' before I hafta hurt you?" At that, the neighboring rancher strained all the harder to free himself, forcing Will to apply painful pressure to his arms. "I said to hold still," he repeated over Pete's pained cry, "else I'll let your brother take a pop at you. I can tell he's itchin' to. Now Grant, here," he continued, looking Evan directly in the eye, "was just gettin' to the part where he was askin' me for Madeline's hand in marriage . . . weren't you, Grant?"

"I—" Evan began.

"You can't do this! You can't! You can't! I won't let you!"

"*Be quiet*, Peter," Jack instructed at the same time Reed gave Pete's arms a hurtful squeeze and growled, "Shaddup!" The burly ranch foreman held the smaller man in front of him, pinning his arms behind his back. "Go on, Grant," Jack said in a deep voice, first nodding at Reed, then giving his brother a quelling look.

"Yes, please. Do go on, brother," Annalisa said in an outraged voice.

Evan swallowed. His heart pumped so forcefully he could feel the pulsations throughout his chest, his neck, even his fingers. Being manipulated into proposing to Madeline in front of a group of vengeful spectators—including his sister, of all people—incensed him beyond belief. Christ! How had it come to this?

But there just didn't seem to be any alternative.

The eyes of all assembled—except Madeline—were upon him, their combined antipathy beating into him with more heat than the late afternoon sun that roasted the back of his neck.

"Evan Grant!" Anna called in an imperious tone that made Evan think of their mother. "You'd better get on with it! If you don't say something right this minute, I'm going to—"

This was more than a man could take.

He exploded in rage. "Will everyone stop badgering me? All of you, stop badgering me! I'm going to marry her, so everyone just leave me alone!" Anger and frustration coursed through him at the indignity of this whole thing, and an ugly obscenity slipped from his lips. He stamped over to where his hat lay and picked it up, brushed off the dirt, and jammed it back on his head.

"Nooo!" Pete shouted, trying in vain to break free, his face contorted in pain. "You can't! I won't let you! She's mine!"

"*I'm not anyone's!*"

Was that shrieking voice actually hers? Madeline decided it must have been; all heads had swung around to look at her. Oh, dear Lord, she wished the ground would open up and swallow her whole. Squeezing her eyes shut, she realized that everyone knew what she had done with Evan. Anna, Jack, Pete, Will. They all knew. . . .

"We'll be wed, Madeline," came Evan's tight voice across the distance separating them, "as soon as possible."

"Amen," echoed Will Reed.

Anna reached out and squeezed Madeline's hand, but Madeline pulled her hand away from her friend. Anger boiled up from deep inside her, overriding her deep humiliation. Marriage? Lord Almighty, where were the words of tenderness, of caring, of devotion?

Of love?

She nimbly dismounted, her feet landing simultaneously on the earth with a soft thud. "Did any of you think about asking me what *I* wanted?" she demanded to know as she strode over to stand in front of the men. "I'm a person, in case you've forgotten! I'm not some sort of *thing* to be ordered about and—"

"Now, Maddie—" Will Reed broke in.

"Don't you 'now, Maddie' me, Will," she shot back furiously. "Because of you, everyone in the whole territory knows I'm . . . I'm—" She couldn't say the word. She felt Evan's gaze burning the side of her face, and she turned her head to face him, meeting his gaze head on. "And *you*, you presumptuous jackass! Do you think I'm going to fall at your feet out of gratitude for your generous and heartfelt offer of marriage?" Her voice dripped sarcasm as she shoved several unruly strands of hair out of her face in a rough, impatient motion, remembering his muteness when she had told him of her feelings for him. "In case you don't recall, Mr. Grant, you made your feelings quite clear to me that last afternoon."

"For Christ's sake," he swore, "I said I'd marry you. Under the circumstances, I think—"

"For Christ's sake," she swore back, cutting him off, "that was no offer of marriage—at least none that I want any part of." She pulled her gaze away from Evan, thinking that not so much as an ounce of tenderness could be seen in his steely blue eyes. The truth was there: he didn't want to marry her. Pain knifed her heart, more pain than she'd ever felt in her life.

"Madeline, be reasona—"

"I'll marry you, Miss Madeline," Pete interrupted the big foreman, struggling to pull his arms free from the larger man's tight grip. Madeline felt faint. "Let me go, Reed," Pete demanded. "I got somethin' to say to Miss Madeline, and I don't want to say it like this."

Slowly Will released Pete's arms. "One false move and I'll tie you up in a knot," he warned.

"For Christ's sake, you near like to tore my arms off, Reed," Matthews complained loudly, working his shoulders. The red blotches on Pete's face had run together until his complexion was nearly maroon. With angry desperation, he turned to Madeline. "If Grant wasn't out here chasin' after his sister, do you think he would have ever come back for you?"

The cold, terrible truth of Pete's words reinforced what she already knew. Though Evan's face was now impassive, she saw the barely perceptible stiffening of his body. He continued to stand apart from the other men, his arms folded across his broad chest. Staring at those muscular arms, she realized that she had never known what it was like having *both* of them wrapped around her. Fleetingly she wondered how his shoulder had healed, if it still gave him pain. . . .

"I guess it ain't no secret I been plannin' on marryin' you, Miss Maddie." Pete's grating voice brought her back to the present with a jolt.

What had he said? Oh, dear Lord, he wasn't really going to propose, was he? *This can't be happening*, she thought. *None of this can possibly be happening.* With horror, her eyes fastened on Peter Matthews.

"Yeah, me and Nate did some talkin' a while back," he continued brashly, jamming his hands into his pockets. The baggy brown-striped trousers rode so low on his hips that Madeline was sure they'd slide right off. "I pointed out to him what a nice little spread we'd have if we . . . well, never mind about that now."

She took an involuntary step backward.

"Didn't we have a nice ride this afternoon, me an' you an' Jack an' Anna? Just think of it, honey, how much more time we could be spendin' together." No one spoke as he took a deep breath and hitched his pants up without removing his hands from his pockets. Studying the ground in front of him, he spoke rapidly. "An' knowin' how you took Grant's proposal, I'd like to say that I'd be proud to take you to wife, even under the present . . . er, circumstances." He cleared his throat. "Madeline honey, I *want* to marry you."

Madeline couldn't listen to any more. "Stop it! Please stop talking! I'm not going to marry anyone!"

"But you have to!" Open-mouthed, Pete Matthews stared at her.

"I don't *have* to marry anyone!" she repeated, repugnance pouring through her at the thought of being wed to such a man. "I'm not *going* to marry anyone. The only reason I'm attractive to you is because of my father's ranch."

Taking a deep breath, she glowered at Will, righteous anger pouring through her. "And you! Can't you see that the only reason I'm attractive to Evan is because—"

"Madeline—" Evan's familiar voice was stern.

"I'm not marrying anyone, and that's final!" Tears were already spilling from her eyes in a torrent as she spun on her heel to flee in shame, and disgrace.

"Stop right there, Maddie," Evan ordered grimly.

"*No!*" she screamed. "Go back to California, Mr. Grant, or go straight to hell—I don't care which. Just leave me alone!"

As she broke into a run, the wind rushed past her ears, mercifully covering the sudden buzz of voices that rose behind her.

Streaks of crimson, salmon, and violet spread out above the white-capped mountains to the west when Annalisa climbed the porch steps and walked into the kitchen of the Spencer ranch house. Pausing a moment after she closed the door, she realized that the good-bye kiss Jack had given her just a few minutes ago still burned on her mouth. Hesitantly she traced the contour of her lips with her finger, remembering the way his tongue had first tentatively, then boldly, parried with her own.

Heavens!

The handsome blond rancher had just returned her to the ranch after taking her to his place for a simple evening meal. Though she had wanted to follow Madeline and comfort her after that awful scene in the yard, Will had advised all of them to leave Maddie alone for a good long while.

Pete had been the first to leave. Making vile, sputtering protestations about what Madeline really needed, he had mounted his horse and immediately ridden off. Then Jack had suggested that Anna accompany him back to the Matthews ranch for dinner. At Evan's curt nod, they'd wasted no time in departing.

She had no idea what had become of Evan and Will; the two were still facing each other with their hackles raised when she and Jack had departed.

For all she knew, they could have killed each other by now.

The house was dead quiet, but she had a strong feeling Madeline was up in her room licking her wounds. Walking toward the stairway, she wondered where Will and Evan could be; it was nearly dark. Pete hadn't yet returned to the Matthews ranch, either, when she and Jack had left after their meal. Uneasily she wondered if Pete would try something foolish.

Slow down, Anna, she chided herself. *Pete's loud and obnoxious, but he wouldn't do anything to hurt anyone.*

Would he?

She shook her head slightly, finding it absolutely perplexing that two brothers could be so different.

The new boots Joker Joe had proudly presented to her sounded noisy on the wooden stairs, and she hoped the racket wouldn't wake Madeline in the unlikely event her friend had found the solace of sleep.

Madeline was expecting Evan's baby! The thought rang over and over in her head as she climbed the stairs, producing in her, if she was honest with herself, a feeling of gladness.

A baby! Her head whirled when she thought of all that had come out this afternoon. That was why her friend so often looked pale and drawn, why she barely touched the food on her plate. It also meant that Madeline and Evan had . . . She swallowed hard.

It meant Madeline and Evan had done what she'd very nearly done with Jack only two nights ago. A sudden thrill passed through her as she thought of the magic of Jack's hands and Jack's lips . . . and Jack's body. With God as her witness, stopping what they'd started the other night had been the single hardest thing she'd ever done in her life. The sometimes chaste, sometimes fevered kisses that had been inflicted upon her in the past by various beaux had not prepared her for the flood of wild, passionate feelings that Jack had loosed inside her. "I want to love you, Anna," he'd whispered in her ear as he pressed himself boldly against her on the blanket he'd laid in the sweet prairie grass. Under the star-studded velvet sky his hands had stoked a powerful fire within her, a blaze she knew only he could quench. "Oh God, Anna, I want you to be my wife," he'd said, "but I don't think I can wait that long. I want you to be mine, for now and for always."

If a next time occurred before Jack had a chance to talk to Evan about setting a wedding date, she didn't think she'd have the strength to say no.

She'd known that something had gone on between Evan and Madeline. The deep sadness in her friend and the ambiguous note she'd seen on the chair in the first floor bedchamber, written in her brother's unmistakable hand, had been her initial evidence. That, coupled with Madeline's unwillingness to talk about Evan, or even say his name, had made her nearly certain that Madeline was in love with Evan—and that Evan had done something abominable.

She was sure Evan didn't do or say hurtful things deliberately; when they were growing up, her elder brother's disposition had been amiable, good-humored, even exuberantly playful at times. But since the breakup of his engagement with Melissa Morris he'd become silent, withdrawn, and cheerless. For the past four years he'd been an utterly unhappy man, a man in need of the love of a good woman.

In her heart she knew Madeline was just the woman for him.

She hoped the two of them could overcome their differences. Hellfire! They'd *better* overcome their differences; there was the matter of her very first niece or nephew to consider.

Pausing in front of the door to Madeline's bedchamber, Anna thought of all the unpleasantness her friend had endured this afternoon. She didn't think she'd ever seen a soul in such torment, such pain. When her thick-skulled brother deigned to speak with her about her running away from Chicago—and she knew that lecture would be coming—she would speak right back to him about how women ought to and ought not to be treated by men.

"Madeline?" she said softly, rapping on the door with her knuckles. "It's me, Anna. Can you open up, please?"

She was surprised when the door opened a moment later.

Madeline looked pale and wan—in a word, terrible. Her eyes and cheeks were swollen from crying, and her hair and clothing were hopelessly rumpled. Anna's heart went out to her, and she felt tears prickle in her own eyes. Making a sympathetic exclamation, she wrapped her arms around her friend and held her tight.

Madeline didn't pull away from her. Sobs shook the blond woman's shoulders for an eternity, it seemed, as Anna stroked her friend's hair and tried to comfort her as best she could. "There, there," she murmured when the worst of the emotional storm was over, "it's not as bad as all that."

"It isn't?" With a loud sniff, Madeline stepped back. Wetness glistened on her face in the fading light.

"Not at all," she responded firmly, reaching into her pocket and fishing out a clean handkerchief. "Here," she said, extending the cloth toward Madeline. "Dry your tears, dear. Surely all this weeping can't be good for your little one. And neither is starvation," she added gently. "Won't you let me bring you up some food?"

Madeline shook her head. "I'm just not hungry." Wiping the dampness from her face with the frilly-edged handkerchief, she raised dark-shadowed eyes to Anna. "Y-you don't hate me?" Madeline asked hesitantly, her voice quavering.

"Of course I don't hate you!" Anna exclaimed, giving her an impulsive hug. "Oh, Madeline, why should I hate you? You're one of the most wonderful people I've ever known, and I couldn't be happier that we're going to be family." Taking Madeline's cold hands in hers, she gave them a reassuring squeeze. "I'll admit I was a bit taken aback when I heard Will roaring to Evan about you being bred like . . . like one of his cows, but you aren't going to be the first of my friends to be delivered of a fine healthy 'premature' child some seven or eight months after the wedding. I suspect it's been happening for centuries."

"B-but Evan doesn't want to marry me!"

"Oh, pish. Evan wouldn't say he'd marry you unless he loved you." At Madeline's protests, she held up her hands. "No, no, now, listen to me. He loves you. He would not have said he'd marry you unless he truly wanted to. I've known Evan a whole lot longer than you have, Maddie, and after what happened with—"

"With Melissa Morris," Madeline interrupted in a distressed voice. Tears welled up in her eyes again and came perilously close to spilling over her dark lashes. "Who is she, Anna? Ever since you said her name that day, I haven't been able to get it out of my head. Is Evan still in love with her?"

"No, he isn't, and I don't think he ever truly was." Anna sighed. "Let's go in and sit down, and I'll tell you some things about Evan he'll probably tan my hide for." She guided her friend toward the rumpled bed in the center of the shadowed room. "You do love Evan, don't you?" she asked, satisfied when she saw the tragic answering nod. "Then let me tell you of some things that happened one summer, about four years ago," she began. "I don't know all the facts—I expect Evan and Melissa are the only ones who do—but I do know enough to have put some pretty good assumptions together."

With a silent shudder of distaste, Anna thought of how close Melissa Morris had come to being her sister-in-law. She'd never liked the sly raven-haired woman and couldn't understand what Evan had seen in her. Thank goodness something had happened to prevent their joining, and judging from the not-so-quiet whispers of Melissa's many indiscretions that had circulated Chicago in the past years, she had a very good idea of what that something was.

Before she could speak, galloping horses and men's shouts could be heard. Turning quickly toward the window, she strained her eyes trying to spy the source of the commotion through the deepening shadows. "What on earth—" she began, as the shouting grew even louder.

Madeline was at her side in an instant. "Something's wrong," she exclaimed. "Someone must be hurt! They wouldn't be making all that noise if someone wasn't hurt! Oh, Anna, if anything's happened to Evan, I'll never forgive myself. . . ."

Already Madeline had left the window and was hurriedly pulling on her boots. "Come on!" she urged. "We've got to get downstairs and light the lamps!"

Amid the fumbling flurry of lighting lamps in the nearly dark kitchen, Anna felt all thumbs. Finally two lamps were lit, just as Artie Hamilton burst in through the door and shouted, "They're bringin' him in here! He's lost a lot of blood, but he ain't dead yet." Artie was scared; his face reflected his fear in the flickering lamplight.

Cold fingers of dread gripped Anna's stomach as Madeline closed her eyes tight and whispered, "Who is it?"

"It's Reed!" exclaimed the agitated man over his shoulder, peering out the door. "Came upon the rustlers . . . got hisself shot."

The sound of Evan's voice rose over the babble of male voices. "Take him down easy, now," he ordered. "Someone's got to keep pressure on this rag. No, dammit, not like that. And someone take care of this horse. We damn near killed it."

The sound of loud moaning came in through the open door. Artie waved his hands urgently. "Up here, up here, come on," he shouted into the darkness. "Did someone go for Ashler's ma?"

An unidentifiable voice confirmed that someone had already left to fetch Mrs. Ashler. "Hope she makes it in time . . . oh, Jesus! Look at that blood! Careful, now! Put him right here on the table." The creak of the porch steps was lost amid the din of thudding bootsteps, male grunts, and Will's piteous sounds of pain as he was maneuvered through the doorway and onto the table.

Anna had never seen so much blood in her life. The foreman seemed to be saturated in it, and a dark trail stained the floor from the doorway to the table. Panic threatened to overwhelm her as Evan strode in after the other men, his face grim.

His sleeves and entire torso were covered with blood as well.

"Maddie," he ordered, "bring us some whiskey, blankets—No! Get me a knife first. We've got to cut his shirt off. Someone set some water to boiling, too. Shit, we've got to work fast. He's bleeding too damn much."

"Anna, bring me the whiskey," Madeline spoke urgently, already rolling up her sleeves. "You know where it is, don't you? Find some sheets and blankets, too. I don't care which ones you use. Just grab anything."

Her friend's calm presence of mind served to check the

hysteria rising inside Anna, and she ran to find the requested items, realizing that the blood covering Evan belonged to Will. So much blood. Could a man lose that much blood and still live? She wished desperately that Jack could be here right now. She needed him, needed his strength.

Will just couldn't die, she told herself. He just *couldn't*. Though the Spencer foreman was as gruff and grouchy as they came, she had grown quite fond of him. Almost at once after meeting him, she had seen through his rough exterior to the soft heart beneath.

"Oh, dear Lord," she prayed, snatching a bottle of spirits from the tall cabinet in the sitting room, "please let him live." The light in the room was poor, and eerie shadows played on the wall, cast by the group of agitated men surrounding the kitchen table.

"Here," she called loudly, dashing to the doorway of the kitchen, "someone take this." The liquid in the bottle sloshed loudly as she handed it off to a terrified-looking young man whose name she couldn't remember. The first floor bedroom was dark, but she rapidly stripped the bed by feel and hurried back to the kitchen, her arms clamped tight around the linens.

"Please don't let Will die." She repeated her plea, not realizing her lips moved along with the words in her mind. The West had shown its savage side to her tonight, and now a good man's life hung in the balance. The crime, the killings, the lawlessness—all the accounts she'd heard about the untamed country west of the Mississippi were true and very real.

Tripping on the tail of the sheet that hung between her legs, she stumbled into the kitchen. Helpful hands took her burden from her, and she had a glimpse of Will's pallid, pain-contorted face before the group closed around him. She was horrified to see that the floor beneath the table shone with dark redness, and that all the men were standing in—and sliding in, and skidding in—Will's lifeblood.

Suddenly she felt sick.

Edging backward toward the wall, she began to recite a prayer from her childhood.

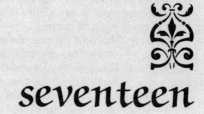

seventeen

"HURRY UP WITH THAT WHISKEY!"

A scared-faced boy of no more than eighteen pushed his way forward. "H-here it is, mister. I got it. Gosh, is Reed gonna die?"

Another cowhand had just finished slitting Reed's shirt open and pulling the fabric aside to expose the injury. Evan looked up from the blood-soaked rag he held against the rasping wound on the upper right side of the ranch foreman's chest. "Not if I can help it. Now open that bottle and pour some whiskey down his throat, pronto," he ordered young Ned Triggs, feeling dark dread course through him at the severity of Reed's injury. "And be damned careful you don't make him choke on it."

The ranch foreman's complexion was gray, his breathing rapid and labored. His eyes were tightly closed, and an expression of unspeakable agony contorted his features. Evan could only imagine the effort it cost the big man to endure his pain without screaming.

"Here, let me help you, Ned," Madeline said firmly, pushing her way forward. "Would some of you please step back? Will needs all the air he can get." The sea of anxious cowboys parted and allowed her to pass. Standing at the head of the table, she gently maneuvered Reed's head into the cradle of her arms and raised it just enough to meet the mouth of the bottle. Together Madeline and the young cowhand managed to get a little of the amber liquid down Reed's throat without causing him to gag.

Watching Madeline as she dauntlessly comforted the injured man—smoothing his hair, murmuring soothingly, pressing soft kisses on his forehead—Evan knew that she was a rare woman indeed. Despite her friend's blood and pain, she exuded a calm confidence as she tended to him.

He wished he felt as self-assured as she looked. He also knew the bullet had to come out of Reed's chest. Jesus! He and Reed had been riding along a low ridge several miles away from the ranch house, an uneasy truce in effect between them, when they spied unfamiliar riders running a good-sized group of cows and calves toward the north.

With a bellow of outrage, Reed had kicked his horse into a gallop and given chase, pulling his pistol from his holster. The noise of the cattle and the dust hanging in the air had disguised the two of them until they'd drawn quite close to the two men riding at the rear of the small herd. Then one of the rustlers had turned his head and spotted them. With a yell to his companion from beneath the dark-colored handkerchief he wore over his nose and mouth, he'd opened fire. The other man, similarly disguised, had also turned and started firing.

Will was struck almost at once, before either he or Evan could get a shot off. With a loud cry, he'd clutched his chest and miraculously managed to bring his mount to a stop before crumpling sideways and falling heavily to the ground. Evan had gone to him immediately, feeling more than one bullet whiz dangerously close to his head.

The rustlers continued to run the noisy, bawling cattle to the north at a dangerous speed as Evan hauled the semiconscious foreman back on his horse, then climbed up behind him to hold him upright and keep pressure on the bleeding hole in his chest. . . .

"Reed ain't got time to wait for no one to git here," a tall, serious-looking cowhand asserted, pulling him back to the unpleasant task at hand and confirming what Evan already knew. "That bullet gots to come out of him right now."

A desperate feeling passed through Evan, making him aware of his limitations—and of the limitations of their circumstances. They had no daylight, no doctor, no instruments. Watching Will Reed's big chest strain to move air in and out, Evan knew that as surely as the sun had set behind the mountains to the west, the life was draining out of the Spencer ranch foreman whose color was even worse that it had been before.

And Will Reed was a man so full of life, whether sitting commandingly astride his horse, going about his duties on the ranch . . . or defending a young woman's honor. He remembered the bull-like way Reed had charged him and knocked him into the dirt only hours before. It was obvious how much the gruff man loved his friend's daughter and—Evan glanced quickly at the blond head bent over the pain-furrowed brow—how much Madeline loved him in return. The thought struck him, also, that only one hour ago Reed had been healthy and whole.

"Anyone ever dug out a bullet before?" His voice came out harsh, thick with emotion.

The room was silent except for the labored sounds of Reed's breathing.

Evan kept steady pressure on the wound, failing to entirely stanch the flow of blood but at least stifling the horrible wet noise. The shot had punctured Reed's lung, he surmised, but where the bullet now rested was anyone's guess.

"Come on, we need a taker!" he said desperately. "I've never done it, either!"

"Reed's done it," Artie Hamilton offered, adding sheepishly, "but I s'pose he can't do it now." The glares of the other men nearly burned Artie to a crisp, and he raised his hands defensively, muttering, "Sorry, but he *is* the only one I can think of that done it before."

Reed opened his eyes and struggled to raise his head, fixing a tortured stare on Evan. "Damn . . . someone better . . ." he managed to say, his wheezing words barely audible, before his eyes rolled upward.

"Do something, Evan!" Madeline lowered Will's head and looked up at Evan, her green eyes bright with unshed tears. "He's going to die if you don't do something!"

A bleak chill settled in Evan's soul at the thought of the big man never rising again. Madeline's gaze locked with his own for a long moment, during which he read the fear and quiet desperation in her eyes. Taking a deep breath and moving the rag aside, he said, "All right. I'll give it a try. Splash some of that whiskey over here."

The young cowhand liberally poured from the bottle, causing whiskey and blood to mix in a swirling pattern on Reed's hairy, hard-muscled chest and run over his right shoulder and down his ribs. A soft, sucking sound issued from the damaged flesh. The bleeding had slowed, Evan noticed, but whether it was due to the pressure he'd held on the wound or because Reed was just plain running out of the stuff, he couldn't say.

Do it, Grant.

He took another deep breath, wiped his fingers on a cold, soapy rag someone had thrust into his hands, and hesitantly inserted his little finger into the hole in Reed's chest, wondering if even this finger was too large to fit. He knew he never could have done it at all if the foreman had not lost consciousness. He couldn't recall ever seeing anyone in so much pain as Reed had been in, and he swore to himself that he was going to track down the bastards who had done this.

Probing gently, he felt a sharp, splintered area where the bullet must have struck a rib. The smell of blood and whiskey was sharp in his nostrils. *Oh, God, Grant, your finger is inside a man's chest.* Though what he was doing seemed unreal, the magnitude of his actions and the terrible responsibility he had assumed brutishly walloped him over the head.

His knees trembled.

Squeezing the muscles of his thighs, he tried to reassert control over his body—and failed miserably. His knees continued to tremble. Sweat beaded on his brow and ran from beneath his arms, and he felt as if he couldn't quite catch his breath.

It was tight in there—damned tight. Gently rotating his hand so the palm faced up, he pushed his finger inside the wound a little farther. Still nothing. Nothing that felt like a bullet, anyway. He cursed to himself, wishing he could use a longer, more dexterous digit. His little finger felt as bungling and unwieldy as the thumb of his left hand.

The ranch hands had spread back from the table, allowing him room to work. Glancing at the head of the table, he saw that Madeline remained there. Tears shone on her cheeks as she silently continued to stroke Reed's hair, and she met his gaze with unspoken support and encouragement.

He had to find the damned bullet; he just had to. Taking another deep breath and ignoring the jellylike quivering in his lower limbs, he changed the angle of his finger and tentatively explored upward. The sharp edge of a rib scraped his knuckle, but still he couldn't feel the bullet. "I can't," he muttered, frustration pouring through him. "I just can't find it. I don't know if the bullet's down under his ribs or—"

"Let me try," came Madeline's plea. She moved around the table to stand next to him. "My fingers are smaller than yours."

"Are you sure you want to—"

"What choice is there? Look at him!"

Glancing at the big man's face, he saw that his color was worse. Even in unconsciousness, Reed's body labored for air. How much longer, Evan wondered, before the struggle would be just too much? The clean, familiar scent of Madeline's hair pushed away the unpleasant smell of blood as she looked up at him in silent appeal. Golden lamplight accentuated the planes and angles of her face, the face he had so often dreamed of in the past weeks, and, as always, he felt as if he were drowning in the brilliant green depths of her dark-lashed eyes.

Nodding, he slowly removed his finger. Without hesitation, Madeline wiped her hands on the cold, soapy rag. Her hand was immediately there to take the place of his, her knuckles brushing against his for a brief moment.

Stepping back, allowing her room to work, he watched as she probed the area around the wound with gentle yet deft fingers before softly sliding the tip of her index finger into the bubbling, hissing hole. An expression of intense concentration crossed her face, and she closed her eyes while she gradually worked her finger into the wound. Her left hand didn't remain idle; with it she continued to push and gently probe the area around the wound in a systematic manner.

Watching her work, Evan was nearly overwhelmed with pride and emotion at her pluck. Not so much as a flicker of revulsion crossed her face as she gave every ounce of her attention to searching for the bullet. He saw, too, that her face had grown thinner since he'd last seen her, but, if anything, she was lovelier than ever, her beauty more sharply defined.

You fool, you almost lost her. The thought frightened him, frightened him ten times more than the thought of marrying her. He studied the dark plum-colored shadows beneath her eyes, drank in the familiar tousled blond hair that sprouted nearly every which way from her braid. As soon as he could convince this golden beauty that he honestly *wanted* to marry her—and, he added to himself uncomfortably, after he'd apologized for the abysmal way he'd left her, and the way he'd proposed to her—he was going to take great delight in turning Miss Madeline Spencer into Mrs. Madeline Grant.

The idea that of becoming a father would take some getting used to, but the thought of their child growing in her womb—and one day suckling at her breast—produced stirrings of warmth and tenderness and, to be perfectly truthful, a great deal of awe inside him.

Madeline's left hand stopped its searching motion. She took in a deep breath, let it out, and pushed with her second and third fingers over the area approximately two inches above the bullet wound. "There," she said softly, repeating the word a moment later in a much firmer voice. "There. I feel it."

Sighs of relief broke from everyone assembled, and a

buzz of sudden nervous male chatter arose in the room, drowning out her next words.

"Shhh. Quiet! Quiet down!" Evan's voice rose above the others.

"Pipe down!" the tall, serious-looking cowboy seconded. "It's as noisy as a calf corral in here, and that bullet ain't out yet. Now, what were you sayin', Miss Madeline?"

A sober, uneasy silence again settled on the room while she spoke. "I said I can't get it," she spoke in a small, defeated voice, opening her eyes and looking around the room. "I can feel it, but I can't get my finger around it. See? It's right here."

The cowhands moved in for a closer look as she first pointed to the spot, then moved her left hand away. With the finger inside Will's chest, she pushed upwards causing a small bulge to appear on the slab of muscle below his collarbone.

"The lead musta gone in there and bounced back an' forth atween his ribs and shoulder bones," a short, kind-faced man spoke from the rear of the group. Looking over the heads of the others, Evan noticed that the man held his sister's hand, patting it awkwardly. Annalisa's face looked bloodless, but she met his quick glance with brave nod.

"What does that mean, Joe?" Anna asked in a shaky voice.

"Well, woulda been better if it'd come straight out—"

"Goddamn, they're gonna pay for this!" another man exploded, interrupting Joker Joe McCaleb. "Stealin' our cattle from right under our noses, like they know right where we ain't gonna be and when, and now shootin' Reed! Each and every one of them dirty fuc—"

A loud babble of dire threats arose, the mood in the kitchen turning ugly and vindictive. Evan saw Madeline say something, but her words were lost in the din. Shouting even louder than before, he made himself heard over the angry, worried men. "What did you say, Maddie?" he asked as soon as the ferocious buzz of voices quieted.

"I said, 'Shame on you all!'" With a quelling look she went on. "You can catch the rustlers and do whatever you will with them—later. Right now Will needs your silence and your prayers. And *I* need a very sharp knife. Who's got the sharpest and cleanest?"

Joe stepped forward from amid the self-conscious murmurs of, "Sorry, Miss Madeline," from the subdued men. "My knife's a good one," he said. "Take it."

"Wash it very well with soap and water first," she ordered. "Is that water boiling yet?"

"It's hot, but it ain't boilin' yet, Miss Madeline," a voice reported. "It should only be another few minutes. I got the stove fired up hotter'n a bitch in—"

"It'll have to do," she interrupted, firing off more orders. "Anna, run and get my sewing basket. Ready me a needle with the stoutest thread you can find, and bring the scissors, too. Someone bring one of those lamps closer so I can see what I'm doing."

Anna left to find the sewing basket, and Joe quickly and obediently set to washing his knife. Two of the men held the lamps so close that Evan was uncomfortably aware of their heat. The quizzical looks on the faces of the cowboys told him that they were every bit as baffled by her orders as he was, and it was on the tip of his tongue to ask her what the hell she thought she was going to do with the knife when he had a flash of comprehension. "You're going to make a cut and push the bullet up through it, aren't you?"

"Mm-hmm," she replied amid the murmurs of understanding from the assembled men. Her eyes were closed again, and with the fingertips of her left hand she delicately palpated the area she'd pointed out—trying to pinpoint the bullet's shape and location, Evan knew.

"Let me make the cut for you," he said, feeling his constitution rail at the idea of cutting into the flesh of a live man, but at the same time wanting to protect her from what was sure to be an unnerving experience. "You shouldn't have to do something like that, sweetheart," he quickly amended, lest she take offense at what she perceived to be high-handedness. "Reed's like family to you. Besides, it would be cumbersome to use your left hand for such a delicate task."

"Okay," she said abruptly, surprising him by not resisting him or arguing. Her eyes opened wide for a long moment, during which he could read the gratitude and fatigue in the deep green eyes that studied him. "Thanks," she added with a little more softness before returning to her task.

Anna entered the kitchen with the sewing materials at the same time Joker Joe placed the clean hot knife in Evan's hand, and suddenly it was time to make the cut. He closed his fingers tightly around the haft of the tool, feeling it sear his skin. Though the inside of his mouth was drier than dust, he swallowed, feeling his heart beating in the back of his throat.

Piercing Reed's chest was the hardest thing he'd ever done, though in retrospect he reflected that the deed had been accomplished rather quickly and easily. "Don't cut my finger," Madeline admonished softly when the tip of the knife entered Reed's muscle. Taking a steadying breath, Evan pushed a little deeper with the knife. Damn, he thought, the man's hide was tough. He'd have to tell him that someday. Blood welled up around the blade, and he wondered what Reed would think if he came to right at this moment.

"You're almost there," Madeline said. "I can feel it."

Thunder rumbled far off, and a strong gust of wind shook the house. Concentrating on putting just the proper amount of pressure on the blade, Evan was only barely aware of the outdoor sounds. They registered in his subconscious along with the muffled whispers and sounds of breathing and the honest smell of men and horses from around him in the close, tense room.

"Stop. Move the knife away," Madeline commanded, just as he felt metal touch metal.

He complied immediately, only too glad to let go of the hot knife. Then, gently as a whisper, Madeline slipped her left index finger into the small cut he'd made. The room was perfectly silent, everyone's breathing suspended, while outside thunder rumbled again. Madeline's eyes had squeezed tightly shut once more, and sweat gleamed on her brow and upper lip.

"Oh, thank you, God," she said in a rush, as her pent-up breath left her. The deformed bullet surged up and out of the cut, followed by a brief flash of the finger that was still inside Reed's chest. "I want more soap and water," she ordered a heartbeat later, "and bring me the needle and thread." Lifting her gaze, she met Evan's eyes with silent, triumphant communication.

The relief of the assembled men was immediate and obvious. "Good work, Miss Madeline," Joker Joe proclaimed as the sighs and murmurs and sounds of shuffling feet died down. "I ain't never seen nothin' like that in my life, and I think I speak for all of us here by sayin' that I'm so proud of ya that I could bust."

"Me, too," Evan mouthed during the chorus of agreement that followed Joe McCaleb's short speech. A pink blush appeared on Madeline's cheeks, and she looked away from him, back down at her hands.

"Even if Reed don't pull through this—" Joe's voice cracked, but he continued—"we all know that it weren't for lack of tryin'." His Adam's apple worked up and down, and he blinked his eyes furiously.

Another, closer, clap of thunder sounded. "That storm's movin' at more miles an hour than I like to think about," Joe said, speaking to the assembled men in a brusque voice. "Come on, we've got plenty to do an' not much time till it hits. Besides, Reed'd be pissed as hell if he came to an' saw us all standin' around starin' at him instead of seein' to the stock."

The room cleared rapidly with a good deal of angry, frustrated muttering about the storm obliterating all traces of the rustlers. Anna handed Madeline the needle and thread, looking as though she might faint or lose the contents of her stomach—or both. Evan put his arm around her and kissed her cheek, whispering in her ear, "You don't look so good, sis."

"I don't feel so good, either," she confirmed, tears welling up in her blue eyes. "And I'm awfully scared Will might die."

Madeline looked up from the first stitches she had made. "Anna, why don't you have Evan take you upstairs to my room, or, if you like you can use the room down the hall from mine. We'll have to put Will in the downstairs bedroom—" She broke off, her gaze shifting uncomfortably from Anna to Evan and back to Anna again.

Was she remembering? he wondered. Did she think of their night together as often as he did?

The first drops of rain hit the house, driven by fierce winds. Thunder boomed and cracked, following closely blinding flashes of lightning. "I'll be back down to help you directly," he said to Madeline, taking a lamp and guiding Anna from the kitchen. From the corner of his eye he saw that Madeline had returned to her task and didn't look up.

After seeing Anna to Madeline's plain but comfortable room, he returned to the kitchen. With her embroidery scissors she snipped a black thread, the little blades gleaming in the lamplight. Noticing him, she said, "It's done." She set the scissors down beside Reed and shook her head. "I sewed up both wounds, but I don't . . . oh, I don't.—"

Evan watched helplessly as she dissolved into tears. Head bowed, she picked up one of Reed's big hands and clasped it between her own. "Please, Will, you just h-have to make it. I don't think I could bear it if you . . ."

Thickness rose in his throat at the pitiful sight of Madeline sobbing over Will Reed's unconscious form. "Oh, sweetheart," he said awkwardly, "we did the best we could for him."

"But what if that's not enough?" she demanded to know, her voice raw with pain.

"Then it's not," he replied gently, moving across the room. "But for now it is." He slipped his hands over her shoulders from behind, noticing that they stiffened slightly. Strands of silky hair brushed his knuckles and made his hands itch to untwist the golden plait and bury his fingers in her soft, flowing tresses. He bent his head toward her, inhaling her unique essence.

"Madeline," he said, not able to help himself from bending his head and brushing a feather-soft kiss over the sculptured folds of a delicate ear. "Sweetheart . . . let me hold you. You need me . . ." Moving around her, he stroked her jaw with his knuckles and raised her face to meet his. "And I need you."

"Don't . . . do this to me," she sobbed, still clinging to Reed's hand.

Gently he disentangled her fingers from the unconscious man's and replaced them with his own. "I'm going to do all kinds of things to you, Maddie," he whispered. "I want to tell you, too, that your father isn't the only hero in the Spencer family. Watching you work tonight . . . Well, what you did tonight was braver than anything Nate Spencer ever did."

Drawing her even closer, he enfolded her in his embrace, realizing this was the first time he'd held her with both his arms. She sagged against him and sobbed harder, the storm inside her breaking open much like the storm that raged around them. Her arms rested between them woodenly, and though a halfhearted hug was less than he had hoped for, he thought it was at least a start.

Just then Reed groaned in the back of his throat. Madeline jumped suddenly, as if she'd been burned by fire. Speaking in a rush, she wiped her eyes against her upper arm, taking great care not to look in Evan's direction. "I have to finish washing the blood off him; then I've got to dress these wounds." Already she had moved away from him and immersed her hands in a basin of water. "Pour some of that hot water into a clean basin, will you?" she directed as she wrung out a cloth. "This water's all bloody. Oh, and you'll have to add some cold to it; otherwise it'll burn him. Then we'll need a couple more men to help move him to the bedroom."

She'd rebuffed him.

He let his arms drop to his sides, staring after her trim figure. He hadn't expected her to simply fall into her arms . . . or had he? Rain beat against the south and west sides of the house, filling the kitchen with the noise. A keen sense of frustration rose in him.

Maybe he should have told her he loved her.

No, he answered himself. *Better to show her.* He knew better than anyone that such words were just that—only words, totally meaningless without truth and substance.

After the way he'd proposed to her . . . hell, she was right. He'd made the kind of marriage offer that no woman in her right mind would want to hear. Right now Madeline didn't trust him . . . and rightfully so.

He didn't have long to dwell on his thoughts before Reed groaned again. Seeing that the big man's grizzled head also moved slightly, he hurried to help Madeline wash and dress the wounds before the foreman fully regained consciousness.

"You done what you could, lamb. There's no use frettin' any more about what you coulda or shoulda done different."

Madeline sighed and looked into Mary Ashler's benevolent face in the darkened first floor bedroom, knowing in her heart that she should have done something more for Will, or at least something different, but not knowing what that something could be. For the past three and a half hours she and Mrs. Ashler had sat watch over Will as he clung tenaciously to life, breath by labored breath.

The lamp burned low on the dresser, just as it had the night Evan had first lain injured in this very bed. And, like Evan, Will now rested quietly, thanks to the pain-relieving qualities of laudanum. She and Mrs. Ashler had managed to coax several drops of the tincture down Will's throat earlier while he was semiconscious.

The hard wooden chair pressed even more uncomfortably into Madeline's back and buttocks as she shifted her position. A vicious gust of wind rattled the bedroom windows, making a shiver run through her. The rain had long since quit, but a harsh wind continued to blow and moan.

"Just listen to that wind carryin' on out there," Mrs. Ashler whispered in the dim room. "If I never get caught in a storm like that again, it'll be too soon. All that thunder an' lightning! Heaven, I thought me an' my Robbie was gonna get blowed right off the edge of the earth on our way over here. He done good with the horses drivin' us here, though I was right proud of him. But I think his heart about broke in two when he came in an' saw Reed. Next to his pa, rest his soul, there ain't a man on earth Robbie admires

more. If Will don't pull through this, it's gonna be awful
tough on him. I wonder how the boy's doin' now? Boy?
Listen to me! Robbie's not a boy anymore; he's almost a
full-growed man." She sighed deeply. "I try not to worry
about him, but there's some things a mother just can't help.
And what about that Mr. Grant? I worry about him, too. He
ain't no cowhand, is he?"

Without waiting for an answer, she continued. "I understand he came back to fetch his sister. I like that girl, I
gotta say. I think she's got an interest in Jack Matthews,
too. Now, them two would make a good pair, wouldn't
they? Jack's a good man. His brother's a little . . . well, a
little too much to take in more than small doses, shall we
say? But Jack would make a fine husband, even though I
think they're really strugglin' to make it with that ranch
of theirs. I wonder how bad the cattle spooked during the
storm? They're prob'ly spread out from Texas to Montana
Territory an' still runnin' for all they're worth. . . ."

Madeline was unable to concentrate while the older woman talked. Evan had left—hours and hours ago—with the
men he'd called in to help move Will. "The Spencer ranch
is down two good men now," he'd pointed out to them after
Will was safely abed, and almost before he could offer his
help, they had recruited him. She didn't know how she felt
about that, but with one of those long looks of his, the kind
that seemed to penetrate right through her skin and into her
inner workings, he was gone, following Wayne Johnson and
Artie Hamilton out the door.

She didn't know how she felt about his sudden turn of
tenderness in the kitchen, either. It had confused her, but
she also felt the beginnings of a cautious optimism. Maybe
he really did have some feelings for her.

He had offered marriage. . . .

Smelling his familiar scent and being held tight against
his powerful chest had felt even better than she'd dreamed
it would. Too, the kiss on her ear had made gooseflesh stand
up on the entire left side of her body. Remembering the way
he'd been forced to propose, though, her optimism faded.

She was back to being confused. And worried about
him.

That was ridiculous, she told herself. Evan was a full-grown man, perfectly capable of taking care of himself. But then again, handling stampede-prone cattle was more than a challenge during dry daylight hours. Here it was, somewhere past the middle of the night, dark and windy and muddy, and he was attempting to do something that even seasoned cowhands would find difficult.

Mrs. Ashler tapped her on the knee, pulling her back to the present. "I said, you're looking mighty peaked, Madeline Claire. Are you all right, dear? You seem a million miles away. Are you feeling unwell? You know, if I didn't know any better . . ." she started to say absently. "Oh, never mind. . . ." She trailed off, sighing deeply. "Why don't you run along off to bed and get yourself some sleep, child? We ain't doin' nothing for this big galoot except lookin' at him and prayin' for him, and I guess I can do enough of that for both of us."

"I don't think I could sleep."

"You don't, huh? Then you should take a good look at yourself in the glass. Your peepers are hangin' at half-mast, an' I don't know if I ever seen shadows so big and purple as you got underneath—"

Will stirred slightly, mumbling something unintelligible. Walking over to the bed, Mrs. Ashler placed one of her plump hands on his forehead. "Shhh, now, Will. Everything's fine. You go on back to sleep." To Madeline, she added, "At least he ain't got a fever. If anything, he's a little on the cool side. His dressings are still dry, too."

"Well, maybe I will go up and see if I can get a little rest," Madeline said, feeling every bit of the exhaustion that seemed to be visible on her face. There was the baby to think of. "Wake me if you need any help."

eighteen

EVAN HAD HEARD OF EATING HUMBLE PIE; NOW he knew what it tasted like.

With chagrin, he recalled his fumbling, inexperienced attempts at handling cattle on the open range. Throughout the long night he'd done one useless, wrong, and ungainly thing after another. It was a wonder the other cowhands hadn't sent him packing . . . or left him to his own devices.

Then, after the storm had passed and the cattle were under control, and as soon as it was light enough to see, McCaleb and several of the men had asked him to take them to the place where he and Reed had seen the rustlers.

To his mortification, he couldn't find the ridge. Not for sure, anyway.

"It's all right, Grant," Joker Joe had said to him quietly, though in a heavy voice, well over two hours after they'd begun searching for rain-washed tracks of a large group of fast-moving cattle. "You ain't familiar with the land here. Besides that, it was half dark, an' you was workin' hard at keepin' Reed on horseback." He'd sighed deeply before shouting, "Any volunteers to keep on lookin'? The rest of you can go on back an' have breakfast. Then we'll divvy up shifts for sleepin' today. Two hours is all I can give you. Wish it was longer, but that's the way it is."

McCaleb quickly had his two volunteers. Evan noticed with satisfaction that the bandy-legged man had the complete respect of the cowhands; the shift in authority from Reed to Joe had occurred quickly and naturally without a struggle. It was good that things had gone so smoothly, he thought, for otherwise the Spencer ranch would have been in a whole lot more trouble than it already was. He wished like hell he knew more about cattle ranching. He knew so little that even ten of him wouldn't equal one Will Reed.

Just then, as if Joker Joe had been reading his mind, he leaned over and said, "You did fine for your first time out, Grant. Lotsa eastern dandies come out here thinkin' that herdin' a few cows is gonna be a cinch. I think we both know it ain't."

Evan felt each and every ache in his exhausted body during the long ride back to the ranch house. The strong winds that had continued for much of the night had softened into a mild breeze, and the bright sun gleamed on the mountains and grassland. It was actually quite a lovely summer morning, he thought, wondering at the same time if Reed was still alive to appreciate it.

After returning to the ranch, he and McCaleb went directly to the house, skipping breakfast at the cookshack. Stepping into the kitchen, he was surprised to see that the room was spotless. If he hadn't seen for himself what a mess it had been last night, he never would have believed that Reed had leaked a bucket or two of blood on the floor. Joker Joe stared at him with wide eyes, undoubtedly thinking the same thing.

Neither of them spoke. The quiet of the house flowed around them, surrounding them. Holding their hats in their hands, the two of them looked around the immaculate, clean-smelling room. Where was everyone? Where was Madeline? Annalisa? Reed? The oppressive silence made him think of a tomb, and Evan wondered if Reed had already died.

Just then the floor creaked, and the short, generous form of Mrs. Ashler appeared from around the corner, startling them. Evan noticed with satisfaction that McCaleb jumped every bit as much as he did.

The kindly, round-faced woman pressed her index finger to her mouth. "Shhh. I got 'em all sleepin' at once, every last one of 'em."

"Then—"

"Reed made it through the night, if that's what you're askin'," she answered Joker Joe in a low voice, her face serious. "But he ain't out of the woods yet, not by a long ways."

Nodding grimly, Joe added, "And Miss Annalisa? How's she holdin' up? Last night she was . . . well, she was havin' kind of a hard time." He turned to Evan. "I don't guess as I've had the chance to tell you how much we been enjoyin' your little sister's company here. She's 'bout as pretty as an ace-full of queens, an' the girl ain't afraid to try nothin'. Wish they made more like her." With a pause and a quick smile, he delivered the ultimate compliment. "I ain't never seen a woman as full of pranks and wisecracks as her."

Evan flashed a brief smile in return, thinking of Anna's spirited, playful nature.

"Well, she ain't tellin' no jokes this mornin'," Mrs. Ashler said. "I ain't heard a peep out of her yet, or Madeline either, for that matter. The poor little lambs must be exhausted." She shook her graying head. "You know, I gotta say that you boys are lookin' a little rough around the edges this mornin' yourselves. Evan dear, you in particular."

"Sorry, ma'am." Evan mumbled, self-consciously running a hand over his stubbled face.

"I wasn't askin' for an apology. I was just pointin' it out. No, sir, you don't have to be ashamed of puttin' in an honest night's work. Joe, am I right in assumin' you've taken over?" At his nod, she bobbed her head with satisfaction. "Good. Will would like it that way. The men like you. Now, Mr. McCaleb, are you going to let this man have some breakfast before you make him climb back on his horse?"

"Yes'm," Joe replied. "I figured I'd give him a couple hours' sleep, too. Say, you want us to bring you up some breakfast up from the cookshack, Miz Ashler? That way you won't have to cook an' mess up your clean kitchen."

An expression of distaste spread over the broad face. "No. No, thanks," she amended. "But bless your heart for askin'. I actually ain't too hungry after cleanin' up all that blood. Don't worry about me, though," she said, gesturing to her ample hips. "I can live off the land for quite some time. Prob'ly a year or two. Say, Robbie's okay, isn't he?" she asked, changing the subject abruptly. "An' you don't have to go tell him I was askin'. A mother just worries, is all."

"He's fine," Joe reassured her. "We passed him not more than an hour ago, on our way back here. Now, if you'll pardon us, ma'am, we'll be out of your way." He put his hat back on. "Oh, and if you need anything from us today, you just let us know. There'll be men around the place, a few workin' and a few sleepin'."

Evan couldn't suppress the enormous yawn that had built up inside him; he was nearly asleep on his feet. Mrs. Ashler clucked over him again as the good-byes were finished, and then they were out the door.

Screw breakfast, Evan thought as the bright sunlight stabbed daggers into his bleary eyes. Climbing back onto his horse, he decided that he was going to get every minute of his two hours' sleep.

Madeline awoke to the sound of voices. Mrs. Ashler's and . . . whose? Evan's? Will's? No, it didn't quite sound like—

"That's Jack!" Annalisa's head popped up from the other side of the bed. "Oh, my goodness, what time is it? Jack's here! Oh, dear, I can't believe I slept so long!" She bounded out of bed and began dressing in a flurry. "Look—the sun's shining. What time did you come to bed last night, Maddie? What time did Mrs. Ashler make it over? I can't believe I slept so hard. Why didn't she wake us? Oh, Maddie, how do you suppose Will is doing? He must have made it through the night. Mrs. Ashler would have woken us up otherwise, don't you think?"

The all too familiar and thoroughly unpleasant feeling in her stomach, the one that visited nearly every morning now and also at odd times throughout the day, started up as Madeline rolled from her side to her back. Adding to her discomfort, her bladder was near to bursting. Her breasts, too, seemed to have grown overnight. Along her sides they felt bulging and taut, and they pressed uncomfortably against her upper arms. The tips, though, were the most uncomfortable. Her nipples rubbed against the fabric of her nightdress, producing a most maddening, irritating feeling inside her.

"Maddie? Oh, honey, you look awful." Annalisa paused while buttoning her blouse. "Are you unwell again? Oh, dear, how much longer is this going to last?"

"Another two minutes would be too long."

"No, I meant—"

"I know what you meant." She sighed. "Will tells me it's normal for a woman in the family way to be ill every morning for a few months—although I don't know why he knows so much about it," she added under her breath.

Sympathy shone in the blue eyes that regarded her. "Can I do anything for you? Would you like me to bring you up some bread to help settle your—" The sound of Jack's voice came clearly through the floor then, distracting Annalisa.

If Madeline hadn't felt so terrible, she would have smiled. Annalisa was like a little filly, her ears almost visibly pricking up at any mention of Jack Matthews. Knowing he was in the same house, only one floor below, was more than her friend could bear. She knew that Anna truly wanted to offer her comfort, but she also knew that what her friend wanted most to do was to pick up her skirt and run downstairs to see the handsome blond man.

"Just go on, Anna," she said. "Jack might not be able to stay long." As enamored as Jack was of Anna, though, she knew the smitten rancher wouldn't go anywhere until he'd seen his blue-eyed Chicago beauty. With great effort, she swung her legs over the side of the bed. "I'll be down directly. I don't feel any different this morning than I have a whole lot of other mornings. You've just never seen me so early, is all."

Annalisa had already taken a skipping step toward the door. "Are you certain there isn't something I can bring you?"

"Yes, I'll be fine," she replied.

A quarter-hour later she still didn't feel fine. Wearing an everyday cotton dress, the green sprigs on the cream-colored background highlighting her green complexion, she was sure, she finished brushing her hair and tied it in a loose chignon.

The aroma of brewing coffee hit her when she descended the stairs, smelling good but at the same time making the sick feeling in her stomach even worse. Tiptoeing to the first floor bedroom, she peeked inside. Will Reed's eyes were closed, but she saw that his chest rapidly moved up and down. She closed her eyes and let out her breath.

He was alive.

"G'mornin', Miss Madeline," Jack greeted her with a nod when she entered the kitchen. He and Anna sat at the table while Mrs. Ashler was busy at the stove. "I just heard about Reed a little while ago," he said, his brown eyes filled with sadness.

"Mornin', dear," Mrs. Ashler called over her shoulder. "Did you sleep well?"

Still half asleep, Madeline replied that she had, belatedly noticing that the kitchen was immaculate. Not a trace of dirt or blood was to be seen. "Oh, my goodness!" she exclaimed, looking about the room and feeling guilty for sleeping as long as she had. The older woman must not have had any sleep at all. "You cleaned the kitchen."

"Had to," Mrs. Ashler replied, turning her head while stirring a pot with a wooden spoon. "Couldn't stand to look at it no . . . Madeline Claire! Would you look at you! Dear, you look like you didn't have no sleep at all! Anna, Jack, look at her! Would you just look at her! Don't you think she's lookin' peaked? Do you feel like you're comin' down with something, Madeline? You know, I didn't think you looked none too good last night, neither. Your face is all drawn, an' your color ain't no good at all." Directing

Madeline with a broad wave of her arm, she continued. "You go on over and sit down. Go on. I ain't makin' no grand breakfast this mornin', but a bowl of oatmeal ought to be good for what ails you."

Jack and Anna gave her uncomfortable, sympathetic looks as she joined them at the table, and under the table Anna gave her leg a quick pat. She wondered how long it would take Mrs. Ashler to figure out just why she looked the way she did. Not long, she supposed, knowing how long it usually took Mary Ashler to get to the heart of a matter. Especially if the sharp-eyed woman saw her gagging over something as bland as oatmeal.

"Mrs. Ashler said Will came to a while ago," Anna began, filling the silence. "She said he asked for a little water."

"I gave him some more laudanum, too." Over on the other side of the kitchen, a serving spoon clanked against a bowl. "He rests better when he gets it. He don't work so hard to breathe."

"Jack also came by looking for his brother," Anna said meaningfully. "He hasn't seen him since yesterday."

"Yesterday?"

"I was wondering if maybe he came back to . . . ah, visit you again yesterday, Miss Madeline," Jack said.

"Oh. No . . . he didn't." A terrible suspicion grew in Madeline's mind. Seeing the looks on Anna and Jack's faces, she knew they were both thinking the same thing.

"Well, maybe he found shelter or put up in a little shack out somewheres last night when the storm blew up," Mrs. Ashler said sensibly, setting bowls of steaming oatmeal before them. Addressing Jack, she continued, "He'll probably turn up at lunchtime, hungry as can be. Now, I don't care if you did already have your breakfast, young man, I want you to eat up. You'll be glad for the little extra you had when you start lookin' for them cows that are prob'ly stretched out over here, there, and everywhere."

"Yes, ma'am," he obediently answered before adding, "They were sure scattering last night. Me and a couple others was busy over by the river. I didn't see Rendner and Goldie and Payson until this morning, but they said they had a heck of a time last night, too."

Mrs. Ashler set a small pitcher of molasses on the table, then walked back to the stove. "Yeah, Evan and Joe McCaleb straggled in here not too long ago to check on Will, the pair of 'em lookin' as limp as neck-wrung roosters. They didn't say as much, but I gathered they didn't have none too much fun last night, neither. Poor Mr. Grant. I wonder what he thought of his first night ridin' herd?"

Madeline's heart fluttered at the mere mention of Evan's name. In a flash, she recalled the way he'd held her last night, the way he'd looked at her. Just knowing he was here at the ranch made her giddy—a feeling she hadn't had since . . . since the last time he was here.

There wasn't much difference between her and Annalisa after all. Digging her spoon into her oatmeal, she watched thick plumes of steam curl upward. Across the table, Jack poured a healthy amount of molasses on his cereal. Transfixed, she watched him set the pitcher of molasses back down, then watched a dribble of the thick syrup run slowly down the side of the container.

Black, smelly molasses.

That was all it took. Tinny-tasting saliva ran sharp and fast in her mouth, and she quickly excused herself and ran out the door, praying she'd make it to the outhouse in time.

"Oh, God! You!"

Evan shuddered. His heart pounded with agitation at being awoken in such a fashion, and the skin on the entire left side of his body rose in goose flesh. Most repugnant of all was the fact that his left ear was wet with . . . cat slobber.

Sugar sat regally on the empty bunk next to him, staring at him in a smug, superior fashion.

"What's all that noise about?" a cross, sleepy voice asked from across the room. "Ain't time to roll out yet, so just keep your yap shut, will ya?" With a loud harrumph and a few choice words the disgruntled cowboy rolled over and punched his pillow before resettling himself.

With a few choice, though silent, words of his own, Evan reached out as far as he could and swung at the grinning cat. The short-tailed feline merely jumped to another bunk, exhibiting all the effort of a pony stepping over a little hole.

Frustrated and angry, Evan grabbed the sheet and wiped the disgusting wetness from his ear. Just that little amount of movement made him aware of the aches and pains reporting to him from all areas of his body. That he'd been roused from his pleasant dreams to *this* made him mad enough to spit.

He'd been dreaming of Madeline, dreaming she was nuzzling his neck. In fact, he'd even heard her purrs of contentment and felt the warmth of her soft hair as she nestled up against him. The tip of her delicate tongue had caressed the ridges in his ear, fanning the flames of his desire, making him long to press his body full against hers and feel her softness beneath him.

Then came the explosive, wet sneeze.

Oh, God, he thought with even more revulsion than before. How long had that ugly fat cat been snuffling in his ear? And what else had he done to him? A creaking noise made him turn his head, and he saw that someone had left the bunkhouse door slightly ajar. So that was how he got in. It was a relief to know the overgrown rodent couldn't walk through walls.

The door creaked again, allowing a fresh breeze into the less-than-fresh-smelling bunkhouse. Tobacco, sweat, and manure were a few odors he was able to identify; the others he didn't care to know. He did know, though, that he wouldn't want to be within ten miles of the place on a really hot day. And this place was better than most, he supposed, judging by the rough wooden floor and white-washed walls.

Flies buzzed maddeningly overhead and against the windows, and he knew there was no going back to sleep now. With a muffled groan he pushed himself to a sitting position. His eyes felt heavy and gritty, and a dull headache pounded in his temples. When he lifted his arms to rub his eyes, Sugar leapt off the bunk and ran out the door.

The little bastard at least had the sense to know he was pushing his luck.

Evan stood, his muscles groaning from fatigue and overwork. He supposed he might as well get up and check on Reed before he went back out on the range to make a fool of himself again. Though McCaleb had assured him his help was greatly appreciated, he was sure that Robbie Ashler, stripling that he was, handled the stock with a dozen times the skill he did.

But to his way of thinking, with Nate Spencer off in Europe doing God knew what and Will Reed lying close to death in the big house, offering what help he could do was the least he could do.

For Madeline.

His clothes were still a little damp, but at least last night's rain had washed most of Will's blood out of them. As slowly as an old man might move, he stepped over the soiled shirt and trousers and rummaged in his bag for clean clothing. Stiff muscles creaked to life from all areas of his body, but his groin in particular caused him outright pain. Severe pain.

He'd ridden before—plenty, in fact—but never with as much bouncing and straining and jarring and leaning over as he'd done last night. How the hell did these men do what they did, he wondered, day after day? Their balls must be as tough as old leather, he surmised, or maybe by being in the saddle so much, they'd all just worn them off into nubs. He wondered, too, how the hell he was going to climb back into a hard saddle and do it all again today.

For Madeline. The answer came to him in a heartbeat. He'd do it for Madeline.

The cool breeze outdoors made him feel a little better, and by the time he got to the steps of the ranch house he was walking nearly normally. An unfamiliar horse stood tethered to the rail, one that hadn't been there when he and McCaleb had been to the house.

"Hello, Evan," Madeline said quietly, startling him.

She was sitting on the corner of the porch with her back up against the house. He had to crane his neck around the horse to see her. "Mornin', Maddie," he said, walking up the steps, taking in her pallor and the listless way in which she sat. "What are you doing out—" A knowing dread struck him. "Reed? It's Reed, isn't it? Oh, damn, don't tell me he's—"

"No, no," she hastened to say. "He's still the same. Maybe even a little better."

"Well, what's the matter, then?"

"I . . . ah, just needed a little fresh air."

"So you're sitting on the porch in that nice dress?" The last few words of his question sounded somewhere between strained and strangled as he squatted down on his haunches. His entire pelvic area rebelled at the movement. Letting out his breath between gritted teeth, he tried to will away his discomfort. Just then, a faint though unmistakable odor wafted from her to him, and he forgot all about his aches and pains. "Madeline," he exclaimed, "you've been sick!"

"I'll be fine in a little while." Without elaborating further, she closed her eyes and leaned her head back against the clapboard siding. Her delicate hands were folded loosely in her lap, and he noticed that tiny beads of sweat gleamed on her forehead and above her shapely top lip.

Comprehension dawned on him, making him feel guilty and helpless at the same time. He'd heard that women sometimes suffered terrible sickness in the early months of pregnancy. *Pregnancy.* His mouth formed the word, and he thought about what a peculiar a word it was, starting with hard sounds and ending with soft ones.

But then again, maybe it wasn't so peculiar after all. A picture of a newborn babe snuggled in Madeline's arms appeared in his mind, and he could almost hear the hushed, soothing sounds she made as she sang to him . . . her? What sex would their baby be? he wondered. What color hair would he or she have? What color eyes?

A baby—his baby—grew inside the still-flat abdomen of the woman before him. Though there was yet no visible evidence of this marvel in the lower portion of her midsection, his eyes traveled higher, taking in the new lushness of her bustline. His mouth ran dry at the sight.

There was his evidence, plenty of it.

What a heel he was, trying to imagine what her luscious breasts would look like now, what their generous warmth would feel like in his hands, against his mouth, when she was so obviously suffering with sickness. He ought to be shot.

"Let me help you inside," he offered, feeling guilty, taking a hold of one of her hands.

"Just leave me." Her voice was weak and pitiful, making tenderness surge inside him.

"Leave you?" he queried, firmly entwining his hand with hers. Raising her pale, slender fingers to his mouth, he pressed a kiss against her knuckles. "Now, why would I want to do that after I came all this way to see you again?"

Madeline's eyelids flew open, her wariness and sudden tension as easy to read as a child's primer. "You came to get your sister."

"That was only part of it." Sudden nervousness quivered inside him, the kind that had always kept him moving in the past. Taking a deep breath, he forced himself to smile as he looked into the emerald eyes in front of him. "I missed you, Maddie. I came back for you."

There, he'd said it. He'd spoken the truth. Forget all the claptrap about hasty weddings and marriage. First things first. Tentatively he reached out and stroked a downy cheek, hoping that one day soon she'd begin to believe him. Believe *in* him.

Her eyes searched his for a long moment before closing again. Gradually her body relaxed, and he noticed with relief that a little color seemed to have appeared in her cheeks.

"Come on, sweet. I'll take you back in the house," he said, helping her to an upright position. He couldn't disguise his wince when he added, "This cowpuncher's got to get back in the saddle."

Though the peace treaty formalizing the end of hostilities between Prussia and France had been signed in May, Nathaniel Spencer had no idea what he was going to find on this foreign soil. From the accounts he'd heard, France was a place of both horror and heroism.

Having seen firsthand the ravages and lingering results of the War between the States, he hoped that by having the advantage of religious sanctuary, Sara had been unharmed. Aside from worrying about her safety during the recent war, he also prayed to God that no harm had befallen her during the past twenty years.

Twenty years. Sara undoubtedly spoke flawless French by now, a skill he wished like hell he possessed right this minute. He could pick out a few words in the babble around him, but most of what he heard sounded like a meaningless jumble of mushy consonants and strangled, nasal-sounding vowels.

Having disembarked at the port of Le Havre a scant half hour ago, he was only too glad to leave shipboard life behind. It was strange but wonderful to have firm land beneath his feet again, and, smelling the early evening odor of cooking food, he decided the first thing he was going to do on dry land was have a decent meal. Away from the waterfront. Sniffing with distaste, he thought that even fresh calf splatter smelled better than a wharf.

Gripping his bag more tightly, he continued to walk away from the port. He hoped he could make himself understood well enough to find respectable lodging. If he correctly understood the directions he'd received, he had another day's travel before he reached the city where Sara lived. With an early start in the morning, perhaps he'd be there by this time tomorrow.

Tomorrow.

He stopped walking, his stomach suddenly feeling as if a herd of stampeding buffalo had run through it. Oh, God, tomorrow? What if Sara wouldn't see him? What if she saw him but didn't recognize him? Worst of all, what if she'd forgotten him entirely?

You'll never know unless you go.

With a deep, shaking sigh, he shifted his bag from one hand to the other and moved on.

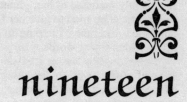

nineteen

 "EVAN GRANT!"

Mary Ashler looked mad enough to eat the devil with his horns on. Wearing her apron, she stood across the kitchen on the opposite side of the table, still holding the spoon with which she'd served the oatmeal.

She knows, Madeline thought with defeat, seeing Jack's and Anna's expressions. Evan pushed the door shut behind him, the arm he held around her first stiffening, then drawing her even closer to him. "You're looking at him, ma'am," he answered blandly.

Sparks flew from Mrs. Ashler's eyes. "Evan Grant, you let her go and come over here right now." Her tone of voice brooked no argument.

"Why don't I just—" Jack started to say, setting down his spoon and scooting his chair backward.

"You just keep your bottom half planted in that chair, sonny," Mary Ashler commanded, shaking the spoon at him with each word. Jack pushed his chair back in place as the older woman looked back and forth between Jack and Anna. "*Both* of you can just sit here and listen to this. Maybe it ain't too late for you two."

Madeline's heart thumped loudly in her chest as Evan assisted her to a chair. Anna's face was white, mirroring the bloodless absence of color in her own, she knew. *Sorry*, she silently mouthed to her, giving her shoulders a helpless shrug. Madeline tried to give her friend a sympathetic smile but failed miserably, jumping in her chair at the force of Mrs. Ashler's next words.

"Come on, boy, move it! I said come over *here*." Evan stepped stiffly over to the other, empty side of the big table, his broad shoulders erect. "Do you see this?" the angry woman asked, pointing to an area on the table.

"See what?"

"See this," she repeated, pointing again.

"See *what*?" Evan's voice was beginning to show impatience, and he reached out to touch the area of the table she'd indicated. "There's nothing—"

Thwack. In a quick arc, the heavy serving spoon struck the back of his hand.

"Ow! Dammit, what are you trying to do, break every bone in my hand?" Madeline saw pain quickly flash on his face before it was replaced with a grim look. Jack and Anna uncomfortably averted their gazes while Evan nursed his gummy hand and wiped the sticky oatmeal residue on his pants.

Mary Ashler brandished the spoon as if it were a formidable weapon. "That ain't the bone that needs to be broke, but it's a start." Shaking her head and lowering the spoon, she tossed it onto the table and placed her hands on her sturdy hips. "Didn't I warn you about this very thing? What in the name of all the saints were you thinkin'?" She exhaled with force. "Well, it's obvious you *weren't* thinkin', not with the head on your shoulders, anyway."

Madeline's eyes widened at the older woman's crude remarks. There was no longer any doubt in her mind that Mrs. Ashler knew about the baby. Evan's face was unreadable as he continued to squarely meet the stout woman's gaze. He stood before her unashamed, uncowed.

Angry pink color suffused Mrs. Ashler's round cheeks. "I reckon you ain't never been in this fix before, have ya?"

"No, ma'am."

"You deny that the babe's yours?"

"No, ma'am."

"You don't, huh?" With each successive word her voice grew in volume. "Well, it don't appear to me that you're feelin' too awful bad about this."

"No, ma'am," he replied for the third time, turning his head and directing a meaningful look directly at Madeline, "I am not."

"You're not?" The bluster seemed to go out of Mrs. Ashler as she caught the look that passed between them. "Well, then . . ."

A shiver passed through Madeline at the intensity in the blue eyes that regarded her. Eyes that could melt her. Eyes that could heat her. Eyes that could turn her absolutely inside out. The unshaven growth on his handsome face served as a startling contrast to their cerulean brilliance, and the discomforts of her body faded as, deep inside, a restless feeling began.

Anna cleared her throat. "There . . . there was talk of a wedding yesterday, Mrs. Ashler," she began, breaking the growing uncomfortable silence. "We didn't get to tell you that part of it before they came in—"

"Maybe there should be some talk of another weddin', too," Mrs. Ashler said pointedly, " 'less we have ourselves another such . . . situation."

Jack blushed a dull red as he looked first at Anna, then at Mrs. Ashler, then at Evan. "There'll be talk of it," he replied, "as soon as it's appropriate. Pete would—"

"Jack, maybe Evan saw Peter last night," Annalisa broke in, adeptly changing the subject. "Did you, Evan?" she asked. "That's why Jack's here this morning," she explained to her brother in a rush. "He hasn't seen him since he left here yesterday."

"Yesterday?" Evan drew his brows together and regarded Jack. His words were slow, grave. "You haven't seen him since yesterday?"

"How did we get from weddin's to Pete Matthews's whereabouts?" Mrs. Ashler demanded, rattling the empty pot on the stove in an unmistakable signal for quiet. "Are you all tryin' to say you think he might be rustlin' cattle? That he was the one who shot Will Reed?" Black skirt swishing, she walked back over to the table and stood next to Jack. "There. I said it. An' I'll also say that your brother ain't no cattle thief. I just know it in my bones. You know, some people spread happiness wherever they go, and, granted, Pete spreads happiness *whenever* he goes, but he ain't got a terrible badness inside him. It's more like bein' different, and bein' misunderstood. He just don't know how to act around folk."

"No one's seen Pete since he left here yesterday," Jack answered Evan's question with a sad, haunted look in his eyes. "Our foreman came in this morning and said he hadn't seen him during the night, either. No one's seen him."

"Who's the law out here?" Evan asked.

"Boswell," Jack replied with a deep, resigned sigh, "but Old Boz ain't around these parts right now."

"I see," Evan said slowly.

"You two don't see nothin'," Mary Ashler snorted, clapping a hand on Jack's shoulder. "Just 'cause you an' your brother's strugglin' to make ends meet don't mean he's turned to thievin'."

Remembering the desperate look in Pete's eyes when he'd begged her to marry him, Madeline wasn't so sure. The timing of the thefts was also disturbing; as one of the men had pointed out last night, it was almost as if the rustlers knew where the ranchers *weren't* going to be, and when.

"I've got to get back out there," Evan said abruptly, his face closed.

"Just hold on there," Mrs. Ashler ordered. "We ain't done—"

"We are for now." Though Evan didn't raise his voice, the authority in his tone was clear.

"I've got to go, too," Jack somberly seconded, rising from his chair. "Many thanks for breakfast, ma'am."

The two men, similar in size but different in coloring, were out the door before any of the women could say a word.

"Thank you, honey," Will rasped as Madeline wet his lips with a damp cloth. Though the weak utterance was a far cry from the gruff, familiar voice that barked out one order after another, nothing had ever sounded so good to her.

Will appeared to have improved over the course of the day. More than a few times since last night his breathing had seemed impossibly distressed and his color purplish-blue, but each of those times, somehow, his body had found the strength to carry on. Madeline and Annalisa had alternated spells sitting with him this afternoon, insisting at noontime that Mrs. Ashler go upstairs and get some well-deserved sleep.

"Well, maybe I will," Mrs. Ashler had said, touching the then-unconscious foreman gently on his forehead, her weariness plain to read on her face. "This ain't been the easiest night an' day a body's ever had." Annalisa had remained behind to take the first watch while Madeline walked out with Mrs. Ashler.

"You feelin' halfways decent now, dear?" the older woman had asked solicitously in the sunlit sitting room, taking hold of her hand. "You looked sicker'n a dead dog when I set that oatmeal in front of you."

"I don't feel too bad right now," Madeline had answered truthfully, feeling embarrassed and awkward under Mary Ashler's shrewd scrutiny.

The plump hand had squeezed hers. "I know a few tricks that might help with the sickness. I used to get it terrible, too. We can have us a talk later on, Madeline Claire. I reckon there's a few other things you don't know."

"I'm sure," Madeline had murmured, not really knowing what to say, feeling her cheeks grow warm as the woman continued to regard her.

"You love him, don't you."

After a long moment, Madeline had nodded.

A gentle half-smile had appeared on Mrs. Ashler's lined face. "Then all will be well." The exhausted woman had grown abstracted. "Me and my Henry had a powerful love for one another, much like what I suspect you and Mr. Grant got. I'm gonna tell you somethin', Maddie, somethin' not too many people know, and I'm only tellin' you because . . . well, I don't know why I'm tellin' you. I just am." She shook her head. "I know I sounded mad enough to kick a bull with my bare foot this mornin', but it's a'cause I only want the best for you, dear. That Mr. Grant," she'd said with a nod of approval, "he didn't cower none, and he wasn't ashamed to claim what he done. No, sirree, he wasn't ashamed a'tall. He loves you somethin' fierce, girl, even if he didn't say as much. I could tell, you know, a'cause you just about set his eyes on fire, Madeline Claire. . . . Oh, what am I sayin'? I'm so tired I'm gettin' off track here."

Mrs. Ashler had yawned before continuing. "Love is powerful," she'd said simply, drowsily. "And I ain't so old that I forgot all about the kind of love you're in. Mr. Chicago's gonna make you one fine husband, dear. Henry did me, even if folks was countin' their fingers on us, too." She'd walked off then, leaving Madeline stunned at her admission.

Mrs. Ashler had—

The weak, wheezing sound of Will coughing pulled her from her thoughts. She prayed he wouldn't have another of his airless spells; a little of her died each time she watched him struggle to keep hold of the rope that bound him to life.

"What can I do for you, Will?" she asked anxiously.

His words were interspersed with coughing and gasps for air. "Get me . . . gun . . . horse . . . kill them . . . son . . . bitches." The coughing spell passed then, as if the idea of revenge brought him peace of mind and body. His eyes closed. He breathed rapidly, and a grimace twisted his lips for just a second; then he appeared to rest more calmly.

Madeline released a long, silent sigh and pulled the sheet up over his chest. With satisfaction she noted that no new blood had wet the dressings on his chest, even with the stress and strain the coughing must have put on the wounds. No signs of festering were apparent, either. Earlier, while Will was sleeping or unconscious, she hadn't been sure which, she'd peeked under the dressings and had been relieved to see that the edges of skin remained neatly approximated, held together tightly with the uniform black stitches she'd made.

As Will appeared to have drifted back to sleep, Madeline returned the cloth to the small basin of clean, cool water and settled back in the chair. Her breasts ached something awful; they had all day. For a moment she supported their new weight with her hands, wondering how much larger they were going to get. Not too much, she hoped, thinking of the full-uddered cows on the range. Sliding her hands down, she cradled her flat abdomen. A baby grew here? It was impossible to believe, absolutely impossible. But soon her belly would begin to grow. . . .

She heard the sounds of men and horses outdoors and guessed they were coming in to get their evening grub from Old Roger. Her heart quickened when she thought of Evan being out there with the others, and she wondered how his day had gone. Remembering her first days on the range, she smiled ruefully. Even an excellent rider had a lot to learn.

But she had no doubt Evan would learn quickly. He was intelligent and strong, he rode well, and he possessed the gift of natural athletic ability. Her mind wandered into dangerous territory as she thought of his athletic abilities—his power, his fluid grace of motion. The aching in her breasts turned into a sort of tingling as she looked at the bed and thought of the night they'd shared.

Would the future hold more of those nights?

The long-unanswered wanting in her body cried out for fulfillment. For Evan. For his kisses, his warmth, his strength; for the magical means he seemed to have to send her body and spirit soaring. Trailing her fingers in the basin of water, she tried ineffectually to cool her heated thoughts while memory after memory of their lovemaking glided through her head and intensified the wanting deep within her.

The creaking of footsteps sounded overhead. Madeline stood. Running wet, unsteady fingers over her face, she tried to settle her wildly erotic thoughts. Will slept on in the curtain-darkened room, undisturbed by the noise overhead and unaware of the tempest inside her. The water momentarily cooled her flushed cheeks, but she knew not even a total immersion under the pump would cool the burning fever of her flesh.

Smoothing the wrinkles in her skirt with excessive vigor, she wondered just what the future was going to hold . . . for all of them.

twenty

PETE MATTHEWS HAD AN ALIBI. HER NAME
was Venus, or as she was more commonly
known, Venus Five-by-Five. Venus actually
stood two inches taller than her sobriquet suggested, but those who had given it to her could
well have been correct about the other dimension. She was
one big whore.

Evan had learned this from Robbie and McCaleb over
a meal of sonofabitch stew and crisped marrow gut two
evenings after Reed had been shot. Word had spread among
the Spencer hands that Matthews had returned from town
late the day before, damn near too drunk to stay on his
horse, claiming he'd been with Venus the whole night.

"Me an' Joe went into Laramie City this afternoon to
check out Matthews's story," Robbie had explained, his
eyes lighting up as he recalled the excitement of his first
visit to a sporting establishment. "Whoo-ee, what a place
that is! I heard of Venus before, o' course," he added with
boyish importance, licking the salt from his fingers, "but I

never figgered she'd be bigger 'round than the hoop on a molasses barrel."

"Whadja think of them tits, boy?" a mischievous voice had called out among hoots and catcalls from the other men. "I betcha just one of them bosoms would be bigger'n your whole head. Them French explorin' fellas mighta give the Tetons a differnt name entirely if they'da knowed about Venus."

"Yeah, how'd you like them painted girls downtown, Ashler?" another voice asked suggestively. "See any that struck your fancy? Did you get a look-see at Imogene or Myrtilla?"

"Robert James Ashler," yet another man spoke, affecting a falsetto, "does your ma know you went down to Front Street?"

The room had erupted into bawdy male laughter as Robbie blushed furiously, his ever-working jaw at a loss. Though the men had their proof that Pete Matthews was in Laramie City the night Reed had been shot, thereby eliminating their most likely suspect, the fact that Reed continued to recuperate at an impressive rate had lightened their spirits considerably.

"That does leave Matthews out of it," McCaleb had said to Evan, shaking his head, as soon as the laughter died down. "Damn, I'da just about bet my last dollar that he was behind it."

"Something about this whole thing smells bad," Evan had replied, frowning.

"Sure does. But I can't figure it. The good thing is that we ain't been hit again, to the best I can figure, since the night Reed was shot. Others are losin' stock, though," Joker Joe had added soberly. "I was talking to Rendner the other day, an' he was sayin' they been losin' a fair number of cows over at the Matthews ranch."

"He said that much?" Jesse Hayford had asked from the next table. "Usually Rendner's about as quiet as a stone fence."

"Yeah." Artie Hamilton had belched loudly. "Usually them Texans are shootin' off their mouths like they eat bullets for breakfast."

"Kinda like you, Ashler," another voice had chimed in.

More laughter and bantering had ensued, the mood never fixing on serious, and the remainder of the meal had been filled with teasing and coarse guffaws as well as boastful talk of capturing the rustlers and exacting various forms of western justice from them.

Though Evan wanted the rustlers dead as badly as any of the other men, right this minute he'd have been happier if every *fly* on earth was dead. Their goddamn buzzing and crawling were going to drive him right out of his mind. With much irritation, he waved an arm about his head and tried to turn his attention back to his roping. Robbie Ashler sat astride a piebald pony about ten feet from him, his reins in his teeth, swatting the air around his head with both arms.

Evan's golden dun whinnied and snorted and shook his head, trying to rid his eyes and ears of the pesky insects. The flies were thick today, the wind not being strong enough to keep them from swarming both man and beast. And, as he had learned this afternoon, cows in fly time were nervous and jumpy and wont to stampede.

All the more reason to practice his roping.

Arranging the coils of the grass rope in his left hand, he prepared to make another pass at the waist-high tree that had been the inanimate recipient of several casts of his lariat.

"Try makin' your loop just a little bigger, Grant," Robbie advised. "You been doin' fine with a tree that don't move none, but them calves don't just sit still an' wait for you to come to 'em, you know. Now, I ain't sayin'—"

"How's this?" Evan interrupted, enlarging his loop by paying out a little more rope. Though he was extremely grateful for the instruction, taking direction from a youth— damn, the boy was only half his age—was irksome, particularly since Robbie could outrope him all to hell.

"Yeah, that's good, Grant. Pretty soon you'll even be as good as Miss Madeline."

"There's a compliment if I ever heard one," he grumbled, kicking his horse into a gallop and approaching the crooked little tree. His right arm ached as he swung the rope aloft and prepared to make another overhand toss. *One, two—*

the pony moved so fluidly beneath him that remaining in the saddle took little effort—*three*. Success. The horse wheeled sharply, automatically, bracing himself for the wrenching pull of a running calf.

"Good one, Grant," Robbie yelled. "Tomorrow we'll give you a calf an' see how you do. Let's go get some grub now, huh? These flies are drivin' me half mad, an' besides that, I'm about starvin' to death sittin' here."

"Sounds good," he called wearily. "Just let me get the rope." The well-trained but undoubtedly baffled dun carried him back to the little tree, his ears twitching and his tail swishing furiously. Reaching over, Evan was able to retrieve the rope without dismounting. "You've probably never been a party to roping these fast-moving trees before, have you, boy?" he murmured, coiling the rope. "If you could give an eastern fellow a little help tomorrow, I'd sure appreciate it. Knowing that both a snot-nosed kid and a woman can rope circles around me doesn't feel any too good."

"You sayin' somethin' to me, Grant?" Robbie hollered. "I can't hear you way over here."

"I said, I'm coming," he shouted back, patting the dun's neck. Shifting himself in the saddle, he was also annoyed at the fact his crotch ached only slightly less than it had a week ago. That was good, though, he supposed, because the few glances he'd had of Madeline in the past week had caused him . . . pain.

He'd barely seen her since the morning Mrs. Ashler had taken the serving spoon to the back of his hand. Making a loose fist inside his glove, he felt a mild, lingering soreness yet from the blow. Glancing quickly at Robbie, he bet the Ashler children had learned to stay in line from a very early age.

After she'd assaulted him with the spoon, though, the older woman had actually been rather nice to him. Pleasant, even. Chatty. Back to normal. He couldn't figure it, nor could he help but check her hands for cooking implements whenever he made his brief visits to the ranch house to check on Reed.

Mrs. Ashler had gone home three days ago, leaving the foreman in the care of the younger women. "I gotta get back home and check on things," she'd explained to Evan one afternoon. "Robbie says that between him and them little Billington girls that are helpin' out, things are gettin' done around the place, but between you and me, *how* they're gettin' done is a matter I ain't entirely comfortable with. Will's comin' along nicely, praise God, and I think Madeline and Annalisa will do a fine job of takin' care of him. Robbie brought the wagon today; he's gonna take me home tonight. I'll be back in another four, five days, sooner if you need me."

After she left, Annalisa and Madeline had stayed mostly indoors, tending to Reed. Evan continued to stop at the ranch house once or twice a day to say hello to the foreman—and to catch a glimpse of Madeline—but other than that the only place he seemed to be, besides the too-short time spent in his bunk, was in the saddle. Getting sorer.

Though the past days had fallen into a pattern of hard work and physical exhaustion, he found in them a kind of weary serenity, a feeling of comradeship with other hardworking men, and a harmony with the wild, rugged land. He also had a good deal of time to think, and think he did, almost constantly, of blond, green-eyed Madeline Spencer.

The woman he loved.

The happy, carefree days of early spring were frequently on his mind, as were thoughts of the future with his wife and child. Though his pride still smarted from her vehement—and public—rejection of his marriage proposal, he couldn't really blame her for it. He hadn't even *asked* for her hand, really, if he recalled the events of that afternoon correctly. He'd just told her, and not in a very nice way, that they would be wed.

Madeline was softening in little ways, though—the way she spoke to him . . . the way she looked at him. He sighed. Her eyes said so much. Each time he saw her a sense of expectancy rose in him, making him forget the hard work and the fatigue. If only they could have a little time together, time alone, for wooing, for courting . . .

For love.

He intended to make Madeline his bride just as soon as Will Reed was well enough to walk her down the aisle. This time, though, he'd make sure to *ask* her to marry him.

"Hey, Grant," Robbie asked, as though he could read Evan's mind, "is it true you're gonna marry Miss Madeline?" The two horses fell into a steady, even gait next to one another as they started for the ranch. "Ain't you scared at the idea of bein' hitched to some woman for the rest of your life?"

"No," he answered after a long silence, finding only truth in his one-word reply.

"You ain't, huh? Well, I would be. In fact, I ain't plannin' on gettin' married a'tall. Them women, all they want to do is hog-tie a man and get him all scrubbed an' clean an' civilized an' slicked down, so he's like a overwashed, whipped little pup—"

"Robbie," he interrupted.

"Yeah, Grant?"

"I know you're young, but you've got eyes in your head, haven't you?"

"Yeah. So?"

"Well, have you ever really *looked* at Miss Madeline?"

"Yeah," he said cautiously.

"And you know her pretty well?"

"Um . . . yeah."

"Well, now that we've established that you aren't blind—or stupid—let me ask you: would you be scared of bein' hitched to a woman like that?"

A wistful look crossed Robbie's angular young face, and a sigh escaped from his chest. "Naw, I guess not." A fleeting smile crossed his lips before his expression grew earnest. "But she's about the only woman in the whole wide world I'd wanna marry. Heck, she works hard, she don't complain about nothin', she can ride herd and shoot a gun and rope pretty good, and I even seen her *spit* before. Yep," he said, nodding, "she don't spit half bad. She don't chew, though. She'd be even better at spittin' if she chewed."

Evan disguised a smile. "That's my woman," he said, nodding in return, wondering what other talents Madeline was gifted with.

He was looking forward to finding out, during the next fifty or sixty years.

"Someday, Robbie," he said, trying to match the boy's serious tone, "you'll find a good woman to love, one who won't want to hog-tie you or holler about your boots being muddy or try to change you into something you aren't; one who will love you for the man you are. Madeline loves me . . ." *At least I hope she still does*, he quickly added to himself. "Despite the, ah . . . despite a few . . . mistakes I may have made in the process of courting her." He shifted in the saddle, trying to find an unsore spot on which to balance his weight. There wasn't one. "I'll be marrying her, in answer to your question, if she'll have me."

"She'll have ya," the youth quickly replied, rolling his eyes heavenward. "Holy smokes, you shoulda seen her when you was gone. It was like all the twinkle went out of her. Yeah," he went on, warming to his subject, "she was all quiet—I mean *all quiet*—mopin' around here with a long face, like she lost her last friend. She worked hard, like always, but there weren't no joy in her, if you know what I mean. I think she even cried," he added, looking at Evan meaningfully.

Feeling as though he'd just been taken down a peg, Evan winced. "I get the idea. Someday, Robbie," he said, flashing the boy a remorseful look before he could expand any further on how miserable Madeline had been, "I'll have to tell you all the things a man shouldn't do or say to a woman."

"In other words, a fella'd probably do best to just keep his yap shut, huh?"

"Well, not exactly." The corners of Evan's mouth turned upward at Robbie's simple logic. "Keeping your mouth shut about some things ends up getting you in the biggest trouble of all. You come talk to me when you find that special girl. I expect I'll know even more about these matters by then."

The youth made a face and shook his head violently from side to side. "*Uh*-uh. No, sir. Ain't gonna be no time soon," he promised with all the fervor a fifteen-year-old could muster.

Madeline sighed with frustration at her recalcitrant patient. "Will, you've got to stay in bed and take it easy. I refuse to let you go out to that dirty old bunkhouse. You're going to stay right here until you're better."

"I *am* better!" The words tumbled angrily from the foreman's lips. "Damn women . . . you're always wantin' to coddle a man, make him soft. 'Can I fluff your pillow, Will?' " he mimicked. " 'Are you cold? Do you need another blanket?' " Picking up the edge of the sheet that covered him, he flicked it hard, causing the smooth fabric to billow with air. "In case you girls ain't noticed, *it's summertime*! You don't need no blankets in the summertime," he roared before reassuming the artificially high voice. " 'Can I get you a drink of water? Something to eat? Read you a story? Cut your toenails? Trim your nose hairs?' God!" he exploded. "I just can't take it no more."

"Do your nose hairs need to be trimmed?" Madeline asked sweetly, hoping a little humor might help snap him out of his foul mood.

"Bah! I need these damned wrappings on my chest trimmed. And them threads! Just when did you plan on cuttin' them little black spiders outta my chest, Madeline Spencer? That's what those stitches look like, you know, is little damn black spiders. Itch like spiders would, too. God in heaven, they're itchin' me to death."

"That means your wounds are healing. You know that," she gently chided. "And I'll remove the stitches in a couple more days."

"Will, we went through the same discussion not more than two hours ago," Anna called from the kitchen. "You should just be glad Madeline sewed you up. Otherwise you might not be here today."

"Yeah, yeah," he muttered. "I guess so." Abruptly he fixed Madeline with a direct stare and changed the subject. "You and Grant do any more talkin' about a weddin'? He comes in to visit, but he's in, he's out, all in about two minutes."

"He's working hard," she answered defensively.

"What I want to know is how hard he's workin' on bein' your husband."

"Well, we haven't talked any more about it . . . yet," she answered evasively, saved from having to say more by the sound of a door opening farther off in the house.

"Howdy-do, Anna," came Mrs. Ashler's voice. "Thought I'd come by. I been doin' some bakin' and thought Will might like a little pie."

Will visibly brightened. "What kind?" he hollered, his voice beginning to sound normal. Madeline brightened, too, at the thought of a slice of the older woman's pie, feeling actually hungry instead of queasy or sick.

"Strawberry," Mrs. Ashler called back. "I got some nice ones in town yesterday. Just came in fresh on the train. I brought some cream, too, and I—"

She was interrupted by the sound of the door opening again. "Hi, Ma," came Robbie's voice. "What you doin' here today? I didn't think you was comin' over here until tomorrow. Oh, and hello to you, too, Miss Annalisa. How are you? We been ropin'—Hey, forget that. Grant, lookit here! *Pie*! You didn't tell me you was makin' pie, Ma! Hey, Grant, it's strawberry! My favorite! You brought enough for us, too, didn't you, Ma? Grant, you ain't never tasted pie so good in your whole life."

"They're for Will," his mother replied. "You'll have to talk to him about it."

"Aw, he can't eat 'em both, can he? Besides that, they ain't no good after they been sittin' around for a couple days. Hey, Reed," he called, approaching the bedroom with rapid, excited steps. "You know how the bottom crust gets all soggy and gooey after a pie sits around, don't you? Ain't no good at all. You wouldn't want to—"

"Have Grant come and help me out of this damn bed into the chair," Will said as Robbie appeared in the doorway, "and ask your mother to cut everyone a slice of pie."

"Yippee!" Robbie shouted, bounding back to the kitchen.

"I'll help dish up," Madeline murmured, not wishing to give Will an opportunity to get her and Evan alone before him. That wouldn't do at all. There was too much heat between her and Evan, heat that flew fast and hot in the glances they gave each other. Heat that couldn't be disguised . . . and could barely be postponed. Will would see it and be out of bed and off to town to fetch the preacher before he'd blinked twice.

In the past days she had slowly come to terms with her love for Evan. It wasn't that she'd ever stopped loving him—she hadn't—but she had tried to suppress her feelings. How futile that had been. All her silly resolve had melted as quickly as a snowball in front of a roaring fire.

Because she loved him.

She didn't know what the future would hold for them, but each day he stayed and worked himself into exhaustion at the ranch she grew more secure in the knowledge that he had feelings for her. Why else would he be here? She had accepted that Evan Grant and the baby—and however many more children God would bless them with—were her destiny.

He was already as far as the sitting room when she stepped out of the bedroom. She stopped, taking in the sight of the tall, broad-shouldered man with pleasure. The red bandanna knotted at his neck contrasted handsomely with the blue of his eyes, the white of his shirt, and the sun-burnished tone of his skin. He looked tired but fit.

"Hello, Madeline" he said simply with a devastating, bone-melting smile.

She took in the way his strong chest and arms filled out his shirt, the way the chaps fit his lean hips . . . and the area over his fly they didn't fit at all. She swallowed hard before moistening her lips. "Hello," she replied, feeling her pulse thrum more forcefully through her body. How did he hold this power over her? "I, ah, I'm just going out to help serve the pie," she explained, moving past him.

He let her go, mostly because the moisture gleaming on her full pink lips tempted him beyond reason. And if he kissed her once . . . well, he didn't think he'd be able to stop. His glance trailed her tempting, feminine swagger, visually caressing her sweetly rounded denim-clad bottom as she moved into the kitchen. With a crooked smile on his face, the thought crossed his mind that she'd probably still walk that way when she was nine months gone.

It was a sight he looked forward to seeing.

"Hey, Grant, you found out anything about them rustlers yet?" Reed's voice called. "Damn it all, am I gonna have to get up out of this bed and catch them bastards myself?"

"I'm sorry to tell you we haven't found any clues yet, Reed." With a quick sigh, he tore his thoughts away from fleshly pleasures. "And you'd better not even *think* about getting near a horse yet," he admonished, "unless you want some trouble from me." Stepping into the bedroom, he was pleased to see that Reed's color was good. His face was much thinner than it had been a week ago, but he knew it would quickly fill out again. Especially if Old Roger and the womenfolk continued to spoil him with his favorite foods and one rich treat after another.

Best of all, though, was the life that once again blazed from Will Reed's eyes. Somehow, as if invigorated by the challenge of cheating death, the vital force within him burned stronger than ever. Evan guessed that lying in bed recuperating had to be driving the normally active foreman right up the wall, and he couldn't repress the smile that curved his lips at the foreman's frustrated, grumpy expression.

"What are you grinnin' about?" the older man growled. "I'm the one who's gonna be givin' *you* trouble. 'Specially if you don't hurry up and turn Madeline into a missus."

"I'm working on it, Reed," he assured him, shrugging his shoulders, "but this ranching business doesn't leave much time for proper courting."

"Seems to me you went a little beyond that before."

"Yeah, well," Evan said regretfully, "I made a few mistakes the first time around. I'm trying to go a little slower this time."

The older man cleared his throat, fixing him with a crackling gaze. "You hurt her, you know."

"I know."

A gruff chuckle escaped from Will Reed's throat. "Yeah, I think you do. She made it real plain, didn't she? But you came back, and that tells me somethin'. And I s'pose there's some usefulness in makin' a mistake if a man learns somethin' from it." He crooked his finger. "Come here, boy, and I'll tell you somethin' I learned over the years. Somethin' I learned the hard way."

Obligingly Evan moved closer, curious.

"Women are sweet, Grant, real sweet." A wistful expression crossed Will's grizzled features. A moment later, stark realism replaced the wistfulness. "But just keep in mind that women got all the sweetness of a honey-covered thorn. They'll prick you, and prick you sharp, if you move out of line."

"What's this whisperin' about?" Mrs. Ashler asked, standing in the doorway with a pitcher and an armful of glasses. "Ain't you even got him outta bed yet, Grant? Come on, haul his skinny little behind out of the sack and into the sittin' room." Her eyes lingered on the injured man, and she added tenderly, "It's good to see you lookin' so well, Reed. You appeared more dead than alive for a while."

"Yeah, well. Felt like it, too."

"I imagine," Mrs. Ashler agreed, nodding her head. "But I got somethin' to tell you that oughta cheer you up some. I decided to go ahead with the Fourth of July picnic this year."

"But Spencer—"

"Now, just rest your jaw and listen," she ordered, shifting her grip on the heavy pitcher. "I know Nate's not here, but I think he'd want us to go through with it anyway. It gave him great pleasure these past two Fourths to put on that picnic for the folk around here. This year there's been more than enough joylessness around these parts, what with all the rustlin' goin' on, and with you bein' shot and knockin' at death's door." She narrowed her eyes, daring Reed to disagree with her. "We need us a happy social event, and next Tuesday we're gonna have us one."

"Amen," Evan couldn't help but second, grinning at the momentarily speechless man in the bed. "Did you get a feel of that thorn?"

twenty-one

ONCE MRS. ASHLER GOT BEHIND SOMETHING, she was a force to be reckoned with.

During the past week, as she'd made preparations for the Spencer Fourth of July picnic, many of the Spencer hands were given special invitations—or, rather, conscripted into one kind of service or another by the stout, rosy-cheeked widow who was determined that this year's picnic was going to be the best ever.

Though Albany County was sparsely populated, word of the event quickly passed from ranch to ranch, homestead to homestead, as had Mary Ashler's declaration: "It's time for everyone to get together and have some fun for a change."

People agreed.

The large number of cattle thefts in the area had caused tensions to run high throughout the past months, so the ranchers and cowhands and rural folk alike looked forward to celebrating the Fourth with great enthusiasm. Most had assumed, because of Nate's extended absence, that there would be no picnic at the Spencers' this year, and the news came as a pleasant surprise.

A gentle breeze touched Madeline's face and carried the sounds of horses and cattle and men's voices to her ears, and she hid her smile as she watched Mrs. Ashler stalk Will Reed. From the kitchen window the older woman had spied the foreman propping a ladder against the side of the barn, and like a pot boiling over, she'd been across the room, down the porch steps, and on her way over to the barn.

Eager for a breath of fresh air, Madeline had followed Mrs. Ashler outdoors, grateful that Anna had offered to stay indoors and keep an eye on the loaves of bread that now baked. The three women had been cooking and baking since dawn, with several cooling cakes and pies and other tempting confections to their credit. Though they'd enjoyed hours of friendly camaraderie, Madeline was distracted, restless, and filled with sharp anticipation, knowing she'd more than likely see Evan today.

And tonight.

At various places around the ranch Mary Ashler's draftees worked diligently on final preparations for the holiday picnic, but the only thing in the older woman's sight at this moment was Will Reed. She was bearing down on him, arms akimbo, dressed in her customary garb— a black dress covered by a white apron—and Madeline knew her sharp blue eyes took in the ranch foreman's every movement.

And his movements weren't too bad, albeit a little slow, Madeline observed with satisfaction, cognizant of the fact that only two weeks ago he'd been lying flat on his back on the kitchen table with a bullet in his chest.

"You watch it up there!" Mrs. Ashler admonished as Will picked up a large coil of rope, slung it over his shoulder, and began climbing the ladder. With large steps for such a short woman, Mrs. Ashler quickly reached the base of the ladder, her mouth working the whole way. "What are you tryin' to do? Bust yourself back open? I mean it, Mr. Think-You're-All-Healed Reed. After all the sleep I lost over you, I'd be purely mad if you were to fall off and break your fool neck."

"Yeah, yeah. You'd cry yourself a river, woman, and you know it. Go back to your cookin' and quit worryin' about me," he called down, stopping for a moment and glancing below. "An' watch out for them lanterns. I got 'em all filled up this morning."

The lanterns, varying in size and height, stood in a neat row against the barn. They would be hung on the rope he was stringing between the barn and the shed that stood perpendicular to the side of the barn, to provide light during the evening's festivities.

Everyone marveled at Will's recovery, for it had been nothing short of amazing. He'd gained ground by gigantic leaps and bounds in the past four or five days, ever since he'd picked up and moved back to the bunkhouse. Poor Annalisa. She'd borne the brunt of his anger and frustration the afternoon he'd erupted.

But getting back into his element had probably been the best thing for him, Madeline reflected, watching him make his way up the ladder. A man like Will Reed who had lived a rough-and-tumble life undoubtedly found the overzealous ministrations of two anxious young women a bit much to deal with.

"Let me help you, Reed," Robbie called, coming around the side of the barn. "Hey, why you carryin' the whole rope?" he asked sensibly. "You're just tyin' one end of it up there. Why don't you throw down the other end, an' that way it won't be so heavy for you to carry."

"Because he's tryin' to *prove* somethin'—like how he's gonna fall off this ladder an' kill himself." Mary Ashler's grumbled reply was intended for Will's ears as much as it was for her son's. For emphasis the sturdy woman gave one leg of the ladder a kick, producing, as if by magic, a string of colorful curse words in the air above her.

Madeline turned away when the heavy coil of rope hit the ground with a thump. She didn't need to worry about Will; Mrs. Ashler was doing enough of it for everyone. Unable to disguise her smile, she walked around the corner of the barn and saw that preparations for the picnic were progressing at a rapid rate. Ned Triggs scrubbed busily on one of several tables that stood in the yard near the house.

Tables and benches and chairs had been arriving since yesterday, courtesy of neighboring ranchers, and nearly all of them bore the wet evidence of Ned's hard work.

Old Roger had set up his camp last night, a short ways from the tables. Robbie and Ned had dug a good-sized cook pit yesterday afternoon, and a freshly slaughtered yearling steer already sizzled on a spit over the fire. Reaching under the curved tin hood that shielded one side and nearly all the top of the animal, Roger painted the near side of the carcass with a dark-colored concoction from the gallon pail at his feet.

"Hey, Miss Madeline," Ned greeted her. "Gonna be a great day for a picnic, ain't it?"

"Sure is," she agreed, walking over to where he labored. The light breeze carried the pungent smell of wet wood to her and ruffled the silky strands of hair that had already escaped from her braid. She felt good this morning, not at all ill, and had eaten an enormous breakfast under the approving eye of Mrs. Ashler.

"Do you know where Evan is?" she asked casually, not yet having caught sight of him this morning. A shiver of anticipation shot through her limbs, and she didn't know how much longer she—they—could go on like this. The tension between them smoldered and crackled and grew enormously with each day that passed, wholly unfulfilled by quick glances and lingering looks or an occasional brushing of hand against hip or shoulder against arm. It was meager fare indeed after the sensual banquet they'd enjoyed in the spring of the year.

Tonight.

Perhaps tonight.

She sighed, thinking that at this point she was past pride. To hell with words and past actions; just to love Evan tonight would be enough. For now. Each time she saw him, his eyes stroked her, caressed her, said things to her, promised her.

Granted, there would be roughly two hundred other persons around, but perhaps they'd find some time to themselves. Elsie had always said that being patient wasn't one of Madeline's strong suits.

Besides, this situation had gone on long enough.

"Your young man is over there past the corral," Old Roger answered her, pointing with his paintbrush. "Him and McCaleb are gettin' set up for the races."

"Thanks, Roger." Madeline felt her face color as she turned and began walking to the corral. Her young man? Were her feelings for the tall, raven-haired industrialist-turned-cowboy so obvious? She hoped all her thoughts could not be so easily read. If so, she'd be jailed.

Reaching the corner of the corral fence, she hopped up onto the second wooden rail in a fluid movement. There was Evan, beyond the corral, just as Old Roger had said. Though he now dressed like the cowhands—dark woolen pants, white shirt, dark vest, low-crowned hat—there was no mistaking his form. How she'd missed just *looking* at him in the past few busy days. His broad shoulders narrowed down superbly to a lean, muscular waist and flanks, while, just as impressively, his long, powerful legs joined perfectly sculptured buttocks, and she thought, not for the first time, that he moved with the mastery of motion and grace of a great cat.

Strong. Sleek. Sensual. A man could not be more flawlessly made, of that she was certain.

The breeze kicked up white dust from a sack on the ground near where he and Joker Joe worked, and she guessed they were chalk-marking the ground for the races. Mrs. Ashler had a multitude of games and athletic contests planned for the late afternoon—some for men on horseback as well as several for men on foot. Remembering the good-natured races and roping contests the hands had had last fall after roundup, she smiled. This day promised just as much, if not more, excitement.

Evan caught sight of her and waved. Waving back at him, Madeline felt her smile broaden and her heart lift. Something snorted and bumped roughly into her toe then, and she looked down to see a fat, glistening pig sniffing her boot. Who had had the unlucky task of shaving and greasing the pig? she wondered. Each year Nate generously donated a hog for the pig-catching contest, the hog itself being the contest's prize. Last year a cowboy from the

Dunlay ranch had captured the pig in record time, amid shouting and yelling from the participants and spectators and earsplitting squeals from the frightened sow.

After several seconds this pig decided that something on the ground was much more interesting than a booted foot at snout level, and with one last snort it moved on. Hoping to content herself with one last glance at Evan before she returned to the kitchen, Madeline looked back up and was surprised to see him say something to Joker Joe, brush his hands on his pants, and move around the corral fence at an easy lope.

He was coming over to her.

Stepping down lightly from the fence, she smoothed her hair, hoping that she didn't have any unsightly smudges of flour on her face. The thought crossed her mind that she should be nervous, but strangely she wasn't. Whatever was going to happen between them was going to happen. Golden sunshine poured down from above, illuminating the man who moved toward her with splendid coordination of body and limb.

Barely out of breath, he stopped about ten feet before her, walking the remainder of the distance. With pleasure she gazed at him, thinking that for all his hours of unfamiliar, challenging, backbreaking labor—simply put, hard work— he looked good. Very, very good.

"That's some fine way you're taking care of my baby," he said, cocking his head to one side. "I didn't think women in your condition were supposed to climb fences."

"What—standing two rails above the ground?"

Was he really angry? A smile threatened to curve her lips at his overprotectiveness. Sighing loudly, with mock despondency, she mischievously remarked, "Oh, dear, I suppose that means you don't want me racing my horse this afternoon, either."

"I absolutely forbid it!"

The expression of outrage on his handsome face was just too much, and a silvery giggle escaped her throat. "I'm just teasing you, silly."

"Oh." Blue eyes penetrated her own, and after a long moment a slow, easy smile appeared on his face. "Are you looking to stir up some trouble, little one?"

Her heart skittered in her chest. "Maybe."

"Well, I might be just the one to give it to you." His lazy words were a challenge, and the blue in his eyes seemed to intensify, communicating his want.

It was just on the tip of her tongue to say, "I hope so," when he spoke again, after clearing his throat. He looked at her searchingly. "You're feeling well, Maddie? Any more . . . ah, sickness?"

"It's better." Her heart was touched by his earnestness, his genuine concern. "How have you been?"

"Just fine."

The gleam in his eyes was back, and she felt a responding shiver when his eyes leisurely traveled her form from head to toe. His familiar scent touched her nostrils, and surreptitiously, deeply, she inhaled of it, feeling it work its powerful magic deep inside her. Her gaze fastened on the dark hair sprouting from the open collar of his shirt, and she wished she could open the garment and run her hands over his hard, muscular chest, feeling the stimulating texture of crisp hair and small male nipples tightening at her touch.

"Madeline. *Jesus.* You shouldn't look at a man like that . . . not if you know what's good for you." He removed his hat and ran his forearm across his brow, and she saw his chest rise and fall in a tense, controlled motion.

"I know what's good for me." She gave him a smile of seductive promise, feeling their intimacy rekindle itself quickly. "Maybe *you* don't, though," she said roguishly, moistening her lips, remembering the potent effect her words used to have on him. "Maybe you . . . forgot."

Putting his hat back on, he made no answer. The pulse in his tanned neck beat steadily . . . more rapidly than before? He stood motionless with an intense expression that told her he remembered everything every bit as clearly as she did.

A wicked thrill shot through her, and she backed up to the fence, laying both arms, outstretched, on the top rail. The new fullness of her breasts tested the buttons of her blouse sorely, and she felt her nipples tighten and rub erotically against the fine fabric of the short chemise beneath her shirt. Desire, more powerful than she remembered, flooded through her, making her knees weak. "In case you don't remember what's good for me," she said breathlessly, "I could remind you . . . step by—"

"I remember what's good for you." His glanced flicked boldly downward, over the hard proof of his desire, before returning to her face.

"Hey, Grant," Joker Joe's voice came from across the corral. "Come on! We gotta get this finished."

"Coming."

McCaleb's words had all the effect of a drop of water on a blazing forest fire, and for a long moment Evan's eyes continued to sear and scorch and devour her, and then, with one great stride her closed the distance between them, standing so close that she could feel the heat emanating from his body.

"And I'm going to show you, the first chance I get," he promised, his breath warm on her face before he turned and walked away.

The sound of laughter and revelry filled the early evening air, punctuated occasionally by shrill whistles, sharp-sounding firecrackers, and even a few gunshots. Adding to the gay hubbub were the last-minute rehearsal efforts of the evening's musicians—seven cowboys who had been hastily designated a week ago, for their varying talents on fiddle, banjo, guitar, harmonica, and Jew's harp.

The festive atmosphere had undoubtedly been helped along by several large wooden kegs of beer that had been delivered from town during the afternoon amid a chorus of cheers, courtesy of Justus Fletcher, an area rancher. Mrs. Ashler's displeasure at the wagonful of malt brew had been unmistakable, but later Madeline had seen her raise a glass of amber liquid and drink deeply when she thought no one was looking.

The sun had disappeared behind the great mountains to the west, and the customary early evening twilight fell across the jovial assemblage. Madeline's stomach was comfortably full, but groans from those who had eaten too much of the bountiful fare could be heard nearly everywhere. Though an enormous amount of food had been consumed by dozens of hungry men and a handful of women and children, plenty remained yet for the partygoers to consume during what promised to be a long night of vigorous dancing.

"Hey, Miss Madeline, your Mr. Grant sure is a fast runner," Robbie Ashler declared, slipping a pile of dishes into the large wooden tub of soapy water in which her hands were immersed. "I thought Noah Horn was about the speediest thing on two legs—he won the foot race last year—but I ain't never seen a man move the way Evan moved this afternoon. He made Noah look about as slow as molasses in Janu . . . Oops," he said with an embarrassed grin, pointing at the soapy trail on her cheek. "Sorry about splashin' you, but like Ma always says, you'll dry."

"But, Robbie, I'm just so sweet I might melt," she said innocently, blowing a handful of suds at him.

Brushing the bubbles from his face and chest, he pulled a face at her. "You're a lot of things, Madeline Spencer, but you ain't sweet."

"I'm not, huh?" she asked, threatening him with another handful of bubbles.

Petite, freckle-faced Emma Billington paused while drying a plate and giggled at their play, and Madeline was struck by how much she had missed teasing the dear, gangling boy-man. A few short months ago one of her greatest pleasures in life had been to render Robbie Ashler speechless or, at the very least, tie his tongue for a second or two.

Now her greatest pleasure in life was something . . . someone else entirely. She had no doubt that Robbie would have been rendered speechless for days if he'd known just what their banter had been replaced with.

"*I* think you're sweet, Madeline." Nine-year-old Camille Dunlay beamed loyally at her from the next table, where she neatly stacked dishes along with her mother. "He don't know nothin' 'cause he's just a dumb old *boy*."

"How's it comin' over here?" Mary Ashler asked, depositing a full armload of dishes and eating utensils on the table next to the tub. Her cheeks were flushed pink from her exertion. "Good! Looks like we got 'em more than half-licked. The music's gonna start up pretty quick. Thank goodness the weather is holding, and the wind ain't bad tonight, either. Say, Robbie," she said, turning to him and arching a brow, "whatcha doin' flappin' your lip over here, anyway?"

"We was just talkin' about Grant winnin' the race this afternoon. You saw it, didn't you, Ma?" At her answering nod, he went on excitedly. "That was some race. Did you see the look on Noah Horn's face? He couldn't believe he was gettin' beat! Them long legs of Grant's just tore up the ground, an' he din't even look like he was workin' very hard. As I live an' breathe," he said, shaking his head for emphasis, "that Grant is the fastest man I ever seen."

"I'd have to agree with you there, dear," Mrs. Ashler said deadpan. Then, so quickly that Madeline wasn't even sure it happened, the older woman turned to her and winked. "Now, Robbie," she asked, turning back to her son and chucking him under the chin, "are you comin' over to help, boy? We got plenty for you to do, an' I bet Emma's even got an extra dishrag over there."

"I . . . ah, gotta get goin', Ma. I cleaned up our table and brought the stuff over like you said, an' I already had to listen to more teasin' about that than I care to tell you." Fidgety, he edged a few steps backward, waiting for a sign of dismissal from his mother.

"Go on, Robert James," she said, relenting, her expression turning serious, "but I'm tellin' you, if I catch you in that beer, you're gonna be one sorry pup."

"Yes'm," he said with a grin, bounding away before she could say more.

"That boy," Mrs. Ashler said, shaking her head, watching him melt into the crowd. "He's havin' fun, though," she added, reaching for a rag, her smile returning for a moment, then fading as her round features assumed a contemplative expression. "You know who I ain't seen in a while, Madeline?"

"Who?"

"Annalisa. The last time I saw her was during the sack races. She was talkin' to her brother." She paused a moment, thinking. "You know, I don't think I seen Jack all day, either."

"I heard Mr. Pete tell my pa that Jack had to work this afternoon," Emma Billington supplied helpfully, "but I don't know where Miss Anna is. She sure is a nice lady. I hope she decides to live here for good. She's so pretty, too," she said, sighing, setting down a plate and reaching for another. "All that dark hair and smooth skin . . . and no freckles."

"You ain't got freckles, dear," Mrs. Ashler said kindly. "Them's angel kisses. And I wouldn't be surprised a'tall if Miss Annalisa settled in these parts."

"The last time I remember seeing her was when they turned the pig loose," Madeline said slowly, trying to recall if she'd seen her friend since then. The afternoon had been quite hectic. "I know Artie Hamilton and about fifty others have been making sweet on her all day." Thinking of all the earnest, hopeful-faced men who had flocked around her beautiful, saucy friend, she added, "Poor Anna, she's been treading lightly all afternoon. I don't know how she does it, but so far she's managed to keep them all dangling without hurting anyone's feelings."

"Oh, well, I'm sure she'll turn up somewhere. Maybe she's helpin' Old Roger or some of the other women," Mary Ashler replied, pushing up her sleeves and sinking her hands into the water. "You run along and have some fun now, dear. You been workin' long enough." In a low voice intended for Madeline's ears only, she added, "I just saw Evan over 'round the other side of the barn watchin' a card game."

Smiling her thanks at the softhearted widow, Madeline quickly dried her hands and set off toward the barn.

Glancing up from a lively game of monte, Evan saw Madeline slowly make her way toward him, smiling and stopping to speak to several men along the way. All interest in the game fled as his eyes feasted on the impudent minx who had traded in her heart-stopping trousers for a simple yet elegant dress of soft-looking turquoise. A buff-colored petticoat peeked gracefully from beneath the artfully arranged folds of her skirt, swaying gently when she walked, and draped around her shoulders and tucked into her neck opening was a matching kerchief. The bottom folds of the lace-trimmed square rested temptingly on the upper swells of her breasts, emphasizing the strong, proud shoulders that majestically supported their fullness.

Her face was just as arresting as her form, however, and he thought again that no woman on earth was as appealing as Madeline Spencer. Her tawny hair was pulled away from her face and tied at the crown of her head with a large turquoise ribbon. In the fading light the cascade of lustrous curls gleamed burnished gold, and he itched to bury his hands and face in the soft, fragrant mass.

He'd been crazy for her all day long.

The tight control he'd been attempting to hold over his thoughts and urges in the past days, with only mediocre success had slipped away from him in a hot, turgid whoosh this morning, the instant she'd looked at him with those seductive green eyes. God, the way she'd teased him should be outlawed, he thought, positive he'd explode if he didn't find some way to see her alone tonight.

"It's just about time for your watch, Grant," McCaleb called out from the other side of the table. Evan swore to himself as the bandy-legged man continued. "You an' Johnson should leave in 'bout an hour or so. Remember, we're keepin' them cows as tight as possible tonight. Reed figures the rustlers'll try an' pick us clean tonight, but me, I don't. I figure they're in town a-whoopin it up, too drunk to sit a horse."

"Thanks for the reminder, McCaleb," he said tightly, feeling any chance of seeing Madeline slip away.

"Don't look so glum, Grant. It's only for two hours," Joker Joe responded with a snort of laughter at Evan's obvious disappointment. "You'll get plenty of time to do some dancin' with the ladies tonight. Maybe you ain't got these kind of parties in la-di-da Chicago," he said, lifting one of several bottles of whiskey from the table. Taking a deep swig, he sighed. "Ah, that's more like it. Yes, siree, Chicago, here in the West we celebrate until the sun comes up, an' sometimes then some."

"Hello, Joe, Wayne, Jim," Madeline's voice said from behind him before adding, more softly, after the men had greeted her and turned their attention back to their game, "Hello, Evan." Her delicate floral fragrance reached his nose even before he turned to look at her, stoking the fire within him. What he wouldn't give right this minute to have her silky-smooth, perfumed flesh naked beneath him . . . or over him . . . or alongside him. Hell, it didn't matter; he just needed to be near her, next to her. Inside her.

Brilliant green eyes searched his face, and he saw a matching hunger reflected in their depths. "You ran quite a race this afternoon," she said breathlessly, the tip of her tongue coming out to delicately moisten her lips. "Everyone is still talking about it."

Bending close to her, he whispered, "Did you know that you use that same voice to speak to me when we're making love? Only then you say things like—"

"Stop it, Evan!" she whispered shakily. "Someone might hear you!" A pulse beat erratically in her neck at his words, and she heard the slight noise she made as she swallowed. Taking a deep breath, she closed her eyes briefly and placed her hand over her chest as if to quiet her heart. "Evan," she said huskily, shaking her head, "what are we going to do?"

"Come with me."

"What?"

"Come with me right now, Madeline," he said, his desire for her making him impulsive, impatient. "How fast can you change into riding clothes?"

"I don't know if . . ." She trailed off, seeing what was in his eyes. "Give me ten minutes," she said decisively. "Where are we going?"

"On my watch."

"Really?" she raised her eyebrows, and a slow, suggestive smile curved her lips. "Well, well, Mr. Grant, I guarantee it will be one watch you'll remember for a long time to come."

"Meet me in the tack shed when you're changed," he said hoarsely, thinking that ten minutes sounded like ten years.

twenty-two

Hurrying down the seldom used steps from the front door—the one that opened from the sitting room to the outdoors—Madeline held her bundle of range clothing tightly against her body. She hadn't dared change into them lest she be questioned about what she was doing and where she was going, so instead she'd hurriedly scooped up her trousers and a blouse and traded her black patent leather boots for her well-worn riding boots.

Edging along the side of the house, she peered around the corner and saw that several lanterns had been lit, including the ones hanging from the rope Will had strung up. A large group had congregated around the musicians, and the glow from the gently swaying lanterns spilled invitingly over the crowd in the deepening dusk.

Good. Maybe she could get to the tack shed without being noticed.

The first notes of a lively tune rang out amid whoops and cheers and a loud clapping of hands. Not imagining that there could ever be a better opportunity than this, she ran quickly along the rear side of the house, slowing her pace to a brisk walk when she was in open view.

Her heart pounded with the thrill of what she was doing—and the thrill of what she was about to do—as she approached the small wooden structure. With a quick glance over her shoulder she opened the door and stepped across the threshold. It was nearly dark in the little shed, with only a little murky light entering from the two windows and the open door behind her.

"Evan?" she called softly. Squinting, she tried to accustom her eyes to the gray-blackness.

Warm, strong hands gripped her arms and pulled her further inside the shed. "Right on time," came his low voice in her ear as one arm reached past her and pushed the door shut. The smell of leather and horse sweat and saddle soap faded from her senses, swiftly replaced by the familiar masculine scent of the man who held her in his embrace. She sighed deeply, feeling as though she had just come home after a journey of years.

"You're sure about this?" he asked huskily. One hand caressed her hair, while the other gently stroked her neck and jaw, angling her face toward his. "I doubt I have the strength to let you go, but I will if—"

"I'm sure." She slid her arms from between them, letting the bundle of clothing fall to the rough wood floor. Standing on tiptoe, she reached out with shaking fingers and stroked the familiar planes of his face, tracing his brows, his nose, his cheekbones, and finally the curve of his lips. "I've waited so long for this, Evan," she murmured, not believing she was finally in his arms again. "Just love me."

His lips captured hers in a searing kiss that told her his waiting had been as difficult as hers. Eagerly she opened her mouth to him, their tongues fusing and swirling in an erotic tempo. Weeks and weeks of longing burst forth in a passionate flood inside her, and she sagged in his arms for a moment, overwhelmed by the intensity of the hunger inside her.

"Are you all right, Maddie? Did I hurt you in some way?" he asked anxiously, breaking their kiss. His arms tightened around her, supporting her weight, pulling her closer to him. Through the gathers of her skirt and petticoat she could feel the erection behind his trousers pressing hot and hard against her belly, and instinctively she rotated her hips, wringing a groan from his throat.

Feminine satisfaction at his reaction made her bold, and she whispered, "I'm on fire for you, Evan. I want you so—"

"By God, Madeline," he rasped, "you can't want me half as much as I want you. Not a day has gone by that I haven't thought of you, dreamed of you . . . dreamed of this." His hands ran urgently over her shoulders and breasts and belly, then curved over her hips to cup her buttocks. "I don't think I can wait until—"

"Then let's not." His hands had fanned the fire that already burned dangerously out of control inside her, and she pulled the kerchief free of her neck opening and began unbuttoning her bodice. "I have to change my clothes anyway."

"Allow me." His hands brushed hers aside, feeling for the neat row of buttons down the center of her chest. "What's this?" he asked, raining feather-soft kisses on her face. The warm fingers on her bodice had already wandered from their task, tracing large circles over her breasts. "A button way over here . . . and a matching one on the other side, too?"

The uncomfortable ache that had been present in her nipples since the beginning of her pregnancy flared into flames of sweet longing, and she sighed with pleasure, hungrily reaching out to trace the rigid contour behind the buttons of his trousers.

With a muffled curse and an impatient motion, Evan stepped away from her and cleared an area on the wide shelf that ran along one wall of the shed. Scooping her up in his arms, he deposited her on the counter and set to unbuttoning her bodice in earnest. Her eyes had adjusted to the dimness, and in the faint light from the window next to her she saw that his expression was tender and hard and loving all at once.

"Madeline Spencer, you have the most beautiful breasts on earth," he whispered, undoing the buttons on her chemise. "Ben thought so, too, but the poor son of a bitch will never get to see them . . . or touch them." His fingers caressed the swells of her naked flesh. "Or taste them." His hands cupped their new heaviness, and he groaned again, lowering his mouth to a turgid nipple.

A stream of liquid fire rippled through her at the touch of his mouth, intensifying as he teased first one breast, then the other. One of his hands slipped under her skirts and traveled with maddening slowness up her leg. The area between her thighs was hot and swollen and slick with need, and she leaned back against the wall to better receive his touch, her back pressing uncomfortably into the straps and buckles of the bridles that hung behind her. Drawing back her legs and tilting her pelvis forward toward him, she felt wicked, absolutely wanton. Nothing else mattered at this moment except the sensation of his hands and lips on her body.

Her breath caught in her throat as he reached through the slit in her pantalets and touched her eager flesh. "Oh, God, you're already ready for me," he growled, his fingers slipping expertly past her tumescent outer lips to stroke the tender, inflamed flesh beneath. "So hot . . . so wet . . ." One bold finger slid upward. "So tight."

"And so empty," she whispered hoarsely, finding it difficult to breathe or swallow . . . or even think. The feelings he created inside her spiraled and grew, and soft whimpers escaped from her throat.

"You've missed this, then?"

"What . . . do you . . . think?"

His breathing sounded as erratic as hers, and he leaned toward her, fastening his mouth once more over hers. His tongue and his fingers invaded opposite ends of her body with exquisite precision and coordination, stimulating her beyond reason.

"Evan," she said, gasping, breaking her lips from his. "I need you . . . inside me . . . so much." Leaning forward, she reached for his waistband. "Right now. Right this second. Please."

"Yes, ma'am." His tone was both urgent and amused, his words rich with promise.

A sudden, ridiculous thought struck her. "I still have my boots on."

"Now, there's a sense of propriety," he said with a ragged chuckle, helping her with the buttons on his trousers. "If it'll make you feel any better, I'll leave mine on, too."

A thump and a clatter just then caused them both to start and Madeline to gasp, and the wee amount of light that came in from the window next to her was blocked by a large, furry silhouette.

A loud, sonorous purring sound filled the air.

"Oh, Sugar, it's you!" she exclaimed, relief flooding through her. "Heavens! You scared me half to death, you sweet kitty." Reaching over, she scratched the cat under his chin.

"Madeline Spencer, that goddamn cat is no 'sweet kitty.' He nearly killed me, in case you've forgotten." The big tom purred louder at his mistress's touch, nearly drowning out Evan's soft but vile string of imprecations.

"Evan!" she said, puzzled at his great animosity toward her pet. "You know, if it wasn't for Sugar we wouldn't be together. After all," she murmured, reaching out for him, "he didn't spook your horse on purpose."

"He damned well did, too. And he watches me. All the time."

"Evan," she purred, quickly losing interest in this line of conversation. She leaned toward him and pulled his hands free from their tight grip on the edge of the shelf. "You're being silly. He's just a cat." Nuzzling his chin, she placed his hands back on her breasts, impatient for their lovemaking to continue.

He pulled his hands back as though they'd been burned. His voice was taut. "He's no cat. He's a damned devil sent from—"

"Hey, Whitney!" a voice came from outdoors, very near the shed. "You seen Grant around? I'm supposed to go on watch with him."

"Naw, I ain't seen him in a while," came the answering voice.

Madeline's heart froze in her chest at the thought of being discovered by Whitney and Johnson, and she stiffened, clasping her hands over her naked breasts.

"Oh, God, why me?" Evan muttered with frustration. She heard the rustling of fabric as he quickly buttoned his trousers and tucked in his shirt. "Stay quiet, sweetheart," he whispered, his breath hot in her ear. "I'm going out there now. You just sit tight until we're gone. Then get yourself buttoned up and back to the party. With any luck I'll see you sometime before midnight."

Quickly, silently, he was gone, out the door, leaving her empty and aching.

And all alone.

Rejoining the party was easy, she hadn't been missed.

The celebration was in full swing when she walked unsteadily back into its midst. The sassy sound of the fiddle and the twang of twin banjos carried over the rest of the instruments, and almost every female from five to fifty was being whirled around the dance area in front of the musicians. Justus Fletcher loudly called out the steps from atop a large overturned wooden box near the band.

Tables laden with cakes and cookies and large bowls of punch had been prepared to refresh the dancers. Strong coffee was brewing at Old Roger's camp, and the hardworking cook was busy separating the remainder of the roasted beef from the bones of the animal on the spit.

A large bonfire had been built in the yard during her absence, and those who chose not to dance sat on chairs and benches and on the ground around the blaze, tapping their feet in time to the music. Alongside the barn, men sat around two tables and engaged in card games and gambling, and much boisterous noise and shouting came from that area as well.

Lust burned unslaked in her belly, her breasts, and the moist cleft between her legs, and she walked through the crowd, nodding and smiling and saying hello, automatically, wanting at the same time to throw back her head and scream for the sheer frustration of it all. These feelings just weren't bearable! Did Evan suffer on his watch as much as she did right now? she wondered.

Hoping physical activity would help assuage the passionate torment inside her, she wandered over near the dancers and, for the next hour, danced one vigorous dance after another, with one merrily intoxicated partner after another. For never having played together before, the musicians did a fine job of playing square dances and waltzes and lively polkas, and of course the ever-popular Virginia reel. Justus, too, did a remarkable job of calling, adding many inventive impromptu calls of his own, many of which produced mirthful confusion and raucous laughter from the dancers.

The activity did help her turn her thoughts from the desire that burned hot inside her, but what helped most of all was the raging pain in her feet. At least a dozen times since she'd joined the dancers her booted feet had been stomped on by overeager cowpokes whose enthusiasm far outweighed their aptitude for following the steps.

In the middle of a slower waltz, an anxious-looking Jack Matthews pulled on her arm, provoking a wail from her partner: "Hey, watcha doin', Matthews? I got her 'til the end of this dance!"

"I've got to talk to you, Madeline," Jack said urgently, pulling her completely away from Jim Culvert. "Sorry, Culvert," he said, nodding to the lanky, sandy-haired cowboy. "It's important."

She had to take running steps to keep up with the tall blond rancher who tugged so insistently on her arm. When they were a good distance from the dancers, he turned to her with undisguised worry on his face. "Annalisa's missing," he said bluntly.

"Are you sure?" she asked, realizing with the first cold touch of dread that she had not seen her friend since midafternoon.

"Positive. I didn't get here until way after supper, and when . . . Oh, sorry, Madeline," he said, releasing the uncomfortably tight grip he held on her forearm. "When I got here," he began again, taking in a tense breath, "no one could remember seeing her for a long time."

"Well, she has to be somewhere, Jack," she said, squeezing his hand encouragingly. "She just can't be *gone*."

"She's gone," he said gravely, pacing in measured steps. "All she talked about yesterday was this picnic and not being able to wait to dance with me. Something's wrong, I just know it."

"Don't get ahead of yourself, now, Jack. She could have had a headache and gone to lie down—" Breaking off, she remembered that the second story of the house had been empty when she went upstairs to fetch her pants and shirt. "I'll check the house to be sure," she said with much more confidence than she felt, adding brightly, "and I'll have Justus make an announcement."

"I can't tell you how . . . how I'd feel if something happened to her, Maddie." He cleared his throat, squeezing her hand. "I . . . I love her, you know."

"I know, Jack," she whispered, feeling tears prickle her eyes.

Approaching Justus Fletcher at the end of the waltz, she quickly told him of her friend's mysterious disappearance. Concern flared in the older man's eyes as he listened, and he pointed at the band and ordered, "Hold it, boys."

Standing up to his full height on his crude rostrum, he shouted, "Attention, everyone! And I mean *everyone*! Someone clear those tables back around the barn, 'cause I want every last man and woman to hear what I got to say."

A babble of curious voices rose from the crowd as people wondered aloud what was going on. Will Reed stepped over to the podium, his expression troubled. "What's up, Maddie? Is somethin' the matter?"

"Anna's missing—" she said just as Justus Fletcher's voice cut her off.

"Can everyone hear me?" Fletcher shouted, his voice carrying clearly in the night air.

To a chorus of "Yeah" and "Go ahead on, Fletcher," he continued. "We got us a problem here, folks. Now, it might only be a little problem, but then again it could be a larger one. It seems that Miss Annalisa Grant is missing, and as you all know, Miss Annalisa has been a guest here at the Spencer ranch for the past several weeks. So what I want you all to do now is give the boys in the band a little break, and each and every one of you take a look-see around for Miss Annalisa. We'll meet back here in a quarter-hour. That's all."

The hubbub of voices was deafening in the wake of Fletcher's announcement. Will's gruff voice was loud in her ear as he put his arm around her shoulders and hugged her to him. "I don't like the sound of this, Maddie. Damn, I knew this party was a bad idea from the get-go. There's men runnin' around the countryside that'd kill their own mothers for lookin' cross-eyed at 'em. Hey!" he shouted, seeing Jack's broad-shouldered form standing next to the smaller frame of his older brother. "Hey, Jack Matthews! Come over here! You, too, Peter."

"Pete was just telling me that he saw Anna last about three-thirty, four o'clock," Jack said loudly over the noise as he approached them, his usually merry brown eyes appearing black with worry.

"Yeah, she was askin' me about Jack," Pete said to Will, trailing his brother, his face screwed up in a disagreeable expression. "Wanted to know when he'd be here."

"And that was 'bout four? Aw, Christ," the big foreman said, wearily running his hands over his face, "that was hours ago. You don't suppose she got a notion in her damn fool head to ride over to your ranch all by herself, do you?" Will asked.

"I didn't see her," Jack said, shaking his head.

"That's my point." Will's voice was grim. "Maybe she never got there."

"Yeah, she coulda been swiped by Injuns," Pete speculated aloud, "or happened upon an outlaw with a hankerin' for a pretty miss."

"I'm going to find her," Jack bit out, turning to leave.

"Hold on there, boy," Will ordered. "It's dark, and you don't even know for sure if—"

"I'm sure she's not anywhere around here!"

Madeline felt sick inside at the thought of a terrible accident—*or worse*, her mind whispered to her—befalling Annalisa. Sweet, impulsive, vivacious Anna, so full of life and love. Madeline felt her throat grow thick with emotion. During the past weeks she'd grown to think of Anna as the sister she never had.

Evan's sister. Oh, dear, she thought urgently, Evan needed to be told about this.

Will reached out and placed an arm on Jack's shoulder. "Just wait until Fletcher gets everyone's attention again. If she ain't been found, we can organize a search." At Jack's curt nod, he went on. "I know you're worried about her, son. I am, too. But we got us one whole hell of a lot of manpower gathered right here, an' we can start lookin' for the girl right away."

Groups of men set out on horseback a scant thirty minutes later.

The big bonfire snapped and crackled in the night air, broken only by the quiet, worried voices of the women seated around it. The house, the grounds, and every outbuilding had been thoroughly searched, but Anna hadn't been found.

After unnecessarily tossing another log into the fire, Madeline sank back onto the wooden bench and watched a plume of sparks flare upward as the hungry flames closed around the dry wood. How much longer until Evan would return? Would Anna be found tonight? Where was she? Had she been injured . . . or harmed?

Her mind whirled with questions for which she had no answers, and dread sat like a lump of cold, congealed grease in the pit of her stomach. Mrs. Ashler came to sit beside her, giving her eyes a quick swipe with the bottom of her apron as she settled her generous form on the bench.

"How you doin', dear?" she asked tenderly, putting a plump arm around Madeline. "Lord Almighty, this waitin's hard, ain't it?"

The older woman's gentle touch was Maddie's undoing. "I-I'm so sc-scared for her," she sobbed, tears slipping from her eyes unchecked. "And I feel so b-bad." Guilt bubbled up inside her. "It's my fault. I should have missed her sooner. It's just that I was—"

"It ain't your fault, dear," Mrs. Ashler said, kissing her cheek and holding her closer. "It ain't no one's fault. I'm sure the men will find her, if not tonight then tomorrow mornin' when it's light. And you know as well as me that she coulda done somethin' simple like fall off her horse an' bump her head or twist her ankle—"

"I know," she managed to say through her tears against Mrs. Ashler's plump bosom, knowing deep down that something else had happened to her friend.

"Let's us do a little somethin' to help Anna out," Mary Ashler said to the assembled women and children, whose faces reflected their uneasiness in the flickering firelight. "Wherever she is, the poor lamb is likely scared to death. My Henry used to find the Twenty-third Psalm might comforting, an' I imagine the words might apply to whatever fix Annalisa's in right now."

"Anna honey," her rich contralto voice rang out across the hush of the yard, past the warm glow of the fire, far above the string of lanterns that burned on above the deserted dance area, and well beyond the unattended, lamp lit tables of refreshments. "Wherever you are, this is for you. There's many kinds of darkness in this world, dear, an' we just want to send you a candle to help you find your way through yours. 'The Lord is my shepherd' " she began, looking around at the assembled group, " 'I shall not want' . . ."

Softly, at first, then with conviction, other voices joined hers. Mrs. Ashler's hand clasped her own, and Madeline saw that many other hands were joined as well.

" 'Yea, though I walk through the valley of the shadow of death, I shall fear no evil . . . ' "

Madeline repeated the words along with the other women, but the fear that something evil had happened to her bright, ebullient friend wouldn't release its grip on her. Crime ran rampant here in the West, and a multitude of horrible possibilities played through her mind, each more awful than the last.

Anna was in danger, she just knew it.

Dispatching silent, earnest words to her Maker, she hoped the men would find Anna and find her swiftly.

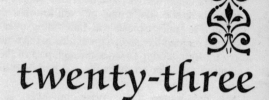

twenty-three

"THE GIRLIE LOOKS KINDA LONESOME SITTIN'
over there, don't she, boss? Maybe I could just
go on over an' give her a little company—"

"Mebbe she don' want your kind of company,
Shiny," another voice interrupted. "Mebbe she
wants mine."

"She'll stay over there, and you'll stay over here."
Rendner's curt reply drew grumbling and groans from the
seven men assembled around the small campfire. "She's
worth money. Lots of it."

Miles away from the Spencer ranch—exactly where, she
knew not—Annalisa Grant decided she was done being
scared. Redoubling her efforts to slip her wrists free of
the rope that bound her hands behind her, she swore to
herself, realizing that her fear had given way to bubbling,
boiling anger.

She was mad, all right, possibly madder than she'd ever
been.

Being forced to ride for hours at gunpoint didn't set well
with her, nor did being manhandled, nor did being denied

food, drink, and even privacy to answer nature's call. Just who the hell did these men think they were, anyway?

They're cattle thieves, Anna, she answered herself, *dirty, rotten, stealing sons of bitches.*

How could she have been so stupid as to slip off to the Matthews ranch the way she had? She hadn't let Madeline know where she was going, or even told her that she was leaving. Her only excuse was that riding over to surprise Jack had seemed like such a good idea at the time. She'd felt sorry for him, having to work through part of the picnic and having to miss out on the races and games and excitement of the afternoon.

She had gotten the surprise, however, as she'd dismounted and approached the Matthews barn, where she'd heard male voices raised in loud discussion. She'd recognized Aaron Rendner's thin, penetrating voice at once; the others she couldn't identify. Sensing that something wasn't quite right, she'd stopped outside the door. Shocked at what she heard, she froze, listening.

A person would have to have been rather dim-witted not to put two and two together.

Aaron Rendner and a group of unfamiliar men—Mann and Shiny were two names she heard—were behind the cattle thefts in the area. *Thank God it's not Pete*, was her first thought, for she knew how reluctant Jack had been to suspect his brother of the heinous crimes. Her knees trembled as she listened, hearing details of their next planned thefts and Rendner's boastful certainty that neither Matthews brother knew anything about his elaborate rustling operation.

Shaking with nervousness at the importance of her discovery, she'd quietly stolen back to her horse and mounted, intent on getting back to the Spencer ranch with her information as quickly as possible. She'd almost gotten away, too, but four new arrivals rode up, and they had guns.

They'd arrived at this place, this valley, after dark. Though it was impossible to see or count the number of cattle the rustlers were holding here, it sounded like a great many. Hundreds, even. After greeting the men who rode herd, Rendner had wasted no time in dragging her from her horse and tying her hands behind her back, then forcing her over to a crude corral. There he'd pushed her to the ground and lashed the other end of the rope to the bottom of one of the wood posts, leaving her with only six or seven inches of slack.

Please, God, she prayed, *help me get loose*. With one last enormous, painful effort, she tried to work her wrists free of the rope, biting the inside of her mouth to keep from crying out. It was no use; Rendner had knotted the rope too tight for her to slip her hands free. Resting the back of her head against the rough post, she wanted to kick and scream with frustration at the hopelessness of her situation. She was tied to a corral, dammit, in the middle of God-only-knew-where, her wrists were chafed raw from her attempt to escape, she was hungry and cold, and a group of criminals sat twenty feet from her and discussed her fate as if she was so much bothersome chattel.

Worst of all, no one else on earth knew where she was.

You'll be fine, Anna, she told herself, glaring at the seven men sitting around their campfire. *Just try to think of this as another western adventure. Besides, you're a whole lot smarter than all of them combined*. The tantalizing odors of their cooking food drifted over to her on the night air, making her even angrier. Her stomach growled painfully, and she realized she hadn't had food or drink since the noon meal.

"Hey, you be good over there, girlie, an' we might give you a little somethin' to eat," came the voice of the man known as Shiny, as if he knew how hungry she was. He was the first man she'd like to take revenge on. He'd plagued her nearly continually since she'd been captured. Shifting her weight from one buttock to the other on the hard ground, she made no reply to his taunt.

"But then again, if you're real good," he continued, "I might could give ya somethin' real big to eat on." He smacked his lips crudely for emphasis.

"Like what?" another man hooted derisively. "That li'l peashooter you call a tallywhacker? She might need herself a pair of them spectacles to find it—or mebbe even a spyglass—"

"Why, you—" Shiny leapt to his feet, all humor gone from his voice, his hands on his holsters.

"That's enough!" Rendner's voice cut through the night air over the sounds of the cattle and horses. "I didn't plan on draggin' this girl along with us any more than you did, but we didn't really get no choice about it. We're stuck with her." He stood, his beefy form silhouetted in stark relief against the glow of the campfire. "And what we're gonna do is let them get good an' worried about her, an' then we'll see how much they wanna pay to get her back."

Unless I find a way out of here before that, she mentally sneered. But for all her bravado, feelings of fear and loneliness undulated through her belly like a snake slithering through tall grass. She wasn't having an adventure; she was all alone and in big, big trouble.

Would she ever see Jack again? she wondered. Or Evan? Madeline? A lump rose in her throat as she thought of her family and loved ones. She'd left Chicago in a bad way, sneaking out of her house in the middle of the night. *Face it, Anna, you ran away*, she told herself harshly. What if she never got a chance to tell her mother and father how much she loved them? Would they know?

She longed for Jack with every fiber of her being, longed for the feel of his strong arms around her, longed for him to nuzzle her ear and whisper that everything was fine. Gazing up into the star-studded sky, she sent a prayer that she might be given a chance to escape from this place and these terrible men.

A quarter after three. Madeline glanced at the clock, and then at the glow of Old Roger's camp in the darkness beyond the kitchen window. Two enormous pots of coffee hung from iron hooks on the pot rack over his fire, and already the cook was preparing breakfast.

Another group of riders had just returned to the ranch after hours of fruitless searching, but she didn't see Evan's tall form among them. He and Johnson had returned from their watch four hours before, already having heard of Annalisa's disappearance from the men who had replaced them. Evan had spoken to Madeline briefly, confirming the frightening news of Anna's absence. Then, grim-faced, he'd clasped her to him in a rough hug before setting out with Johnson to join one of the search parties.

"You should try an' get some sleep, dear," Mrs. Ashler quietly said to her from the doorway of the kitchen. "The rest of the women are bedded down, though I don't know how many of 'em are sleepin' for worryin' about their men out there in the dark. All the children are finally quiet, though, even that fussy little tyke of Rosemary's."

"I can't rest when I know Annalisa's out there somewhere," she said simply, jamming her hands into her pockets and turning to face the older woman in the faintly lit room. She had changed from her dress to her denims and a loose blouse a few hours ago, wanting to be ready if someone needed her assistance. She simply felt more comfortable in her range clothing.

"Another bunch of men just get back in?" Mrs. Ashler asked.

"Yes."

"She's not with them, either, is she?"

"No." Madeline sighed deeply, turning back to the window. Several men milled around the fire, eating stale party refreshments and drinking hot coffee. Will Reed had gotten back from his search a short time before this latest group of men had arrived. Talking quietly, he moved among them, shaking his head.

More hoofbeats sounded, and all heads turned to see who was coming. Hope flared once again inside her, and she pressed her face closer to the window to see if Annalisa might be one of the riders.

"I don't even want to ask anymore," Mrs. Ashler said from behind her in a somber tone. "But I have to."

"It doesn't look like Annalisa's with these men, either," Maddie said just as heavily, her voice sounding muffled against the glass. Tears gathered in the corners of her eyes. "But I think I see Jack and Evan walking toward the fire." Indeed, both men made their way toward the growing gathering near the chuck wagon, their steps heavy and wooden, and her heart twisted at their obvious dejection. Two sets of broad shoulders slumped, and both heads shook negatively when Will Reed went to speak to them.

Evan rubbed his hands across his face then and looked at the ground. Her heart nearly broke at the sight of his grief, and she wished she could enfold him in her arms.

"I wonder which one of them is hurtin' more?" Mrs. Ashler asked, moving to stand beside her, sighing deeply. "God in heaven, I can't help but think what it's gonna be like for her poor ma an' pa to find out about this."

"They're going to find her today," Madeline said bravely, blinking back her tears, hoping that if she believed her words enough, they would come true.

"Of course they will, and we can't lose heart, not even for one minute," came Mary's reply. "I imagine we can't make Jack feel a whole lot better about things right now, but you have the power to salve Evan's spirit, dear. Go on out to him."

Needing no more encouragement, she gave the older woman a quick, wordless hug and walked out of the kitchen. A chill had settled in the air since the last time she'd been outside, and she hugged herself for warmth.

"Holy smokes, Miss Madeline!" Jim Culvert exclaimed soberly as she descended the porch steps. "What are you still doin' up?"

"You want a cup of coffee, ma'am?" another voice offered. "You can take this one. I ain't drank out of it yet."

"Thank you kindly," she said to a cowhand from the Dunlay ranch, she guessed, gratefully accepting the tin cup of hot, fragrant liquid. Taking a sip of the coffee, she continued to make her way over to where Evan and Jack spoke with Will.

She didn't know which of the two younger men was hurting more over Annalisa's disappearance. Both loved her fiercely—each in a different way. Though their faces were grim and otherwise free of visible emotion, their posture spoke of their worry and frustration and hopelessness. She saw the strain in their eyes as they looked up at her.

"Hi, Maddie," Will said dully. "We're gonna regroup here for now an' let the men eat an' get a few winks of sleep." He sighed deeply, and she noticed that he seemed unsteady on his feet. "There ain't nothin' to be found out there in the dark. We'll start searchin' again at first light. The other ranches are sparin' us all the men they can."

"Are you all right, Will?" she asked with great concern, knowing he wasn't up to all the hard riding he'd done tonight. "You should go lie down—Will!"

The burly foreman visibly faltered, a grimace of pain contorting his features. "I'm fine," he growled at her, his chest rising and falling rapidly, "an' it's over my dead body that the outlaws around these parts are gonna keep gettin' away with doin' what they damn well please."

"You're right about the 'dead body' part," Evan said grimly as he and Jack took Will's arms. "Say good night, Reed."

Madeline followed them to the bunkhouse, greatly troubled at Will's slow, shuffling gait despite the stream of invectives he managed to send out into the night air. Anxiously hovering near the door, she waited until Evan and Jack came back out.

"How is he?" she asked, shivering in the chill air.

"Madder than hell," Jack said, shaking his head. "See you later, Grant." He walked slowly back toward the chuck wagon, leaving her alone with Evan.

"I warned Reed not to get out of bed for at least a day," Evan said, sighing. "He exhausted himself looking for Anna. . . ." His voice trailed off, and in the feeble light cast by the distant fire she saw the anguish on his face. His mouth moved as if he might say more, but then he closed it.

Answering grief welled up inside her, and instinctively she moved closer, whispering, "It's going to be all right, Evan. We're going to find her."

"I . . . hope so." Worry and sadness made his voice harsh, and he dared not speak more out of fear that the burning hotness in his eyes and throat would give way to unmanly tears. Annalisa had been taken miles from here by now, he thought with despair, wondering at the same time what ill use his baby sister had suffered in the past hours. *If she's still alive to suffer*, a dark part of his soul murmured, making him want to howl with rage and pain and frustration.

Madeline's soft arms encircled his torso, and before he knew it his arms were around her and he was hugging her back, burying his face in the mass of silky, fragrant curls. Sweet, sweet Madeline. Her tenderness and caring washed over him, slowly filling the black, empty reservoir inside him with hope and strength, as well as with the courage to face the outcome of this search, whatever it might be.

Love and family. *That's what it all comes down to in life, Grant. Love and family.* Dear God, how could it have taken him twenty-eight long years to come to that simple conclusion? With his back against the rough plank siding of the bunkhouse he continued to hold on to Madeline as if he were holding on for dear life.

"I love you, Evan," she tearfully whispered against his chest. "I'll love you always and forever." *Always and forever.* A hot tear slipped from his eye at her words, and for an endless moment he stood with his arms around her, realizing how richly he had been blessed.

"Madeline Spencer," he said, pressing a gentle kiss against the top of her head, knowing he couldn't live even one minute longer without telling her how he felt. Disengaging her arms, he took her hands in his and moved along the side of the bunkhouse, putting a small distance between them. Maneuvering their positions so that the dim light from the distant fire caught her full in the face, he knelt before her.

"I've got something to ask you, sweet," he began, "and I'm determined to do things right this time." Did his voice tremble slightly? Did she notice? Suddenly he felt more nervous than he'd ever been in his life. What if she didn't . . .

As he gazed up at her, his fears fled into the night. The bunkhouse, the men over near the chuck wagon, the hard ground beneath his knees—everything faded from his consciousness except the hopeful radiance shining from Madeline Spencer's face. God, how he cherished this woman, this plucky, unconventional, precious woman who had taught him the meaning of love.

"I love you," he said simply, seeing twin glistening trails appear on her cheeks at his words. "I love you, Maddie," he repeated, this time in a stronger voice, "and I want to marry you if you'll have me."

"I—"

"Hurry up an' say you'll marry him so I can get some sleep!" came Will Reed's cross voice from the bunkhouse window. "God, I can't hardly stand the suspense no more."

"Evan!" Madeline's jaw dropped. "He's been listening to everything!" Wiping the tears from her cheeks, she called toward the window, an expression of good-natured outrage on her lovely features, "You're an old snoop, Will Reed!"

"Yeah, well, it's kept me alive this long. Now hurry up an' tell the boy he can make an honest woman outta you. Then go do yer kissin' under someone else's window."

"Yeah, hurry up and tell the boy he can make an honest woman of you," Evan repeated softly, smiling and shaking his head. With his thumbs he traced circles on the velvety skin of Madeline's inner wrists.

"This is as romantic as it's going to get?" She stepped back, pulling her hands away from his and planting them on her hips.

"He told you he loves you," came Reed's gruff voice from the window. "What more do ya want?"

"Oh, *I* don't know!"

"I love you, Madeline Spencer," Evan said again, sensing that there was a part of her, beneath the playful sarcasm, that wanted to hear more. He walked on his knees toward her, a sharp *pop* sounding from one of his aching joints as he moved. *You're getting old, Grant*, he told himself, sucking in his breath as a sharp stone bit into his other knee, *but you're going to get old along with the most wonderful woman in the entire world*. He wrapped his arms around her hips, pulling her close.

"I'll love you more than any husband could love any wife," he promised, looking up at her a long moment before pressing his face against her belly. "And I'll love each of our children more than any father on earth could love his children."

"I didn't hear that last part there, Grant," Reed's voice declared. "You're gettin' all mumbly-mouthed."

Lost in the spell of the moment, the two of them ignored the nosy foreman. "Oh, Evan," Madeline whispered, easing his hands from behind her delightfully rounded hips. Kneeling before him, legs against legs, torso against torso, she brushed her full lips against his. "I'll marry you whenever and wherever you say," she replied softly, kissing him again, her breath warm in his face, "and I promise to love you more than any wife could love any husband."

"You're kissin' out there, ain't you? I told you to take that business somewhere else!"

"We wouldn't kiss, Reed," Evan called primly toward the window. "We're not married yet." He cupped Madeline's chin in his hand and slanted her face toward his. As he captured her sweet lips beneath his own, Will Reed's disgruntled sputterings quickly faded from his ears. At first sweet, the kiss rapidly flared into something hot and urgent and demanding, and it was with great effort, a scant half-minute later, that he pulled away from her.

God, what was the matter with him? Annalisa was missing. Any number of terrible things could have happened to his baby sister, and here he was, horny as hell, ready to take Madeline right to the ground.

"It's all right, Evan. I feel the same way." Her breath came in rapid little pants, and she leaned against him heavily. "Come with me," she whispered in his ear as if she knew his every thought, his every feeling. "I know a place we can go. It's a quite a ride, but I don't think either of us is going to get any sleep tonight anyway."

Later, much later, in the peaceful, grassy area at the bend of the creek, two young lovers sealed their commitment and devotion to each other in the pale predawn light. With their worry for the woman they called sister and friend heightening their emotions, their lovemaking was both hungry and tender, urgent and deliberate, pure and healing.

Their love words and inarticulate cries of pleasure joined the sounds of the plain as beside them the waters of the stream burbled along tranquilly, as if quietly sighing its approval of their union.

twenty-four

THE FOLLOWING DAY PASSED WITHOUT ANY SIGN of Anna, as did the following night.

The next morning Evan looked tiredly over at Jack Matthews, wondering if the younger man ever needed sleep. It didn't seem he did, judging by his appearance. The fair-haired man looked at least twenty times more alert than Evan felt. Pulling the brim of his hat down farther to shield his eyes—two peeled eggs that rolled around in beds of gritty sand—he studied Jack's strong profile.

"So how long are you and Grant gonna be gone?" Pete Matthews stood on the steps of the Matthewses' tiny ranch house, wearing his customary sour expression. "Fletcher got hit last night, you know. Lost thirty, forty."

"What are you saying, Peter?" Jack tossed down the bundle of belongings he'd gathered, planting his hands on his hips. The tension between the two brothers was thicker than ever. "And you'd best keep in mind that we're searching for this man's sister—*and my future wife!*"

Arms gesticulating, Pete took one step down. "I'm sayin' that you two ain't gonna find a trace of her. You haven't yet! You ought to leave the searchin' to the authorities and get back to tendin' our cattle! Rustlers are runnin' the countryside, an' I been up all night bustin' my hump while you and Grant"—he spat out Evan's name as if it were poison—"are plannin' on takin' off for God knows how long to look for a girl that just ain't gonna be found. It ain't like we got the help to spare—"

"Why, you—" Jack started toward him with a dangerous glint in his eye, but Evan stopped him.

"Hold on, Jack." Something Pete had said disturbed Evan deeply. "Fletcher's ranch is way south of the city, isn't it?" he asked Jack quietly.

The blond man stopped his struggling. "It is," he said slowly, a terrible comprehension dawning on his face. A vile curse escaped his lips. "And whores are to be bought, aren't they?"

Turning stiffly, he pulled his arm free of Evan's grasp. "If Fletcher got hit during the night, Peter," he said harshly, "how come you know about it so early?"

"Rendner told me!"

"Rendner told you." Jack's disbelief was apparent in his statement. "Where were you last night, Peter?"

"What are *you* sayin', brother?" Pete hollered, rapidly descending the steps and walking over toward them. "Rendner told me this morning when I was headin' back here."

"Where's Rendner?"

"He's out on the range."

Evan stepped back silently, allowing the long-brewing battle between the two brothers to erupt. Jack Matthews was no more behind the cattle rustling than was the man in the moon; of that he was now certain. In the past days Evan had developed a grudging respect for Jack; if there was any man in the world tailor-made for his spirited young sister, it was Jack. Though it still felt strange to think of Annalisa being someone's wife, Jack Matthews was a man he'd be proud to call brother.

Pete Matthews, now . . . Evan still had strong suspicions about the homely, disagreeable rancher despite the fact that he was with Venus Five-by-Five on the night of Reed's shooting.

"I ain't a cattle thief, Jack!" Pete cried. "God, is that what you think of me?"

"I don't know what to think of you." Disgust dripped from Jack's words, and he stabbed his finger at his brother accusingly. "But I do know it's a good thing Ma ain't alive to know you anymore. She'd be sick at your meanness." He took a step backward and retrieved his bundle. "*I'm* sick at your meanness, and you can count me out of this ranch as of this second."

Turning on his heel, Jack walked stiffly to his mount. Evan followed behind, proud of the way the younger man had handled himself. The door of the ranch house slammed behind them, but Jack's step didn't falter.

"You sure about this?" he asked as Jack lashed his bundle behind his saddle.

"I'm sure. This has been a long time coming."

"All right, then," he said, nodding, satisfied with his friend's answer. "Let's get back over to the Spencers' and pick up the rest of our supplies. With any luck we can be on the trail by noon."

Madeline stood silently in the golden sunshine of late morning, watching Evan and Jack make final preparations for their trip. Next to the fresh mounts that were to carry them, two packhorses stood impatiently as the men loaded their provisions evenly on the animals' backs. Gun belts rode low on the hips of both men, a grim reminder of the danger of their undertaking.

Unlike Madeline, though, Will Reed was not able to keep quiet. Edgy and ornery, he paced about the yard, hollering words of caution and instruction and advice to the two younger men. "You wired your pa yesterday, didn't you, Grant? An', Matthews, you put word out about Anna in Cheyenne, didn't ya? You got a heavy coat, Grant? The air gets damn cold up there in the mountains, you know. Oh, hell, I wisht I was goin' with you. You boys don't even know what you're dealin' with. Could be Injuns or desperadoes—"

"We'll be careful, Reed," Evan said without turning his head, the fabric of his tan shirt stretching taut over his powerful back and shoulders as he hoisted another load onto the back of his packhorse. "What's more, we'll bring Annalisa back," he finished resolutely.

Madeline drank in the sight of the man she loved, trying to crush the rising anxiety inside her that hissed, *This might be the last time you see him alive.* She no longer doubted his love for her, but both of them felt that their wedding would have to wait until the mystery of Annalisa's disappearance was resolved one way or another.

With a shaky sigh she folded her hands low over her belly, praying that Anna would be discovered, safe and unharmed. Though she couldn't bear the thought of anything bad happening to her lively, vivacious friend, the very real possibility existed that she might never be found.

Or that she was already dead.

Tears she thought had been used up ran again. What if she never saw Anna or Evan again? She didn't think she could bear losing one more thing in her life. . . .

"Hey! You hear that?" Will's tone commanded them to be quiet and listen.

"What?" The men stopped their work for a moment. Evan cocked his head to one side before turning to face Madeline, a curious expression on his face. Straining her ears, she could hear something over the glad song of the meadowlarks. A distant note? A cry? Running to the corral, she climbed to the top rail and stood balanced with one foot on the rail, the other on the post, looking into the distance.

A rider approached from the north, his horse at a dead run. The sounds of the flying hoofbeats were now distinguishable, as were the cries of the rider.

"Is that Ashler?" Evan asked from beside her.

"He's gonna kill that horse!" Reed bellowed from behind them as Robbie Ashler approached, "if he don't break his own fool neck first."

"Don't you even think about jumping," Evan warned as Madeline quickly eyed the ground for a safe place to land.

Taking his proffered arm, she lightly descended the rails, pulling him along. "Come on, Evan!" she cried impatiently. "What's he saying?"

Old Roger had come out of the cookshack at the shouting, wiping his hands on his apron, the few men who had gathered for lunch trailing out behind him. All watched as Robbie approached at breakneck speed, his head bent low over his mount.

"I saw her! . . . I saw . . . I saw them," he shouted hoarsely as he entered the yard, vaulting from the foamy, heaving dun even before the animal had come to a stop. "Up there." He pointed, pacing wildly. "I saw them! . . . They have her . . . an' I—" His voice broke, and he swiped at his eyes with his fists. "An' I . . . an' I couldn't do nothin' about it, so I came back an'—"

"Whoa, Ashler," Evan said, enfolding the tall, nearly frantic adolescent in his arms. "Settle down. It's all right now. You're not hurt, are you?" At the rapid negative shaking of Robbie's head, Evan broke the hug and looked down into the young face. "Just take a deep breath and tell us what you saw, Robbie."

For all his seeming patience, Evan's tension was evident in his big frame, and not for the first time Madeline thought of the muscular form of a big, sleek cat. The rest of them crowded around, anxious to hear the details of Robbie's discovery.

"Well . . . I saw these two fellers ridin' a blue streak to the north," he began, his breath coming rapidly, "an' I jus' had a funny feelin' about 'em."

Relief and anxiety mixed uneasily in Madeline's breast as Robbie explained how he'd trailed the men to a distant unoccupied valley.

"And you don't think they saw you?" Jack asked when the boy paused for breath.

"Naw, they didn't see me," he said confidently. "They didn't even turn around." Looking back at Evan, he continued. "I followed 'em for what seemed like forever, hangin' way back, an' then they rode straight down into a little valley that I ain't been to before. There was a bunch of bawlin' an' yellow smoke comin' outta that valley," he said, raising his head to glance at Will Reed, "an' I knew right away that they were—"

"Branding." Will breathed the word with venom. "Jesus, Mary, and Joseph, they're brandin' *our* cattle down there!"

The immediate babble of angry voices was deafening.

"Forget that!" Jack roared. "They're branding mine, too, as well as everyone else's!" The blond rancher appeared ready to explode. Clapping his hands roughly on Robbie's thin shoulders, he put his face next to the boy's. "Ashler, you said 'They have her.' *Did you see Annalisa?*"

"I did! That's what I'm tryin' to say! An' what's more, I saw your foreman down there, too." Swallowing loudly, Robbie shrugged himself free of Jack's grip. "Rendner appeared to be in charge of the rustlers. They got themselves quite a setup," he said, his words tumbling out quickly now. "They got a camp an' a corral an' a little crick—"

"What about the girl, Ashler?" Will Reed said, impatiently. "Right now we just want to know about the girl."

"Well, there's just so much to tell, an' I'm tryin' to tell you everything—"

"It's all right, Robbie," Evan said quietly. His face was filled with hard purpose. "You're doing fine. Just tell us how Anna looked and how many men are down there, and we'll take it from here. You can lead us back there, can't you?"

"Yep." The angular face bobbed up and down importantly. "I sure can. Went right by your place, Matthews."

"*Ashler*," Reed warned, "get to the point."

"Well, jeez!" Hurt was apparent in the young voice. "I was just gonna say that Miss Annalisa appeared to be all right. Looks like they got her tied up, though. An' there were seven men in all," he quickly added, nodding. "Seven. I counted 'em."

"Armed?" Evan asked.

"To the teeth. I saw—"

Madeline let out her breath in a great sigh of relief. Anna was alive. God willing, she'd be home for dinner tonight. But how were they going to—

"And we'll stop by your place and round up all the men your brother can spare, too, Matthews," Evan was saying to Jack. "There are five of us here right now, plus what we can—"

"Six," Madeline said stubbornly, looking around. "I refuse to sit here and twiddle my thumbs while my friend is—"

"Seven," Will declared, folding his arms across his chest, daring anyone to defy him. "She goes, I go."

"Neither one of you is going!" Evan shouted, clearly outraged. "Dammit, Madeline, don't you realize that we've got to kill those men to get Annalisa back? And you!" he gestured angrily at Will. "Riding the other night just about did you in, Reed. In case you forgot, you just hauled your sick, sorry ass out of bed yesterday afternoon."

"We'll be ready to go in five minutes!" Wayne Johnson called as he and Jim Culvert and Roger Reilly ran to get their mounts.

"I'm going, Evan," Madeline repeated, knowing instinctively how much her friend would need the presence of another woman. Especially if she had been . . . Madeline couldn't even bear to think of the word. Planting her hands on her hips, she lifted her chin. "We're not married yet, Evan Grant, and I do not have to obey you until that day."

"God! As if you ever would!"

"I mean it. I'm going! Anna needs me," she repeated, narrowing her eyes at the angry, equally determined man before her. "You'll have to shoot me to keep me here."

"Don't tempt me, woman." His hands drifted to his holsters, and he cocked his head to one side. When he spoke again, his voice was rough. "What if the wrong side wins, Madeline? Have you thought of that?"

"Then we'll die together. I don't think I could live

without you, Evan." she finished softly, touching his arm, appealing to the steel blue glint in his eyes.

"Save the mush for later, you two," Will said gruffly, clearing his throat. "Come on, let's help Jack unpack these horses so's we can get goin'."

twenty-five

AT EVAN'S SIGNAL, THE FIRST GUNSHOTS RANG out in the warm July afternoon. A cold shiver passed through Madeline as she watched him and seven other brave men disappear over the rim of rocky grassland into the valley below. She, Will, and Robbie waited on horseback, out of sight, near a clump of low bushes.

"Just sit tight." Will made a face and mimicked Evan's words. He tightened his grip on the rifle he balanced on his saddle horn. "And just how the hell are we supposed to do that?" he asked angrily as more gunfire sounded. "Settle down, horse!" he ordered, pulling on his reins. He looked tired, his face pinched. "An' I ain't so sure that blastin' in there in broad daylight was the smartest thing to do."

"Well, Jack an' Evan said—" Robbie started to say, his young face looking white and scared despite his tan. Rings of sweat bloomed beneath his arms, and he scratched his nose nervously with the butt of his revolver.

"Don't you 'Jack an' Evan' me, boy," Will snapped, "an' careful where you're pointin' that thing . . . Oh, damn! Now what are they doin'?"

Gunfire and shouting and the bellowing of cattle carried clearly out of the little valley. Fear and nausea churned heavily in Madeline's stomach as she listened to the fighting. They had ridden out here at a merciless pace, and her nerves were stretched to their limits. Thank God, though, the rustlers had not posted a guard. Whether they'd become so confident that they would not be discovered or whether they had simply grown careless over time, she couldn't say.

Pete Matthews had insisted that they attack immediately, pointing out that as long as they had the advantage of surprise, they might as well also make use of the daylight. Remembering the pain and shame on his ruddy face when he'd learned of Rendner's involvement in the cattle thefts and Annalisa's disappearance, Madeline felt her heart soften slightly toward the antagonistic rancher. He'd been quick to offer her a brief, agonized apology to all assembled. Then he and two of his cowhands had quickly joined their little army.

How would he fare in the battle? she wondered. It was hard to say which one of them—Evan, Jack, or Pete— was the hungriest to see justice served. How would any of them fare, for that matter? Was Annalisa still unharmed? Madeline swallowed, her mouth as dry as tinder.

Was Evan safe?

The screaming of a woman rose above the other sounds then, making her scalp prickle and her blood stop cold in her veins. "That's it!" she exclaimed, kicking her horse into a gallop. "I can't sit here anymore." She heard Will and Robbie shout behind her, but she only urged the gelding on.

A gust of wind blew her hat off as her mount cleared the ridge in a fluid motion and began to descend the hillside. Dust rose high in the air as the thundering hooves of hundreds of cattle pounded against the hard-packed ground. The beasts were off, running wildly toward the open end of the valley. Four bodies littered the ground around a makeshift branding pen, and beyond that, on the ground next to a small corral, sat Annalisa, screaming her head off.

Gunshots boomed in the distance from the men who continued their battle and simultaneously tried to turn the herd, but Madeline's attention was on Anna. Was she hurt? Had she been shot? Why did she scream and shake her head so?

Just then, Robbie appeared at her side. "Maddie! Grant's shot! Grant's down!" he hollered, pointing. "Look! Over here—hurry!"

Grant's down.

Horror overwhelmed her as she spied Evan's inert form on the ground roughly seventy-five yards beyond the corral. Oh, God, that was what Anna had been screaming about. Urging her horse forwards she was oblivious to everything except reaching the man she loved.

Pete Matthews reached Evan just a few seconds before she and Robbie did. "He picked off three of 'em before he went down. I saw him fall, but I went after the bastard that shot him," he shouted to them as he dismounted. "Got him, too." Kneeling next to the unconscious man who lay face down with his left arm sprawled at an impossible angle, he announced, "He ain't dead."

"He's bleeding!" Madeline cried, clambering down from her horse and cupping her face in her hands, feeling as though she were about to swoon. "Why is his head bleeding? Why is he—" Great sobs shook her as she sank to her knees. "You can't die, Evan," she wept hysterically. "You just can't . . . n-not now. . . . Oh, I love you . . . so much. Oh, God, please . . ."

"I don't think he's gonna die, Miss Maddie," Pete said awkwardly as he untied his handkerchief, looking between her and Evan as if he wasn't certain who was in greater need of attention. Concern was the only emotion on his plain, ruddy face.

"Here, take mine, too," Robbie offered, hurriedly unknotting his neckerchief. "Gosh, Matthews, do you think his shoulder popped outta joint again? Just look at his arm layin' there like that."

"Yeah," Pete agreed, "I think it did. Let's get him turned over, now, before he comes to."

Through her tears she saw the two men turn Evan to a supine position, and though her head felt thick and stupid and numb, she saw that Evan's chest rose and fell in a regular rhythm.

Pete had spoken the truth: Evan wasn't dead.

"Thank you," she whispered. "Thank you, thank you."

"You okay, Miss Madeline? Your man's gonna be fine, really." Emotion filled Pete Matthews's voice as he stopped his work and stared at her. "Maybe you should lay down or something. You know, you gotta think of the—"

"Hey, it looks like Grant's wigglin' his face a little bit," Robbie announced.

"Come on, Ashler, we've got to get Miss Madeline's man put back together here," Pete said with a sad smile, his gaze meeting hers a moment longer in silent, accepting communication. "Are you holding that cloth up to his head tight enough to stop the bleeding?"

"How's he doin'?" came Will Reed's gruff voice as he drew his cantering mount to a halt next to them. Evan groaned as the big man dismounted and knelt next to him. "He's startin' to come to, eh? Good. Yeah, them bastards put up a tough fight, but we got 'em all," he continued grimly, looking up for a moment and pointing to the distant end of the valley where the small group of Spencer and Matthews hands rode toward them. "Damn cows are gone, though."

"And Rendner?" Pete asked in a low voice.

"Wasn't no decent tree around to hang him from proper, so they shot him, just before I got down there. That black-hearted sonofabitch! Stealin' every one of us blind for God knows how long, an' all the while pretendin' to be our friend. I should go put another piece of lead in him, just for good measure! And ain't this dandy!" he exclaimed, studying Evan's arm. "Do I see what I think I see? Is this boy's shoulder outta place again?" He pressed his thick fingers gently over the deformed joint. "Oh, damn. Let's get this bone back in the socket. An' when he wakes up, tell him I'm gonna start chargin' him for this!"

"Did any of our men—" Pete asked, backing up and giving the Spencer foreman room to work.

"Nope," Will answered proudly. "Old Roger got winged, but otherwise all our men are accounted for. Our women, too," he added as Jack Matthews streaked by on horseback, headed for the makeshift corral. "That ol' Cupid's been shootin' his arrows like crazy around here. Your brother's a goner, you know," he declared, shaking his head. "I'm predictin' a wedding for those two before snow flies."

"Yeah, I imagine," came Pete's distant-sounding reply, his eyes on Jack as he all but flew from his horse and ran to embrace Annalisa. Sighing, Pete pushed himself to his feet then, turning his back on them and the touching scene in the distance. "Well, guess I'll see if anyone else needs help," he muttered, brushing his hands on his chaps and walking slowly toward his mount. "Anyone got any predictions for me?" he added so softly that Madeline wasn't sure he'd even spoken at all.

twenty-six

"THE PREACHER'S HERE, THE PREACHER'S HERE!"
High horsetail clouds swept the azure sky over the snowy peaks to the west as Robbie Ashler ran noisily up the porch steps and threw open the kitchen door with such force that it banged against the opposite wall. "Hey, Grant! Ma! Miss Madeline! The preacher's here! Reed got the license an' brought back the preacher!"

A chorus of male whoops and loud laughter sounded from the sitting room while Mary Ashler's "Settle down, everyone!" rang out with authority from the kitchen.

The voices carried to the two women in the upstairs bedroom of the ranch house not only on the warm afternoon breeze that stirred the curtains but also clearly through the floorboards.

"A ranch wedding—another western adventure," Annalisa said, laughing softly and shaking her head. "I can't say as I've ever been to a wedding like this. Listen to them carrying on down there, Maddie. I wonder how Evan will stand up to their kidding?"

If she hadn't been so nervous, Madeline might have laughed with her friend. But she *was* nervous. Heavens, this wedding had been put together in the space of a single morning!

"The only thing for me to do, woman, is marry you quick before anything else happens." Evan's disgruntled words to her at breakfast had been taken quite literally by Will Reed. They'd been talking about the cattle rustlers, with Anna providing many details of her capture, when Evan had expressed—for the hundredth time in a day and a half— his great displeasure at Madeline for disobeying his orders and rushing into the midst of the fighting.

"Marry her quick before anything else happens, eh? That's the best idea I heard outta your mouth yet, boy," Will had said, slamming down his fork and clapping his great hands together over a half-finished stack of Mary Ashler's flapjacks. "I know your shoulder an' head are still painin' you, but if you can stand on your feet for ten minutes this afternoon, we can turn you into a bridegroom. Hell, you can do it sittin' down, for that matter." Pushing back his chair, he'd reached for his hat and was out the door before any of them could say a word.

"He's serious, isn't he?" Evan had said irritably, looking around the table, his eyes settling on Madeline. As he shifted his left arm beneath the uncomfortable-looking binding, a slow, wolfish smile had spread across his face. "Good."

The smoldering heat in his blue eyes had played havoc with her insides, and she'd scarcely been able to finish her own flapjacks for thinking that today this magnificent man would become her husband. Aside from his dislocated shoulder, his injuries were not severe. A thrill had run through her when she realized that he would be perfectly capable of performing any husbandly duties she might require of him.

And she had several such requirements in mind. . . .

"Oh, dear, a *snubbing post*?" Annalisa said with wide-eyed amusement, pausing as she pinned her brooch to her bodice. "Poor Evan, what kind of terrible song are those cowboys singing to him now?" Giggling, she added, "He's really getting teased. I wish Ben could be here today to see it."

"And I can't believe all we had to do was let the hem out of your grandmother's dress," Anna continued, kneeling before her and arranging the folds of Madeline's skirt. "Oh, honey, you look just beautiful in it." Tears shone in Annalisa's sapphire eyes as she looked up at Maddie. "The ivory is perfect with your coloring, and your grandmother did such fine detailing on the sleeves and bodice. I can't believe it's as old as it is. Are you ready to go down now? . . . Oh, dear, Maddie, don't cry. You miss your grandmother, don't you? You must miss her terribly."

Nodding, she realized how much she missed Elsie. And Albert. They were the only parents she'd ever known. Unwrapping Elsie's wedding dress this morning had been a bittersweet pleasure, as well as a painful reminder that her family situation was as unsettled as it had been since she received Emmett Brinkman's letter all those weeks ago.

Don't forget that Nate's your real father, a small voice reminded her, adding dismally, *wherever he is*. She sighed and wiped away her tears as the voice spoke again. *And don't forget poor Sara Brinkman.*

"Bring her on down, Anna!" Will's voice called up the stairwell. "We got a hold of the groom by his hind legs, an' the preacher's in place."

Another round of rowdy cheers and pounding feet shook the floor beneath them. "It sounds like you're getting married, honey," Anna said, standing and brushing a soft kiss on her cheek. The brunette's face was sunburned and a little thinner, perhaps, after two days in the company of her kidnappers, but she was otherwise unharmed. "I've always wanted a sister," she whispered, squeezing Madeline's hand reassuringly as she pulled her along.

As if in a dream, Madeline descended the stairs and took Will Reed's arm. The sitting room was packed full of freshly washed Spencer and Matthews cowhands wearing their Sunday finest, and another loud cheer arose as she appeared. She noticed that both Jack and Pete Matthews were in attendance as well, the latter nodding and giving her an honest, encouraging smile as she passed.

A path opened through the group of men, and her gaze was drawn immediately to the tall, dark-haired man standing in front of the window. The room's boisterous sounds faded from her ears, and all melancholy vanished from her soul at the sight of her husband-to-be. Straight and proud and true, even with one arm bound to his chest, he stood beside the minister and watched her approach, and she knew in that moment that his virile form would never fail to stir her. *I love you*, his blue eyes communicated to her across the room, filling her heart with warmth and joy.

They exchanged their vows, and the brief ceremony was over before she knew it, and when tall, thin, kindly Reverend Marks called for Evan to kiss the bride, the room erupted into cheering and clapping and shouting such as she'd never heard.

"I think they want us to kiss," Evan said loudly, eliciting a chuckle from the minister and even more enthusiastic encouragement from those assembled. Gathering her into his good arm, he smiled down at her, tiny crinkles fanning out from the corners of his eyes, and Madeline felt her spirit soar as his strong arm and his love encircled her when they kissed.

"Hey, you two gonna stand there starin' at each other all day?" Joker Joe hollered above the voices of the others. "Ain't your necks gettin' sore? Come on, finish up already an' let's dig into that sugar cake I saw in the kitchen."

"The refreshments are gonna be served outdoors," Mrs. Ashler announced in a tone that brooked no argument, "an' I'm lookin' for some volunteers to help me finish cartin' all the food out there."

"Shall we lead the way to the refreshments, Mrs. Grant?" Evan murmured, breaking the kiss. "Before we have a stampede on our hands?"

"Congratulations, you two," Will said gruffly as the room began to clear. Planting a kiss on Madeline's temple, he said, "I know your pa woulda been every bit as proud of your choice of husband as I am, Maddie. And even though my name ain't Spencer, I'm happy as hell to welcome you to the family, Grant," he added, clasping the younger man's hand in a firm grip. "Oh, and I picked you up a piece of mail when I was in town today. Here you go," he said, reaching into his vest pocket. Slitting open the envelope with his pocket knife, he withdrew the folded sheets of paper and handed them to Evan. "It's from your brother."

"Thanks, Reed," Evan said, taking the pages and scanning the words. "Would you like to know how Ben's—" he started to say. "Oh, Jesus! Ben's been snooping," he announced, struggling with the fingers of his right hand to get to the second page of the letter. "Talking to Brinkman's attorney." Furrows had appeared in his forehead as his eyes flicked back and forth down the page, and a peculiar sense of foreboding filled Madeline as she snatched the first paper from his hand and began to read.

"Oh, my God, Madeline," Evan said sharply, interrupting her before she'd made it through the first two lines. "Nate went to France to find your mother—your *real* mother!"

"Her real mother? She's dead . . . ain't she?" Reed's expression was incredulous.

"Not according to this," Evan continued, shaking his head. "Listen."

Shock rooted Madeline's feet to the floor and prevented her from moving or speaking, as her husband read the rest of Ben's missive aloud. His younger brother had been very thorough in uncovering facts and information from the attorney and from Caroline Brinkman, Sara's unmarried younger sister, and Madeline felt her disbelief increase with each line Evan uttered.

"So what he's sayin' is that Nate went off to France to fetch Miss Sara, and that Madeline an' the two sisters inherited the whole estate to split three ways?" Will interrupted. "Shee-it, Maddie! Do you know what kind of money that old bastard was worth?"

An inheritance? That meant nothing to Madeline compared to knowing that Sara Brinkman was alive. Exiled to France, but *alive*. The excitement in her breast turned to sorrow, though, as she tried to imagine what it must have been like for her young mother to undergo the heart-wrenching tragedy of giving birth to a child she was told was stillborn and then to be cast away in disgrace from her family to live in a foreign land.

What had become of Sara Brinkman in the past twenty years? she wondered. Would Nate be able to talk her into coming back to the States?

"Are the bride an' groom comin' out to have the first pieces of weddin' cake?" Mrs. Ashler called from the kitchen. Her round face wore a gentle smile as she appeared in the doorway and gazed at them. "Anna's mannin' the cake table an' having one heck of a time tryin' to hold back all them hungry cowpokes."

"They'll be along in a minute," Will answered, walking over to take the older woman's arm. "How 'bout we give the bride an' groom a few moments alone?"

"We done good, Willis Reed," came Mrs. Ashler's voice as they walked away. "Didja see their faces when they was sayin' the words? Just think—I was the first one to see love bloomin' between the two of them."

"*You* were? You didn't even—" The kitchen door closed on the rest of Will's response, leaving the newlyweds alone in the house.

"What are you thinking, sweet?" Evan asked. "That's an awful lot to take in at one time." His eyes didn't leave hers as he set the letter down and tenderly traced her jawline with the knuckles of his right hand. "Hell, even I'm feeling overwhelmed."

" 'Overwhelmed' describes it nicely," she replied, feeling his intense blue gaze and potent nearness affect her as much as Ben's information had. "But I hope Nate and Sara can . . . Oh, never mind," she added softly, "I'm just being silly."

"Hope is never silly," he murmured, brushing his lips against hers. "And neither is love or faith or patience. You taught me that, sweet wife, among many other things."

"Really?" she purred, leaning carefully against his good side. "And just what might these many other things be?"

"Oh, Madeline, promise me you'll never change," he said huskily against her mouth, capturing her lips in a passionate kiss while the sounds of merry revelry from the outdoors carried in to them and a furry gray form leapt down, unnoticed, from the top of the hutch.

Evan took her hand in his, and they walked out together into the warm July afternoon.

epilogue

GOLDEN AUTUMN SUNSHINE SPARKLED DOWN from a sky of lapis, its brilliance put to shame by the radiant happiness on the faces of the bride and groom as they stood at the top of the gaily decorated Spencer Ranch porch steps.

If Jack Matthews was handsome in his new black suit, then Annalisa Grant was an absolute vision to behold in an intricately wrought bridal gown of creamy white poult-de-soie. Matching sprays of tiny wildflowers graced both her coiffure and the bouquet in her hands, and, fluttering slightly in the soft breeze, a long veil cascaded over her shoulders and down her back.

Hannah Grant had brought the wedding attire all the way from Chicago last week, and both she and Elsie had suffered a great lack of sleep since that time in order to accomplish the gown's final fit. Looking over to where Elsie sat next to Willis Reed, Madeline smiled. Her grandmother's health evidently wasn't as frail as she had thought.

Instead of answering Madeline's letter—the long letter in which Madeline had told her grandmother almost everything that had gone on during the spring and summer— the gray-haired woman had simply traveled to Wyoming Territory to see for herself what kind of funny business was going on at Nate's ranch.

Taking everything, even the advanced state of Madeline's pregnancy, in stride, Elsie had easily settled into the ranch routine. Her kind, gentle nature had quickly won the hearts of all, and she and Mary Ashler had spent many pleasant afternoons sewing baby clothes and planning every detail of Annalisa's wedding.

"I wonder what my mother had to say to get my father to come?" Evan whispered to Madeline, pointing to Hiram Grant. Two rows ahead of them, the broad-shouldered, silver-templed man tugged impatiently at his collar. "I still can't believe he's here. Last I heard from Ben, the old man was so steamed about Anna running away and his leather deal falling through that he said he wouldn't come." His words ended in a chuckle as Hannah pulled surreptitiously but ruthlessly on a lock of her husband's hair and gave him a quiet earful of wifely advice.

"I guess you women have your ways, don't you?" he said, putting his arm around her and drawing her close.

Just then Reverend Marks cleared his throat and asked the guests to quiet down and take their seats. Turning her head to look behind her, Madeline saw that the neat rows of benches and chairs in the yard were nearly filled with hatless, subdued, slicked-down cowboys. Jim Culvert and Joe McCaleb looked so foreign in their Sunday best that her eyes almost skipped past them without recognizing them.

"Why do you suppose they couldn't have behaved like this at our wedding, Evan?" she asked, turning back toward her husband. "Look at them all sitting down like timid little mice."

"Well, either Mrs. Ashler warned them to behave, or else they've never seen a bride in full wedding regalia before, and it scares them."

"Dearly beloved," Reverend Marks began, preventing her from making a reply, "we are gathered here today to . . ."

As the minister spoke, Madeline's mind drifted back to the day when she and Evan had stood before the tall, kindly man and spoken their own vows.

So much had happened since then.

Both Will and Evan had recovered completely from their injuries, thank goodness, and the ranch again ran smoothly. Most of the stolen cattle had been recovered, and so far the area had not been plagued by any more rustlers.

And gone was the intense, serious, preoccupied eastern industrialist she had once known; Evan's happiness and contentment with life in the West were easy to see. Despite the hard work, his manner was relaxed, his laugh easy, his love steadfast and true. With great enthusiasm he spoke of starting their own ranch one day soon, of raising cattle and horses.

Madeline had received a letter last month from Basil Merritt, Emmett Brinkman's attorney, in which he'd detailed the specifics of Madeline's grandfather's will. Madeline had been staggered to learn of the large fortune she stood to inherit, but a part of her knew she could never accept Brinkman's money. The instructions in her grandfather's will that called for the three women—Madeline, Sara, and Sara's sister Caroline—to come together in San Francisco . . . now, those were instructions she looked very much forward to following.

In fact, Caroline had also written Madeline a friendly letter last month, telling her how much she looked forward to meeting her, and inviting her to San Francisco for a visit. No one had heard from Nate or Sara, however. That was the only pall on this otherwise perfect day.

Reverend Marks's voice rang out over the assembled group. "And do you, Jack William Matthews, take this woman to be your lawfully wedded wife?"

"I do," came Evan's deep voice in her ear as his arm tightened around her.

His words and the soft kiss he placed upon her temple might have started the flow of moisture from Madeline's eyes, or it might have been the sight of the bride and groom, so obviously in love, reciting their vows beneath the garlands of ribbons and bright-colored asters that hung from the eaves; she didn't know. Dabbing at her eyes with a handkerchief, she noticed that several other women did the same, as did a few of the men. Next to Robbie, Mrs. Ashler cleared her throat and unashamedly blew her nose into her white handkerchief.

Reverend Marks pronounced the young couple man and wife just as the sound of pounding hoofbeats could be heard. All heads turned toward the rider who came into sight a moment later, a young boy on a piebald pony. "Got a wire for Miss Madeline!" he shouted, slowing his pony in the yard. "I knowed you was havin' a weddin' today, but the instructions were to deliver this immediately!"

Evan was on his feet and over to the boy in an instant. Speculations and the buzz of curious voices filled the air, and Madeline remembered Evan telling her that Nate's last wire had been delivered from town in much the same way.

"Here we go, Madeline Spencer," he said, walking back toward her with an encouraging smile on his face. "It's from someone who doesn't know you've been turned into a Grant."

Nate?

She felt everyone's eyes on her as she took the envelope with shaking fingers. Withdrawing the sheet of paper, she began to read.

"What's it say, Maddie?" boomed Will's voice. "Come on, you gotta read it out loud!"

"I-I can't," she said, having quickly scanned the words. Tears clouded her vision and spilled down her cheeks. She handed the message to Evan. "Here."

As he read, a broad smile quickly replaced his concerned expression. "I love you, sweet," he murmured in her ear, first pulling her into a firm embrace, then bounding to the porch.

"Nate's coming home!" he declared from the second step. Great whoops and shouts met his words, and he held up his arms for everyone to be quiet.

"And that's not all," he continued with a flash of even white teeth, his eyes meeting his wife's across the distance separating them. "Nate and his new wife, Sara, expect to be home by the end of the month."

The assembled cowhands remained silent for a long moment, then burst into a tumult of noisy, surprised racket. Through her tears Madeline saw Will and Elsie embrace, and she knew her grandmother's happiness must be even greater than her own.

As if sensing its mother's feelings the baby stirred within her belly, its tiny limbs tapping a delicate message against her gently rounded abdomen. Pressing her hand to where she'd felt the movement, with love and pride she watched her husband make his way down the steps and across the yard toward her.

The balmy blue of the Indian summer afternoon bathed the joyful gathering in its warmth and gentleness, and in this perfect golden moment, Madeline knew that no joy could be more complete than her own.

NOTE

The author welcomes mail from her readers. You can write to her at Box 333, Circle Pines, MN 55014.

FREE
Romance
(a $4.50 value)

Send in the Coupon Below

To get your FREE historical romance and start saving, fill out the coupon below and mail it today. As soon as we receive it we'll send you your FREE Book along with your first month's selections.

Mail To: **True Value Home Subscription Services, Inc. P.O. Box 5235
120 Brighton Road, Clifton, New Jersey 07015-5235**

YES! I want to start previewing the very best historical romances being published today. Send me my FREE book along with the first month's selections. I understand that I may look them over FREE for 10 days. If I m not absolutely delighted I may return them and owe nothing. Otherwise I will pay the low price of just $4.00 each, a total $16.00 (at *least* an $18.00 value) and save at least $2.00. Then each month I will receive four brand new novels to preview as soon as they are published for the same low price. I can always return a shipment and I may cancel this subscription at any time with no obligation to buy even a single book. In any event the FREE book is mine to keep regardless.

Name _____

Street Address _____ Apt No _____

City _____ State _____ Zip Code _____

Telephone _____

Signature _____
(if under 18 parent or guardian must sign)

Terms and prices subject to change. Orders subject
to acceptance by True Value Home Subscription
Services Inc.

965-X